Monsoons and Potholes

Manuka Wijesinghe

Perera Hussein Publishing House

Published by the Perera Hussein Publishing House, 2006

ISBN: 955-8897-07-8

First Edition

Monsoons and Potholes is a work of fiction. Historical figures and events are presented in a fictitious context. The perception of reality is not intended to correspond to fact nor is it intended to misrepresent persons or events. The right of the author to be associated with this work has been asserted.

Cover design by David Blacker
Printed and bound in Sri Lanka by Samayawardhana

Monsoons
and
Potholes

Manuka Wijesinghe

Perera Hussein Publishing House

By the same author:

Books: Silhouettes for justice

Plays: The Mad Cow
Flight 582 to Zurich
Karma 2016
My Way

To Conall -
     my friend and fantasy,
and Albrecht -
     my lover and reality.

Prologue

The dark, coarse-haired child held onto her hand and refused to let go. She had been gone long. Too long. He did not know her. She did not know him either. But he wasn't a stranger. She had watched him grow up. Every word he spoke, every picture he had drawn, every bruise on his body had been documented. Every photograph of him had been pasted. She was old, her memory was long; but he was a child who had no memory. Not of her. Of who she was, but not of her. She could have been anybody. He refused to let go of her. He wanted to know where she had been all those years. She tried to tell him. But he only listened with his eyes. She had seven ear studs in her lobes. He only knew people who wore two. She knew that human beings could not listen with their eyes. So she tried to show him. But first she had to show him who she was. Who she really was. She went to the cupboard where her past been pasted in albums, documented and wrapped in plastic to keep away termites and decay. She put her hand into its darkness. But the cupboard was empty. The past was gone. Someone had robbed her childhood. Who? She wanted to cry, but the little dark child kept listening intently with his eyes.

I

The Anatomy of a Pathological Birth

His name was Dasharatha,
  A raja of renown,
Noble and compassionate,
  Of famed Ayodha town.
His eldest son was Rama,
  The darling of his heart
Enchanting as the full moon
  And skilled in every art.
Protector of his people
  Upholder of his word,
The terror of his foes,
  And Dharma's faithful lord.
Commanded by his father,
  Obedient Rama went
With Sita and with Lakshmana
  To forest-banishment.
When Rama killed the rakshasas
  With which the woods were rife,
Infuriated Ravana
  Abducted Rama's wife.
In his search for Sita
  Rama has a friend
Sugriva on whose orders
  I run from end to end,
Leaping over oceans
  Mountainously wavy,
Till I succeed in finding
  The lotus lovely devi.
Now at last I've found her!
  Oh, the signs are clear!
Her grace, her charm, her sweetness
  She is here, she is here!
(Sung by Hanuman, Book five, the Ramayana of Valmiki)

I was born on the soil upon which king Ravana died.

Karma oversaw my arrival. The X and Y chromosomes that parented me were assured the birth of a single male child with a horoscope that glittered like a multi-facetted diamond; but his lustre alone could not illuminate the fading lights in the household into which I was to be born. Therefore, karma decided to be benevolent and grant me the gift of life.

There are many interpretations to my story. Fables, fabrications, fallacies and facts. When the past finally reached the present, it mutated. No longer what it had been; a structure of confabulation, the conditional having conquered the past participle. Truth had departed. I have taken the liberty to enhance the tale. Adding, subtracting, multiplying, dividing and re-writing.

It is my life, my story.

Achi would say, 'this child did not want to be born,' when I fell ill every week or threw up the milk I was fed. Nenda, my protector, who descended into our household shortly before my birth, would say that my brother's diamond karma was not supportive of a younger sibling. Kiriamma, my paternal grandmother would lament 'How can this child grow up to be healthy when her parents' joint Karma permits the birth of only a single male child?'

But I was born. Female. Second child. Not in the rosy pink glow of a newborn babe, but a gasping, blue hued apparition, cocooned and strangled by a python-like umbilical cord, which in this particular pregnancy developed a life of its own. Only one of us could survive. A manic gynaecologist with hitherto unknown gynaecological skill, disentangled me from this morbid monster, removing my fashionably blue hue and made me appear as common and pink as all other babies.

Despite obvious Karmic obstacles, destiny required my birth since my family lived in an upstairs house. It began like this:

Siya had suffered a heart attack while driving his Austin Morris Minor and was forbidden to work, drive Morris Minors or climb stairs. Achi, on hearing of my grandfather's heart attack, hyperventilated, creating such supreme chaos with her cardio-vascular system that her own heart had no choice but to enlarge to the size of a watermelon in order to fulfil her full course of Karma. Ammi, who regarded life as a frolicking party decided her superficial existence was not compatible with her nascent intelligence and registered herself in all advertised classes, courses, schools and lectures: from cake making to karaoke singing in order to discover what Karma had planned with the deviating headline on her palm.

The family's lives had to be re-structured. Siya had to be moved to a house without stairs in order to pacify his heart; Achi had to sacrifice her wedding cake manufacturing service on account of *her* heart and Ammi's intellectual endeavours had to be financed even though they had nothing to do with a heart. None of this sounds too complicated, but our family, or rather the family I was to enter had no money. Caste, creed and social respectability to spare, but the coffers were empty. Siya's upper caste respectable Govigama father had gambled away ninety-nine percent of a part of Colombo he had inherited from his forefathers, and the remaining one percent had to be divided between twelve siblings. After one hereditary object had been divided by twelve hereditary objections, we as a group of descendents of my great-grandfather could have moved into an ant hole, but not a staircase-less house.

As human beings, we each have a pair of primogenitors. My maternal grandmother, Achi, being the second daughter of the second wife of a Govigama civil servant who already had three daughters from his first marriage, had inherited two teak chests of Rosenthal crockery, sterling silver cutlery and a few odds and ends of glitter. A twenty-two carat gold chain without a clasp, a diamond ring without the diamond, a set of two bangles - of which one was lost and a choker of diamonds, rubies and sapphires, where zircons had replaced the diamonds and Indian glass the sapphires. Alas! My grandmother's teak-chest inheritance was inadequate to sponsor the family's needs.

But, I still had the non-negligible Y chromosome. My father, Thathi, a victim of: a meticulously planned marriage, correct planetary positions, correct Lagna, correct caste, age and wealth, unfortunately suffered a major setback immediately following his marriage to my mother. His father died. Although he had left his first-born son fertile fields of plenty ready for harvesting, he had also left five unmarried daughters ripe for marriage. Thathi's primary duty following his own marriage was that of unearthing suitable husbands for his sisters. It had been no easy task. But he did it.

Eventually, when my mother went about the process of liquidating the land her land-owning husband had brought into the marriage, she realized that the five opulent weddings and the even more opulent dowries had left them with a capital that was not enough to buy a staircase, let alone a house.

It had been a question of either bountiful paddy fields with barren sisters or erstwhile paddy fields with bountiful sisters. My father, without uttering a word to my mother had chosen the latter.

Astrology or no astrology, Karma or co-incidence, it was a bad start to any marriage. As Ammi ranted and raved, Thathi got his first ear infection, which left an eternal buzzing in his ears. Not during the monsoons, but during the dry season when even the oceans left our island and swimming pools went dry.

Nenda, an ardent devotee of my father's causes, eternally found comparisons between Thathi and protagonists of the Jataka tales, who were always sacrificing something in order to enter the realm of Nirvana. Justifiably, Ammi was unimpressed by his similarity to the characters of these tales and declared a cold war between my father's family and us. 'Go to Nirvana,' she would say to him, 'or go anywhere you want, take all your sisters… why not your entire clan? But don't think you will get in there. Neither you, nor your sisters, nor their husbands… perhaps not *here*, but I know that up there, there is some justice. They will look at you pug nosed people in the face and send you straight to hell. Why? Because you left nothing for your wife and children, that's why.'

It was all Karma and had to happen the way it did. Despite the natural tendency to rant like a fisherwoman at St. Johns fish-market, my mother was pragmatic and above all a survivor. She knew she had to now consort with Karma for us to enter into the future. A future in a staircase-less house.

And that is where I was to appear in the family album. I suppose if the past had not been the way it had been, and the present was not the way it was, there would have been absolutely no reason for my birth and I would have never reached for pen and paper to tell my story: The anatomy of a pathological birth, impregnated by Karma.

My birth caused a sensation. Not because I was fashionably blue or engulfed in a living umbilical shawl, but because my death, which was imminent even before my birth, would be the ultimate Karmic disappointment to the family's finances. I'll try not to talk in parables. But, it is difficult to be *unparabalic* when talking about the death of a creature as yet unborn. Only predicted.

The story was related to me in bits and pieces: a certain astrologer, generally ostracized due to his passion for alcoholic beverage, had predicted to my grandmother, that a daughter would be born to her daughter in order to increase the family's wealth. Please don't jump to the conclusion that I was born either brainy, beautiful or unusually handicapped. If so, I would not be wasting my time and yours, writing this story. My birth was to have a strange and wonderful influence on the family's planetary constellation. I was predicted to be the infant of planetary re-organisation, necessary due to two enlarged hearts.

Jupiter and Mercury would battle with Saturn and the dragon's head, conquer them, take de-facto residence of the tenth house of income and eleventh house of profession to increase fortune. My birth was essential. My survival was vital. But as I came out, strangled and cyanotic, Achi dropped the bucket with my mothers vomit, spraying the bile on to the gynaecologist's trousers and the nurse's hairy legs, ran out to my granduncle Kandapola Siya's driver who had been urinating behind the croton bushes outside the labour room, ordered him to stop pissing at once, buy a cock and sacrifice it immediately at the goddess Pattini's temple in Maradana, come back and continue his piss behind the crotons. Podian the driver, totally perturbed at the mistresses orders as his sarong had been tucked up, had forgotten to put it back down and had bought a goat instead of a cock and sacrificed it to Kataragama God's temple instead of the Pattini temple. While I resisted the removal of the pulsating necklace, Achi returned to the labour room, picked up the empty pail of vomit and continued to chant the single Buddhist hymn she knew. '*Aney manda, aney manda, aney manda, aney manda...*' (I don't know, I don't know...)

Pathiraja was the only person who had predicted my birth. But he seemed to have overlooked my imminent death. However, my grandmother had seen death in this cyanotic creature fighting for breath. My salvation, then, lay not in the unpredicted words of Pathiraja, but in the prowess of the pint-sized warrior/gynaecologist and Achi.

Let me talk of Pathiraja first. His predictions were brilliant under the influence of alcohol and dull when sober. My grandmother, being a woman of great perception, had invited Pathiraja for a dinner of fried rice, wild boar, mutton and chicken liver, given him half a bottle of Arrack and somewhere along the post-dinner, nocturnal route to intoxication, made him predict the otherwise unpredictable. My birth.

Despite repetitious predictions by repetitive astrologers who repeated that Aiya's Karma did not enable the birth of a second child, Pathiraja stated that *Bodhi Pujas* on seven consecutive Tuesdays after Aiya's third birthday would ensure the birth of a female child who would bring them financial gain.

Now, to return to my birth. As Dr. Wijedasa acquired Herculean strength in order to disentangle this Medusa like creature from her snake, Ammi kept throwing up green bile on Achi's pastel blue poplin sari with its pink rosebuds, while the nurses cursed under their breath, staring at the clock where the time read eight minutes past eight. PM. Their shift had ended but they were still at work.

When I did emerge amidst this bilious commotion, the assistants of labour were so concerned about cleaning the bile from their hairy legs that they had forgotten to give a thought to my time of birth. Hence, I was born without a time.

The time of birth dictated whether a person born at a particular time would be beautiful or ugly, live or die, marry or be celibate, study or be an idiot, be fair or dark, fat or thin, etcetera. In other words 'time' was everything. It was the axis upon which the earth rotated. It was the heartbeat of existence.

Astrologers could tell us many things. The past, the present, the future, the occult, the esoteric... everything. But the basis of this knowledge is time. Hence, when 'time' was not available, the architectural prediction of karma, the prescription for a justified existence was a mirage.

'So, Dr. Wijedasa what time was this child born?' Achi asked him while the labour room assistants were busy cleaning bile and not looking at the clock.

'Its eight-eight now, that's the time,' he replied.

'No, no, don't you think Doctor, we should note the exact time when the child came out, not after you won the battle with the umbilical cord?'

'You are right Mrs. Marasinghe, now let me think… it took me about five minutes to disentangle the child from the umbilical cord…'

'No, no Doctor, it took about twenty minutes.'

'Definitely not Mrs. Marasinghe, maximum fifteen minutes, not more. Mrs. Weerasinghe what do you think?' the question was directed to Ammi.

'Aney, I don't know Doctor, it felt like a lifetime and I was so busy vomiting on mummy's sari and feeling so bilious…' It was evident that my mother possessed a gory delight in describing excrement.

'So we have agreed, the time of birth was ten minutes before eight-eight. That makes it seven fifty-eight.'

Suddenly the nurse butted in. 'Doctor, if you look at that clock for the time of birth, all the children born in Ceylon in the last four months have been born either at eight-eight in the morning or eight-eight at night.'

'Ah! Why is that?' asked the Doctor putting on his horn-rimmed spectacles to inspect the clock more closely.

'Why do you think? It's broken, that's why.'

'Not to worry,' said the doctor, while Achi was in a cold sweat and Ammi was oblivious to the dilemma of time. 'Let us convey to the father that he has fathered a daughter.'

Then, while the doctor searched out my father who was seated amidst thousands of expectant fathers reading 'Doctor Spock's Guide to Infants', Ammi and Achi concocted my time of birth.

Thathi entered the room in ecstasy. Doctor Spock was in one hand, the note pad and Parker fountain pen in the other. He had the paternal task of noting the time of birth and making a dash to the astrologer.

'So what time was she born?' he asked staring at my face.

'Eight-eight pm,' replied Achi without batting an eyelid.

He noted it on his notepad, glanced up and saw the clock where time had stood still and said: 'Oh my goodness! My time is wrong, let me adjust my watch.' And he adjusted the correct time on his watch to eight-eight on the broken labour room clock.

'So I'll go now, straight to Mr. Pathiraja's residence and give him the time of birth.' He stood there without going, staring at me through his spectacles. He had a round face, round head, round nose, dangling ears and hairy forearms.

'Why are you standing there? Go.'

'Mali, let him look at his daughter.'

'Go. You put me through all this pain and you stand there grinning like a jackass. Go and do what you have to do.'

He pecked her on the cheek and was about to leave the labour room obviously oblivious to her tantrums.

'You will come back with the letters?' Achi had a worried look on her face. Not due to the fear that my father may not return with the syllables with which I should get my correct astrological name, rather, she was afraid that the concocted time of birth would predict that a child born at this concocted time was not a child but a rat, a dog or a cockroach.

'I will return as soon as I get the letters, mummy.' he replied.

'Don't bother, send Kandapola uncle's driver with the letters. I don't want to see your face,' said my mother.

He pecked her face again and left the room grinning.

We remained in that hospital room where time stood still at eight-eight.

3

When a female child is born, there are two topics of conversation for visiting relatives and friends. Her looks and marriage prospects. In my particular case the astrological highway was in actuality a Karmic freeway and permitted ample room for speculation. Relatives could not be barred from visit. Hence, this topic needed to be avoided.

'Who knows which planet was placed in her house of birth in order to complicate such an uncomplicated pregnancy?'

My grandmother was having tea with her friend Dotty.

'You know, I heard a story from my neighbour Mrs. Weeramuni's sister-in-law at her father's funeral that all the astrologers they had consulted said that Saturn's period was definitely bringing death and destruction and that there was…'

'Yes Dotty,' Achi broke in, 'that maybe so, but you can't generalise these things. This child was lucky to be alive because Dr. Wijedasa was a brilliant doctor and it was not the planets, but he who saved her life.'

Was? Dr. Wijedasa was obviously no more!

'What a tragedy that such a great man had to die so early. In fact, I was telling my daughter that when she gets labour problems she should only go to Dr. Wijedasa.'

'Your daughter is so old already?'

'Apo no! But who knows if I will be alive to see her having children?'

'Don't talk nonsense, why should you die? You are not even fifty no?'

'Apo what fifty, thirty-eight! Aney, but look at Dr. Wijedasa! Did anyone think he would die so young? And such a great man too.'

'All good people die young,' replied Achi.

'Aney, but why did he have to hang himself? He was such a successful doctor, and his children are still quite young no?'

That was my revenge for his destroying my umbilical scarf and removing my fashionable blue hue.

'There, there the baby is crying, she must be hungry,' said Dotty peering at me through horn-rimmed glasses and putrid breath.

I am not hungry you cow! He probably tried to copy me by wrapping things around his neck, and got strangled in the process.

'My foodness aunty,' she muttered between her cowcatcher, 'she has a strong voice, very unlike a girl, what did the astrologer say about her line of profession?'

A change of conversation was needed.

'Yes Dotty, he was such a great man!'

'Who?'

Added to the bad breath, she also had a bad memory.

'Dr. Wijedasa of course,' replied Achi in exasperation.

I had stopped squealing by then. Dotty's putrid breath had brought me to silence. She dropped me back onto the mat and returned to the saucer chair next to my grandmother. In the meantime, I continued rolling and beating my head into shape, upon the hard floor until it fitted the proportional norms of society.

'You know sister Beet,' Dotty peered around to make sure no one was eavesdropping, 'Without mentioning names, I heard from a reliable source that Doctor Wijedasa's wife had been having an affair.'

'But that is nothing new no?'

'You heard about it too?' Extreme disappointment was evident on Dotty's face for not being the primary bearer of the sordid tale.

'What do you expect from a low-caste woman? She did the same thing that her mother did years ago.'

'Her mother?' Obviously my grandmother's advanced age had given her more access to historical information.

'She, the mother, was a servant who got pregnant by some gentleman who had visited their home, and Dr. Wijedasa's mother, a very kind and good hearted lady, raised the woman's child as a part of her family.'

'Ah! How gracious, just like you, sister Beet,' Dotty's mouth opened so wide that her bad breath reached down to my mat.

My grandmother had the same graciousness as the doctor's mother? I still did not know this story. But no matter, I had just moved into this house, I presume there was a lot to scavenge around for during the course of life.

My grandmother smiled happily. She liked to be described as gracious.

'And she allowed her son to marry a servant's child?'

'The mother and the daughter, they were shrewd creatures. They fed some charmed food to old Mrs. Wijedasa and got her last will changed.

Dr. Wijedasa had to marry that girl if he was to inherit his mother's property.'

'Poor Dr. Wijedasa, I didn't know he was forced into marriage.'

'Fortunately, she was a fair skinned, attractive girl. So it wasn't that obvious that she was a servant's daughter.'

'And low-caste too,' added Dotty. Her mouth did not close again. 'Chee, chee, chee,' she said.

'What to do?' replied Achi, 'that was the poor man's karma.'

'Aiyo! But those people are Christians no, they don't believe in karma.'

'Yes. But Christian or no Christian, you can't escape karma,' replied Achi philosophically, enjoying her spiritual guru of the saucer chair position, with slaves such as myself rolling on the hard floor at her feet, and cavernous minds with putrid breath in the form of Dotty nearly strangling herself on every word she uttered.

'Chee, chee, cheekay… I would never have guessed sister Beet! And that woman spoke such good English no?' From the depth of the cavernous structures of her brain Dotty had finally discovered a topic of slander. The English language.

'That was after elocution classes.'

Just then the servant brought Dotty a cup of tea.

I opened my mouth and tried to tell them that Dr. Wijedasa looked like a gecko in spectacles and that he should have left me where I was, for it was far more comfortable where I came from than on this hard floor.

'There, there she is hungry,' muttered Dotty unenthusiastically. She did not like being disturbed while fu, fu blowing her tea, which she had poured onto the saucer and was fu, fu blowing to cool.

I am not hungry you cow! I want to tell you what I think of that Wijedasa man!

'Oh my goodness, she has a really loud organ. Sounds like she has donated gongs to the temple in her last birth. What was it you were telling me about her horoscope?'

The topic was immediately changed. 'Mali, Mali,' Achi screamed. Mali was my mother. It was her cue to stick her breast into my mouth and shut me up.

Yes, it was far more peaceful where I lived, before I was forcibly taken out of there and placed on this mat. Serves that Wijedasa man right.

Nenda emerged. 'Why is the child crying?'

'She is hungry. Where is that Mali?'

'She must be hanging on the telephone as usual,' replied Nenda angrily, looking at neither my grandmother nor at Dotty. She didn't like visitors, but she loved me. She raised me from my mat and continued her soliloquy directed at Achi, Dotty and others. 'Yes, if not for me, this poor child would be starving to death. Yes, because this child has done enough good deeds in her previous birth, karma has been kind to her, and brought me to this house. But, what to do? Even karma can't help when people who are supposed to be looking after her are too busy with their teatime parties and telephone affairs! *Aneyyy, chooti putha*, don't cry. I will take you to your mother even if she can't be bothered to come and see why you are crying. If only the other people in this house had half the compassion that I do!'

Needless to say Nenda was completely off-track regarding my cries. But her soliloquy made me shut up. I was learning to become an opportunist. Nenda, whose relationship to the rest of the household I had not quite figured out, since she was neither sibling, nor relative nor servant, was the only person who gave me her undivided attention. So, if I could not change destiny, I was going to change my attitude towards destiny. Doctor Wijedasa had pulled me out. I could not go back. I would at least try to make the best of it. I stopped crying and smiled at Nenda.

She was my ally.

And my teller of tales.

4

Brutally woken up at five forty-five am, bathed at five fifty-five am, smothered in Ponds baby powder, eau-de-cologned with Johnson's baby eau-de-cologne, clad in a skimpy sexy backless frock, four black plastic bangles twirled on each wrist, black cord around neck, cold scratchy golden amulet on cord, a large black spot on forehead, Karapincha twigs bored through plainly festering ear lobes and a life cast in Meena lagna (Pisces) I awaited the arrival of my 'Daughter, Welcome to the World' guests.

Meena. Why not Kanya?

Kanya (Virgo). Female child. The beautiful translucent spirit like virgin. Heart shaped face, bronze, freckled, dimpled cheeks, golden skin and long blonde tresses. Instead, I was a slimy, slithering fish carousing with crabs and prawns hiding in mud holes and covered in slippery seaweed. Was karma responsible, or was it the broken clock?

Karma, the single word for cause and effect. The bridge that connects birth and death, had cast me into the most unfavourable zodiac sign a girl could possess. If I were to remain a child until eternity, it would not have mattered, but the natural law of nature was such that a girl child would become a woman. Then what? A female fish? *A mermaid?*

Meena. Pisces; dark skin. Short. Height similar to breadth. Fingers stout. Toes bulbous. Shoulders muscular and spherical. Hair, texture of coconut husk. Nose, like lorry-run-over *Jambu* fruit, constitution sturdy, profession favourable, monetary matters: saving advisable. Female Meena child positive influence to father. Mother: no positive or negative influence. Positive influence to older sibling if male child. No indication of further siblings. Venus exalted, Mercury debilitated, Saturn strengthened and auspicious…

I awaited the arrival of my guests.

They started strolling in, a double-decker bus-load of short, stout, dark people. Women in simple cotton saris and white lace jackets with stained armpits and stained cowcatchers. Men in ankle length sarongs and stained teeth suspended on a single nerve, smelling of soil, beetles, frogs, bark and sweat.

Then came the trousered gentlemen smelling of cigarette smoke, with cowcatcher-less ladies smelling of cheap jasmine perfume. A carload, not a bus load. They all squawked and squealed without paying much attention to me. They kept rotating their position on the pretext of looking at me, suffocating at Ammi's breast. Each visitor presented me a packet of biscuits or a bottle of eau-de-cologne. I was all set for a scented life and decayed teeth.

Suddenly, I realized that there was a certain metronome like precision and a change of smell attached to my suckling sessions. Beetle smell gone, cigarette smell in. Breast came out and Ammi did not seem to care if I suckled or not. The breast remained out. Out of the bra and out of my mouth. Out. Evident.

Cigarette smell gone, beetle smell in. Breast was brutally tucked into the padded bra and I was left to gulp oxygen molecules and eat the fabric fibres of the Angelina breast supporters. I began to experiment with the subtle art of observation. Doing justice to my slithering zodiac sign, without a cry or whimper, I turned my head and checked the origin of the cigarette smell.

Thirty-ish, balding, trousered, male. Language of communication: English. Blatant nervousness. Perhaps a reaction to oozing breast. Fumbling fingers haul pack of cigarettes from bulging trouser pocket. Trouser pocket is multi-adaptable, has triple usage quality. Successfully conceals cigarettes, car keys and semi-erection. Drops car keys in aggravated nervousness. Perhaps continued reaction to further oozing breast. Bends and picks up car keys resting on Ammi's rubber-slipper clad feet. Head of smoker shining like freshly polished brass oil lamp. Shirt collar covered with dandruff. Non-suckling female Meena child observes movement on shirt collar. *Lice?* Triple usage trouser pocket owner re-positions himself vertically.

Bones creak in process. Sticks cigarette in mouth with shaking hand. Fumbles trouser pocket in proximity of semi-erection for matches. Trouser pocket now quadruple usage. But matches not in trouser pocket, matches in shirt pocket. Matches light wrong end of cigarette. Cigarette changes ends. Re-lights. Sucks cigarette into mouth. Relative calm is achieved despite exposed breast. A female voice breaks the calm. 'Apo! Are you mad to be smoking near a new born child?'

'Sorry, sorry,' mutters trouser pocket owner and searches possibilities of extinguishing cigarette without removing eyes from breast. None visible. Female voice shouts again. Trousered male leaves room with burning cigarette. Breast re-enters the Angelina bra.

Change of smell. Trees, barks, leaves, toads and beetles. Breast remains in Angelina bra, and bed jacket covers thorax. The scent of wilderness appeals to me more than acrid smoke. I observe. Only similarity with trouser clad male is gender and the human race. New person; fifty, sixty or maybe eighty. Bald crown. Remaining hair above neck tied into knot like the ladies. Face weathered. Like gravel road after monsoon. Mouth and surrounding facial muscles engaged in a permanent chew. Expert in carrying on conversation on paddy harvesting while in a permanent chew. Occasionally thick red sputum discharged through mouth and through window. Chew stops, and mouth opens. Reveals strangulated red teeth hanging on wasted red gums. Fewer teeth than my mother, but more than me. Continues with detailed description of paddy harvest. Removes ingredients from sarong pouch at waist and makes further concoction for chew. The chew begins. Subject changes. Paddy harvesting becomes coconut retail market price fluctuations. Self splattered with shower of beetle juice spewing from the gaps between strangulated teeth. Self irritated. Wanting his departure. But mother finds coconut retail-market price fluctuations extremely entertaining and ignores red splattering from oral cavity.

'Ko? (where?) Ko? Where is the little girl?' A belligerent female voice is heard above the coconut retail-market price fluctuations. The chewing person reacts to female voice. 'Ah listen, sister Seela is here.' My mother is indifferent. 'You continue,' she tells chewing man, 'your conversation is far more interesting than Seela's nonsense.' He continued. 'Aiyo, Mali sister, twenty-five rupees now becoming twenty-two rupees, difficult making living out of prices going down all the time. Government only talking about doing something, but bugs destroying coconut tree when government only talking. Coconut cultivation becoming cursed cultivation, but paddy doing much better.' So their conversation returned to the paddy price fluctuations.

The loud female continued outside. 'Aiyo aiya, hariyata traffic!' (Aiyo big brother, lot of traffic!). 'Aney, and we are coming and coming for the last three hours at a snail's pace. Cars and lorries bumper to bumper. Accident! Out of all days today!' The belligerent female had arrived to pay her respects to me.

As she chatted outside the door about the traffic jam, Nenda came into the room and began enlarging the spot on my forehead. Someone of extreme evil-eye had obviously descended into our house. 'Aney Mali, where is the Chooti little girl?' And she barged into the room. Ammi covered my face. 'Don't shout. She is trying to sleep.' A blatant lie. But my mother was not willing to uncover my face until the black spot had dried. 'What nonsense,' she said, 'She is not sleeping, her eyes are wide open.' My curiosity had pushed my mother's hand away from my face. She was large. 'How can anyone sleep when you are around Seela? When you open your mouth even the dead will wake up.' She was large and white. 'Ho, ho, ho,' Seela laughed. Her corpulence insulated her against my mother's dislike.

'So let me wear my specs and take a look at the child.' Wearing her specs with the precision of a forensic expert, she studied me. I prepared myself for a gong donator's loud declaration about my neo-natal cuteness.

'Aiyo,' she began, 'her ears are as black as night.' She then inspected my ears from all directions, while her lamentation became lugubrious. 'Aiyo, poor thing! She is black. And how black! If it was a boy it would not have mattered, but for a girl? Aiyo!!! Aiyo!!! Aney Mali, what a pity! Now see your son? He is fair no? It should have been the other way around. Putha should have had her ears and she should have had putha's ears.'

I had just begun to realize that there was a fundamental difference between my mother's first born and myself. And it was not the difference of sex. He had that which I should have had. I started lamenting weakly. In a deep state of shock.

'For a girl, her chances are always better if she was fair.' Seela knew the advantage of colour. She was my father's third sister. A ray of whiteness in a family of total female blackness. The only sister to receive not one, but many proposals from not one, but many moneyed suitors. The others had to collect the remaining crumbs. The colour had made the difference. My lamentations grew louder. Why me?

'Must be the bad Karma.' As my lamentations increased, Seela's gong donator cacophony increased. 'Don't let the child play too much in the sun; actually you should protect her from the sun completely.'

'Did you come alone?' inquired Ammi, preparing for battle with Seela and the rest of her family. My father's flesh and blood garrulous siblings: each one louder, more corpulent and more garrulous than the other. Unfortunately for my mother, Seela was white; hence in the battle of colour, we were no match for her. Nor in the battle of corpulence. But this battle could not be fought yet, it had to wait. Seething, my mother waited. It was still the early sixties. Anorexia, bulimia or emaciated shapeliness was not in vogue. Fatness was considered a symbol of affluence, and blackness, a symbol of hopelessness.

'You all took your own sweet time to come and visit no?' said Ammi cattily. It was her retaliation to Seela's comments on my blackness, which in actuality were an indirect hit on Ammi's sharp-nosed black attractiveness in contrast to Seela's pug nosed white ugliness. 'Yes, yes... you all are very busy getting richer and fatter no? In fact your Aiya was commenting, rather disappointed in fact, that it was very strange that you all had not come or even called.'

'Aiyo, Aiya was wondering why we didn't come?' Seela was perturbed. A dutiful sister.

'Yes, yes, he was quite upset,' said Ammi adding fuel to her disturbed state.

'Aiyo really, but...?'

'No but. Yes. He said, if my sisters don't bother to come, what's the use?'

'Aney, but we gave a call and said no, why we won't be able to come earlier.'

'I don't know about that, I only know that he was quite upset,' replied Ammi, enjoying Seela's unease.

'Aney, Aiya was upset? Let me go and talk to him, I just left him in the dining room with the other sisters and he didn't say anything about being upset no.'

'So y'all all came together? Like going on a pilgrimage?' retorted Ammi, sharpening her razor blade tongue.

'Coming to see our brother is as honourable as a pilgrimage,' replied Seela, slowly regaining confidence. 'But then Mali, how would you know?

You were an only child no.' and before Ammi could reply she said, 'Here I brought some things for the baby.' She put the package directly next to my nose. I squinted in curiosity. 'Some clothes and Ponds baby powder.'

'Apo Seela, you can take it back and give it to someone else. We only use Johnson's baby powder on our children.'

A battle of quality. The cheap, indigenous, sub-standard, made in Ceylon baby powder versus the expensive, non-indigenous, imported made in England baby powder. Colonial superiority. My mother was full of it. It was her weapon against my father's family. Missionary school education versus native education. English versus Sinhalese. Nearly twenty years after the end of colonization we tried to be more English than the English. And those of missionary school education had a distinct advantage over the others. The advantage was the English language.

I peered through the made in India cello tape that had removed itself from the temporary function of concealing the Ponds baby powder beneath the made in Ceylon brown paper, far more appropriate as sand paper than packing paper. True, there peered at me the faintly familiar symbols of the Ponds baby powder, with which I had been powdered since my birth. The sacred Buddhist precept, 'Thou shall not lie,' was not applicable to my mother. Not in her battle with Seela. 'You had better keep it Mali, she'll need all the powder she gets to make her fair,' and she exited before Ammi could concoct a suitably cutting reply.

My nearly ceased lamentations increased in volume and grew into a cacophony. I vowed to take my revenge on Karma. Today I did not know how, perhaps tomorrow. Why me? I began to howl like a chicken about to be slaughtered. Ammi offered her only identified solace, the breast. I bit it with all the strength in my toothless gums, so hard that she dumped me onto the pile of Ponds powder and ran in search of ice cubes to pacify her breast. Bra undone, breast bared, milk oozing. A two legged cow through the conglomerate of jungle and cigarette types patiently awaiting their lunch after the tiring task of visiting a black-eared female child stuck to a shapely breast.

My chicken cry increased in volume and became that of a goat on its way to the slaughterhouse. Achi rushed in and out of the room pressing my abdomen from different angles. Occasionally her fingers were accompanied by oils and undecipherable words borrowed from someone's obsolete Lexicon of Medicine.

Karunawathie the servant girl came in with smoking incense in an iron pan which she held under me, on top of me, beside me, behind the cupboards, in the cupboards… until Nenda came and screamed at her, ordering her to return to her work without prying into cupboards. 'Aney putha don't cry,' she cajoled. Carrying me from the mountain of Ponds baby powder she began to sing *doi doi doi doiia baba, bai bai bai baiiababa.*' My goat's cry became that of a calf. Nenda rocked me faster and the song became louder. Ammi returned to the scene. Breast covered.

'What, she is still crying no,' said Ammi, stating the obvious. 'What do you expect? You all are too busy entertaining guests, no! And no one pays attention to this little child. She must be suffering from an overdose of evil eye. What else? With so many greedy people staring at her,' retorted Nenda. She didn't like visitors. And she was blind. Who else would think that anyone would caste an evil-eye on a black-eared baby? Black ears did not fit into the accepted norms of Asian beauty. Asian beauty had white ears, not black.

'It has nothing to do with the visitors, she is suffering from 'mpherghtasnmsn' Achi mumbled, drawing blank looks from everyone present. 'Without standing there looking at each other's faces, go and call a doctor,' Nenda retorted. 'It will go away, replied Achi, all babies suffer from (*the word again*)'

My calf cry became a bellow. 'Nothing is going away,' replied Nenda, 'can't you see that her crying is getting worse? The child is in tremendous pain! Do something.'

'Mali, then go and call a doctor, some people seem to think that we have not brought up children no?' Evidence of anger in her tone… 'Which doctor shall I call, Dr. Wijedasa is dead no?'

'Spends hours on the telephone, but there are more important things to talk about than finding a good doctor for a new born baby.'

'Aney you just shut up and wait, as if you know what important things I have to talk about.'

A nasty storm was brewing. I had to go in for a crescendo.

'Mummy, I'll call Dagma she is well informed about doctors.'

'That woman is a donkey,' replied Nenda.

'Should I find a doctor or not, woman? You are shouting and telling me to do something and when I want to do something it is not the right thing!'

'Yes, but hurry up and come back without talking other unnecessary things on the phone.' Ammi huffed as Thathi entered. At this late stage he had heard the commotion in the bedroom, above his five baritone sisters.

'Maybe she is hungry,' said Thathi with the typical male naïvety that the only problem I was allowed to have on this planet was that of unsatisfied hunger. My father was a simple man, a believer in the theory of the killer ape. We were descended from the apes. All we needed was food. For food we would kill. Buddhism differentiated us from apes. The Buddha taught us dharma, the dharma taught us moderation and moderation taught us the path to eliminate hunger. Without hunger there was no killing. The ape that killed knew no dharma, and killed only to satiate hunger. Being a baby, I was more like an ape than my father the evolved Buddhist who knew of dharma.

'Apo! You are an expert on child rearing no,' replied Ammi. She was angry with him. My mother believed in reincarnation, not in the killer ape theory. 'Without making Tissa Aiya deaf with your screaming go and call the doctor so that this child will finally get some rest,' shouted Nenda.

No one seemed to have realized that I had stopped screaming. Their cacophonous ranting and raving were beginning to hurt my black ears. 'Who is shouting? You are the one who is shouting no,' said Ammi about to do battle with Nenda for siding with Thathi. 'You are the one who is making us all deaf! And of course all those sisters who have donated not bells, but gongs to all the temples in their previous births!'

'Tissa, why don't you take the child out and show your sisters,' suggested Achi. She was the United Nations Secretary General of our home front. 'I suppose they are too good to come into the bedroom to see the child,' said Ammi angrily. Without responding, Thathi carried me to his sisters like a proud anthropologist exhibiting the first human specimen of the killer ape. *Australopithacus Asiaticus Ceylonaise!*

Nenda waddled behind him on her bowlegs trying to increase the size of my Pottu. I screamed again. Seela's coarse tongue was following me. I didn't want the Pottu; I wanted to retain whatever whiteness I had without rubbing more sepia ejaculations on myself. But Nenda was not to be deterred. As I continued to scream she rubbed and rubbed my forehead. I presume I looked like night, before the creation of day. Thus, I was presented to my fathers' sisters. 'So, this is my daughter Manuka,' he said proudly.

'Until this moment I didn't realize that I had been given a name. A guttural, rhymeless, expostulation. Like a molecule from that bile filled pail in the hospital labour room where time had stood still at eight-eight pm.

'Aney, chooti duwa,' cooed one sister stroking me with her rough palm.

'Aney, Akka, our daughter looked like this too no, you remember?'

'She was fairer no,' that was Seela.

'No, no she wasn't much fairer,' again the same voice.

'What are you talking? Of course she was much, much fairer.' Another sister.

'Aney, Putha open your eyes and look at your aunties.'

I pressed my eyelids down, even harder.

'Yes, Putha, this is Seela Nenda…, open your eyes and look at your Nenda will you?'

Seela went *Gnung, Gnung, Gnung* in baby language that only she understood. I did not.

'This is Kamala Nenda.'

'Aney, *duwe*, open your eyes and look at me.'

I kept my eyes shut. The world was like a big black hole. But Seela barged into my spiritual landscape like a rabid albino elephant. 'Aney, Aiya, she looks just like you.'

Lo and behold! There was another person on this planet who was as ugly as I. My father. We were bonded forever. I opened my eyes, dilated my pupils and adjusted my amphibious position to observe my father's black ears.

Until today I cannot say if my father's ears are blacker than the rest of him. But that which was important when eyes were closed, ceased to be important when eyes opened. Four chubby cheeked, double chinned, cow-catchered, black sisters confronted me. Except of course, Seela. But, under this faint shimmer of sunlight that tried to creep out of the heavy grey monsoon sky, Seela's whiteness didn't appear to be that white. Not next to the white walls, the white curtains, her sister Kamala's white brocade sari and the white teacup she held at her garish pink lips. In this moment of monsoonal ambivalence, her whiteness seemed quite tarnished. And the other four sisters, needless to say, were blacker than night.

I opened my eyes even wider, dilated my pupils even further, unwrinkled my forehead in sheer happiness, stuck my index finger into my mouth and with my own spit enlarged the black spot on my forehead. I had only my black ears to worry about. My aunts had all their black sensory organs to worry about.

I smiled like I had never smiled before. I laughed like I had never laughed before. Karma was finally about to give me my own moment of glory. 'Aney look, she has finally stopped crying.'
'She is smiling, sisters. I think she likes your faces!' If only Thathi knew.
'Here, here, you want to carry the baby?'
'Come let me carry her first, let Akka go and wash her hands.'

And so I went from one chubby hand to another. Pressed, pampered and smothered. Each pair of chubby hands that carried me, carried a face that brought optimism into my life. 'Come Chooti *Petiya*, smile, smile with your Aunty Seela'.
'Not Aunty, *Nenda*…we are not foreigners are we?' said Ammi cattily, passing by like a rainbow illuminating a bit of cattiness. She who called her parents Mummy and Daddy like the English, insisted I address my relatives in native vocabulary. A long life was too short to comprehend her logic.

'Mage podi haawa pena, pena aawa…' my aunty Kamala attempted a nursery rhyme. It did not bother me. My cries had been louder. In fact, her cow-catchered lisp was so amusing from my horizontal posture that I had no choice but to smile with all the elegance available to a toothless newborn. Thathi expounded on the fondness I showed towards his siblings.

A stream of Aney's and Aiyo's and giggles and cackles circulated around the room as Thathi and his siblings discussed the fertile route of our common karma. 'There! I called the Doctor, he told me to bring her immediately,' announced Ammi entering the living room like a thunderstorm.

'What for?' asked Seela 'She is smiling and laughing so happily.'

'Yes Mali, the moment she saw my sisters' faces she stopped crying at once.'

'No wonder! She must have recognized her pug nose on your faces.' She walked out of the room like Cleopatra. Nose first.

My happiness was undone.

5

My early existence consisted of smothering breasts, urinating, defecating, rolling to and fro, being bathed, eau-de-cologned and powdered, with sculpture treatments (ninety five percent nose, three percent forehead and two percent legs) and finally, make up of sepia ejaculation against the evil-eye. Music accompanied me eternally. Wolfgang Amadeus Mozart had been reborn into our family. As my brother. His latest composition was a new interpretation of '*Twinkle twinkle little star*' dedicated not only to the Milky Way, but also to all existing galaxies - known and unknown.

It all began with the efforts of a four year old who had not quite mastered the intricacies of pronunciation in the English language. 'Tinkle, tinkle little star, hau I vander wat yu are...'

'Not Tinkle, tinkle, Putha, it is tuwinkle tuwinke,' corrected Nenda. Having gone to a village school up to the third grade, having learned only the native tongue, she now had a PhD in household English. It was a PhD acquired through hearing, logic and common sense. Nothing more.

'No, it is Tinkle tinkle little star,' replied Aiya adamantly, 'that is how Miss Nandamalini taught me to sing.'

'Aney those *goday* teachers from the village don't know how to talk proper English,' retorted Nenda angrily. Living in a Colombo household had given her an overload of the Queen's English from the colonial masters who had left their ghosts in the souls of dark-skinned natives living in the city. We were more English than the English. Nenda too.

My brother's singing teacher, Miss Nandamalini, had a Karmic defect. The wrong name. Nandamalini was the name given to Nenda's third sister. The only sister who had never left their village. Hence, one and one added up to a conclusive three. The missing numeral was filled with logic. If her sister Nandamalini could not speak English, neither could Aiya's Montessori teacher. Nandamalini was a goday name, and even the acquisition of English would not remove the goday mantle from a person who possesed the unfortunate karma of being named Nandamalini. Once goday, always goday. Goday was the opposite of fashionable.

'Miss Nandamalini is not goday, she talks more English than you.' In those first few years of his life my brother had all the impertinence he lacked in the latter part. 'Don't be too wise for you age,' replied Nenda crossly, 'even if I may not talk, I know more English than your Miss Nandamalini.' The king coconut liquid I was being spoon-fed was suddenly gorged by my wind-pipe. I burst out in a fit of coughing. No one cared. 'Tinkle, tinkle little star, how I wonder how you are…,' sang Aiya loudly, ignoring Nenda. 'Wrong, wrong, wrong, wrong… don't ask me anything again if you are too posh to accept what I say. I may be from humble origins, but we are not foolish. We have more powers of perception than you city people who have been brought up on fancy pastries and chocolate cakes.'

My windpipe was as stubborn as my brother. It refused to release the king coconut liquid. My black face turned blue. Nenda blew onto the crown of my head like a helicopter. 'Tuwinkle, tuwinkle little star…,' Aiya showed the first signs of confusion when at the mercy of a dominant woman. He knew neither what he had said, nor what he wanted to say nor even what he should say. But music was his soul. I called him TM Mozart.

Nenda shook her bowlegged knees and kept tempo. I clutched onto her sari petrified I might fall through the bowlegs, on to the ground. Hail thunderstorm! Ammi appeared. A double PhD in English printed on her soul. Missionary school education had brought her closer to the English colonialists than Nenda. 'Cheekay, what is that you are singing? Don't tell me Miss Nandamalini taught you to sing like that?'
'Yes she did,' replied Aiya, who had already forgotten his interlude with Nenda. 'Certainly not! You are singing like a goday child! Just like your father's sisters' children, not to mention his sisters!' TM Mozart ignored her and sang. Loud. Feeling sorry for him, I gave him my undivided attention, even though his tinkle, tinkle was about to create in me a permanent state of starlight tintinus.

'Tuwinkle, tuwinkle little star… hau I wonder what you are…' 'Stop, stop!' shouted Ammi above the din, 'Not like that, like this. Tweenkle, tweenkle little star, how I won-der what you are. Up above the world so high, like a di-a-mond in the sky…' She smiled at him in a melodious moment of inspired maternity and said, 'Now sing like I sang, sweetheart.'

He opened his mouth, took a deep breath, strung on an imaginary guitar, kept time with his extra large feet and sang. 'Tuwinkle tuwinkle little star, Tuwinkle tuwinkle little star...' My mother turned a darker black than a night without a single star. In less than twenty-four hours, TM Mozart began elocution classes with the first available teacher. Miss Wendy Wellesley, a fair skinned lady. Ancestry assumed English due to whiteness of skin but probably burgher.

Miss Wendy Wellesley lived opposite the Prince of Wales College. She was married to a Weerasinghe. Some of her students from the Prince of Wales College spelt her name as Walesly, not Wellesley. They received extra classes. Normally, a Walesley or a Wellesley married to a Weerasinghe would also be a Weerasinghe. But Weerasinghes were not descendents of the English. They were as native as the king Ravana of ancient Lanka. They were like us.

Thus, a musical maestro with perfect pronunciation was born under the tutelage of Miss Wendy Wellesley. I cannot say much about the tune, but he would point his mouth like a woodpecker when he sang. Wolfgang Amadeus Mozart's genetic construction was a Karmic decision. Miss Wendy was my mother's decision. My brother was TM Mozart.

6

The uncomfortable aspect of bathing, a daily ritual performed at least twice a day was my greatest irritation. I can not say that I had a pathological fear of water, or that I experienced revulsion when water touched my body, but it was a tiresome ritual that hindered my earthly observation routine. The bathroom with its grey walls, grey tiles and grey ceiling was a morbid contrast to the world outside. Enclosed within these walls of drabness, the colourful characters of my existence metamorphosed into demonic oppressors. The dirty white plastic bathtub on the grey cement floor, in which my miniscule frame was scrubbed, was an existentialist trap. I was its victim.

When the first person came to undress me before the ritual of bathing would begin, I would begin to shout. I would squeal before being put into the water and I would squeal while in the water. I would splash and splutter, like a dying fish, so that everyone responsible for my cleanliness would become wetter than I. The drying session followed the bathing process. Every finger, every toe. When the body was eliminated of dampness, the scenting sessions began. Johnson's baby eau-de-cologne between every part, and then Ponds baby powder between the same parts.

Then the orthopaedic sessions to bring me into planetary inhabitant standards of female proportions would begin. Stretching of the bow-shaped legs, elongation of the forehead, shaping of back of head so crown would not look like a serving tray, and finally the stretching of pug nose. This was the longest and performed by many household persons, for each person had a different opinion of super-model standards.

'She wet me right down to my underskirt,' muttered Nenda increasing the diameter of the black sepia dot. 'If this wretched rain continues I wonder how I am going to get my clothes dried.'

'Cheekay, you are not wearing an underskirt?' asked Ammi cheekily, pulling my nose with all her strength. My nose was her top priority, obviously to distinguish me from Thathi's pug nosed sisters.

'*Aey mae*, don't be so cheeky, we village people don't wear *sukuruththang* (intricately complicated) clothes like you town people.'

'Aney, why not? I am sure it will suit you very well.'

'Don't annoy my tongue to say something it might regret!'

Ammi laughed heartily, obviously visualizing Nenda in feathered bras and sequined panties; bowlegs raised on platform shoes.

'Without laughing like a Jak fruit which is about to split, you had better try to do something about this child bringing the house down while bathing. I must say, I have never seen a child like this. Normally children love the water.'

'So what can we do about it? The only thing we can do is not to bathe her and keep her in filth.'

'Easy for you to talk,' replied Nenda crossly, 'you are hardly here, it's always Mummy and I who are deafened by her cries. It breaks our heart.'

'If you can't bear it put some cotton wool in your ears.'

'You shouldn't be a mother, you should have been born a rattlesnake. Aney chooti putha what would you do if I wasn't around to protect you?' cooed Nenda into my ears. 'There, finally in dry clothes.' Achi entered the room.

'*Anty*, I don't know, Mali doesn't seem to care at all, but you should check with an astrologer as to why this child cries when she sees water.'

'As if astrologer's know such things!'

'Of course they know. Maybe it has something to do with her last birth. Maybe she has a fear of water due to some accident with water. Maybe she drowned? Or was killed by a crocodile in a river? Or maybe she fell off a ferry? I remember! It was about ten months ago, that a ferry-load of people died while trying to cross the Kelani river during the monsoons. There was even a whole group of school children on that ferry. I heard the mothers crying and relating the incident on the radio.'

'Why the Kelani river, maybe she was on the Titanic,' replied Ammi laughing.

'You laugh! But it does not make any sense that a child born into the Meena lagna cries so much when she sees water. Normally all Meena lagna people love water. After all they are like fish and a fish cannot exist without water. Unless of course she is not a Meena lagna, but something else?'

A hush entered the room. Ammi's laughter froze. Only for a moment…

'Of course she is Meena lagna,' replied Achi hurriedly clothing me and trying to drag me away from Nenda's contemplations. 'What else could she be if not Meena lagna? Three astrologers assured us that she was a Meena lagna.'

'Then why…?'

'I know Meena lagna people who hate water.' Ammi had found words again.

'Who?'

'Why there is…'

'Yes.'

'Dan and Seela, they smell so much because they never wash. And they are Meena lagna.'

'Who are they, I don't know them?' Even Achi looked a bit confused.

'See you don't know everything do you?' replied Ammi. The moment's contemplation about Meena lagna was over. Ammi took me out of the room and out of Nenda's realm of contemplation.

Was I Meena lagna or not? Due to the saga of the broken hospital clock, I was given a karmic possibility. A Meena lagna of possibility, not of certainty. And the less one spoke about my non-Meena characteristics, it was easier for Ammi and Achi to live by the lie they had created. My grandmother and mother were masters of karmic flexibility. The rest of us were the unthinking players of their game.

If they would initiate me, I would have liked to play the game with them. I liked flexibility and I liked the idea of the Titanic. Yes, the more I contemplated, I was sure that I had been on the Titanic. Somewhere in the labyrinth of my mind I began to see water. It was water that was different from the bathtub water and the king-coconut water. The Kelani river ferry was traditional, native, goday and pastoral. The Titanic, on the other hand, had been a historical calamity. I liked being a part of a historical calamity. In the middle of historic calamity, a flat nose and black ears lose the prominence they have in a life which has no historic calamity.

Incidentally, just to get the facts straight. I never had a dislike for water. I did not love it either. Perhaps I was not a true Piscean, more of an amphibian sort. Unfortunately the zodiac bore only fish and crustaceans, even when time stood still. On the other hand, I believe, on that day when time had stood still at eight-eight, the zodiac had not given birth to a fish, but an amphibian. Myself.

I cried because there was nothing to laugh about. Time was killing memory. What had happened to the Titanic?

7

True to astrological prediction, the family fortunes began to change after I was born. At first, slowly. Achi re-opened the boarding school she had before she began her wedding cake manufacturing business. Siya's heart was discovered to have exceeded the size of a mango and was becoming the size of a watermelon, like Achi's heart and ordered by the doctor to stop climbing stairs. It was not possible, for Siya and Achi lived in the upstairs part of our house while we were in the downstairs part. The doctor asked him to move into a stair-less house. But stair-less houses cost more than stair-cased houses. Even though I had been born for the purpose of moving planets, it was evident that my slow growth was not ready to deal with planets - not yet. Multi-vitamin syrups, cod liver oils and vitamin C cordials supplemented my meals, but they were as ineffective as my planetary movements. Since I could not be returned, other options were sought. Hence, on a rainy Sunday morning when the national newspapers were not delivered due to the weight of the monsoons, we exchanged places. Furniture, beds, cutlery, crockery went up, while Thathi's newspapers and Ammi's head-line text books came down. The only items that remained where they were, were Siya's whisky bottles. Not because Ammi or Thathi drank whisky, but whisky apparently contributed negatively to growing hearts of elderly people. Just like the staircases.

Achi, her domestics and her boarders moved downstairs. I moved upstairs with Ammi's milk filled breasts, TM Mozart, Nenda and Karunawathie the servant. Thathi did not move up or down. He was like the whisky bottle. If he got tired, he just removed his shoes and slept on the closest horizontal piece of furniture.

It is not correct to say that I could not move planets. I did. Perhaps not in the way my family expected its movements, but things did change.

Nenda's cowcatcher teeth fell out. The empty crater was replaced by a perfect set of man-made teeth that no longer spluttered when she sang tuwinkle tuwinkle little star.

My planetary feats went beyond the limits of the capital where we lived. Kiriamma, who lived in the village of my father's birth, found the hundred rupees she had lost two years ago. It had been in a box of wooden building blocks that was rescued from a cupboard filled with termites and taken out and cleaned in order to be sent to me as a part of my 'welcome to the world' gift collection.

Aiya, was discovered to be not only a little TM Mozart, but a cricketing genius as well. He became the only known miniature personality in the cricketing history of Ceylon, to play in a cricket team of under-eights while being only four. My mother bought a new table to keep his cricketing trophies. The vendor had sold her a cheap chest of mango wood, but on closer inspection at home, through the genial eyes of my uncle Buddhi, it was discovered to be mahogany and not mango. Now my mother's planets were moving positively as well. She liked to get a good deal for Thathi's money. Furthermore, TM Mozart's voice improved. Instead of singing 'tinkle tinkle little star' to me, he now sang it to his trophies.

All these changes were trivialities as karmic happenings. The most important benefactor of my birth was Thathi. He was suddenly sent by the highways department to Japan to follow a course on building bridges. My father had been a master of roads. The roads he made survived the most amount of monsoons. But he was a stranger to bridges. So why did the government decide to teach him bridges? Was it due to the superiority of his roads in contrast to all other roads that disintegrated with the first rains? Or else, was it because of his relationship to an immortal bridge? The bridge over the river Kwai.

When David Lean and his entourage of celebrities came to our island to eternalise the atrocities of the Japanese in World war two - in Technicolor, Thathi's cousin Buddhi, a creative genius who could build a radio with a string hopper mould and two hair pins or a motor-bike with a rusted kitchen knife and a salmon tin, had been chosen to build the bridge on the river Kwai over our drought ridden Kelani river. Coconut trunks instead of Burmese teak. The bridge uncle Buddhi built had been far superior to the original bridge on the river Kwai, so people began to say that if uncle Buddhi had built the bridge for the Japanese, the Allies would never have won the war.

Amidst this celebrity status, the Japanese government offered a scholarship through the Ceylonese government to uncle Buddhi to come to Japan and learn to build bridges. Uncle Buddhi knew how to build bridges. He didn't have to learn from the Japanese how to build them. So, it was evident that the real goal of the Japanese had been, on the pretext of teaching uncle Buddhi the craft of building real bridges, to siphon his creative knowledge and start the war all over again.

Uncle Buddhi could not take up the scholarship; the Ceylonese government never offered it to him. Instead they offered it to my father. No one knew why they did so, but they did. He reaped the glories of connection and tropical logic. If one cousin had the creativity to rebuild a famous bridge for a film, the other cousin would certainly have the vision to build one for posterity. The Ceylonese government had the final say. And to the Japanese, we all looked alike. Descendents of the black bellied, black eared Ravana.

Thathi went to Japan. He learned to build bridges and returned in three months. On his return, the highways department was renamed the department of highways and bridges. One minister and one secretary attended to fiscal matters. My father attended to all other matters. A few months later, due to certain fiscal irregularities - internally politicised, the bridges part of the highways department was removed from the department of highways and bridges and was put under the department for canal and canal development. It now became the department for canal, canal development and bridges. The minister, his wife the junior minister and two secretaries were responsible for the fiscal matters. My father was responsible for all other matters.

A few years later, a new junior minister, a new secretary to the junior minister and new fiscal irregularities, the bridge part was removed from the department for canal and canal development and was put under a brand new ministry fundamentally funded by the Japanese. The ministry for Mahaveli development.

The Mahaveli development ministry remained the ministry for Mahaveli development and the bridge part got sucked in, but remained nameless. Like the massive funding the Japanese contributed for the equal distribution of the Mahaveli's waters for cultivators of the dry zones.

The new minister promised the elimination of drought, an abundant Mahaveli and an end to the ferryman - all with Japanese funding. The funding remained unchanged. But not the minister's promises. Drought was not eliminated. The Mahaveli was not deviated and the ferryman remained, with only a ferry and no water. The minister who had lived in a rented annex with his humble wife and three humble children now moved into his own mansion. The wife became no longer humble. And the three children were no longer seen in our country. Paris, London, New York... elsewhere.

Now my father became a top senior employee for three ministries. The highways department, the canal and canal development department and the Mahaveli department. We saw very little of him. He was extremely busy drawing plans for the deviation of the Mahaveli's waters when the rains came. During the rest of the time he supervised the elimination of potholes for the highways department.

Incidentally, in the ministry of canal and canal development, Thathi remained a non-functional top employee occasionally invited by the minister when they inaugurated new canal development projects. They would spend a few minutes on the deck of the motorboats; contemplate the eradication of mosquitoes before the minister would descend onto land to the sound of drumbeats and traditional dancers. The minister would then be engulfed in giant Jasmine flower garlands and Thathi would take an anonymous seat reserved for an anonymous top employee. Then, while the minister held his monologue about a wretched past, a bountiful present and a mosquito free future, if he should remain in power, Thathi would silently leave his seat in search of potholes. The minister was captivated by his own rhetoric. Ministers did not talk of potholes; they only spoke of new roads.

Then, the ministry for the elimination of Malaria was founded. Thathi was not offered a top employee post; rather the ministerial post. A minister without a party. Needless to say the Ministry for the elimination of Malaria had no fiscal problems since no developed country with fiscal excesses seemed to be particularly interested in funding a ministry for the elimination of Malaria. Countries with fiscal excesses preferred to manufacture the medication for the battle against Malaria. Thathi yo-yoed between accepting at once and accepting after thought. Not because he had a clue as to how he should run a ministry for the eradication of Malaria, but how could he refuse? Democracy, in my country was a thin layer of personality. Feudalism was character. We had been a nation of descendents of great kings. Now, without a king, the minister was king. My father, a humble civil servant could only accept. He was not of a defiant nature. A man could not refuse a minister.

But Ammi put her foot down. She still believed in kings. In the absence of a king the minister never became king. Not to her. Hence, like great Lord Shiva bringing the world to an end with one stamp of his foot, she put her foot down. She became Shiva, the destroyer of my father's career. Government jobs brought a certain prestige and household walls decorated with laminated photographs of handshakes. But it brought no fiscal gains. Not to us. A great question mark shadowed their bedroom. IF?

Needless to say, my father could not participate in bringing our country into a mosquito free future. Instead, he became a victim of a happening no astrologer had predicted. The question mark in the bedroom had been exorcised. But that is another story. For now I must return to the present. To Thathi's return from Japan. To Karma and Consequence.

8

Thathi returned from Japan with two materialistic acquisitions, which were to change my life. A Hillman car and a 'Made in Japan' camera. Camera in one hand, instruction pamphlet in the other, he set about the task of immortalizing me. Under the Araliya tree, beneath the Guava tree, in Nenda's arms, in Achi's arms, in Kiriamma's arms, in his sister Seela's arms, on the armchair, on the saucer chair, in the Hillman, on the Hillman, beside the Hillman… and many more. I obliged him and sustained excellent behavioural patterns. Even with Seela. After all who does not want to be immortalized?

Then came that fateful day when Thathi returned with a handful of snapshots and I had the opportunity of observing my appearance. I think God wanted to make a buffalo out of me. But, just before manufacture he opted for a Meena Lagna girl. My hairless head was shaped like a curved triangle with the foundation for horns being laid, but no horns. The chin was like a valley, in drought. My cheekbones protruded below the outer cantus of my eyes, giving me the appearance of a child born to the Dravidian mistress of Genghis Khan. A few barely evident strands of hair flattened with coconut oil made my head look like a butter nylon sari. The nose! More puggish than Seela's. Like a Jambu fruit run over by a bullock cart. My mouth and eyes were a saving grace. Eyes, not abnormal, somewhat elongated. But that could have been an integral part of the Made in Japan camera that made non-slit eyed Asians, slit eyed. Mouth, not abnormal, lips somewhat crooked, but a negligible deficit. The outcome of my hair was still in the stars. If karma was on my side I would inherit Ammi's straight and silky tresses, if karma was against me, my father's baldness and if karma was ambivalent, my aunt Seela's grizzly mane. I made a mental note to not be obnoxious and please karma. My ears seemed to have lightened, or rather did not seem to be as dark as Seela's description. The photographs were black and white and my ears were gray. I suppose I ought to thank black and white photography and not my karma. Finally, body and legs were in a united haze. Body was always clad in miniature bed jacket and the legs were always folded or carried. I did harbour some doubts whether I could be suffering from some muscular atrophy due to the incessant rubbing sessions, which had probably slimmed my legs down to the size of joss sticks.

Despite this depressing summation of individual sensory organs, as a compound or a whole I could not be described as an ugly. In fact, in certain shots I did look quite pleasing. Pleasing as opposed to ugly. Especially in over-exposed snapshots where the colour chart between black and white lightened, like TM Mozart playing a lower octave on the piano, when uncle Buddhi came to sing.

By the age of four, the blackness of my ears had spread to the rest of my body like an urticaria. I could no longer seek satisfaction in black and white photographs. Fujicolor had invaded the nation. Everything was now coloured. The white Hillman was painted green to look better in the coloured snap-shot. The Phillips refrigerator, turquoise blue and Achi's grey hair raven black. I occasionally scrutinized an over-exposed, blurred photo for molecules of prettiness, but these blurry moments had become rare. Thathi had studied and re-studied the instruction manual and become quite an expert in non over-exposed photography. Fortunately his attention towards family waned. After the Ministers took special care of appointing him the most senior employee of all their ministries, the condition of roads in our country took priority over humans. Potholes got preference to people.

He now not only covered up each and every pothole, he even photographed them. Before the monsoons and after the monsoons. Before repair and after repair. With the lapse of time the potholes became more interesting than I. I was sacrificed to the silver fish that nourished themselves on photograph albums that lay untouched in wooden cupboards belonging to a non-Fujicolour black and white past.

9

At the age of four, I was scrubbed, powdered, eau-de-cologned, hair flattened with coconut oil; un-oiled section tied into a coconut tree with white ribbon at root and sent to school. A Christian, missionary, English speaking school for female children. I was not a Christian child. But since my mother had attended the same school, my non-Christianity was unimportant.

This school had two mediums. The Sinhala medium and the Tamil medium. When my mother had been in this school, they had even had an English medium. Then the native government brought in the native languages and came to the conclusion that there were no native English in the English medium. The three mediums became two.

We still learned the same things, but in different languages. Tamil teachers taught the Tamil children and Sinhalese teachers taught the Sinhala children. The other minority teachers taught both mediums. We did not mix with each other. But we sat together during the morning assembly. Only the Christian children did not sit with us and went into the school chapel to sing their hymns and thank the missionaries for bringing Jesus Christ to Ceylon and starting our girls' school. The Tamil children sat with us in a big hall with rickety fans that made a great din and sang the national anthem in Sinhalese. I think the Tamil children only moved their lips. Then we went in separate lines to our separate classrooms. Only the mixed children were lucky. The Tamil-Sinhala or the Burger-Sinhala or the Muslims could choose their own medium. Most of them decided to go to another school and study in English.

This school's children wore the ugliest school uniform ever created. Square neck, square pleats, square pocket, square armholes and square buckle. White. On that first day I felt like a pot of treacle unevenly covered with curd. My rounding frame bursting out of the square mis-creation. I looked so hideous, that I swore neither to be seen nor to be heard. Never. On the other hand 'never' was too long for a four year old so I decided to continue my 'never' during hours clad in square attire.

I hid myself at the back of the classroom between the A,B,C posters and the cupboard with paint tins and hoped I would not be noticed. A few girls tried to make an odd attempt to smile with me, but I pretended to be otherwise engaged. The Ant under the letter 'A' had six hairs on its head. The butterfly under 'B' was blind in one eye. The cat under the letter 'C' had four whiskers on one side and three on the other. The piano under the 'P' did not have a middle C and the Xylophone under the 'X' was a mouth organ, not a xylophone.

It wasn't difficult to be obscure on that first day. Most of the girls were either crying or hanging on to mothers or servants. I had no one to cling on to. My mother had dropped me off in the green Hillman and gone for a chat. Since she was absent there was no point in crying. The teachers were occupied eating hot-dogs and drinking tea, talking about holidays and pregnancies. I spent the day between blue and red paint tins, quite content observing the sobbing children and their excitable mothers who had metamorphosed from neatly attired women to a flock of cackling birds.

A thud, a slob, a rolling… and I stood in the middle of the red and blue paint tins, fallen onto the ground and meandering into the colour purple… or was it brown? Hush. The twittering ceased and the teachers' hot-dogs got stuck in their oesophagus. I did not stay to find out whether the colour was brown or purple. I ran.

I ran as fast as my skinny legs could carry me. Psychedelic footprints remained in my tracks. I kept running as the blue powder paint dried and hardened on my left leg, and the red powder paint hardened on my right leg. But where could I run? I knew neither the entrance nor the exit to this school and I did not know my way home either.

I wished the earth were a square so I could fall off when I had reached the end, but the earth was a ball and I could run forever. *Forever!* The thought augmented my panic. I was not a very athletic child. I stopped. I was standing near a drain. Behind me was a building with three rooms. Uniformed girls sat at their desks and listened to their teachers. In front of me the sound of drumbeats and a meticulous clutter of feet were projecting through the open windows. To my left was a garden of Shoe-flowers and Crotons. To my right was a dark doorway. Sari clad ladies were walking in and out. Suddenly, from the corner of my eye I saw my mother's familiar frame in the midst of an animated conversation with someone I didn't know. Pity the world was not a square. As I was about to hide in the drain, she saw me. A blue left leg and a red right leg, cracked like sub-standard marble work. Fire blazing from her eyes and smoke emanating from her nostrils, she darted and grabbed me in the midst of a verbal avalanche, put me into the green Hillman and drove home. In silence.

As the world was not a square and the calendar had no end, the day evolved into night and the night evolved to day. Bathed, scrubbed, re eau-de-cologned, re-oiled, two brown legs, two white socks, two black shoes, a white uniform, a new day and another chance. I got into the green Hillman at 7.30am. I arrived at school. Punctual. In silence.

She was still fuming. My mother. Like a dragon with a scorched tongue. Not so much about me looking like a reincarnated fresco, rather for making a dent in her spotless past-pupil reputation. I was obviously a product of erratic genetics. Too many village chromosomes inherited from my father and his sisters.

As much as my mother was loved and adored by her teachers, past and present, I was to be deplored and detested. Her love for school was my hate. Her moment of joy, my moment of misery. But, as my chief karmic negotiator and the trustee of my karma, she was indispensable to my existence. So, the stream began to flow and the current too strong for me to get out. If I tried, I would crush my head against a rock, get jolted around, hang on a while on a floating log and sometime, along this karmic journey flow again. I learned how to avoid the rocks - and survive.

Obscurity became my strength. I became a chameleon, capable of changing colours, immaterial of time or space. I walked into the classroom just as the bell began to ring and thirty five eager pupils ran to their desks and thirty something mothers and nannies left the school premises. I assumed an aura of authority, despite the cackling sounds of a few pupils who had obviously seen my previous day's escapade. I occupied the free desk in the last row of the classroom and pulled the chair away from the desk and sat. There were about three feet between the table and me. This time it was the Sinhala alphabet above me to the right. A, Amma (mother), cross-eyed. Aa, Aatha (grandfather), emaciated. Ae, Aetha (tusker), feeble. Obviously a zoo tusker, not a temple tusker. Aäe....

Two ladies entered the classroom. The teachers. A fair, small nosed, dainty teacher in a Punjabi suit, with a thick, black plait hanging down to her waist. The other: fat, black, cut away blouse, hipster sari, grizzly curls on head like the rain forest, pug nosed. The Dravidian and the Aryan. The Punjabi suited, doe eyed, lotus lipped victim of Ravana's passion and the big bellied, big-breasted sister of Ravana, nobody's passion.

'Good morning children,' said the two. Loud and clear. In unison. 'Good morning teacher,' said about five variously pitched, non-united voices, while the rest of the twenty-five held their tongues. I belonged to the twenty-five.

'Oh, why is it that only a handful of you are saying good morning?'

'The others are not having a good morning teacher,' squeaked an over-eager pupil. I couldn't see her face from where I stood, but her arms and legs were a beautiful shade of marshmallow pink.

'Never mind lets try again,' said the black teacher, ignoring Marshmallow's over-eager commentary. The dainty, Punjabi clad teacher twirled her plait, which hung over her shoulder.

'Good morning children,' again both teachers in unison.

'Good morning teacher,' repeated five loud voices, about twenty quiet voices and the rest simulated the words. I belonged to the latter. Marshmallow belonged to the first five.

'That was very nice,' said the black teacher, 'Now try to say good morning with both our names, you all remember our names don't you?' I did not know due to the blue and red turbulence of the previous day.

'Yes, yes teacher I remember very well, you are Miss...,' that was Marshmallow again, jumping up and down with a raised hand like an electrocuted pudding made of pink gelatine.

'Yes, yes, we know that you are a very attentive child, now let us see if the others know,' Marshmallow stopped jumping, but her arm retained its pointed position directed towards the ceiling.

'So now think children, this is Miss... ,' she was pointing to the Punjabi clad teacher who had temporarily ceased to twirl her plait and had assumed the position of Queen Viharamahadevi, moulded into a statue after the flood.

'Fatima, she is Miss Fatima,' there was no need to look. It was none other than Marshmallow.

'Right dear, you are correct,' said the black teacher with a tone of exasperation lurking within her sentence, 'but I told you let one of the others answer the questions.'

Marshmallow. An only female child, an only fair skinned female child in a family of dark skinned pastry shop owners. She had been fed with butter and pastries; we had been fed with rice and vegetables. She knew no limits. And the teachers did not intervene. They had already been bribed for the day with a sumptuous breakfast of Chinese rolls, prawn pies and cutlets. Marshmallow had by now removed her hand from its towards the ceiling posture and was smiling avidly at the rest of the children.

'So now say good morning to Miss Fatima,'

'Good morning Miss Fatima,' needless to say, Marshmallow again was loud and clear. The rest of us had evolved into a murmur. The black teacher, in her battle between discipline and a sumptuous breakfast was overruled by the breakfast. For the moment.

'Now do you all remember my name?' The black teacher.

'Yes, yes Miss you are Miss Lili... Lili... Lila...,' the pastries were beginning to lose their enchantment.

'Close, very close. Does anyone else remember my name?'

No one even tried to remember. We were happy when Marshmallow's pastry fed brain cells absorbed the material for the rest of us.

'Lilamani...' It was evident who had spoken.

'Not quite, my dear, try again.' Like a puff pastry, un-puffing when the oven door opened, she pouted, she frowned, she puffed. Her eyes, nose, ears and mouth lost their compact gelatinous structure and turned into a melted pink liquid, like a Faluda; the fat teachers name had escaped her.

'Miss Lily Marlene.'

All eyes turned towards the last row left side of the class. There stood, stooped and lanky, Chandrika. Meaning, the luminous radiant moon.

But, as black as night and as thin as a scorched papyrus on the banks of the Nile.

'Correct, now say good morning Miss Lily Marlene,'

'Good Morning Miss Lily Marlene,'

'And Miss Fatima?'

'Good morning Miss Fatima.' All.

'Very nice children, now before you introduce yourselves to us, we are going to sing the school hymn together.'

Singing was an integral part of Miss Lily Marlene's karmic constellation. She began her song, the hymn. She sang and she sang. All sixteen verses from the depths of her corpulent being. She sang of grandiose achievements, of missionaries, of sewing, of reaping, of harvesting, of fathers, of sons, of lords and a numerous collection of persons lying under the tombstones of the Christian part of the Colombo cemetery.

I stared in awe at this creature, with her grizzly head and abundant frame, as she dilated her lungs and manoeuvred her lips to sing the words of a song about happenings long gone, and people long dead. Despite chameleon qualities, I could not help being beguiled by the luxuriousness of her voice and the clarity of her words. The carbon compounds of the dead were restructured into glittering diamonds as they left her throat.

Meanwhile Miss Fatima twirled her plait and sang her version of whispering hope. In silence. As the song ended even Marshmallow's pastry fed mouth was ajar. 'That was a very nice song Miss Lily Malini,' donated the precocious beast.

'That was not a song, that was a hymn and if you think a bit before you speak, you will realize that my name is not Lily Malini, but?...'

'Lily Marlene,' said the black radiant moon.

'Now children I want you all to sit down and let us begin with today's lesson.'

I had learned my lesson. Only a Lily Marlene was able to sing a hymn. Not a Lili Malini.

We sat making a great racket. I pushed myself further away from the table and sat almost pasted on the wall. I don't know why, I just did

it. Perhaps I had not been given the correct auspicious moment to start
my learning process. Perhaps the first step needed to be taken to the left
and not to the right. Perhaps I ought to have entered the school from
the North entrance and not the South? Perhaps everything was
absolutely right, but a Gecko had squeaked when I was leaving and we
had not heard hear it. Gecko squeakings were a bad omen. No matter,
something was radically wrong. Everything I did or tried to do had
either misfired or was to misfire and I was to feel a misfit. Perhaps it all
boiled down to the broken clock in the labour room, or perhaps not. I
could not change my karma.

I sat on the chair and kept a three foot distance from the desk.
I became more a part of the wall. This obviously did not please Miss
Lily M. 'You can come forward my dear,' she said. I pretended to
be deaf and donated my undivided attention to the squirrel that was
prancing about on the branches of the Jam tree outside. 'Darling, you
can come forward with your chair.' I was still deaf.
'What is your name darling?'
Silence.
'*Hello*, my dear, what's your name?'
Silence.
'She is Manuka. Her mother told me...' Marshmallow's pastry fed mouth
decided to become my mouthpiece. All the more reason not to talk.
'Manuka, don't be shy just pull your chair to the desk.'
The squirrel had now jumped onto another branch. Then the language
changed.
'*Manuka putuwa adinna meseta,*' the Sinhala language tinged with a
Tamil accent. Miss Fatima had finally spoken. I decided to react, but
delayed the reaction. As I turned my head towards the two teachers,
they had put their heads together and were conducting a conversation
of utmost conspiracy. 'You are Malini's daughter aren't you?' They had
uttered the magic word. I was petrified of my mother's wrath. She was
not far away.

My mother's deviating headline had brought her to school along
with me. She was now the primary school Buddhism teacher. I didn't
think she knew anything about Buddhism. If she did, she had not taught
it to me as yet. Nenda had taught me whatever I knew about

Buddhism. But Ammi was here, near me. While other mothers stayed in their kitchens and baked Betty Crocker's chocolate cake, my mother competed with Jupiter in the house of wisdom and followed me to school.

I was incarcerated. Every step, every move, every act of disobedience was noted and reported. It flew to my mother's ears faster than an Apollo rocket. In order to avoid wrath, I had to blend. Blend into the massive learning machine. I pulled the table towards the chair.

But, it was not right. Children were not supposed to pull the table towards the chair, only the chair towards the table. I was not supposed to look at the squirrel, but at the teacher. I was a part of the geometric structure of the classroom, seven in a row and a total of five rows. When I pulled the table towards the chair I was no longer a part of the row and was destroying the geometrical structure. Who knows, perhaps Newton and Copernicus started the same way I did? Or, perhaps Laurel and Hardy?

At eight fifty-five am on that seventh day in January I learned that the chair belonged to the table and not the table to the chair. Even though I now stood outside the class with my face to the wall, the geometric structure of the classroom had been maintained. Miss Fatima released her plait, and pulled the chair towards the table. I was punished. Outside with the squirrels.

The interval bell rang. Marshmallow bit into her prawn pastry while thirty four hungry mouths swallowed spit. I bit in to my tissue paper thin *Mallung* sandwich. No one watched and no one swallowed spit. Sliced green leaves between two slices of bread was no reason for envy.

The bell rang again, I was unpunished and we resumed the process of learning. Chapter: communication – subtitle: names.
'So now children we do not need to introduce ourselves any more,' said Miss Lily Marlene. Miss Fatima re-braided her plait.
'You all now know our names…?'
Marshmallow contributed as usual.
'So now that you know our names, begin with your names.'
Like a fresco falling out of the Sigiriya rock, she twirled, swayed her pigtails, tucked her hands on her belted hips and said: 'My name is Madhubakshini.'

'Very nice dear, but I want to hear all your names and in order. One after the other. Let us start from the left side of the class. Do you all know which side is the left?'

'In Ceylon we use the left hand to wash our backside after doing kakki.'

Miss Fatima stopped braiding her hair and stared at pastry M in mortification. Speechless. Why? She was right. The right hand was used to eat rice and the left to wash the back. That was the first thing we learned in our lives. Differentiating the right hand from the left was an integral part of our education. It had nothing to do with table manners, but went deeper. It was culture. It distinguished the good from the bad, the sacred from the un-sacred. Rice was sacred, shit was not. Only foreigners were excused when they came to our country and made the cardinal mistake of eating rice with the left hand. But they were not a product of our civilization. Their civilizations were somewhat doubtful anyway. After all, their Jesus died like a half naked beggar on the cross, but our Lord Buddha was a prince with royal luxury. Of course he had decided to give up this luxury, but that was his problem, not ours. We children needed no mothers, fathers or loving relatives to teach us this wisdom of the left and the right. It was communicated by the servants, who usually had to carry out the unholy task of washing out backsides after the big job. Therefore, the earlier we learned to distinguish between the left and the right meant the lessening of domestic chores for servants.

I don't know why Miss Fatima looked so baffled. Out of all the nonsense Marshmallow had donated in the course of our relatively brief school exposure, this was the most intelligent statement she had made. Either Miss Fatima who was Muslim, used the rice eating hand to wash her back, did not wash her back, or perhaps did not eat rice. As I pondered the norms of Miss Fatima's Muslim civilization in comparison to our Buddhist civilization, the left side of the class had been discovered.

I tried to concentrate on the names, the voices and the volumes. In my thirty-fifth position within this geometric equilibrium it was not possible to see the faces belonging to the names. A bit of height and a bit of girth was all that was evident from the rear.

I tried to associate the names with the rears. But it was a difficult task. The box pleats at the back were the same as the box pleats in the front. And the box pleats to the right were the same as the box pleats to the left. Name remembering, based on the differentiation of box pleats was a Herculean feat for a non-genial four year old. Obviously my parents and co-inhabitants of the household had been lax in brain training this four year old.

The life of a child was something like the Karapincha tree. When it was needed for adding flavour to the curry, it was plucked and utilized. Thereafter, discarded. When it rustled a bit too much in the monsoon wind the dog would bark all night long. The dog would be removed from the kennel and tied onto the Karapincha tree. He would then stop barking and piss on the tree all night long. But, because of that precise indefinable taste the Karapincha leaf possessed, it was a requisite for that inexplicable element that differentiated Ceylonese curry to Indian curry. Karapincha made us a unique island and India a part of a common massive subcontinent. Hence, watered and cow-dunged for that special something, Karapincha was essential.

Names, names, names. Thirty-four new names to remember. Complicated names. I had never heard them before. In the last four years of my birth I did not have to remember a single name. Not even my own. After all when did I have to call myself by my own name? The inhabitants of my household communicated with me with individual interpretations to my being, never my name. Little girl, darling, baby, daughter, chooti, etcetera. The people around me were either relatives or servants. Addressed with due respect or disrespect. Occasionally I would be confronted with a new servant and a new name. But if I shouted 'Kakki', she would wash my back and I needed to memorize no name for that. Now and then I would remember a name. I remember Karunawathie. She was only a few years older than I was and did not wash my back. But in six months she was gone. Either the Sinhala New year, the Tamil New year, the Prophet Mohammed's birthday or Vesak. They usually chose not to return. I was granted another six months to learn a name or to continue with Kakki.

Anyway it was no complicated task. Village people were not so fancifully complicated as Colombo school children, they only had about five names that circulated around the entire community. Karunawathie, Sumanawathie, Leelawathie, Somawathie or Premawathie if they were Sinhalese. Podian or Letchumi if they were Tamil. Hasan, Husein or Mohommed if Muslim. And Mary or Joseph for the rare Christian.

In the English speaking missionary school it was different. Many complicated tongue twisters occupied the desks in the classroom. Madhubhakshini headed the list. I was saturated. I locked my ears. Silence.

Should I look out of the window at the squirrel…? The branches of the Jam tree swayed minus the squirrel. 'You are next my dear, why don't you introduce yourself to us?'

I imagined the squirrel. Brown. No, golden brown. Fat. Three black stripes on the back. Prince Rama's fingerprints. Prince Rama had stroked squirrels in the forests surrounding Lanka, having no Princess Sita to stroke. Sita had been kidnapped by Ravana, the Raksha king and imprisoned in his kingdom of Lanka. Doe eyed, lotus lipped Sita and doe eyed, lotus lipped Rama were separated. So the squirrels got their stripes.

'You over there, in the corner…'

My name did not match any of the other names within this structure. It had a strange angular twist. Dry. Barren. Hard. Like a desert. Why were my parents not more of the mass follower types? Sai Baba devotees, born-again Christians, Hare-Krishnas, whatever. But they were individualists. They had to give me a name that no one else in this world had, or would dream of having. A linguistic novelty. Manuka. How could I now change hues like a chameleon when destined to stand apart with such a name?

'We are waiting my dear.'

'Who, I?' I whispered, finding it difficult to communicate in English, having spoken with Nenda and the servants in Sinhala for the past four years.

'Yes you.'

I stared at her with a blank expression as thirty four heads turned towards me 'Oyata therenawada?' Miss Fatima with the Tamil highlights taking over the task of integrating children with linguistic autism. I was submerged in a riddle. Miss Fatima spoke a bad Sinhalese tinged with a heavy Tamil accent, proudly, fearlessly. And I had a morbid fear of communicating my deficient English with its heavy Sinhala accent.

'*Therenewa neda?*'

I nodded. Eyes on the blackboard.

'*Ithin kiyanne nama.*'

'Miss, I know her name,' Marshmallow shouted, 'Makuna.'

'A bit louder, dear.'

'MAKUNA,' Marshmallow shouted. They all laughed. Even the teachers.

Makuna was a bug. Manuka was the girl.

Now, I the girl was a bug.

BUG.

Marshmallow's language had been fertilized with cream bun éclairs and puff pastries. Mine with rice and curry.

She was a lady, I was a bug.

10

I was determined to find out from which flea infested garbage dump my parents had salvaged my name. But before I could do so, Ammi had supplementary plans for my future. The autistic laboriousness of divulging my name had reached her ears and the illness swiftly diagnosed: genetic malfunction of English language due to karmic connection to my father and his sisters.

That very afternoon I started elocution classes with Miss Manel White Ratnayake. I never understood why she had so many surnames and when I tried to ask Ammi, she asked me to be quiet and listen and not talk since I had a pathological knack of embarrassing her in whatever I did and wherever I went. She had globalised my karmic molecular activities.

Miss Manel White Ratnayake had facial muscles of elastic. When she spoke the words that had once been uttered by the kings and queens of England, they looked quite dramatically ridiculous. I could visualize George the First, gout ridden and obese, spurting Beetle juice out of his paralytic lips and speaking the language of kings. English. With the help of Miss White, I embarked on the journey towards verbal coronation.

Miss Manel White Ratnayake could extend the English alphabet beyond its twenty six letters. Her words never ended and her sentences flowed like streams, never encountering drought. Occasionally, like an amphibian requiring a shot of oxygen, she would pout her lips and emerge from the stream of words to articulate a word beginning with an 'O', then dive inside and swim further. I suffered facial muscle exhaustion learning elocution under Miss White Ratnayake. But she instilled in me a love for the dramatic. And somewhere in the labyrinth of my chameleon brain I retained her wonderful mimicry for later use.

BUG:

The New revised English Dictionary. 200,000 entries. 800,000 definitions. 600,000 facts. 30 dictionaries, glossaries and reference works in one.

Bug: Between buffoonery and bugaboo (origin unknown).

Bug: An insect or another creeping or crawling invertebrate. An obnoxious insect. Bed bug. Head louse.

Any of the order of Hemiptera. Insect with sucking mouthparts. Incomplete metamorphosis. Destructive plant pest. (true Bug)

An unexpected defect. Fault. Flaw. Imperfection.

Disease producing germ. Or a disease caused by it.

Fad. Enthusiasm. Enthusiast.

Concealed listening device. (Origin unknown. Same as bugaboo)

Solving the meaning of my bug related name by referral of a dictionary had not been successful. There were too many explanations. Possibly, I could salvage one to fit my description. Perhaps concealed listening device? Not quite satisfactory. Black ears given too much prominence. I could perhaps browse under the word Manuka. But, between 'Manufacturer' and 'Manumission' there was no Manuka. Not even an empty space for later discoveries or inventions. Manufacturer preceded a hypothetical Manuka and Manumission followed. Emancipation from slavery. Origin known.

I had only one option. That was to break Ammi's silence. Miss Manel White Ratnayake's facial elasticity was now required. I placed myself in front of the mirror. Ignored all black and flat sensory organs, and worked on my facial muscles. Finally satisfied with a cross between Miss White and King George, I entered my parents' bedroom.

It was shortly before dinner-time and Ammi was seated at the dressing table transferring 4711 Eau de Cologne from a family sized bottle into a pimple size bottle. She saw my reflection in the mirror but ignored me and concentrated on the act of suction and transport between the two bottles and her mouth. She was evidently seething. Nothing new. Ammi was a deadly volcano, capable of spewing lava further than any volcano on earth, the oceans or Mars. I switched on my expression. 'Ammi what does my name mean?'

'How do I know?'

It would have been untactful to ask her why she did not know the meaning of her daughter's name for it was obvious that she was involved in the global search for a name that no human being living or dead had ever possessed. 'You don't know?'

Silence. The pimple bottle for the dressing table was now full. She began filling a smaller pimple bottle for her handbag, in case pimples attempted to protrude while attending deviating headline classes. 'Who would know?'

'I don't know, ask your father.'

'But he is not here.' Thathi was finished with building bridges and was now back to building roads. Not the usual covering potholes, but real roads. From the beginning. Roads where no human tread, only monkeys tangoed on the trees. Where Hanuman, the son of the god of wind, the monkey warrior from India had obviously procreated like an amoeba before rescuing Princess Sita from Ravana.

There was no explanation for Thathi building roads in this area. There were no people there, only monkeys. Perhaps my father wanted to make it easier for Hanuman, in case he needed to invade Lanka again.

We did not see our father often. Sometimes once in fourteen days, sometimes once in ten. When Ammi placed a trunk call and blasted him for neglecting the family, he would come home again. 'Ammi?'

'Then wait till he comes,' she said without looking at me.

She locked the family size eau-de-cologne bottle in the dressing room cupboard, put on a dressing gown with gene manipulated flowers found only on dressing gowns, not in nature, wore her new bath cap from Japan, which had arrived in the same shipment as the Hillman and the camera, and with more cherry blossoms on her head than in the whole of Japan, she took the toilet size bottle of eau-de-cologne and went for a body wash. I was left in the room with the two pimple sized bottles and silence. Another source had to be sought out. Nenda?

Nenda was in the pantry, in the middle of a usual third person verbal battle with Magi who was in the kitchen. Nenda and Magi always fought. They had nothing in common except the cowcatcher, but even after Nenda's cowcatcher had been replaced by a perfect set of man made teeth they still fought. Nenda was in charge of home affairs, Magi in charge of kitchen affairs. Nenda was Ammi's protégée; Magi, Achi's. Magi had one son, Nenda had none. Magi was black, Nenda white. They had absolutely nothing to do with each other so they fought

with each other. Usually about different topics. Nenda shouted from
the pantry and Magi from the kitchen while the dog barked in-between.
Nenda: I don't know why certain people are getting unnecessarily
excited when no one spoke about them.
Magi: Yes, yes, we know even if we were not spoken to that when
certain people say that sugar is finishing very fast, they really mean that
we have stolen and eaten the sugar.
Nenda: I don't know why certain people's ears are always open to
commentaries that do not concern them.
Magi: Today it is sugar, tomorrow it is rice, day after tomorrow it is
Maldive fish...
Nenda: When certain people are always talking about stealing and
eating when they have not been spoken to, they must know what they
are talking about.
Magi: Yes, yes, we know that certain people have been given special
powers and they are only happy when the others leave and return to
their villages. Then they can steal and eat alone without any fear.
Nenda: If the people who are stealing and eating had a home to return
to, they wouldn't be sitting in a sooty kitchen haunted by cockroaches
and stealing and eating.

This verbal battle in the third person conducted between the
pantry and the kitchen was one that had crossed many rebirths. It needed
foreign intervention. Me. *'Nenda, Thathi ai kawaddha enné?'* (Nenda,
when is Thathi coming again?)
'Ooong weekend ekata ei' (Ooong, he should be here for the weekend.)
'Ei ei, kata-arala balaagena inna enakal. Yai Amma balanna.' (Open your
mouth and wait till he comes. He will go to visit his mother.) 'That is
more important to him than his wife and children no.' Ammi had no
hot water for her body wash as the gas geyser had not been turned on.
She had been shouting from the bathroom until she was blue in the
face, but the battle about the sugar thief had reached a crescendo and
her shouting had not been heard.

'Aney, if you open your mouth you only say sinful filthy things,'
said Nenda. She could not bear anyone speaking negatively about my
father. Truth was subjective. My father was always right. Noble and
beyond fault. Various individuals saw with different eyes. My left eye

differed from my right eye. Together, they were influenced by reason.
But when reason is defeated? Was I then blind? When it came to Thathi,
Nenda was certainly blind. And right.

'What do you mean sinful things, I am only portraying the truth
the way it really is. This child needs to talk to her father about an
important thing and she can't do so. He is not here. In fact he is never
here.' I had begun to exist again in Ammi's life. Her anger had changed
direction. It was now my father's turn.

'Putha you can talk to Thathi when he comes for the weekend,'
Nenda tried to console me.
'As if he'll come.'
'He'll come.'
'How do you know?'
'I know.' Nenda possessed a telepathic nearness to Thathi. Ammi
possessed the exact opposite. Perhaps karma had confused the two
women and given the wrong one to my father as his bride.

'How many days do we have for the weekend to come?' I was
getting rather desperate. This search for the meaning of my name had
begun to blow out of proportion. It had been easier for Columbus to
discover America.
'Today is Monday, another four days.'
'But I can't wait that long, I have to ask him something today.'
'What do you need to ask him?' asked Nenda.
'I want to know my name.'
'Your name is Manuka no.'
'I want to know the meaning.'
'Why do you need Thathi for that, Ammi knows the meaning as well
no. After all they chose it together.'
'Aney, I don't know. Your precious Tissa Aiya is the one who picked it
up from somewhere.'
'From where?' Tears were beginning to make an appearance.
'From Australia,' replied Ammi.
'Where is Australia?'
'At the bottom of the world where Kangaroos live.' And she left for her
body wash. Like a live pot plant, Made in Japan.

'Does my name mean Kangaroo in Australian?' My world was
coming to a rapid end and I too was sinking to the bottom of the earth

where those Kangaroos lived. Nenda became sensitive to my trauma. Instead of concluding her third person battle with Magi, she took my hand, left the pantry and went towards the bedrooms.

'Let us ask Aiya,' said Nenda knocking on his bedroom door. TM Mozart the first was an infant prodigy. The suffix 'the first' due to becoming first in all he attempted. I was probably going to be Manuka the last.

'I am busy,' he said as we went in.

'We have to know something important.'

'Come later.' TM Mozart the first was being difficult.

'It can't wait till later.'

'Then ask someone else.'

'No one else knows.'

'Alright then, but bring me a crackerjack without nuts when you come.' Chocolates were only distributed in our household after meals. It was now in-between meals. But in a state of emergency, rules had to be broken. Nenda and I proceeded to Ammi's room where the gods under the roof, atop the Almirah, protected the chocolates. Nenda drew the chair to the Almairah, I climbed and took the old milk powder tin from the top and took out a crackerjack without nuts. Thereafter the tin returned to the gods. Chocolates were rare, precious and devoured by all. In our family it had more value than gold. We took the crackerjack and returned to TM Mozart's territory. He looked like a reincarnation of Emperor Nero. Strumming his fiddle while I was in flames.

'Putha, what is the meaning of Nangi's name?'

'Wait, listen to this song first.'

We waited.

'City stop walks, burning cat walks, dressed in whole daeiy's style, in the air there is a feeling of Christmas. Children walking, people talking, winning smile after smile and in every street corner we heeer. Silver bells, silver bells, it's Christmas time in the cityyy…'

It was nearly February. And time for a tantrum. I began.

Silver bells stopped ringing and TM Mozart grinned. 'Let me think… Ah, yes I now remember Thathi once telling me, yes… On that particular day we were counting potholes on the Nawala-Nugegoda road, that the word Manuka, or Makuna which it is actually supposed to be, means a giant Australian bug, bigger than a cockroach... no, no even bigger... about the size of a bandicoot and you know what it does?' I was paralysed.

'It sits under the bellies of pregnant kangaroos and sucks their blood until the babies die. But the kangaroo doesn't even know it. Only when the baby is born, DEAD does the kangaroo mother realize that the Manuka bug has killed the baby kangaroo. She orders the father kangaroo to eat it, but the Manuka bug is a very UGLY bug. A cross between a mammal, an amphibian, a reptile and a dinosaur, and when the father kangaroo sees it he gets such a shock at its absolute ugliness that he turns into stone. The Manuka bug then goes into the belly of koala bears and continues to kill their children.'

Nenda took me out of the room. Scolding him for being a civilized Colombo child who attended a respectable Buddhist school but did not have a molecule of compassion towards his sibling. The final phase was initiated. Nenda took the telephone receiver and booked a trunk call to Maskeliya. The monkey homeland where Thathi was building roads.

'This is 94938, I have to book a call to Maskeliya 554.'

'No, no, not Waskeliya. Maskeliya.'

'554.'

'*Na, na* not 557, 554.'

'*Na, na* not Waskeliya 554, Maskeliya 554.'

'*Hari*?' (OK).

'What is the delay?'

'Apo, that is too long. This is an emergency.'

'*Peya dekak?* Two hours? Didn't you hear I said it was an emergency?'

'In two hours the patient is dead. Can't you all hurry up a bit?'

'If the lines are blocked, unblock them. Those people blocking the lines must be talking protracted nonsense.'

'Apo but one hour is also too long.'

'Not Waskeliya, Maskeliya 554.'

She replaced the receiver berating the Ceylon telecommunications department for hiring people from the Deaf and Dumb Home to work as telephone operators.

Either two hours flew faster than expected or the deaf telephone operator was not deaf after all and had bought the emergency part of

Nenda's fabrication. 'Hallo, hallo… I'm calling from Mr Weerasinghe's residence, it is an emergency can you kindly call him to the phone at once.' Nenda was playing with fire. Thathi was a stickler for the truth. For him, truth was the truth and there was only one truth. Whether this etymological emergency that cast a shadow on my existence fit into my father's concept of emergency, formed a repulsive question mark on my ardent quest. Would he submit? Or be enraged? Would I ever learn the truth?

Nenda was clever. As soon as Thathi said hello she handed the phone to me. My father was a victim to his daughter's wiles. Thathi did justice to the word trunk call. He blared and trumpeted through the telephone wires like a wild elephant lost between vociferous monkeys. Either it was his tinnitus or he never comprehended the functions of a telephone. The longer the distance, the louder he had to shout. Maskeliya to Colombo was loud. But not intolerable. I was relieved that the quest for my name had not begun when he had been in Japan.

'Hello Thathi,' I said mildly, on the verge of realizing that the path to the truth was the actual truth and beyond that, there was no truth. Like Columbus discovering America when he was searching for India and finally saying, '*Oh shit, I can't be bothered anymore,*' and simply naming the natives he found in America 'the Indians' and thus solving the problem of the elusive India. If Indians lived in America, America must be India. QED.

'Hello Chooti, you called me? You started school today no?'
'So you have two teachers, one or two? Let me think, usually there are two so you must be having two. You must listen to them very carefully. What are their names?'
He didn't wait to listen.
'Always listen. Concentration is the most important part of life. If you concentrate, ninety nine percent of the problem is solved. You don't even have to waste time studying if you concentrate. Remember, it is quality that matters, not quantity. Don't ever forget; everything you have in life can be robbed from you, your money, your house, your wife, your wealth.'
I had nothing to worry about.
'Only your knowledge can never be robbed.'

I didn't even know the meaning of my name.

'So concentrate and learn. That is all you need to do in life. That is happiness. After all, what are we human beings searching for in our lives? Happiness. Cars, houses, money bring no happiness. Only knowledge brings happiness.'

I still didn't know my name.

'Knowledge is Nirvana.'

Perhaps I should terminate my quest. I was not in the mood for Nirvana's nothingness.

'So you must be having a lot of friends now?'

Did I have friends? I was searching for the meaning of my name.

'You know I was five years old, only five, when Kiriamma sent me to Colombo to study. I saw her and Aththa only during school holidays. That was the best they could do for me. In fact I wanted to send you and Aiya to the hostel to learn to be real men and women, capable of fending for yourselves…'

Thathi neither changed a light bulb nor repaired the car. We always needed a mechanic, even to change the gas cylinder.

'But your mother wouldn't hear of it. She was spoilt by Achi and Siya. Didn't learn the proper way I did. I am not belittling her. She has wonderful qualities. But the fault lies with Achi and Siya, and the way they educated her. She cannot cook, cannot sew. Even to sew a button she needs a seamstress.'

Ammi always knew where to find a good mechanic. One for lights, one for the car, one for the gas cylinder. If we waited for Thathi, we would be without electricity, without food and without transport.

'Study. And learn to be independent.'

Why had I called?

'So Chooti, the driver has come and I have to go to the site now. Tell Ammi if she has something important to say she should call. It is easier to catch me after six in the evening, or else early morning before going to school. Cheerio.'

And he hung up

I stared at the dead receiver. Perhaps it was time to create my own meaning.

Ammi had just finished her bath and was flip flapping through the corridor like a penguin in wet Bata rubber slippers. She saw me, distorted and confused.

'Whom are you talking to?'

'To Thathi.'

'So where is he?'

'Gone.'

'If you finished talking then put the receiver back.' she said flip flapping past me.

'I didn't finish talking.'

'Then why aren't you talking?'

'I didn't have time to.'

Ammi stopped her flip flapping and squinted at me between the droplets falling from the wet cherry blossoms.

'First take that finger out of your mouth and speak like Miss Ratnayake White taught you to speak. Did you talk to your father or not?'

'I did.'

'So what did he say?'

'He spoke about Kiriamma sending him to the hostel at five and …and he told me that if you have to tell him something you can call.'

'I have nothing to tell that bugger. What did he tell you about the meaning of your name?'

'Nothing.'

'What do you mean nothing?'

'Nothing.'

'Did you ask him what you wanted to ask?'

I nodded like Noddy.

'Why not?'

'He didn't let me.'

'He didn't let you?'

I wasn't lying. Nor was I telling the truth.

'He spoke and spoke and then he cut off. He said if you want to talk to him you can call.'

'If? I'll tell that fellow what I think of him.'

With her speech and volume at an absolute crescendo she got Thathi on the phone. In superlative ultra crescendo she told my father he was the worst father and the worst husband God had ever created. God. In such moments God was far more effective than karma. God had more

of a monopoly on the unreasonable and the inadequate; much more
than karma. Karma tended to be more burdensome. A long journey of
obscure births. We didn't have time for such complications.

'Now talk,' she said handing me the receiver and walking away
spluttering and swearing about God, Karma, men, potholes, everything.

'Hallo Thathi,' I whispered meekly.

'What do you want to know, *magé Duwa*?'

'Thathi, what does my name mean?'

'Which one?'

'Manuka?'

I sensed him smiling on the other side of the receiver. Proud of
his choice of name. I made myself comfortable on the chair, preparing
myself for another monologue. 'Manuka…' I heard him thinking. My
father, the nomenclatural archaeologist. Clad in a bush shirt. A torch in
one trouser pocket, a snakestone in the other. A ballpoint pen and a
note pad in the shirt pocket, trekking along the discovery channel.
'Manuka yes, yes I remember where I saw it. It was in a suburb in
Canberra. The natives call it Maanuka, but I decided to change it a bit
and call you Manuka.'

A small consolation prize. Not that it would have made much of
a difference. They both sounded equally weird.

'Thathi, but what does it mean?'

'What does it mean?' Thathi was like a cow chewing the cud. Whatever
I said he would repeat before parting with a word. 'What does it mean?
I don't know, I am trying to think what it means. Chooti, funny I don't
know what it means. Come to think, I don't think I ever bothered to
find out what it means. I saw the name written somewhere, liked the
sound and jotted it down in the notebook I always carry with me.'

I wished he had lost his notebook.

'You know you should always carry a notebook. When you see
something interesting you can always note it down. I have some extra
notebooks in the drawer of my bedside cupboard, you take one and put
it into your uniform pocket before going to school in the mornings.'

I made a mental note not to carry a notebook. If not for his notebook
this ugly meaningless name would still be in Australia, not on me.

'Thathi, we don't have a pocket in our uniform.'

'Oh, I see. You know I wanted to send you to the Devi Balika Vidyalaya, but your mother wouldn't hear of it.'

'They have a pocket in the school uniform?'

'I think so. Most school uniforms have pockets. But really, you should always learn to carry a notebook for then you can always note down new words you hear. Memory alone is not sufficient.'

My name was not a new word. I didn't need a notebook to remember it. 'Chooti, I will try to find the meaning for you when I come to Colombo. I still have some friends in Canberra whom I can write to. In the meantime if anyone asks you what it means just say it is an aboriginal name.'

'Right, Thathi. What is Aborigine?'

'Aborigines were the first people in Australia. Like the Veddha's of Ceylon.'

I won't comment on my psychological state.

VEDDHA. A dark skinned tree climbing Neanderthal, who had inhabited this island before the Aryan princes invaded and occupied. There were still some left. Naked, illiterate and black. Worshipping devils and snakes, not Bo-trees and gods wearing expensive Indian silks.

I should have used that umbilical cord to strangle rather than adorn myself. I may be black and flat and look like a Veddha, but I was surely a product of blue blooded, golden skinned, lotus lipped, and doe eyed Aryan ancestry?

11

TM Mozart entered an all island essay competition. The title of the essay had been 'MY COUNTRY'. Not exceeding thousand words, hand written. No one asked me to enter the competition. I couldn't understand why. I may not have the same opinion as TM Mozart about my country, but I lived in the same country, and had the same indigenous right to enter the competition as TM Mozart.

MY COUNTRY

My country is Ceylon. It is an island in the Indian Ocean situated beyond the South-Eastern tip of India. There are twenty-four miles of water between my country and India. This twenty-four mile stretch of water is called the Palk strait. To the east of my country is the Bay of Bengal, to the west the Arabian Sea.

Prior to being called Ceylon, my country has had many names. In ancient south Asian mythology, it has been known as Lanka. The Greek and Roman traders had called it Taprobane. And a famous fairy-tale, 'the three princes of Serendip', meaning my country, has given to the English dictionary the word 'serendipity', meaning the faculty of making happy.

The first king we have had in this country has been the Aryan Prince Vijaya. He came from India, conquered the demonic natives and spread the Aryan race. King Devanampiyatissa was the first king to convert to Buddhism, which enabled my country to become a Buddhist country. The last king of my country was King Sri Wickrama Rajasinghe.

My country has experienced four hundred and fifty years of colonization. First, the Portuguese, then the Dutch and finally the English. It is only during the times of the English colonisers that my country got the name Ceylon. In nineteen forty-eight we received independence from the British and D.S. Senanayake was proclaimed the new prime minister. My country received independence without having to shed a drop of blood.

Seventy-five percent of the population are the Singhalese people. They speak the Sinhala language as their mother tongue. This language is not spoken anywhere else in the world except in my country. Besides the Singhalese, we have Tamils, Burghers, Muslims, Malays and other small minorities. We have always lived in peaceful co-existence with each other.

My country is primarily a Buddhist country. Most of the Singhalese people are Buddhists. Besides the Buddhists we also have minority groups of Hindus, Christians and Muslims. It is believed that the Lord Buddha had come to my country three times during his lifetime. During his last stay in my country he left behind a footprint, which is still on top of the mountain called Adam's peak. We also have the Buddha's tooth relic. It is kept in the Kandy temple. Once a year there is a perehara (pageant), where the temple's tusker carries the tooth relic and shows it the world outside the temple. Fire-eaters and Kandyan dancers contribute to the glamour of the pageant. Tourists from all over the world attend this pageant.

The Sinhghalese people are descendents of the Aryans. The first Aryan king was Vijaya. They were lighter skinned and better looking than the natives that inhabited the country. Vijaya was the son of Sinhabahu. And Sinhabahu, the son of the bandit lion. The Bandit lion had kidnapped the Princess Suppadevi from the north and given her two children; Sinhabahu and Sinhaseevali. When the lion went out to hunt he had kept his family locked in his cave for he feared other jungle creatures harming them. But his son Sinhabahu did not like being locked in a cave. He made his mother and sister betray their father and they all escaped to India. The lion was traumatized through sorrow and agony. Travellers visiting the kingdom of Sinhabahu's escape, related to the prince tales of the traumatized lion. Thereupon the son raised an army and returned to kill his father. Sinhabahu means the lion slayer in our language. Vijaya was his son.

Prince Vijaya was a very bad person of bad character. People in Sinhabahu's kingdom told the king to kill his son. But the king could not do so. He had killed his father; he could not kill his son. So he put the prince and five hundred of his friends upon a ship and put them into high sea. Prince Vijaya and his friends landed in my country. They saw the copper sands and called the island 'Thambapani'. The land of copper sand.

The island of Thambapani was inhabited by Rakshas, Naga's and Devas. The Raksha's were the protectors of the forest; the Deva's were worshippers of the gods and the Naga's, the cobra worshippers. The Rakshas were the most powerful. They were dark skinned, fat and extremely fearsome. The Raksha Princess Kuveni saw the light skinned and handsome Aryan prince and fell in love. She betrayed her Raksha people and gave him her kingdom. The Rakshas had to retreat to the forest. They had been betrayed.

After giving birth to two children, Prince Vijaya no longer desired Kuveni and sent for a light skinned Aryan princess from India. Upon her arrival, he got rid of Kuveni. She had no choice but to return to the Rakshas, with her two children. But the Rakshas had not forgotten the betrayal. Upon arrival, they stoned her to death. The two children managed to flee. They began the Veddha tribe that exists in my country until today. Prince Vijaya and his new Aryan queen started the Sinhala race, of which we are descendents.

The origin of the Rakshas, to which Kuveni belonged, is uncertain. Most history is documented in Pali and since we are not taught Pali in the schools, it is not possible to say what is written in the Pali books. But it is believed that the Rakshas are the descendents of the wicked king Ravana who had ruled Lanka. He had hundred heads and two hundred arms. King Ravana had kidnapped the Princess Sita who was the wife of Prince Rama from the city of Ayodha in north India. Thereafter Rama got the monkey Hanuman to help him to rescue Sita from her prison in Lanka. Hanuman jumped across the Palk strait, set fire to the whole country and rescued Princess Sita. Rama killed Ravana in the final battle. That was the end of Raksha supremacy.

In my country we have fifteen million people. The capital of the country is called Colombo. We have two natural harbours, Trincomalee and Galle. Our main export is tea. Rubber, spices and coconuts are other exports.

My country has the most colourful flag in the world. We call it the lion flag. There is a yellow lion in the middle carrying a yellow sword. Since the Sinhala people are the descendents of Sinhabahu the lion slayer, the lion with the sword is a symbol for the Sinhala people. It is a lion of justice. The yellow on the flag is the colour of Buddhism.

The red background upon which the lion is standing is the red colour that represents the Singhalese people. The orange stripe to the left is for the Tamils and the green is for the Muslims and all other minorities. The four Bo-leaves above and below the lion, upon the yellow borders is a further symbol for Buddhism.

My country is a beautiful country. It has golden beaches, blue waters and green mountain peaks. It has no volcano and we have never experienced an earthquake. We have been known throughout history as the pearl of the Indian Ocean. We have no war and all minorities get on with each other. Christmas, Vesak, Thai Pongal and Ramazan are national holidays. The people listen to the Lord Buddha's dharma and follow his middle path.

THE END

I found his essay stupid. The Rakshas were not ugly. They were black and attractive. The Aryans were white. Whiteness does not make a person beautiful. Whiteness is only colour, not beauty. I hoped he would not win the essay competition. Furthermore, he had forgotten to mention that Kuveni had cursed the Aryans for what Vijaya had done to her. But even before Kuveni, Ravana had cursed the Aryans.

But he won. Ammi removed my framed painting from the wall claiming it was time I did a new painting. TM Mozart the first, winner of the all island essay competition now occupied my place on the wall. In fact, come to think of it, I think he occupied all the walls.

His head grew bigger before my eyes.

12

I wished the night would not end and the day would never begin. But it did. A new day dawned and I still had my Veddha name. The half a tube of Signal toothpaste and the three quarter glass of salt water I had drunk the night before did not give me the slightest temperature or vestige of indigestion. I had the constitution of a Raksha. I returned to school. The Veddha name followed me like an unwanted shadow.

I sat, pulling the chair towards the table. A new girl had come to my class. A superlative. She was now the blackest and the fattest. Marshmallow and the teachers were riveted by her black exuberance. They made no more references to my Bug definition.

'So you are new today?' said Miss Lily M, plainly perturbed that a child would dare stay away without excusing herself.

'Yes teacher.'

'And why weren't you here the last few days?'

'My grandmother died teacher.'

'I am sorry to hear that, when did she die?'

'I don't know… some time back.'

'Then why didn't you come earlier?'

'How to? First, seven day almsgiving, then one month almsgiving, then the three month almsgiving.'

'And you couldn't come to school because of the almsgivings, I think I should have a talk with your mother.'

'She is not there.'

'Where is she?'

'She is busy.'

'Arranging the six months almsgiving I presume?'

'Aiyo teacher, you know nothing no! There is no six months almsgiving; there is only, the seven-day almsgiving, the one-month almsgiving, the three-month almsgiving and the one-year almsgiving.'

'I can see you are well informed on such matters. Are you equally well informed about the alphabet?'

'If I was, I wouldn't be here no. Then I will be at home helping my mother, Sumana Nenda, Soma Nenda, Richard Mama and Norbert Mahappa to organize the one year almsgiving.'

The flies flew into Miss Lily M's open mouth.

'Yes teacher, we have to do these things or else Achi will be re-born as a cockroach and will creep all over our toilet at night eating kakki.'

'Eeeeee, Miss. I can't hear this any more. I think I will vomit…,' and out ran Marshmallow with her hands covering her mouth. She didn't vomit, but ate all her prawn pies alone. She left just one Chinese roll, for show.

'I will later have a conversation with your mother, in the meantime tell your name to the rest of the class.'

'Sakuntala Shiranee Rukmanidevi Amerasinghe.'

She was the happiest fat black girl I had ever seen. I wished I could be like her.

During the interval I put on my 'Don't bother me, I am extremely self sufficient' face and tried to formulate a non-obvious contact with SSR Amerasinghe – to be known as Saku. She was laughing and singing and jumping up and down in the sand pit. Marshmallow was having a conversation with the teachers about all the different kinds of pastries and cakes she had eaten in her short life. I observed Saku without joining the mass insanity in the sand pit. She was far too happy in the midst of whiteness. A traitor to black solidarity. I bit into my transparent *Mukunuwenna* sandwich. Two tissue paper thin slices of bread held together with a Mukunuwenna and green chilli mass, no butter, no margarine. It was repulsive! I bit and swallowed – just one bite. The rest I crumbled and distributed amongst the Crotons.

'Makuna, Makuna, catch me, catch me.' Marshmallow had finished her pastry descriptions and was ready to irritate fellow human beings. She had planted herself at the other end of the back garden, past the netball courts and was playing with the acoustic variations of my name.

I observed the squirrels who had offered Prince Rama their bodies. Those days India and Lanka had been one mass of land. Then a huge wave had come and India and Lanka had separated. Rama remained in India. Sita, Ravana and the squirrels in Lanka. The wave of karma. Fortunately Rama met Hanuman who could fly across the water, for Hanuman was the son of the wind god. He came and burned us to cinder. I did not like monkeys. I liked only squirrels. Despite their ugly stripes.

'Makuna, Makuna,' the sound increased.

Without quite realizing why, I ran towards the netball court, was about to proceed to the other side, but didn't. I hung on to the steel frame of the goal when it suddenly gave way, crashing to the ground like a coconut tree sabred at the root. A flash-back of memory assured that no one was standing in its vicinity. I hurriedly turned to salvage the damage done, before anyone could notice that the great white post had crumbled in the middle of the back garden. But, reality had taken a different path to memory. Under the post lay a uniformed student oozing blood. I saw her and fled. I ran as fast as my un-athletic legs could carry me. I ran. Away from my crime. Away. Praying, that my negligent karma would erase this nascent deed. It was no longer a question of mixed paint tins or of pulling the table towards the chair. It was now a question of life and death, of which I knew neither. Would I be reborn as a cockroach? Was that girl under the post dead? I found my way to the only unoccupied building, reeking of uncalculated gallons of Uric acid; unflushed. I stayed in this room of many uncoordinated emissions of many emergencies, from nephritis to myopia. I inhaled this putrid air and sacrificed my respiratory organs for a replay of past events. With a different ending. A vertical netball post. And a vertical child.

Hours and hours later the bell rang. Amidst the vociferous screams of a thousand children on their way home, I emerged from the toilets and mingled like a chameleon amidst the exiting hoards of schoolgirls and found my way to the driver and the car that was to take me home.

That afternoon, as the rest of the household indulged in their siestas and the servants were washing the lunchtime's crockery, I crept into the corrugated iron trunk and stole a tube of Punch and Judy toothpaste and emptied it into my stomach. Thereafter I mixed Signal toothpaste with a glass of salt water and drank that too. It did the trick. As cockroaches travestied the toilets during the night, I emptied my endless bowels. As the cock began to sing its morning serenade a crippling temperature overcame me. School had to wait. This time it was not karma.

As I lay in bed, I listened to Siya reading the daily obituaries. He always read the obituaries loud enough for Achi to hear while she made milk toffee in the kitchen. But there was no obituary caused by a falling netball post. Perhaps karma had cleaned up the act for me. Or had it all been imagination? I waited for the telephone to ring, or the police to come. But neither did the telephone ring, nor did the police come. Nor did Ammi go on a verbal strike. Excluding my bowels, the rest was normal. Perhaps I had made an unknown sacrifice? Perhaps my nose had disintegrated after the pungent uric acid? I touched it. It was there, still as flat as a Jambu fruit run over by a bullock cart.

The fever subsided. I went back to school. I could no longer differentiate between the smell of a Mukunuwenna sandwich and the smell of urine. My nose was dead. 'Look Miss, Makuna is back.' Needless to say, Marshmallow ran the commentary.

Please Lord Buddha, I will no longer complain about my name if you bring to life the girl who died under the netball post. I will be willingly called bug, flea or even cockroach. Anything. Just bring that girl back to life.

In our country people do not ask Lord Buddha to solve problems, since he is dead. He was not like God who looked down at his creations and came to help. Lord Buddha had not created us and he did not help. Lord Buddha had taught us how to help ourselves and how to disappear to Nirvana. Either he had not taught us well enough, or human beings not in Nirvana were fundamentally a foolish lot. I do not know, but no one I knew was capable of solving problems without the assistance of another source. Sometimes a Bo tree, sometimes a Buddha-statue but invariably it was a Hindu God: Brahma, Shiva, Pattini, Ganesh, Vishnu, Krishna, Kataragama... the Hindu pantheon was large and served many purposes. But who was what? At this particular moment, I could not visualize a single Hindu God. Did Lord Kataragama have a head of an elephant, or did Lord Vishnu? Even if I could have sorted out the heads would they come all the way to Ceylon to help me? And even if they were willing to help me, by the time they got here on peacocks, or on the back of bulls, the girl under the netball post would surely be dead. And I did not know which god travelled on the bull and which god on the peacock. I decided it was safer to stick to the Lord Buddha. He had a human head and legs long enough to travel from Nirvana, which probably was not as far as India. Perhaps he would have enough compassion to leave Nirvana and come to my mercy. 'Please Lord Buddha, *help me, help me, help me*. I promise never to trouble you again.'

'Nice to have you back dear, I hope you are well now.'
Perhaps I had discovered something - like that person who had discovered the earth was not a disc, but couldn't prove it.

School progressed like it always had and no one made any comment about either a netball post or a dead schoolgirl. Had it ever happened? Had Lord Buddha fulfilled my wish? I was on the threshold of a new discovery. Buddha normally never fulfilled wishes, or so I had been told. He was just a teacher, nothing more, nothing less. A simple human being who entered Nirvana after many lives of suffering and washed his hands of the human race. Perhaps he was not in Nirvana? I looked around for a missing person. A table and chair minus a child. There was none.

During the interval, I ate the Mukunuwenna sandwich without crumbling it between the Crotons and I did not swallow spit at Marshmallow's pastries. I followed the Buddhist thesis that good intention was one of the roads towards the elimination of sorrow. I had all the good intention of eating my Mukunuwenna sandwich and eliminating the sorrow of hunger and murder. I observed heads. Bandages, plasters, stitches, or headless students. Every neck had its own head. I looked towards the netball courts. A ghost, a tombstone, a funeral pyre? Nothing. The netball post was vertical and the lawn had been freshly mowed.

Buddha who had not gone to Nirvana had saved me. I accepted my bug name, the black ears and the Jambu run over by a bullock cart nose. The Buddha had said, 'be detached.' Detachment eliminated sorrow. I was detached – for the moment.

But I made a mental note to sort out the gods belonging to the Hindu pantheon. Who knows when I may need assistance again? Perhaps by *that* time the Lord Buddha would have become a fossil and would no longer return to me.

13

Looking back at those days at school, I must admit that I never learned anything of particular importance. A bit of this and a bit of that and however I may have performed was more an act of karma than the erudity of the teachers - or myself. Miss Lily Marlene will be remembered for her voice and corpulence and Miss Fatima for her plait. The English, Sinhala and Tamil alphabets will be remembered because of their geographical location on the walls and the primary colours through the red and blue saga of the paint tins.

Then the alphabets came down and a world map came up. I recognized our little island. Lying at the foot of India like a sucked mango seed disposed by Hanuman the monkey, before his departure. 'It's not a mango seed, it's the pearl of the Indian Ocean,' Marshmallow would correct me. 'No. Are you blind?' I corrected her, 'Look! The mango seed has been sucked from the bottom to the top and all the fibres have pasted together and formed the Jaffna peninsula.' Then the world map came down and nothing more came up on the walls. Not even paint. For seven years.

She came like a seven-year itch. Mrs. Bandaranayake, the widow. A phoenix from her husband's funeral pyre. She held a nation and its people hostage for the termination of her husband's life. SWRD, her husband, was killed because karma had turned off the switch, not because of anything else. But, in death he did more harm than he had in life. He had cloned his political myopia and distributed it among his political progeny. Wife and children. The future was bleak and we were not even able to itch. Malnutrition. Of body and soul.

The Sinhala and English alphabets went into the cupboards. The Tamil alphabet was tattered and eliminated. The world map was posted to Mrs. Bandaranayake's residence.

The education system was simplified. Equal opportunity and the elimination of good and bad were introduced. Physics, chemistry, botany and zoology disappeared into a nutshell called General Science. History, Geography and Ethics mutated to Social Studies. English language and English literature condensed itself to simple English, where Charles Dickens' David Copperfield lost weight and became a dainty twenty-five page new literary achievement, without Uriah Heep. Uriah Heep was too humble for the new government.

Sinhala language, Sinhala literature and Sinhala history was condensed to the new government's condensed milk tin, which carried a black and white picture of King Parakramabahu the sixth. Due to the high quality of condensed milk, I learned that Parakramabahu the sixth had been a great king. He had brought our country to a brief period of self-sufficiency. Like the condensed milk tin. When we ate the sweetened condensed milk, we needed no rice. Rice was a carbohydrate and carbohydrates broke down into sugar for the necessary bodily functions, but condensed milk was sugar. Break down was unnecessary since it was already broken down. Thus, Mrs. Bandaranayake brought in an era of condensation, simplification and minimization. Similar to condensed milk.

Further to the condensed milk and the condensed syllabus, Geometry and Algebra became extinct and Mathematics reappeared as New Maths. Instead of the Abacus we now began to play with matchsticks and marbles. Then marbles disappeared like the world map. The English owners of the marble companies were sent back to England. Marbles were not required for Mrs. Bandaranayake's policies of condensation and minimization. Only matchsticks. Lion brand matchsticks were introduced to new maths. They were safe for mathematics, for they never ignited.

A new subject grew out of condensation and minimization. Pre-Vocational studies. This pre-vocational study had two parts. Popularly known as PV one and PV two. Uncle Buddhi's second son who was about my age studied basket weaving for PV one and carpentry for PV two. I did not have basket weaving or carpentry. I was a girl. Girls did not become carpenters. In my girls' school we studied textile weaving and home science. PV one was further condensed into the theory of textile weaving. We neither visited a textile mill nor wove a centimetre of fabric. But we created floral designs that were never used in the mills that produced the cotton fabric that our nation clad itself in and which smelled like a canister of kerosene oil. In the meantime, Mrs. Bandaranayake adorned herself in Chinese Silk. The Chinese had come to her assistance.

PV two was home science. Home science had become an all-important subject with a profound syllabus. I learned the exact ingredients for roasted curry powder used to make chicken curry. Only ingredients, not quantities. Quantities were not a part of the profound condensed syllabus. Nenda, who had not attended school under the Bandaranayake regime, measured the quantities and put it into my school bag when the preparation of chicken curry was required for better grades. In the meantime, Mrs. Bandaranayake's three children attended foreign schools without pre-vocational studies or condensations. The world maps posted to her residence were subsequently destroyed. Her brood was now abroad.

One subject did not appear to have been minimized. PT or Physical Training. For many hours a day we would perform strange contortions under the blazing son. Miss Lily M. and Miss Fatima stood under their parasols and protected their respective blackness and whiteness. I ended up looking like a hyper melanotic jellyfish, while the others acquired various darkened hues. Even Marshmallow began to look like burned gelatine. Parasols and hats for children were not permitted. They did not fit into the syllabus of minimization. Were we being trained for the red army?

It was a pregnant question. Mrs. Bandaranayake did have a special rapport with the Chinese. It was rumoured that she was contemplating substituting her widow's robes for Chou En Lai's red silk bed sheets, even though the Kandyan sari was best draped with cotton fabric, not silk.

In the meantime, her three children got fatter and fairer on Baguettes, Roquefort and Brie. They received no red army training. The Chinese national day was celebrated along with our Independence Day. All Chinese restaurants closed on that day, in homage to a country that had built one of the seven Wonders of the World. We too participated in the veneration and made chicken curry with a dash of Soya sauce. It was called Chicken Chou En Lai. In this particular red spirit it did not matter if the chicken curry was edible. The Chinese restaurants opened when the national day ended. And the Sinhala, Tamil and Muslim employees returned to work as usual.

The silk bed sheet policies of minimization made me very hungry. My karma had brought me to a family where an edible meal depended on the cook's mood. I could not change that karma, and Magi the cook was a part of it. But did Mrs. Bandaranayake also have to be a part of my Karma?

Interval. School. I bit into my Mukunuwenna sandwich because I was hungry. Magi had been in a bad mood since Mrs. Bandaranayake came into power. Malnutrition. Red rice with gem-size kernels of sand, dhal with brilliant like particles of sand, ground red bricks instead of chilli powder, and yam. Not rice, not potatoes, but yams.

First the stones had to be eliminated from the rice and the dhal. Thereafter that weeks' ration of two pounds reduced itself to fourteen ounces and each and every one of us had to minimize our consumption. Men and growing boys got the most, servants the least. I was an in between. If the stones were not removed from the rice we would have had more to eat. We were hungry, so we ate stones.

Injured teeth became a primary problem. Teeth began to break during each mealtime. Learned people practicing dentistry had emigrated. Patients had increased, pay had minimized and health care was nationalized. Doctors now practiced medicine for the good of the human race, not for personal gain. Mrs. Bandaranayake had brought us all back to the root of Hippocrates. But when Hippocrates had lived and died, there had been no cost of living and every man was a philosopher. Magi was right to be angry. She had no teeth and was extremely hungry.

'*Kkkkrs...*' A typical sound at the dining table during meal times, usually lunch. Rice and dhal were a part of the meagre lunchtime buffet of three dishes. The third was pol sambol. Grated coconut mixed in chilli and seasoned with limejuice and Maldive fish. Pol sambol had no stones. Coconuts and limes had no stones, not because they grew on trees, but when purchased they were still in their god created form. But the chilli was a problem. Not a daily problem since one did not buy chilli daily, but still a very important problem.

Chilli was usually ground chilli, and the grinding of chilli was usually performed in grinding mills, which sold their chilli to vendors who in turn sold it to us. Vendors became geniuses under Mrs. Bandaranayake's minimizations. They discovered the similarity of colour between red brick powder and chilli powder. Most of the time, that which was purchased as chilli powder, was not chilli but red brick powder. Fortunately, my Achi never accepted minimization and would return to the vendor and berate him with all the strength of her mighty vocal chords, so that he eventually replaced the red brick powder with chilli powder, and we could have a decent pol sambol. Furthermore, in the beginning, Maldive fish which was as essential as chilli powder and limejuice for the seasoning of the pol sambol was not minimized. I think they just forgot to do so.

'*KKKkkkrrrrrrssss…*' A gem-sized piece of stone had been crushed by Ammi's teeth.

'Magi, come here at one. What do you see?' She had emptied the mouthful onto the plate.

'How to see, we are starving so eyesight is weak no?'

She then received the old pair of spectacles belonging to my grandfather. The next day, '*Kkkkrrssssss…*' even louder, and a part of Ammi's tooth had broken.

'Magi, come here. AT ONCE. What is this?'

Magi entered the dining room wearing my grandfather's old spectacles.

'It is a black grain of dhal,' she replied.

'Woman, are you blind, it is not a grain of dhal, it is a stone.'

'It is the same shape.'

'In future, you take out all coloured pieces, immaterial of shape.'

'Then we have nothing to eat.'

'I don't mind starving.'

But Magi minded starving.

I took a second bite of the Mukunuwenna sandwich. Now home grown. Fertilized by the dogs. Moraji Desai in India was drinking urine, so the dogs were fertilizing not only the Karapincha, but also our Mukunuwenna.

'What are you eating, Makuna?' It was Marshmallow.

'My name is not Makuna.'

'What are you eating?'

'None of your business.'

'It looks HORRID,' she said fondly, opening and closing her lunch box without consuming the contents inside.

'It is not,' I defended my sandwich and took an extra large bite nearly choking with revulsion.

'Manuka... (I noted the changed name, perhaps I had a certain utilitarian value), if you are my friend, I will give you a bite of my Chinese roll.' And she pulled out the most scrumptious looking Chinese roll, crisp and golden, bathed in quality coconut oil. Mrs. Bandranayake's dead husband's father had been a coconut baron of quality coconuts. Coconuts had not entered minimization.

She stretched it towards me. Perhaps I would end up dead like Snow White, biting into a poisoned Chinese roll instead of an apple? But I didn't care. The months of Bandaranayake minimization was giving birth to its own kind of slit eyed wisdom. I bit into that Chinese roll and became Marshmallow's friend. There is a cloud at the edge of every silver lining. Or was it a silver lining at the edge of the cloud? English minimization was becoming evident. I no longer knew where the silver lining was.

Marshmallow's friendship did not consist of only sharing Chinese rolls. I had to collect her daily lunch from the pastry shop courier who was not permitted to enter the school premises since he had 'an unknown male' status. Someone had to go to the front of the school and collect the lunch box he left with the school security guard. That someone was me. Then, I had to do homework for her, I had to let her copy from me during tests, and on the first of every month I had to steal a crackerjack from the milk powder tin on top of the Almirah and give it to her. I was not an exceptional student. But, next to Marshmallow I could have been Albert Einstein. She had the wealth of pastries but a brain made of candyfloss.

Chinese roll: one bite if beef. Two bites if fish.

Cutlets: one bite.

Chicken pie: two bites.

Bacon and egg pie: 3 bites (she hated it. But didn't hate it enough to give me the whole pie.)

Prawn pie: No bites. If crackerjack chocolate was delivered the same day a bite was permitted.

Then Karunawathie, Ariyawathie and Sumanawathie, the servants were sacked because crackerjacks were getting lost. Karma and greed battled in my nightmares giving me many sleepless nights and finally, I submitted to karma. This birth was imperfect, but if I stole further, the next birth would be worse. In this birth I had a nose that looked like a Jambu fruit run over a by a bullock cart, in the next birth who knows, it may be run over by an elephant carriage. I did not steal any more crackerjacks. Neither did I say who had stolen them. I repented. That should suffice. Angulimala, in the Buddhist Jataka tale was a murderer who cut the thumbs of his ninety-nine victims, threaded and hung them around his neck like a jasmine garland. But he still attained Nirvana, after repenting. Why should I not be absolved? I had only stolen crackerjacks not human thumbs! On the other hand I had absolutely no intention of going to Nirvana. Nirvana was vegetarian. I wanted pastries. I committed a last crime. I stole the prawn pie. Actually, I did not steal it, I ate it.

Marshmallow had sent me as usual to collect her lunch from the courier. Somewhere in-between the front gate and our classroom which was near the back garden, I opened the lunch box and gobbled the prawn pie. Fast. Before the taste buds could deliver the message to the brain that I was in the process of munching on a cherished prawn pie, it was gone. The act over before it had begun. No satisfaction, no elation, no after taste. Only a hammering sensation of guilt remained. I handed Marshmallow the lunch box and refrained from taking bites from the Chinese rolls.

'It is very strange, but my Thathi told me that he would be sending a prawn pie today.'
'Maybe he forgot.'
'My Thathi never forgets. He was Ceylon's chess champion for the last ten years and remembers every move he has made and his opponents have made.'
'He must be reincarnated from a forget-me-not.'
'It is not funny. I wonder if the boy who brought the lunch box would have stolen the prawn pie?'

I could not afford to jeopardize my karma. Three servants had been sacked because of crackerjacks, now the bicycle boy because of a prawn pie. Should I tell the truth, or should I assume that karma was having a siesta. 'You are such a bad girl. How can you accuse innocent people of stealing your prawn pies? In fact, last week when I collected the lunch box, that poor boy wearing a torn shirt, patches on his shorts and no slippers, told me, 'I don't know how these Colombo children can eat meat, or fish, or prawns without fearing karma.' He is a vegetarian. But what I also don't understand is how this boy is working for your father and he doesn't even have enough money to buy a pair of slippers. Your father must be like uncle Scrooge - stingy.'

I was playing with fire. I didn't even know what the bicycle boy looked like. The school's security guard took the lunch box from the courier and handed it to me. After all, the boy with the lunch box carried the unknown male status. The security guard was a known male. Transactions between schoolgirls and unknown males were not permitted during school hours. Or in school uniform. Once upon a time there had been known males as teachers. But a schoolgirl in uniform had eloped with the male teacher, hence there were no more male teachers in our school and all males, except the security guard received the unknown male status. A female security guard would have been preferred, but none were available.

'But my Thathi does not usually forget.' Marshmallow put on her thinking cap. 'I know why.'
'Why?'
'Poya.'
'*Poya?*'
'You are very stupid. When there is Poya, the tide is very high and there is too much water in the sea. So, water replaces the meat in the prawns and the prawn fishermen observe Sil.' (Lord Buddha paced up and down in the same place on twelve consecutive full moon days, which somehow aided his reaching enlightenment. A combination of pacing and full moon was necessary for enlightenment. But, since we are mere mortals who had not experienced as many births as the Lord Buddha and have a lot of pacing to do before we learn to eliminate greed and reach enlightenment, in our mere mortal way we paid respect to our great teacher on Poya days and observed Sil. During Sil, one wore white and ate a vegetarian meal before noon. Sat on the ground and meditated in order to prevent the mind from wandering into the territories of bad thoughts. No dinner was permitted. This was classical Sil. I never observed Sil. Neither did Marshmallow. But prawn fishermen did. They were catching prawns, not actually killing, only

catching. Since prawns could not live out of water, catching them was the same as killing them. Hence, prawn fishermen needed to boost their karma by observing sil, but not us.) 'But never mind, come take a bite of a Chinese roll. Actually you can eat the whole Chinese roll. Because you are my best friend I want to give you a whole Chinese roll today.'

I don't know what caused her change of heart, nor could I think or eat. I had begun to itch. I itched in school. I itched at home. I itched day and night, night and day. My body was covered with a circular relief work. Urticaria. Karma had obviously not been having a siesta.

It was my time for crime and punishment. Mrs. Bandaranayake had her own form of crime and punishment. She told the Americans and the Israelis to go home. And the slit eyed North Koreans who looked like Chou En Lai's brothers, moved into the recently vacated residences of the others. She ordered flowers and drummers and welcomed them to our humble island.

When the itching stopped and I returned to school, we invented a new game. I spy. 'I spy with my little eye, something beginning with B.'
'Backside. I see Miss Fatima scratching her backside though she tells us that we should not scratch our back sides.'
Mrs. Bandaranayake's slit eyed North Koreans multiplied. Because they all looked the same, Mrs. Bandaranayake did not realize that they were multiplying. The Russians financed their multiplication.
'I spy with my little eye, something beginning with N.'
'Nose, Miss Lily Marlene is digging her nose because she thinks no one is looking.'
The multiplied Koreans penetrated into the villages and made friends with the rural unemployed youth who had aided Mrs. Bandaranayake's victory, but were still unemployed.
'I spy with my little eye, something beginning with E.'
'Eyes. They were slit eyed, we were not. But we saw less.'
The bell rang. The interval was over.

14

We were asked to vacate our No. 58 home in three weeks. Ever since I remember, we had been living in house number 58. Before I had a memory, we had been living in house number 35 across the street, but after my birth and the change of family fortunes, we had moved to house number 58. It was bigger and accommodated more boarders. Achi was able to make more money even though Thathi paid more rent. We were compelled to live in a house with an even number. The fortunes of the family members were such that when we lived together as a family, the house number had to be divisible by two. That was not much of a difficulty, since fifty percent of the houses in the world had numbers divisible by two. But, when we were rejected from house number 58, we had only three weeks to find a house that had a number divisible by two. And precisely at that point of karmic turmoil, there were no houses divisible by two. It was a serious problem.

Thathi now came to Colombo every five days and searched for houses divisible by two for two days. He came on Friday and searched on Saturdays and Sundays. Saturn was an odd number and influenced Saturdays, therefore it was not a favourable day for the search for houses divisible by two.

Sunday was different. It was a good day, influenced by Jupiter. Jupiter was an even number and predominant in Thathi's present karmic sub period; but the house owners who were willing to rent houses divisible by two were usually out of town on Sundays. Therefore when Thathi left after his two-day search, the family would return to normality though no house had been found. Everyone would continue with what they were doing and hoped that karma would rent us a house divisible by two. TM Mozart sang and played cricket, Ammi attended her classes, Siya read Buddhist books during the day and played cards at night, Achi made milk toffees, the dogs barked and pissed on the Karapincha tree and I attended school and learned to divide by two.

But, two people came out of their usual routine. Nenda and Magi. They ceased to fight and ruminated about the sexual antics of Mr. Karunaratne, our landlord who was now asking for house number 58.

Mr. Karunaratne had married a non-govigama burgher who had given birth to three children and run away with a dhobi caste. Now he chose to return to house number 58 minus the wife, but with the three children. This was wonderfully juicy material for Nenda and Magi. So, as they continued to ruminate about why a burgher wife would run away with a dhobi, which was worse than being burgher, I revelled in Mr. Karunaratne's ill luck. I hated this house.

In fact I was elated. The front of house No. 58 faced the road like most houses did, but the back of the house faced the Colombo cemetery. My room was at the back, and there were ghosts there.

Ghosts. I had no reason to fear ghosts. In fact I had no reason even to think about ghosts. Buddhism had no ghosts. There was Nirvana and there was reincarnation. Nirvana is something like a black hole into which one disappears never to return. Reincarnation was not fearsome either. I did not have to bother with other people's reincarnation problems, only mine. As long as I secured my karma, my future was safe. If others were reincarnated as dogs or monkeys, it was not my problem. Above all there was nothing to fear. Of course it is not correct to say that one is totally devoid of fear, but this fear is a certain tangible fear, a fear of the predictable, rather than the unknown. But, the ghosts who jumped onto the balcony at the back of the house were not Buddhists, they were Christians. Christian ghosts.

These ghosts copulating on the balcony and peering through the back windows were beyond my tangible Buddhist territory. They came from the Christian part of the Colombo cemetery, to my room, which overlooked not the Buddhist or the Muslim parts, but the Christian part. Here, the bodies were buried in boxes under the soil. I wondered: what happened thereafter? The bodies were devoured by termites and maggots, was the soul devoured as well? How did this soul escape the termites, when the heart and the brain were devoured? Or could it be possible that termites did not attack the dead bodies and they rose up in the night as ghosts. The more I thought, the more confused I became. It was like the black hole. It was so black that I could not see where I was heading. Where did dead Christians go when Nirvana and reincarnation was forbidden to them? Where was heaven?

Where was hell? What was purgatory? Was it like a Buddhist funeral pyre? Or was it more like my balcony? When I asked, I would receive the usual Buddhist reply.

'You don't have to worry about what happens to Christians when they are buried, if you are bad in this life you will be born as a cockroach or a cripple in your next life, and if you are good you will go to Nirvana and never be reborn.' End of Christian question.

'But they can't spend the rest of their dead lives in coffins, under the earth.'

'Let that not be your problem, you are a Buddhist.'

'But...?'

'Don't but me. It is not your concern. Think about your problems and your possibilities of going to Nirvana.'

If I could not change my destiny, I ought to change my attitude towards my destiny. If I was not permitted to talk of Christian burials and the Christian after life, perhaps I should talk of Nirvana. Better something, than nothing. I had heard some Christian ghosts scratching on my windowpanes with long dirty fingernails early on in the evening and I did not want to return to my bedroom.

'And what happens in Nirvana?'

'What should happen, you will stay there and never have to suffer the agony of being reborn.'

'Being reborn is not an agony.'

'Chooti don't say stupid things. You obviously have a lot to learn.'

'What?'

'I don't have time now, ask your father.'

'Thathi is not here. Why can't you answer me? You teach Buddhism in school.'

'If you listen properly in school, you will not ask such stupid questions.'

'Of course I listen. But you only talk about the Jataka tales and the Lord Buddha's life and his boring up and down pacing and his boring enlightenment. I cannot understand why on earth a prince would give up all the beautiful things he has and go to the jungle where there is nothing. If I was a prince I would certainly stay in my golden kingdom and eat all the food one does not get in the jungles or in Ceylon.'

'That is why you are not a prince, and you are your father's pug nosed daughter.'

I ignored the pug nosed part. She always used it when she was angry with Thathi. I don't know why she was angry this time, but she was angry most of the time.

'I want to know what happens to Christians when they die.'

'You are not a Christian. You don't need to know.'

'Why not?'

'Don't waste my time asking stupid questions.'

'I am not wasting your time, you are only putting Cutex on your toe nails.'

'I need to concentrate. Go and ask Nenda.'

'She has gone to the cinema to see 'Love in Tokyo'.'

'Then wait until she comes.'

Ammi finished her toenails and searched the pages of the Sunday Mirror for advertised classes until the toenails dried. Her headline was still roaming.

'Ammi, if nothing happens in Nirvana, what's the point of being there? They probably don't even advertise classes in the Sunday newspapers, which is if they have newspapers at all.'

Nirvana had the appeal of a plate of unsalted rice with neither pol sambol nor curry.

'For a human being to appreciate Nirvana you have to come to the point of enlightenment that removes you of all greed and selfishness. Only then will your karma enable you to go to Nirvana, or even appreciate Nirvana.'

'Do you want to go there?'

'Why, do you want to kill me?'

It was difficult to have a detached conversation with my mother. All roads originated and ended at her Cutexed toes. 'Well if nothing happens there like you say, I don't care how enlightened I am I will pray and pray that I will never go to Nirvana when I die. I don't want to live in a ball of cotton wool for the rest of my life.'

'It is not cotton wool, it is nothing.'

'Why can't we go to heaven like the Christians? I am sure it is an interesting place to be in. With lots of pastry shops and chocolate factories.' Since Mrs. Bandaranayake's condensed minimization, the crackerjack chocolate tin on top of the Almirah had submitted to minimization and the tin was empty.

'We don't have heavens, we have hell and we have nirvana.'

'Of course we have heavens I have heard of angels in Buddhism.'

'Yes, but they are not like you and me.'

'Then who are they?'

'They are angels and they only live in the heavens.'

'Then they must be Christians? I am sure there are Christians in Buddhism and those angels who were supposed to have looked at Lord Buddha when he was preaching were surely Christians looking at him from the heavens.' I had just unified Christianity and Buddhism. And I needed to be further educated in order to separate Christianity from Buddhism. There was no unity between the two and separating a child's unity was beyond my mother's Buddhism teacher capabilities. It was not in her syllabus.

The following Sunday, and all remaining Sundays for the next few years I was sent to temple to learn the true essence of Buddhism. An eighty-year-old somnambular Buddhist priest, spraying me with beetle juice and grey frothy phlegm, missing the life size spittoon at his feet, related and re-related the same Buddhist texts. In Pali.

Questions were not permitted. Buddhism was crystal clear. Not understanding was karma. It was neither bad teaching nor Buddhism. Karma should have given birth to me in Pali. Not Sinhala. The old questions remained. New questions arose.

In the meantime, I transferred my energies into creating special Air Ceylon flight routes for Christian ghosts between heaven and hell, without a purgatory transit on my balcony. Sometimes the flights re-routed. Was karma to blame or the Chinese?

Mrs. Bandaranayake's red silk bed sheets were bringing us many benefits. The Colombo Air Port had been re-built by the Chinese. It was named the Bandaranayake International Airport. Mrs. Bandaranayake, her three children, her brothers, their wives, their children and their relatives climbed Air Ceylon planes and flew to meetings, conferences, summits, political events, representative events and etceteras around the world. It was after all the Bandaranayake International Airport. It was our new world wonder.

Growing up in the middle of minimization on an island, our concept of the world was limited to our glorious airport. We were proud.

Of it, of us, of the Chinese, of Mrs. Bandaranayake. Her widow's wiles had given to us a Chinese airport to call our own. Every Saturday and Sunday, while Thathi searched for houses, Ammi, the servants, the boarders and I, visited the Bandaranayake International Airport and watched the Air Ceylon planes take off and land with the Bandaranayake family onboard.

Soon uncle Buddhi and his family joined us. Then uncle Roland and his family joined us. Thereafter, uncle Harry and his family. Uncle Buddhi converted his car into a van and we all went to the Bandaranayake International Airport on Saturdays and Sundays, together. Each family brought their own tiffin carrier with one portion of rice and different curries, to share with each other. Additionally there was cake for teatime; iced coffee made with King Parakramabahu the sixth's condensed milk and condensed milk toffee for the in-betweens.

One day my father joined us. Since all of Colombo was watching the aeroplanes at the Bandaranayake International Airport during the weekends, there were neither landlords nor realtors available to show him houses divisible by two for rent. My father handed the job of searching for a house to karma, and joined us. But he was not like the rest of us. Instead of looking up at the planes as he accompanied us to the airport, he looked down at the potholes. The length, breadth, diameter and the hypothetical monsoon history of each and every pothole on the airport road was noted in Thathi's notebook. When he travelled with us in uncle Buddhi's van, we would see more potholes than aeroplanes. Uncle Buddhi tactfully suggested to him that he should perhaps follow in the Hillman. He said, 'Tissa, since your Hillman is lower than my van I think you have a far better chance of seeing all the potholes on the airport road than when you travel in the van.' The thought of missing a pothole did not appeal to my father. So he followed in the Hillman. When he eventually joined us at the airport, the tiffin carriers were empty. But he was in time for Parakramabahu the sixth's iced coffee and milk toffee. It never bothered him that he had missed lunch. For my father, potholes were a welcome compensation. And as essential as rice and curry.

15

Buddhist destiny was easy. Life was like a game of snakes and ladders. The snake was karma, so was the ladder. The quality of this birth was equivalent to the carat weight of karma. Death was the phase of life beyond this birth; it was life's stepping-stone to another birth. One day the stepping-stones ended and the Buddhist entered the realm of Nirvana. Thereafter, there were no more births.

When the Buddhist pyre was lit in the Buddhist part of the Colombo cemetery, except for the stench of burning flesh, the time for contemplation ended. Karma decided on the rest. But for Christians, God decided. How did I know how God thought? Did the Christian know how God thought? How did he manage to get them out of their coffins? Did the devils help? I tried to ask my Christian friends in school. But Christmas was around the corner and they were more interested in carol singing and Christmas presents than God and death. It was not unnatural. Their windows did not face the Colombo cemetery, mine did.

The flights I routed during the day, re-routed themselves at night. Marys, Josephs, Johns and Elizabeths sprung onto my balcony, drank whisky and copulated with their burial mates. I tried telling Ammi about it, but her toenails were more important. I tried telling Thathi about it, he asked me to tell him after the monsoons. Then I related it to TM Mozart; he related it to Siya, Siya related it to Achi, Achi related it to Ammi and Ammi to Nenda. It became a large karmic cascade and I got an electricity-saving blue light to scare off the ghosts at night.

It was no solution. The ghosts liked the blue light. With Mary, Joseph, John and Elizabeth, Belinda, Lucy and Samuel came as well. I spoke to Nenda. She scolded Ammi, Achi, Siya and Thathi. The karmic cascade reversed direction. Finally Nenda moved into my bedroom with me. My single bed and Nenda's single bed were removed to the boarder's room and the empty space in my room was replaced by a double bed. Thathi paid for the double bed and Achi received two rents for the same space.

But the ghosts returned while Nenda slept. They scratched on the windowpanes and recited passages from the Old Curiosity Shop.

Charles Dickens had written about hell; I felt it came alive on my balcony! Perhaps my balcony was the platform to purgatory. Perhaps those going to hell had already reached it. Through the coffin, through the earth, past Australia and the south-pole... into an unknown hot planet of chilli trees, rivers overflowing with chilli sauce, and hundred headed men like King Ravana checking visas with rabid dogs functioning as the police force.

In eight days we had to leave, but no house had yet been found. During daytime I laughed back at the ghosts who were laughing at me at night. In eight days and nights they could hammer on the windowpanes of Mr. Karunaratne's half govigama, half burgher children and scare them to death. I did not care.

Seven days more. No house. Achi spent the hours counting her silver cutlery and the Rosenthal crockery and noting the exact amounts on an exercise book, that when we eventually arrived at our new house not a single fork, knife or spoon would be missing. I don't know what difference it would have made since we only ate with our fingers. When visitors came Achi would take out the silver cutlery, but the visitors too ate with their fingers. When foreign visitors came one would expect them to eat with fork and knife, but they too would try to be like us and eat with their fingers. Of course they did not know the difference between the right and the left hand and usually would use the left hand and we would have to inform them that in our country one does not eat with the left hand. They would wash the left hand and begin again with the right. What we needed were not forks and knives, but finger bowls. But, Achi did not count them since they were not silver.

Six days more. No house. Nenda and Magi united again for a small moment in the history of time and packed the Rosenthal crockery and the crystal goblets in Daily News and Lankadeepa newspapers collected since Nineteen forty-eight. The year of independence. The year my father came to my grandmother's household looking for board and lodging. Magi packed, Nenda entertained. Mrs. Bandaranayake was minimizing everywhere, except in our kitchen.

In our kitchen D.S, Chelvanayagam and SWRD reigned. From backdated newspapers. D.S. propagated freedom from the English, became the first prime minister, fell off his horse and died. SWRD propagated freedom for the Sinhalese. Chelvanayagam propagated freedom for the Tamils. The British were gone and the Sinhalese were free. Chelvanayagam propagated freedom from the Sinhalese. SWRD wanted freedom for the free. Chelvanayagam said English. SWRD said Sinhalese. Then Chelvanayagam said Tamil. D.S. was dead. Chelvanayagam said, Tamil, English, Sinhalese, together. SWRD said 'not together'. Sinhala Only. Red coloured people embraced Karl Marx and fuelled the SWRD revolution. The Buddhists monks liked the red colour and joined them. The Sinhala Buddhist revolution. Sinhala only, Sinhala Buddhist freedom. Karl Marx converted. He became a Sinhala Buddhist.

Nineteen hundred and fifty-eight in our kitchen in house number 58. Sinhala Buddhism, Nationalism and Patriotism were at a peak. Sinhala hooligans were destroying Tamil homes, Tamil businesses, Tamil people - for the freedom and the expansion of the Sinhala language. SWRD then made a pact. With Chelvenayagam the Tamil. But the Sinhala Buddhists did not like the pact. They had not seen the pact, but they did not like it. So SWRD broke the pact. SWRD was literate. The hooligans were illiterate. As long as Sinhala triumphed, the Sinhalese did not need to learn to write their name in their language, or any other language. Sinhala triumphed. Who cared about definitions of literacy? Democracy too had triumphed. The Sinhala Buddhist had left the path of the Buddha and entered politics. They had their freedom. The Sinhala freedom. SWRD's freedom. SWRD's thoughts, backed by the Sinhala hooligans' deeds.

Did SWRD have second thoughts? Hard to speculate. He said one thing, but did another. Then he was killed. Shot. A man in Buddhist robes killed him. For freedom of the Sinhala. And for the freedom of the Buddhist. Was the Buddhist now free to kill? Had they escaped the clutches of reincarnation or had reincarnation submitted to 'Sinhala only' and left the country with the mass migration of burghers to Australia? Buddhism had been re-defined.

The Sinhala Buddhist Karl Marx translated it. He spoke neither Sanskrit nor Pali. Just a few bits and pieces of broken Russian, like the Sinhala hooligan's literacy. SWRD was dead. May he rot in the idiocy of Sinhala only. Karma had just turned off his switch. 'All politicians are idiots,' said Nenda, summarising before giving Magi the newspaper to wrap the Rosenthal crockery.

When we reach the new house, the newspapers were not going to be re-utilized as newspapers. Only garbage. It was planned that Ammi, Achi, Nenda and the servants were going to tell Thathi that the lorry drivers shifting our belongings had stolen the newspapers. D.S., SWRD, Chelvanayagam died. Sinhala only lived on. SWRD metamorphosed into Mrs. Bandaranayake and lived. It was like reincarnation. The Sinhala Buddhist Karl Marx continued the SWRD revolution with Mrs. Bandaranayake. It was like a homeopathic remedy. Increased energy, despite dilution.

Patriotic euphoria had risen in the grass roots, and no one questioned whether it was the wrong remedy. It was the new age of literacy. Free education provided education free of charge to all layers of society. But obviously free education could not provide wisdom. If Buddhism had failed, why should free education succeed?

Five more days. Ammi continued with her daily routine. She was now a part time Montessori teacher trainee. The Montessori school system did not give holidays to trainee teachers moving houses. Siya began to do his share of work. He began the day with choler. Cursing the women of the household for using the Daily News and Lankadeepa newspapers to wrap the cutlery before he could study the 'houses to let' part. He would then walk to the boutique to read the daily papers in all the languages. Even the languages I had never heard him speak in my life. I don't how he read, for his reading glasses would be wrapped in a handkerchief and hidden at the back of the bedside drawer while the Lankadeepa and the Daily News would be concealed in places where only a child would dare to pry. Siya would return after supposedly reading all the papers, smelling like an ashtray after a Marasinghe card party and disappear into the bathroom for half an hour. In the bathroom he would gurgle like a belligerent sea god and re-emerge smelling like an old spice after-shave factory. He would then go to the kitchen and tell Achi, 'No luck again today old girl, people are not renting houses. All because of this mad woman running the country. What do you expect? Would you rent a house to people in this bloody country? Once a tenant gets into the house, they don't leave. As long as this woman is ruling we will have to sleep on the streets.'

'Yes, but we are not like those people,' Achi would reply.

'What difference does that make? The people who are renting houses do not know what we are like. Bloody curse of a woman, that idiot shouldn't have killed SWRD, he should have killed her!'

Achi remained silent. I don't know if it was Mrs. Bandaranayake or Karma, but none of the national newspapers ever had a house for us to rent. Even if they did, how could Siya see it when his reading glasses were in his bedside cupboard drawer when he was reading newspapers in the boutique? Since my grandfather's heart had enlarged to the size of a watermelon, it was not only whisky he was prohibited. He was not allowed to smoke cigarettes either. The roadside boutiques not only sold newspapers, they sold cigarettes too. When my grandfather returned, he always smelled like an ashtray.

Four days more. Still no house. The Rosenthal crockery was wrapped and put into empty boxes. The silver cutlery was wrapped and put into empty suitcases. Achi locked everything with a padlock and hung the key with the million other keys around her waist. Nenda and Magi's friendship had now entered a new karmic sub period of unity, with the advent of Dudley. They were now wrapping cheap pavement pudding bowls that were cheaper than old newspapers.

Dudley was now the prime minister in our kitchen. Dudley had never married. Nenda and Magi had not married either. Ceylon under Dudley was a golden era for virgins and spinsters. Nenda loved him. Magi loved him. The female boarders loved him. All unmarried women loved him. Dudley brought hope to the women of Ceylon. He symbolized availability and he symbolized hope. As long as Dudley was prime minister, all unmarried women of Ceylon would hope. Hope brought happiness that marriage never would. Magi and Nenda were hopeful.

'Magi, just look at this.' Magi peered at the paper with her illiterate eyes. 'Look at the prices of things those days. Onions, rice, coconuts, all so cheap. He was a great man our Dudley.'

'Don't I know! Those days I did not have to ruin my eyes looking for stones in the rice and the dhal.'

'And look at this, houses, houses, houses to rent everywhere, in every page of the newspaper.'

'Pity that we have to look for a house now, and not then.'
'And look at the films. All Hindi films. Not like the Sinhala rubbish of today.'

But Dudley lost the election and moved out of the newspaper. Still unmarried.

'Good people have no place in politics. Politics is only for rogues,' concluded Nenda. The Dudley newspapers were utilized.

Then Mrs. Bandaranayake entered the newspapers. There was only one newspaper left to wrap what remained of the household. Mrs. Bandaranayake had begun nationalization. Nationalization combined with minimization and condensation reduced the size of the newspaper and the sum of newspapers. The remaining household items had to be transported unwrapped.

Three days left. No house. My granduncle Cecil visited us with his wife Dagma. Dagma was fifty, pregnant and had filariasis. Her right leg looked like that of the elephant man. Her black face with the red lipstick and the puff pastry like hair-do made her look like a woodpecker. That was neither the pregnancy nor filariasis. That was Dagma in person.

Granduncle Cecil and Dagma had not come on a purely social visit. Three days before shifting houses no one comes on a social visit, since all the teacups are packed. But, granduncle Cecil and Dagma came, unannounced. 'Don't those people have any shame?' Nenda muttered to Magi as they unpacked the packed teacups. It was not shame. It was an emergency.

My grandmother was not only a professional milk-toffee maker, she was also a medical expert. A diagnostic specialist who diagnosed each and every infected appendix before rupture, even before the doctors. In our house, every family member and the boarders had their appendix in little bottles filled with formaldehyde. Except me. My appendix had still not become infected. Since I was still young and obsessed with pastries and chocolates, I had not eaten enough indigenous fruits with indigestible seeds that usually infected the appendix. Dagma's appendix was also in formaldehyde, so appendicitis was not her problem. Her problem was that she was fifty, pregnant and looked like the elephant man.

My grandmother needed to be consulted. Fifty could not be changed, but the question was, did Dagma need a gynaecologist for the pregnancy, or a parasitalogist for the Filariasis. Only Achi knew the answer since Dagma was a foolish woman. It was a precarious situation. Even for my grandmother it was a difficult decision. She thought longer than usual and used her fundamental reasoning to ensure that Dagma and uncle Cecil's child would have Dagma for a mother and not the elephant man. 'Karma will take care of your child, but karma will not take care of the Filaria,' she said.

So, without a cup of tea she sent Dagma and uncle Cecil to the Buddhist priest at the Pamankada temple who performed the unbuddhistic task of destroying whatever it was that caused Dagma to look the way she did.

Before going, uncle Cecil divulged that he had been occupied with the study of palmistry the last five years since retirement and he would check our palms and find the reason for our not being able to find a house divisible by two. Achi stretched her palm. The right and the left. Achi's sub period was suitable for new houses and a move was indicated. Soon. Exact dates were not indicated on the palm. Siya refused to show his palm. He was still angry with Mrs. Bandaranayake. He believed it was Mrs. Bandaranayake and none other who was blocking our ideal-home karmic journey. Ammi's palm was okay. Nenda's and Magi's too. TM Mozart and I were too small to check palms. Thathi was in the monkey civilization. There was obviously no plausible reason for us not being able to find a home, except karma. 'But, nothing to worry,' granduncle Cecil said, 'be patient. The present karmic sub-period is ending in eight weeks and two days and thereafter, not to worry, life will be like a newly tarred road.' New beginnings were indicated. Not only for us, but also for the whole world. Patience was required for eight weeks and two days only. We practiced patience.

Mr. Karunaratne, our Landlord was not in the same sub-period. He was not patient. Thus, in a matter of two days everything was packed into two lorries. Ammi, TM Mozart, Magi, the boarders, the servants, the four dogs, two cats, two rabbits, tortoise and squirrel got into the lorry. Thathi, Nenda and Thathi's books into the green Hillman. Siya, Achi and I got into Kandapola Siya's Morris Minor which Podian the driver had driven down all the way from Nuwara Eliya to take us to wherever we were planning to go.

Siya sat in front, Achi and I at the back. 'Ennappa Hamu, sir,' began Podian the driver. 'I am not underisting why it is not possible to you for finding a house in this Colombo. This is big capital. Houses, houses, houses everywhere, this morning I am walking down road to the boutique to buy beetle leaf and boutique owner telling me, 'I say Podian… vary funny Marasinghe and Weerasinghe family not finding houses when most houses empty since Mrs. Bandaranayake Madam coming to power,' then I tell boutique owner 'Where show me house?' he show me three houses. Boutique owner talling me, 'Master sir Marasinghe coming every morning to boutique, but doing other things, not talling boutique owner master needing house to move.' Siya told him to shut up and drive without killing us in a road accident with his nonsensical chatter.

True, we did not have a house. Not our own house. But, we had all been generous people in previous births. Owners of rest-houses, motels and hotels. We were not likely to endure hardship without a roof over our head. Not in this birth. Not even for eight weeks and two days.

We moved to Mount Lavinia. To my Aunty Lydia. Our collective Karma was strong. And good. Aunty Lydia could not say no. 'Enappa Hamu, sir,' said Podian as we drove into aunty Lydia's garden. 'I am but a poor man from plantation estate, we are all living in one tin house, but I am not underistanding why rich Colombo peoples like you having to move into madam Lydia's ismall house where there is not even room for Madame Lydia's own family. When you have only been talling me you are needing a house, I would have come *pata, pata* to Colombo and found nice big house for all of you's. Ennapa! But Hamu, I am not uneristanding you? You are sending Master sir to boutique to find houses, Master sir not searching for houses in boutique, Master sir is…' Siya raised his hand to hit him. Podian grinned and jumped out of the car to help Magi out of the Lorry. Her cloth had got caught on a nail and she was hanging like a flag at half-mast.

16

Aunty Lydia was Christian. She had a Christian husband, Christian children and a Christian mother, who was now dead. Her Christian mother had a Buddhist husband who was my grandmother's brother. And it was this brother's driver Podian who had sacrificed the goat instead of a cock, enabling my birth. Now, it was the same Podian who had driven us to aunty Lydia's.

Aunty Lydia and her family lived in a house close to the sea. I knew the sea was near because the house was in Mt. Lavinia and even under Mrs. Bandaranayake's minimization syllabuses we learned that Mt. Lavinia was near the sea. But I never saw the sea from a single window of her upstairs house. Not even from the roof. On the Galle road, as we travelled from house number 58 to her Mt. Lavinia house, I did not see the sea either. But the sea had to be there. That was elementary education that even Mrs. Bandaranayake could not minimize. I loved the sea. I had never really seen it, but I loved it. It was big, spacious, and had no cockroaches or ghosts. I always wanted to live near the sea. But karma placed me near the cemetery. Until now.

Aunty Lydia's house was full. We accommodated ourselves in every corner and in every space. Space was not the problem. The problem was corrosion. Mt. Lavinia caused corrosion. For us, people who had never lived near the sea, corrosion was an extremely grave problem. In fact it was the greatest problem. Ammi worried about the refrigerator, Siya worried about the Hillman, Achi worried about the silver and TM Mozart worried about the guitar strings. I worried about the absent sea.

Space was a problem. We were not what one might consider a small family and aunty Lydia had her own family. Four children, a husband and a servant who all lived in the upstairs part of the upstair house. The downstairs part of the upstair house was occupied by the house owners. Ammi slept with aunty Lydia and her husband in the master bedroom. Sometimes aunty Lydia's third child slept with them. Achi and Siya slept with aunty Lydia's child number one and child number two. Aunty Lydia's child number four slept with Nenda, Magi, and their own servant. TM Mozart sometimes slept between Achi and Siya and sometimes between Ammi and aunty Lydia. I slept between

Nenda and aunty Lydia's servant in the servants' bedroom. The servants slept under the beds. The boarders and the animals slept in the garage and under the coconut trees. The coconuts were not ripe and the monsoons were still in the east coast. Thathi was not with us. He dropped us and returned to the monkey civilization since there was no room in aunty Lydia's house.

I didn't like aunty Lydia's house. It was a dark Christian house. I don't know if the walls were dark or the ceilings, I don't know if the windows were of glass or of wood, but I know that aunty Lydia did have windows since I spent most of my time hanging on the window hoping to get a glimpse of the sea. Mt. Lavinia had been near the sea before minimization programmes had removed the world map from the wall. So where was it now?

The new map was being printed. It was not going to be a world map. It was to be a map of Ceylon. But first, the printing companies were being nationalized. Maybe the sea would come back once the companies were nationalized? But nationalization took time. Everything that had been written in English had to be written in Sinhala. The translators had to learn English before they began to translate the English into Sinhala. It's not that we didn't have people who could translate English into Sinhala. We did, but Mrs. Bandaranayake did not like those people and she did not like their translations. She liked people who were not versatile in English to translate English into Sinhala since then, every word would not be submitted to translation, and minimisation and condensation would be enacted along with nationalization. She could kill two birds with one stone.

When aunty Lydia's upstairs house had been built, there had been a sea at the window. That is why the windows were so high. But that was then. Now the sea was gone and no one had realized it. Not aunty Lydia, not her Christian husband, nor her four Christian children. They realized it was not there only when I came and asked to see it. Uncle Lionel, aunty Lydia's husband put a chair at the window for me to get higher in order to see the sea, but it did not appear at the window. Until the next planetary change I was destined to live in a dark Christian house that once had a window near the sea.

My life did not become easier. Aunty Lydia's house had no balconies where ghosts copulated but every nook and corner of the house had a symbol of Jesus Christ. Most of the time he was on the cross with blood pouring down his body and head. The rest of the time he had risen above the cross and looked like the ghost Samuel on my balcony. Wherever I went in this dark house Jesus Christ followed me. If his eyes were not behind me, his cross was in front of me. If his eyes were in front of me the cross would be behind me. A sense of persecution attached itself to me like Dagma's Filariasis. I didn't like living in this house. Life here was dark, morbid and gloomy. How could it be any different when crosses and bleeding bodies covered the walls? I longed for our house number 58. For the colourful Buddhist statues, the multi-coloured Hindu Gods, the burning incense and I realized why Samuel, Henry and the other Christian ghosts partied on my balcony. It was far nicer with us than with their traumatic decorations of crosses and bleeding bodies of men who looked like unwashed hippies. I was glad that reincarnation was my karma and not heaven. Imagine if heaven was something like aunty Lydia's house? Even the sea that was once at the window had now left.

The greatest fear was realised. Mrs. Bandaranayake's minimizations struck again. The Hillman corroded. We had to travel by bus, recently nationalized. I travelled with Ammi for two days and stopped. On the second day, a trousered product of Mrs. Bandaranayake's saronged minimization who had helped her fuel the revolution began to feel my mother's shapely back in the nationalized bus which was filled like a can of dead Sardines. Thereafter, my mother became the chief propagator of anti-minimization and anti-Bandaranayakism.

I would have preferred to go to school. Not because I enjoyed school, but the white posterless walls looked happier than aunty Lydia's dark walls. But children's opinions were never considered. TM Mozart went to school by bus. His back was not as shapely as my mother's. Aunty Lydia who was a senior school teacher, travelled by bus. Her back was somewhat lopsided. Uncle Lionel who worked in an office, travelled by bus. He was backless. Aunty Lydia's four children travelled by bus. They had inherited their father's backlessness.

Though I didn't see the sea, I got a taste for it. Aunty Lydia's servant formed a karmic affiliation to me and served me sprats at my window post. Battered sprats, fried sprats, devilled sprats. I liked eating them. Battered sprats were my favourite. I got a sense of the taste of the sea. Salty.

Ammi discovered Mrs. Dickinson's seafood cookery class down the road and learned to make sweet and sour sprats. I ate it only once. It was so horrid that I nearly lost my yearning for the sea. Achi continued to make milk toffee with Parakramabahu the sixth's condensed milk. She made and made, but no one visited her to eat them. She then packed eight milk toffees in paper bags and sent them to Colombo with uncle Lionel, who sold them in his office. Uncle Lionel's colleagues liked Achi's milk toffees and the demand began to grow. Then aunty Lydia's four children took milk toffees and sold them in the school canteens and brought my grandmother the money. The demand still grew. TM Mozart tried his hand at it too, but only once. He was pick-pocketed in the bus where the robber had taken only the milk toffees, not the ten rupees in the pocket. But Achi did not give him any more milk toffees. Aunty Lydia took milk toffees too. But only for personal consumption. She refused to demean herself to the level of a milk-toffee saleswoman. Then, at the height of demand, production had to stop. Minimizations struck again.

This time it was cashew nuts. Mrs. Bandaranayake prohibited the sale of cashew nuts until the nationalization of the cashew industries had been completed. Milk toffees without cashew nuts were not the same as milk toffee with cashew nuts. The nationalization of the cashew industry was also a complicated matter with many candidates of the Bandaranayake clan willing to head the list of nominees for the top post in the nationalized cashew industry. It dragged on and on. Parakramabahu the sixth's light brown coloured condensed milk became black and hard with age. When they finally reached a settlement, a fungus struck the cashew trees and cashew nuts entered a new era of non-planned minimization. My grandmother gave up the production of milk toffees.

Bandaranayake minimization had its positive moments. The cooperative store opened. Most times, the shelves were bare since the nationalized transport services were not as quick as the non-nationalized transport services. But, as we stood around and waited for the nationalized delivery of rice and dhal, Ammi becoming irritated with my eternal 'Ammi how long more?' bought for me that which was never out of stock. The blank paged drawing book and the box of

Homrun pas crayons. I drew. I no longer stood on the chair at the window searching the sea. I drew the sea.

My gloomy days were filled with as yet non-minimized colour. The sea was blue and had no waves. The coconut tree on the beach never got fungus and the ripe coconuts on the tree never fell on the head of the elephant standing underneath it. The boat near the horizon never had a fisherman on board. He had drowned. The sun was always setting. The horizon was sometimes straight and sometimes curved. Curved, when the monsoons were nearing, and straight at other times.

The quality of the colours varied, but the essential substance remained. I could now give the re-appeared Mt. Lavinia sea different hues. Light blue, dark blue, green blue... It was almost better than having the sea at the window.

The Hillman was still corroded. Siya no longer sat around reading Buddhist books aloud; he contributed to the elimination of corrosion. Every morning he would go to the garage where the Hillman was being repaired and stay there until the mechanics left for the day. It was an important job. The Hillman belonged to an era of non-nationalization. In this era of nationalization, the removal of essential car parts and their resale as spare parts was a lucrative business. Especially when these parts were imported. Our Hillman had gone to the garage only for further corrosion prevention, but if my grandfather did not sit there and watch the mechanics, very likely our Hillman may have been returned to us as an un-corroded skeleton, lacking internal organs.

A week went by. No Hillman, no school. The corrosion had been worse than could be seen by the naked eye. Ammi learned to make savoury sprats. The boat in my sea without the fisherman now had a fishing net. But still no fisherman.

Two weeks went by. No Hillman, no school. Ammi learned to make sprats in sauce. The sprats tasted better than the sauce. The fishing net on the fishing boat without the fisherman had now caught one fish. A goldfish. The corrosion had been arrested. The Hillman had to be repainted in order to avoid further corrosion.

Three weeks. No Hillman, no school. No sprats. Ammi was fed up with Mrs. Dickinson's cookery classes after sprat salad and sprat soup were pronounced inedible. She craved for the Hillman. My fishing net had a gold fish and a crab. The green paint for the green Hillman was not available. The paint industry had been nationalized and green paint was no longer produced. Green was the colour of the opposition. It was Dudley's colour. Mrs. Bandaranayake was blue. Ammi and Siya did not want any paint on the Hillman. Corrosion was preferable to blue. Achi did not care. Aunty Lydia and family were not interested, they travelled by bus and were not bothered with what they considered the trivialities of colour.

Nearly four weeks later, the Hillman drove through Aunty Lydia's gates. It was blue. Thathi had visited the garage before visiting us and ordered the Hillman to be painted blue. My father was a traitor. He had become a Bandaranayake supporter.

A fisherman appeared on the boat in my drawing book. The boat was blue like the sea. He had no fish. I was wondering if I should put some green seaweed in the fisherman's net? But I was torn out of my Homrun pas world! The Hillman was back and I had to return to school. Ammi did not drive the Hillman; she refused to drive a blue car. She told Siya who was not supposed to drive cars to drive the Hillman until the government changed and the nationalized paint industries produced green paint. I sat in the back, Ammi sat in front with Siya and we drove to school. I wished Thathi didn't have the Hillman painted blue. I had nothing against the colour, but I preferred to stay in aunty Lydia's house and draw the fisherman in the sea.

There was no happiness at re-union. The girls barely glanced at me, nor did they ask me why I had not been at school. Perhaps they all had the same dilemma with the green car turning blue that they needed no words to understand my absence and plight. They were all quieter. So were Miss Lily Marlene and Miss Fatima. Miss Fatima did not twirl her plait and Miss Lily Marlene no longer sang. They tried to teach us about my country, the mango seed in the Indian Ocean.

'Children,' she said, 'It is nothing but good fortune and good karma that all of you are born in this wonderful country.' Miss Lily Marlene's words were hollow, her eyes kept darting back and forth to Miss Fatima. It was as though she did not want to say what she was saying, but had to. 'This country was once called the pearl of the Indian Ocean. I suppose you all know what a pearl is?' No one said anything. Not even Marshmallow.

'Right. Upon this pearl of the Indian Ocean, there is magnificent vegetation, rare birds and animals no country has ever seen. We have many rivers that supply us with water and electricity, we have two monsoons during different seasons in the two parts of the country, but above all, what you all should never forget is that this is one of the few countries in the world where no earthquake happens nor volcanoes erupt. We do not have a single volcano. We are safe.' She then looked at us with darting eyes as though she was unsure if she had said the right thing. 'Understood?' Silence. 'Good,' she continued. 'We in this country have the most beautiful flag in the world.' She took out a cloth flag from her handbag and Miss Fatima held it. 'Now the yellow borders represent Buddhism, the Bo-leaves are also Buddhism because Lord Buddha attained enlightenment under a Bo tree. A branch of this Bo tree was brought and planted here. Perhaps your parents can take you all to see this Bo tree one day when…' She checked her sentence and began again. 'The green stripe to the left represents the Muslims and other minorities such as Burghers, Malays, Chinese, Boras and Sindhis, the orange stripe, the Tamils. The lion in the middle of the flag represents the Sinhala people. Sinha, the lion. The Sinhala people are the people of the lion. Tell your parents to tell you all the story of Sinhabahu and Sinhaseevali the children of the lion.'

'And the sword Miss, why is the lion carrying a sword?' Miss Lily Marlene and Miss Fatima looked at each other. I think they did not know why the lion carried a sword.

'But Miss, no animal can stand on three legs. Look at that lion on the flag. It is standing on three legs and carrying the sword with its front leg. If any animal stands like that it will fall down and cut itself.'

'Let us discuss that later. Now we shall continue with the flag. Now, the red surrounding the lion. The red is for…'

'Blood,' said a quiet voice.

I had never heard that voice before. I turned my head to look at her. A new face, a new girl. Her eyes brimming with tears and her body shaking in agony. Miss Fatima and Miss Lily Marlene stopped the lessons and sent us out into the garden. Only the new girl remained in the class.

Her name was Deepa.

17

The eight weeks and two day karmic sub-period had ended, but we were still living in aunty Lydia's house. Though she never said a word about our extended sojourn, I think even her good Christian heart was becoming irritated at this bunch of people who did not seem to be making an effort to search for a house.

Thathi no longer came to Colombo on weekends and Ammi, despite her initial anger at the green Hillman turning blue, got uncle Buddhi to remove the black lenses from her sunglasses and replace them with yellow ones. She now drove the Hillman which was blue to the world, but green for her. Ammi loved green. It was Dudley's colour. Now, not only the virgins and the spinsters, but even married women were beginning to fall for Dudley.

Mrs. Bandaranayake's minimizations were reaching an egalitarian peak. The saronged man in trousers who had stroked Ammi's back in the bus was now educated. He wanted a car. Not just any old car. A red car. But first, he wanted to destroy all the blue cars.

He was a new phenomenon. The new educated unemployed. He did not want to plough the fields and cultivate the rice; he wanted to industrialise the fields and eat rice. He was the supreme product of free education. He had helped Mrs. Bandaranayake to win the election. Defeating Dudley, who favoured ploughing. But Mrs Bandaranayake's minimized egalitarian equality called free education had not taught him that a blue car could be painted red and needn't be destroyed.

I knew it. Magi knew it. Nenda knew it. But not this free educated saronged man in trousers who had bumped up the statistics of literacy in Southeast Asia. While Mrs. Bandaranayake practiced minimization on the privileged in the cities, this newly trousered man no longer wanted to stroke my mothers shapely back in the bus. He was busy breeding like a rabbit in the countryside. It was the red fungus.

This red fungus was angry with Mrs. Bandaranayake. She had not fulfilled the promise she had made to them prior to her election. So she tried to console them. She took land from the rich to give the poor. But it never got to them. Instead, it got stuck somewhere within this long word she liked so much: nationalization. The rich no longer had land, but neither did the poor. The red fungus became angrier. They burned the land, they burned cars, and they burned houses.

Emergency was implemented at night. The blue Hillman stayed behind the gates and so did Ammi. Thathi's arrivals became scarce. The red fungus was jeopardizing the nationalized transport service and the nationalized incompetence and lethargy began to intensify.

Though aunty Lydia was cross that we had still not found a house, uncle Lionel was not cross. He told me stories of the sea that had once been at the window before minimization. In the evenings he sat with Siya, drank whisky, smoked cigarettes and discussed politics. On most evenings, aunty Lydia went to church. She did not walk the main roads, but crept through barbed wire garden fences to get to church. When she didn't go to church and remained at home, uncle Lionel and Siya discussed politics without cigarettes or whisky. Aunty Lydia was an Anglican. Uncle Lionel a Catholic and my grandfather a Buddhist. Siya practiced moderation in cigarettes and whisky while uncle Lionel practiced no moderation. The Catholic Church was opulent and Latin, not austere and Buddhist. Even if moderation was introduced to the Catholic Church like minimization to Ceylon, uncle Lionel would not have understood. He knew no Latin. It was like Pali and me. But aunty Lydia was different. She understood everything and practiced reformation. Reform the minds of those who waste money drinking spirits and smoking tobacco. She was a good Anglican.

Uncle Lionel had a heart attack and history repeated itself. We all changed places. The owners of Aunty Lydia's house moved up and we moved down. Uncle Lionel could no longer climb stairs. The window where the sea had once been, now belonged to the owners of aunty Lydia's house. I had no window. The sea disappeared forever.

The Homrun pas blue crayon became qualitatively inferior to other crayons. Red was red. Yellow was yellow. Green was green, but blue became something extra terrestrial. It appeared blue to the eye, but colourless on paper. A slimy slithering wax. Without colour there was no sea. The coconut tree and the elephant lost their appeal without a sea. My drawing book remained blank.

The downstairs part of the house was not as dark as the upstairs part. The walls were pink and the ceilings yellow. The bleeding Christ began to lose his fearsome power. Then Christmas neared. Aunty Lydia attended church every morning and every evening. Her four Christian children attended church every evening. My grandmother, somewhat depressed since the depressed sale of milk toffee, now concentrated her culinary energies on Christmas cake- without cashew nuts.

In the middle of minimization, which had progressed beyond the nationalized cashew cooperation beginnings, people were happy when they got a piece of Christmas cake at all. They were no longer fussy about cashew nuts. Ammi drove the blue Hillman to Christmas decoration classes and learned to make Bonbons. With the help of the Chinese, the firework industry had reached a peak it had never experienced before. My mother made quality Bonbons and Cargills Limited bought them all. Each and every Bonbon my mother made cracked when pulled. Inside the Bonbons she had metal whistles and plastic dolls imported from China. They were not particularly appealing, but the loud crack was a satisfying compensation.

Siya and Uncle Lionel began decorating the house with glittering garlands. Aunty Lydia said 'church is more important than garlands.' Uncle Lionel said that church was bad for his heart. Aunty Lydia said that garlands were bad for his heart. But Christmas kept getting nearer.

Kandapola Siya's driver came in the Austin Morris Minor with a large Christmas tree from his master's garden. Now more garlands were required. Uncle Lionel, Siya and the driver Podian drove to Pettah in the Morris Minor to buy garlands. Achi escorted them to buy dates and pumpkin preserve required for the Christmas cake. As the story goes, despite the lack of quality garlands, Siya and uncle Lionel had got themselves so excited about the non-minimized price of garlands, that, in the middle of the dusty humid shop, uncle Lionel had clutched his heart and suffered another heart attack.

Podian the driver had rushed out of the dusty shop, into the Pettah Kovil and dashed a coconut at Lord Kataragama's feet and begun to pray. Siya was now left to drive the Morris Minor with Uncle Lionel to the hospital. Podian was still prostate.

When Achi came out of the condiment shop with ten pounds of pumpkin preserve instead of the intended five pounds, (five pounds of dates had to be substituted with pumpkin preserve, since the nationalized port authorities had not cleared the last shipment of dates from the Middle-east in due time, and the dates had rotted in the harbour) neither Siya, nor uncle Lionel, nor Podian, nor the Morris Minor could be found in the whole of Pettah. Achi walked from shop to shop carrying her ten pounds of pumpkin preserve but did not find them.

In the meantime Podian, after dashing the coconut and prostating himself at Lord Kataragama's feet had stood up, wiped his feet with the edge of his sarong, climbed onto Lord Kataragama's lap and removed all his garlands. He knew that uncle Lionel and Siya had not bought garlands before the heart attack and since he had no money to buy the garlands, he borrowed them from Lord Kataragama. It was no crime. He was Hindu. Lord Kataragama was a Hindu like he was. If Lord Kataraganma did become cross, he would say to him, 'Ennappa, my Lord Kataragama, when you are angry with me for taking garland to decorate Madam Lydia Christmas tree, not be angry please Lord Kataragama. I will bring Christmas cake piece from madam hamu Beet and keep at your feets. She is making the best Christmas cake in the world, even when Madam Bandaranayake is eating all necessary condimens alone. But when you are still angry, not be angry great Lord Kataragama, I am bringing garland back when Christmas is finishing and putting on yours neck.' So the matter was settled and he ran out of the temple before the Lord could have second thoughts.

Achi saw him, running from shop to shop looking like a two-legged Vel cart which travelled the city with coloured trinkets in honour of Lord Kataragama. 'Ko, ko… where are the masters?' Like a tidal wave he covered my grandmother with a spit-sodden tale of the happenings. In Tamil. In his excitement he had forgotten the Sinhala language. It was a Bandaranayake lead Sinhala only era. My grandmother did not understand him.

Achi grabbed him, got into a bus and returned home with the ten kilos of pumpkin preserve and started cutting it up for Christmas cake while Podian decorated the Christmas tree with Lord Kataragama's garlands. In the middle of the garlands was a twenty two carat gold Thali, sacrificed only that morning by a young Hindu woman whose old Hindu husband had been run over by a lorry. The husband did not die. He seesawed between life and death. The Hindu god's could not decide on his destiny, so the young bride wanting to make it easier for them sacrificed her 22 carat gold Thali to Lord Kataragama and asked him to please save her husband's life. But the weight of the lorry was more than the carat weight of the Thali. The husband died. The young widow returned to the Kovil to reclaim her Thali from Lord Kataragama's neck. But, Lord Kataragama had no Thali.

The Thali had replaced the Angel with the torn dress on top of aunty Lydia's Christmas tree. The police had been alerted. But, in the middle of minimization, the Sinhala police did not go to Hindu Kovils. The Sinhala only police had the important task of eliminating Sinhala only red fungus, which was now beginning to infiltrate the cities. A solitary Tamil journalist reported the news of the stolen Thali in the non-nationalized Tamil newspaper. We did not buy Tamil newspapers since we did not know the language and Podian, who knew the language was illiterate.

Some weeks later the same incident was reported in the nationalized English newspaper. Since the news too had now submitted to minimization and some news was needed to fill the blank pages, the Tamil widow had bribed a Sinhala nationalist for the Tamil article to appear in the Sinhala only newspaper in English. The title of the article was 'Thali robbed from Lord Kataragama's neck. Finders Rewarded.'

Aunty Lydia read the article. The date, the time and location corresponded to uncle Lionel's heart attack. Thereupon, aunty Lydia added her senior schoolteacher logic to the article and pulled down the gold decoration from the top of the Christmas tree for comparison with photograph on newspaper. It was the widow's Thali! All hell broke loose!

I would have kept the Thali, so would my mother and grandmother. But aunty Lydia who had a Christian god, feared the unknown. I do not know if she feared the Thali, the widow or Lord Kataragama, but instead of contacting the newspaper to fulfil the finders rewarded part, she muttered 'Oh my dear Lord, Oh my blessed Lord, Oh sweet Lord, Oh my Lord…' and dragged the Christmas tree out of the house and burned it up with all of Lord Kataragama's garlands including the widow's Thali. I did not recognize aunty Lydia's sweet Lord on the pink walls or the family photo album. But I hoped that this sweet Lord would aid the Hindu woman who had lost her husband and now her Thali. Lord Kataragama was obviously not a good caretaker of Thalis. 'Aunty Lydia, who is this sweet Lord?' I asked. 'Don't talk,' she said, 'I do not want to hear one more word about that gold chain.' The twenty-two carat gold, five sovereigns Thali became a common chain. Like the half a sovereign gold chain hanging from the neck of aunty Lydia's eldest marriageable daughter. 'It is gone and it is forgotten.'

'But?' I tried again. 'Not a word. We have to now concentrate on Lionel's heart. That is now the only priority. Nothing else.'

18

Uncle Lionel did not die. After two days of hospital he returned home without even being examined. Minimization and bribery had entered the hospitals. The Sinhala only had evicted the foreign Christian nuns who had worked in Sinhala hospitals without accepting payment or bribes. In their place Sinhala only medical staff had been hired in order to provide free medical services where the rich and the poor were treated alike. Aunty Lydia was against all forms of bribery and corruption. My mother pleaded with her, 'Lydia Akka, if you are against payment, I shall do it for you,' but aunty Lydia refused, 'Nangi, never in my life will I support such corruption, not even for the love of Lionel,' and she got uncle Lionel discharged and brought him home. It was another typical theoretical utopia!

Achi's Christmas cake did not function either. Christmas cake needed more than just pumpkin preserve to be called Christmas cake. Uncle Lionel's heart weakened and aunty Lydia applied to the commonwealth. Our nationalized health services that required a bribe for proper examination to treat the rich and the poor alike could not treat uncle Lionel's heart, only the commonwealth could.

I was thrilled that our little island was not as isolated as in the times of Hanuman the monkey and that we were a part of the commonwealth. But my delight was short lived. TM Mozart saw me ecstatic and began his favourite task of de-ecstacizing me. 'Not for long,' he said, 'the person of your sex who is running this country is having her wonderful love affair with the Chinese and the commonwealth is contemplating dropping us into the Indian ocean like a hot potato.'

This time I double-checked his story. It was unfortunately true. Mrs. Bandaranayake's minimizations had brought a shadow to our commonwealth. The Commonwealth did not like Mrs. Bandaranayake's love affair with the Chinese. It was another non-functional function.

Ceylon. The source of Ceylon tea. The pearl of the Indian Ocean. The pride of colonization. A segment of the British commonwealth. Minimized, to a Bandaranayake common wealth. Uncle Lionel's heart could not be healed as long as the Bandaranayake's monopolized the theoretical commonwealth's common wealth. Aunty Lydia had no choice but to apply for a teaching post abroad in order to save uncle Lionel's heart. The commonwealth understood her problem and asked her and her family to come.

Between teardrops Achi tried to find a culinary connection between the Christmas cake and the pumpkin preserve. Aunty Lydia was her favourite daughter. Even though Achi had given birth only to one child, my mother, aunty Lydia was her favourite daughter. The love between aunty Lydia and my grandmother far exceeded the love between my grandmother and my mother. It was a Christian kind of love. They kissed and stroked if ever they saw each other or passed each other. We Buddhists kissed only on birthdays. And that too was too much. I was not a kisser. I hated being kissed and I hated kissing. When I had to kiss someone for a Birthday, I would hide under the bed and would have to be bribed or threatened and brought out to kiss. I loved eating Birthday cake though. 'No kiss, no cake,' said my mother. So, if I wanted to eat cake, I had to kiss.

The kiss ought to be eliminated. Perhaps I ought to write a letter to Mrs. Bandaranayake and ask her to eliminate the kiss. If that did not work, perhaps she could nationalize the kiss. Then she and her people could utilize the kiss and I could eat the cake.

Christmas was still around the corner. But what was Christmas without a Christmas tree and Christmas cake? And with uncle Lionel's feeble heart? And with the problem of the commonwealth? Aunty Lydia was distracted and worried. Every night before dinner she repeated at the dining table, '...and thank you my sweet Lord for the generous gift of food. Let us appreciate what we have and not ask for more. The sweet Lord has blessed us that we are not starving. Thank you sweet Lord.' I too repeated, 'Thank you sweet Lord,' though I wished this sweet Lord would put on our tables something other than red rice and dhal boiled in water, with neither coconut milk nor salt.

Coconuts caused cholesterol and salt caused high blood pressure. Siya had cholesterol, uncle Lionel had cholesterol and high blood pressure, my grandmother had cholesterol and my father could get high blood pressure for his father had died of it. Their debilitated and debilitating hearts needed to be protected, and I protected my un-debilitated heart at the same time. It was karmic unity of aunty

Lydia's Christian family who did not believe karma and my mother's Buddhist family that believed in karma. And this sweet lord of aunty Lydia's served rice and curry that tasted like toilet paper.

That was not the worst. The worst was yet to come. Aunty Lydia was in a mood for monologue. 'My darlings, let us thank the sweet Lord for what we have and not ask him for more. If he should give us what we do not have, let us be thankful and thank the sweet Lord for that which he has given us. We must not ask him things that we think we might need. We must learn to accept the sweet Lord's gifts graciously and not tax his sweet soul.'

Since the nationalization of the sugar and chocolate industries I had forgotten the sweet taste of sweet. Aunty Lydia had found a compromise between minimized sweetness and the sweetness of the Lord. I could not do so. I had not met her sweet Lord. There was more to come. 'My darlings, I know that Christmas is near. The sweet Lord has given us more than we need, we shall not ask for more. Lionel has a weak heart and we have to concentrate our energies and ask the sweet Lord to help Lionel strengthen his heart, and that is not an easy task for even the sweet Lord. Lionel you have provoked the Lord. Your lying, your gambling, your smoking and your drinking! At least now, thank the sweet Lord that you are alive...' aunty Lydia continued her monologue before uncle Lionel could formulate a suitable reply. She was the personal protector of his heart. 'And my darlings, this Christmas we shall not ask the sweet Lord to give us any gifts and for the first time in your beautiful young lives there will be no presents at the foot of the Christmas tree. Thank the sweet Lord that we are happy, a family, we have a roof over our heads and we are alive.'

My first Christmas in a Christian house! And I had to thank the sweet Lord for salt-less food, a window without a sea and Christmas without a present. One day we were going to return to a Buddhist house and Christmas was going to end up like the Hindu widow's Thali. Forgotten. Karma followed us like a shadow, even into Christian houses.

Christmas came and went. No presents. Red rice with dhal and chicken boiled in water. Aunty Lydia's application to the commonwealth was accepted. Achi cried. Aunty Lydia cried. All her children cried and the pumpkin preserve aged. Achi worried about aunty Lydia's eldest

marriageable daughter. She worried about aunty Lydia's departure. The
future was bland and morose. I was sad that aunty Lydia and family
would be leaving us. I was willing to stop yearning for the sea if only
they would remain. I would miss them. Perhaps not as much as Achi
would miss aunty Lydia, but I would miss them. Furthermore, aunty
Lydia was the only person I knew who had a house in Mt. Lavinia with
a window that had once overlooked the sea. I even liked her four
Christian children. They were nicer to me than TM Mozart, whose
fiddle playing had increased. Music had become his only source of
communication. I was not sure if he could speak. I had not heard his
voice in years, except in song.

The paper industries were nationalized and paper minimized.
Books were minimized since the book markets did not publish Sinhala
only. The English books became too expensive since salaries were
minimized. The published word had reached a minimum and pioneers
were needed to raise us out of this created quagmire of minimalist
reading. And so, like magic, second hand bookshops sprouted in the
city. Read and return for payment. Suddenly books were galore. All
second hand.

Thathi visited us with a book for every member of the family. I
got a non-minimized David Copperfield with a Uriah Heep who was
non-existent in my school condensed version. Ammi got a book on
Maria Montessori and Achi a book on Astrology. Achi now found a
temporary diversion from the ageing pumpkin preserve in the glass jar
on top of the kitchen cupboard. Aunty Lydia's move to the source of the
commonwealth was astrologically analysed.

Aunty Lydia would move. It was astrologically predicted. Her
eldest daughter would marry late. Again astrologically predicted. Uncle
Lionel's chronic heart was also astrologically predicted. Venus was the
villain. Times would get worse before they became better.

Jupiter with its early marriages and sedentary women had left
the earth and given the reigns to Venus. Venus having nothing better
to do, had raised the minimum age for marriage and created career
women. Women were throwing off the yolks of tradition, crossing seas
and bearing fewer children. Venus was weakening the male. Uncle
Lionel's weak heart was the fault of Venus. His Roman Catholic

non-moderate excesses were not the reason for his weak heart. Venus was the villain.

Venus was not only a villain, she was also a vehicle. Hence, there was no preventing aunty Lydia and her family getting into a plane and crossing the skies to the source of the commonwealth. England. Her four pathetic children were destined to have a sad future of inter-cultural marriages. Venus was certainly a villain. A female planet. A female villain. Like Mrs. Bandaranayake.

My grandmother cried and prayed and hoped to die before aunty Lydia's four loveable children married foreigners who did not wash their backs. It was no longer a problem of right hand or left hand; the rice eating hand or the non-rice eating hand, foreigners did not wash their backs. Period. They only used toilet paper and were unsuitable for marriage.

Achi could not change Venus. She re-sold the astrology book to the second hand bookshop and kept the money from the sale. People like Achi were not profitable for second hand bookshops. Normally people going to such places always bought a new book when they returned the old book. Achi did not do so. Not because she was a Mrs. Bandaranayake supporter, rather because she was angry with Venus. Aunty Lydia's departure could not be prevented, not for another four hundred and seventy five years. In four hundred and seventy five years Venus would have to go and Aquarius would come. In the Age of Aquarius all men would be sages. What about Mrs. Bandaranayake? The astrology book had said men, not women.

Achi's pumpkin preserve on top of the kitchen cupboard was not going to see the Age of Aquarius. She contemplated packing the pumpkin preserve into sealed plastic bags at the marketing department and sending it with aunty Lydia to England. But aunty Lydia refused to take pumpkin preserve to England. 'You can give people pumpkin preserve as presents,' Achi tried to persuade her. 'Oh my darling aunty,' aunty Lydia would say, 'the English do not eat pumpkin preserve, they eat fish and chips.'

'Yes but they can have pumpkin preserve for desert.'

'Oh my darling aunty, the English only eat mint chocolates and cucumber sandwiches.' To which Achi countered:

'I am sure once the English get a taste for pumpkin preserve they will no longer eat mint chocolates.' Mint was not a part of the Ceylonese diet. Garlic, ginger, curry powder and pumpkin preserve, but not mint. 'My darling aunty, I cannot take pumpkin preserve. The English will think I am completely mad and send the family and me back to Ceylon.'
'Then why don't you take the pumpkin preserve for you all to eat?'
'Darling aunty, the pumpkin preserve has been on top of the kitchen cupboard since Lionel's heart attack and not even the mice have tried to eat it. I don't think either Lionel or the children will eat it.'
'Then you can eat,' said Achi.
'Darling aunty, I loved your Christmas cake, but I cannot bear pumpkin preserve.' That was that. Aunty Lydia was a polite and cultured senior schoolteacher. She did not fight. She did not argue. But she always got her way. I think she was meant to live in the source of the commonwealth, not in our minimized mango seed at the tip of India. A person like aunty Lydia would certainly enhance the commonwealth. She was wasted in the Bandaranayake common wealth of Sinhala only, which did not appreciate her senior schoolteacher English.

Achi began experimenting with pumpkin preserve. Aunty Lydia's love for Christmas cake and her hate for pumpkin preserve released the search enzyme in Achi's brain. Determination was her karmic asset. She was determined to send the ten pounds of pumpkin preserve to England. She did not care how.

Achi had a streak of genius. Pumpkin jam, pumpkin cake and pumpkin chutney were the result. She made, she packed and she disposed without anyone's knowledge. When aunty Lydia and her family reached England after disposing their last rupees on excess luggage, which was discovered to be excess only at the airport and not in the Mt. Lavinia house, her second daughter had three bottles of pumpkin jam in her luggage. Her third son had four bottles of pumpkin chutney and two bottles of jam; the eldest daughter had two and a half pounds of pumpkin cake and the youngest daughter, who had the least amount of personal luggage, carried the rest. Jam, chutney and cake. I presume aunty Lydia became extremely cross. After all she had honest Christian commonwealth qualities and not flexible Ceylonese Bandaranayake common wealth qualities. But sorrow was greater than anger. Achi was her favourite mother, and she the favourite daughter. They never exchanged a word about pumpkin preserve in their letters.

The pumpkin preserve didn't have the karmic competence to survive the commonwealth. The pumpkin cake was inedible. The minimized brown sugar was not as sweet as the white sugar of bygone days. The pumpkin jam recipe had been created for fresh pumpkin and not preserve. The jam was like a Bandaranayake lollipop. One could suck and suck, but it did not get sucked. The pumpkin chutney, needless to say became a victim of a typical minimized product to which Achi had mistakenly added red brick powder instead of chilli powder. Thus, the ten pounds of pumpkin preserve filled the first garbage sack on the first day of garbage collection in aunty Lydia's new house in the commonwealth.

Aunty Lydia and her lovable family had left us for good. They were the first of many who were to leave during the era of minimization. There was nothing left to be minimized and now the human beings began to minimize. Mrs. Bandaranayake had enough of the revolt of the red fungus in the countryside. She began to minimize the countryside and the red fungus began to accumulate behind bars.

My family and I were still a part of the blessed, permitted to live in minimized freedom. Aunty Lydia's youngest daughter gave me her foreign rubber doll before leaving. She did not want to, but kind-hearted aunty Lydia forced her to practice Christian charity. I now had a doll that did not fit into the system of minimalism. She was fat, pink, blonde, had open and closing blue eyes and a nasal 'mama' in the stomach. The 'made in china' plastic dolls available on the Colombo pavements were thin (minimized), with scanty hair, had arms falling out of shoulder sockets, legs suffering the same fate as arms, eyes not open and closing - only open, no nasal 'mama' and naked (the height of minimization). But my doll and I were now members of the commonwealth. It wasn't that bad that aunty Lydia and her four children had left. I now had a doll that said 'mama.' I spoke to her in English and told her of the sea that had once been at the upstairs window in aunty Lydia's upstairs house in Mt. Lavinia.

Nenda lamented in the kitchen. Nenda, Magi and aunty Lydia's servant had formed a happy triangle of rumination and ponder. Aunty

Lydia and her family could not take their faithful servant. The commonwealth only issued visas to senior schoolteachers and their families, not to servants. Aunty Lydia had tried very hard. But the commonwealth did not want all of Ceylon's common wealth. Nenda's ruminations reached a conclusion. 'Only sinners were left in Ceylon.' Aunty Lydia and her Christian family had not sinned. We had. So, like the fearsome Raksha king Ravana, we were to remain in this forsaken island, placed like a sucked and thrown mango seed from the mouth of the wind god's son Hanuman, tormented by Mrs. Bandaranayake and about to perish at the hands of the Chinese. Aunty Lydia and her family like the Princess Sita and Hanuman, left. To the kingdom of the north. We sinners remained in the south. 'Enappa,' said Podian showing off his new twenty two carat one sovereign gold chain which aunty Lydia had given him before departure, 'I having a very big job to do. Lydia madam crying and telling me, 'Podian, I am leaving my darling aunty and my darling father in your care. Look after them like your own parents. Enappa, for me, Tamil man, difficult job... no, no, no, no Hamu... oh my gods don't carry that pot. Much too heavy for you,' and he ran after Achi trying to carry her pot which did not even weigh an ounce since it was empty. But, he was committed to aunty Lydia's word.

Podian was the only person I knew who was happy to remain in Ravana's kingdom and did not think that he had sinned. Rather, the opposite.

19

Uncle Buddhi's wife was the next victim of minimization who went to a non-commonwealth country in the northern hemisphere. Aunty Lydia's servant died of sorrow and left her property to aunty Lydia's youngest daughter. A gold Thali. Aunty Lydia's dead servant's gold Thali weighed five sovereigns. Ammi did not tell aunty Lydia about the Thali which her youngest daughter had inherited from the dead servant. Aunty Lydia was a very honest member of the commonwealth. My mother locked the Thali in the vault of the People's Bank and re-wrote her last will. 'If I were to die before the marriage of Lydia Akka's youngest daughter, she, Pamela should receive this five sovereign gold Thali as a wedding present from those who are responsible for the execution of my last will.' My mother had her own sense of honesty.

The red fungus was eating up the country. Two employees of the highways department, avid co-searchers of potholes and colleagues of my father submitted to minimization and left the country. TM Mozart's cricket team of eleven players reduced to seven. The burghers and Anglo-Asians who had remained despite SWRD's myopic 'Sinhala only' now began to leave. Miss Manel White Ratnayake left. The Sinhala only policy had no necessity for my elocution teacher's superior English. Only the sinners remained. And a house found us.

We did not find a house. A house found us. Mrs. Adonis: seventies, widowed, mothered. Six of her seven children had left the country. She had built herself a one bed-roomed small house, with a wall around it and waited to sell the rest of the land upon which her dead husband's ancestral home stood. She wanted to sell only the land. The house just happened to be on the land. It was an old dilapidated house infested with cockroaches and rats where members of Mrs. Adonis's husband's family had lived and died for hundreds of years.

Karma brought Thathi to Mrs. Adonis with the first monsoon breeze. As the first breezes of the monsoon were heading towards the west coast and Thathi was performing his usual job of inspecting the standard of potholes, Mrs. Adonis had opened the small gate of her one-bedroom house to speak to her neighbour Roswitha about the culvert that had been blocked during the last monsoon. Her Daschund, Cleopatra, had run onto the main road where Thathi had been inspecting potholes. Mrs. Adonis wobbled behind the dog. Although a Daschund was a karmic mis-creation that needed at least six legs to prevent being victimized by gravity, Cleopatra was still faster than Mrs. Adonis with her seventy something years. 'Cleopatra, Cleopatra…,' Mrs. Adonis had shouted running behind the dog. My father on hearing the name Cleopatra had raised his head from the pothole and begun to run behind the dog. My father does not usually run behind dogs. He believed that if a dog was foolish enough to venture onto the road, it was karma's duty to use wisdom and not compassion and kill it since it was a mortal risk to drivers. But Cleopatra was different. This difference lay in her name.

My father was a lover of Roman civilization. The finest words ever spoken, had been spoken by the Roman Mark Anthony. He had often told me, 'I come to bury Cæsar, not to praise him, the evil that men do lives after them… my heart is in the coffin with Cæsar, and I must pause till it comes back to me.' That was one Roman my father admired, the second was Cæsar himself, and they had both loved Cleopatra, the queen of the Nile. So my father jumped out of his pothole, caught Cleopatra and saved the Roman empire from collapse. Or so he thought in that fleeting moment. In his agitation he had forgotten that Cleopatra was a part of the Egyptian civilization and not the Roman. But Cleopatra was saved, and my father got some plus points from either karma or the Egyptian god Ra. For, Mrs. Adonis, in absolute empirical gratitude invited my father to tea and confided her worries about the blocked culvert. My father, a former boy scout, brainwashed into performing one good turn a day, promised to call on the minimized municipal service and bodily bring one of their employees to dredge the culvert. Failing which, he would do so himself. My father was a double hero.

After solving the problem of the culvert, Mrs. Adonis brought my father a second cup of tea and related the story of the land. She wanted to sell it; her children did not want to sell it. But, it was written in her name and her children were abroad. So she was selling it. Unfortunately, on this land there stood a house that should in actuality be razed to the ground if she was to sell the piece of land. How could she sell a piece of land when it had a house on it? Thathi offered to look at the land. He was obviously capable of judging the land even if a house blocked his sight. He looked and saw nothing amiss. He told Mrs. Adonis that if she reduced the price of the land, which covered the cost of razing a great ancestral home to the ground, he would buy her land. Mrs. Adonis was elated. Thathi, her double hero, now became her triple hero.

Mrs. Adonis's dead husband's ancestral home was dilapidated and wet. It was infested with reptiles that slithered though the Ceylon tiles during day, mice that caroused at night, cockroaches that were not limited to the toilets, but flew around the dining room like giant Archaeopteryxes, humongous spiders that did bungee jumping from the walls, pythons that ate bandicoots in the dog's kennel and geckos that squeaked when one entered and exited the house. The number of the dilapidated house was one hundred and eighty six, which was divisible by two. For my father, it was the most liveable house he had ever seen.

Thathi finished his tea, jumped a double-decker bus to aunty Lydia's house in Mount Lavinia, packed my mother, grandparents and myself into the blue Hillman and brought us back to Mrs. Adonis's the same day. He was as proud as a rooster. He had not only found a house, but he had found a house that superseded Bandaranayake minimization. It was big. And it was free.

As Mrs. Adonis took us around the house and explained the life and death history of each of the ten bedrooms, Ammi's face poured like newly canned Parakramabahu the sixth's condensed milk. Thathi smiled like the full moon. I looked like a grapefruit. Christian folk had died in the rooms! Achi and Siya glittered like sequins and thanked karma for bringing Mrs. Adonis into their lives. They had lived many births together and had just found each other in this birth. Achi and Siya added brilliance and lustre to Mrs. Adonis's story and made the life and death of her relatives, a sequel to their own story. Ammi was silent. In the house, during tea and in the car. I don't know if she liked the house. She didn't say anything. Her lips were sealed as though a bottle of gum had fallen into her mouth. When we returned to aunty Lydia's house Thathi asked her again, 'So my dear what do you think?' She replied somewhat angrily, 'It is a tragedy that Adam's peak is not Vesuvius.' And drove off to an unknown destiny in the blue Hillman, wearing her yellow tinted glasses. I could not make head or tail of her statement.

And I could not ask. My father went in one direction and my mother in the other. They did not talk to each other for the next three days.

Adam's peak was our mountain. Like Everest was India's mountain. Only, it was better. Everest had been conquered by Yeti's, sherpas and Hillaries, but Adam's peak was conquered by Adam, Buddha and St. Thomas. They did not plant a silly flag on our mountain but left something more tangible and valuable. A humongous footprint that resembled the yeti's. The Buddhists said that Buddha's footprint was on Adam's peak, the Christians said it was Saint Thomas's and the Muslims said it was Adam's. There was only one footprint on the peak, so, it was a karmic cosmos, meaning the opposite of chaos, that the Buddhists, Christians and Muslims climbed the peak at different times to worship the same footprint of different persons with the same foot size. All three of them had the same foot size, but who was Vesuvius my mother had spoken of? Was his foot also the same size?

On the fourth day my mother and father spoke to each other again and were more or less coming to an agreement about house number 186 when the first monsoon torrent fell, along with daytime emergency.

It was Hello and good-bye.

They did not see each other for another three months. Minimization had gone wild and created absolute lunacy. The country was ablaze. The red fungus was burning and destroying the monuments of colonialism that had united the independent kingdoms and brought the country into the twentieth century. I do not know if the red fungus wanted to return to the Stone Age, or to the age of the killer ape. But I must say these people looked more like chimpanzees than humans. Facial hair took the place of civilization's clean shaven-ness.

My father, a government servant had orders to return to the monkey civilization and guard his newly built road from the chimpanzee rage. It was a wonderful time for me. Three months of no school. My drawing book started to get some colour. A circular railway track. A female child in a red dress. An English cottage with a red roof next to the railway track. The background was still white and incomplete. Green or grey? The female child in the red dress would have preferred green, it suited the English cottage by the railway track, but I chose grey. Hanuman had once burned this island. The grass had not yet grown.

And it was burning again.

Three months of emergency and curfew. Mrs. Bandaranayake dispatched her forces to eradicate the red fungus. They were succeeding. One after the other the chimpanzees were being captured. The newspapers carried many photographs. Next to the clean-shaven constables, the chimpanzees looked pre-historic creatures in trousers. My grandfather did not like Mrs. Bandaranayake. But, even he would look at the captured chimpanzees in the newspaper and proclaim Mrs. Bandaranayake's greatness. She did not fear karma. She was finally shedding her bondage to the dead SWRD and emerging as her own man.

Emergency prevailed. We were at home. No school, no classes no nothing. Only two hours a day to run to the cooperative store with the ration cards and buy the rationed food for a week. Ammi took care of the rice and dhal. Siya hunted Maldive fish. Achi palled up with the retailers and searched the cooperative stores for fresh coconuts and sugar in the lightest shade of brown. TM Mozart practiced his batting strokes in front of the full-length mirror. Ammi changed the colour of her nails at least three times a day on days that she did not visit the co-op. Nenda and Magi speculated on the Bandaranayake survival strategies and Siya played cards every night with the army who were supposed to be capturing the red fungus that was beginning to infiltrate the city.

My granduncle Hubert was in the army. He was Siya's fourth brother. I don't know if he was a colonel, major, general or whatever, but he must have been quite important for he sat in the back seat of his army vehicle while the other uniformed army people sat in front. He had one car in front of him and another behind him. All army, with awesome guns dangling on their shoulders and elegant uniforms covering their bodies. Granduncle Hubert looked smart in his army uniform. In fact all those people escorting him looked extremely smart in uniform. I liked looking at them. I hoped they succeeded in eradicating the red fungus. They deserved to eradicate the fungus, because they looked better.

Every day, as the sun disappeared into the horizon of aunty Lydia's upstairs window where the sea had once been, three army vehicles drove into her garden. They closed the gates that were always kept open.

Granduncle Hubert entered the house, while the others in uniform hung around in the garden flirting with the female boarders. My granduncle, my grandfather, uncle Lionel's neighbours and two of their neighbours joined them at the dining table and played cards. One and a half bottles of Arrack were usually consumed. Arrack was not in the ration card allowance. But since granduncle Hubert was the only person without a ration card, he had access to things we did not. People without ration cards were better off than people with ration cards.

My mother, who had taken over aunty Lydia's habits of complaint and usually complained about everything, did not complain about the drinking, the card playing or the army officers flirting in the garden. She was in awe of granduncle Hubert's uniform and always tried to distract him from his cards asking irrelevant question about the progress of the red fungus. But it was obvious that the red fungus was not an interesting topic of conversation for him. He preferred to play cards and stroke Karunawathie the servant's leg when she served him ice cubes to cool down his Arrack. Sometimes granduncle Hubert brought me chocolates. I liked emergency, I wished it would last forever.

Before the stroke of midnight, granduncle Hubert and his army left. And we had dinner. Under normal circumstances Achi would have made dinner for the entire army, but our ration card system of emergency did not permit it. It did not matter, I think the army was happier in aunty Lydia's garden than capturing the red fungus. But, there were certain days when Achi made dinner for these smart army people. Those were the days when granduncle Hubert's non-ration card allowance brought us an extra sack of rice and a recently killed wild boar. On those days, more than the usual one and a half bottles of Arrack were consumed. But Arrack was never a problem, for even though granduncle Hubert would sometimes forget the rice and the wild boar, he never forgot the Arrack.

Then granduncle Hubert got transferred. Emergency began to lose its appeal. Siya, again furious at Mrs. Bandaranayake for the endless emergency and the tasteless food one day went to the cooperative store to bribe the retailers into selling him Maldive fish for pol sambol. Maldive fish had the same importance as salt and chilli.

Arrack drinkers especially, needed more Maldive fish than the non-Arrack drinkers. But Maldive fish was not included in our ration card services. It did not fit into Mrs. Bandaranayake's concept of minimization and condensation. Maldive fish came from the Maldives. I think it suffered the same fate as the dates: Port authority fungus due to delayed clearance. Siya was getting impatient. Symptoms of a Maldive fishless diet were evident in Siya's person. He left the house as soon as the emergency ended. He had had enough. Of Mrs. Bandaranayake, of minimization and the lack of Maldive fish.

But he did not return by the time emergency was implemented. We could not search for him because of the curfew. 'Shoot on movement and shoot on sight' was the new law of emergency. Achi got into a frenzy. She tried to talk to the neighbours over the walls, and then she shouted to the other neighbours across the road. No one had seen Siya. And no one had eaten Maldive fish for three months. In fact, most of the neighbours were more curious about knowing the whereabouts of Maldive fish than worrying about the dilemma of my grandfather's absence. She called granduncle Hubert. He came during daylight hours. He told my grandmother, 'not to worry,' and then disappeared. We heard a shot. Ammi climbed the guava tree, but that was like aunty Lydia's window by the sea. Then another shot. Ammi tried to climb the coconut tree since it was higher than the guava tree. She contorted and strained, like trying to release two weeks of constipation, but she could not raise herself on that tree.

Yet another shot. Ammi could not climb any higher. Coconut tree climbing was a profession that required training and special genes. Like Hanuman's. Only daytime's coconut puckers who became night time's toddy tappers were able to climb coconut trees. My mother was neither. More gunshots were heard. Ammi groaned, stuck in her primordial position on that coconut tree. The gunshots increased. Emergency had lost its silence.

Women screamed in anguish. Nenda came outside. She saw Ammi pasted to the coconut tree like a Manuka bug in labour and screamed at her. 'Have you no shame? A grown woman hanging onto that tree like a monkey, did you think you were Hanuman? Come down at once before people start laughing. And pull your dress down; you don't have to give the neighbours a free show! Shamelessness! People are being killed on the streets and the lady of the house has nothing better to do than try to climb coconut trees like a monkey.' My mother came down. She did not like being compared to a monkey.

All the men in the family were gone. My father in the monkey civilization, my grandfather in the Maldive fish queue and my granduncle Hubert in search of my grandfather. Only TM Mozart remained and practiced his batting strokes in front of the mirror during three months of emergency. It was good to have a man in the house.

Achi's heart enlarged further. Ammi stopped painting her nails and chewed them instead. She was still angry about the coconut tree. She preferred to be compared to Sita the princess, not Hanuman the monkey. We received a telegram informing us that my other grandmother had vanished. Women were disappearing too. Were we all about to disappear?

The road
to the Left

Our new address was 186, Cemetery Road, the Socialist Republic of Sri Lanka.

A new house, a new country.

Ceylon was no more.

My father returned with a second hand atlas from the second handbook shop on his way back from emergency. I opened to page 74 where my former country was placed under India... No longer like Hanuman's mango seed but like a giant teardrop.

I knew why she cried. She was dead. Her existence was now limited to second hand bookshops selling second hand atlases printed prior to her re-incarnation in that place where Hanuman had thrown his mango seed into the Indian Ocean. She had not wanted re-incarnation; not Mrs. Bandaranayake's re-incarnation! But here she was. No longer who she had been, the mango, a teardrop; Hanuman dead.

Or captive?

My father stood in our new dining room and asked the whole family to assemble and listen to a speech. The leader of the red fungus chimpanzees had made the speech before he had been locked in jail. 'He has been found guilty,' said my father, 'for conspiring to wage war against the queen. Conspiring to wage war against the queen is punishable under section 114 and 115 of the penal code.'

'But we have no queen,' I corrected him. Personally, I would rather have had a queen than Mrs. Bandaranayake. 'It does not matter, we are still a part of the commonwealth and the queen is the leader of the commonwealth,' he replied. His explanation was meaningless as the red chimpanzee trying to destroy all the blue and green cars for his one red car... 'Listen,' said my father, 'Listen to his defence.' We remained alert. 'One cannot refrain from admiring his eloquence,' continued my father without beginning. 'Can you hurry up please,' urged my mother, 'the curries will burn in their pots.' My father stood with his legs apart and began.

'A representative of one social class is addressing the representatives of another social class. A representative of the exploited and the oppressed proletariat is addressing the representatives of the exploiting and oppressing class. We should not forget that the living reality, which transpires here, is the struggle for the fulfilment and the class interest of the oppressed social class.'

I did not know what my father was trying to say. But I remembered Deepa, the new girl in my class who had come to our school after the chimpanzees had begun to burn the country. They had set fire to her house. Her father had perished trying to save it. Deepa was my age and had lost her father.

'I am a Marxist-Leninist,' continued my father from the piece of paper in his hand, 'I am a modern Bolshevik. I am a proletariat revolutionary. A Marxist Leninist is not a conspirator, he is a Bolshevik. I am a Bolshevik, I am not a terrorist.'

Deepa's little brother had burns all over his body. Every night he cried in pain for the scars contracted and his skin had lost its elasticity. Sometimes he could not raise his head, sometimes not his arms. Deepa's mother would then come into the bedroom and rub oil on the scars and try to ease his pain.

My father continued from the paper. 'As a proletariat revolutionary, I emphatically state that I am committed to the overthrow of the prevailing capitalist system and its replacement by a socialist system.'

Deepa, her mother and her brother had run for miles in their pyjamas and nightdresses, barefoot. Thorns cutting their feet and blisters bursting on their burns until they had reached a neighbour's house.

'The capitalist class is temporarily victorious. I call this a retreat, not a defeat. It is only a phase from which it is possible to recover and to march again to victory. No revolutionary movement has had a non-stop march to victory from start to finish. Forward marches followed by retreat are quite common in a revolutionary movement.'

Deepa had watched her father burn to death. Now she had nothing. She still had thorns in the soles of her feet from fleeing barefoot across the land and not along the roads. The red fungus, singing their revolution, carrying cans of kerosene to augment the fire had occupied the roads.

'I remain an unrepentant Marxist and I am defending here Marxist principles rather than myself. For, as a revolutionary Marxist I have nothing else to defend. See these blossoms strewn on the earth and withered lie, their fragrance shall abide, shall never die. To raise its sweetness high to limits limitless, more buds will bloom and bloom and multiply.' My father ended the paper in a high crescendo and awaited applause.

He admired rhetoric, I think, more than content.

Ammi got up and walked into the kitchen to help Magi with the curries burning in their clay pots. She normally did not do such things, but on that day, she did. Achi followed her. Siya sat where he was and shook his head. Only Nenda dared to retaliate:

'I do not know how you can have the audacity to bring this paper into this house and read it with such pride. I am a simple village woman, I know nothing about this Bolshoi they are talking about in that paper, but I know when a man is a criminal who deserves to be hanged and when a man is a guru who needs to be lauded. That man whose speech you are carrying with such pride should be hung. Or better still he should be burned alive, as he has done to others. He can talk about this Bolshoi you seem to be so impressed with, but I was with Chooti at the Bolshoi ballet in the Bandaranayake Memorial International Conference Hall, and that was a different Bolshoi. That man is a liar who is destroying even the Bolshoi. If Mrs. Bandaranayake cannot lock him up she should get the Russians to kill him for defaming their Bolshoi.' My father tried to interrupt her, 'Nanda, the Bolshevik is different from the Bolshoi…' She did not let him interrupt her, 'Don't waste your time being impressed by nonsense. Burn that paper and see that man for what he is. A criminal. And no amount of beautiful words can obliterate his sins. I hope he goes straight to hell.'

Nenda was right. Nearly all these kerosene-oil carrying chimpanzees were Sinhala Buddhist youth with a free education. Buddhism taught compassion and that one should not kill. I wondered whether free education Buddhism taught something which we did not learn. Poor Deepa, she now got a free education in my private missionary school where the rest of us paid fees. I wonder in what shirt pocket the chimpanzees concealed Buddha's compassion? At least the Christian missionary school gave a Buddhist girl free education when the Buddhist youth robbed her of childhood, her innocence and her father.

My country was no more. In its place a Socialist Republic of Sri Lanka was supposed to be born. Not reborn, just born. Karma had submitted to minimization and left. Mrs. Bandaranayake was the mother. The father, SWRD was dead. We lost our place in the commonwealth. The 'new' Bolshevik proletariat could no longer wage war against the queen. Unless of course, Mrs. Bandaranayake proclaimed herself queen.

Where did I belong? That teardrop under India was once a mango seed. My mango seed. It was my home. A home where mango trees sprouted from mango seeds and gave birth to new mangos. Hanuman's heritage.

The red fungus was now jailed. Their revolution was dead. Mrs. Bandaranayake had won.

The North Koreans who had arrived and opened their embassies amidst Jasmine garlands and Kandyan drummers were asked to leave. Without pomp or pageantry. Mrs. Bandaranayake did not bid them farewell. The Chinese ambassador stood alone at the Bandaranayake International Airport and waved a red silk handkerchief. The leader of the chimpanzees wrote a letter of thanks to the North Koreans, from jail.

The Roman Catholics, the Christians, the Hindus and the Muslims were cross. They were more than cross. They were angry. The Socialist Republic of Sri Lanka, unlike a secular Ceylon, was a Buddhist republic. And a Sinhala republic. Preference had been given to the descendents of Sinhabahu. The son of the lion, who killed his father and married his sister. Patricide and incest! I certainly had no intention of marrying TM Mozart the first. My brother. One did not need free education to know that incest produced handicap, retardation, ignorance and idiocy.

Dagma gave birth to her child. An ugly child. She had the features of Sita and the colour of Kuveni. It should have been the other way around. They called her Kusita. A combination of Kuveni and Sita. The Aryan and the Dravidian.

1

I now lived in house number one hundred and eighty six, Cemetery road, The Socialist Republic of Sri Lanka. The female child in the red dress in my painting now had brown ears. The pink Homerun pas crayon was eliminated in the new socialist republic and a brown crayon entered the box. The railway track without a train anywhere in sight had made a circle and reached the cemetery we had left behind. A karmic circle, there was no train.

Our sojourn by the sea at aunty Lydia's was over. Karma had brought us back. The cemetery was our karma, like the house with a number divisible by two. Despite being on cemetery road, house number 186 was not close to the cemetery. Cemetery road was long, and whereas house number 58 was at the beginning of the road, house number 186 was at its end. Perhaps there had once been a plan to expand the cemetery along the road, but due to minimization and Mrs. Bandaranayake preferring captivity to death, plans for the extension of the cemetery had been halted. The Socialist Republic still had the Buddha's footprint on top of the mountain peak. And Buddha was against the death penalty.

School re-opened. Miss Fatima had emigrated to the east. Miss Lily Marlene to the west. But we had new teachers. New teachers who could not sing like Miss Lily Marlene. Who could not hold a tune. But they sang. We followed them. The song had been redefined in the new Socialist Republic. Words without melody were still a song. A bark instead of a lilt was also a song. A poem would have been a better description, since songs usually had a melody and poems only words. But poems did not fit into the syllabus of minimization, so the new Socialist Republic poem became our song.

On our second day at school we were taken to the new museum that had opened in the new Socialist Republic. Instead of dinosaurs, whales and stuffed birds, this museum had a single exhibit of a blood stained Ariya Sinhala shirt and a blood stained Ariya Sinhala sarong. They had once been crisp white and freshly laundered. Before SWRD had been shot.

The museum too had been re-defined. SWRD's bloodstained clothes entered museum status while Palaeolithic tools and costumes of Kandyan kings lost theirs. I was glad that Mrs. Bandaranayake had opened a museum instead of expanding the cemetery. The museum was not on Cemetery road. It was on the Bandaranayake Memorial International Conference Hall Road.

Minimization had given birth to long names. The Socialist Republic of Sri Lanka, the Bandaranayake Memorial International Conference Hall, the Bandaranayake International Airport. All those people who aided her in making my mango seed into a teardrop got their own road. They usually had long names with initials nearly as long as the alphabet.

My father was back from the monkey civilization. The final phase of construction had been halted. The new Socialist Republic was re-organizing fiscal matters allocated to the construction of roads, and the new ministers of fiscal matters were uncoordinated about the new fiscal policies, and until such time my father had to occupy himself at the head office with utopic projects whose fiscal materializations were pre-destined to enter the bank account of the minister for fiscal matters. My father noticed the deficits. But he could not write them down in the pocket-sized notebook. For, further nationalization of the paper companies had minimized pocket-sized notebooks to extinction. He then resorted to post cards.

Since the mango had become a teardrop, new postage stamps appeared for old postcards. Large colourful SWRDs and Mrs. Bandaranayakes covered these new, colourful stamps. The postage stamps were nearly as large as the postcards. There was very little space to write.

My father was angry. He was pacing. He always paced when angry. He had a pen in one hand and a stack of postcards in the other. He paced. He stopped. He wrote something on a postcard. Then paced again and wrote again. He looked at the Karapincha tree outside the window. Paced again, tripped over the carpet and all the postcards fell on the ground.

The new postage stamps were beautiful. I liked them.

On that day my father dropped his stack of postcards addressed to Mrs. Bandaranayake, Prime Minister, Temple trees, Galle Road,

Colombo, The Socialist Republic of Sri Lanka, I became a stamp collector. I hoped the rest of the world had as beautiful stamps as us. Silently, I helped my father pick up the fallen postcards. They were all addressed to Mrs. Bandaranayake, in the socialistrepublicofsrilanka. One big word. There was no room for spaces.

'Thathi,' I interrupted him meekly. Before commencing I had to ensure whether he was communicative or non-communicative. Communicative meant he would talk, and I usually enjoyed listening to him talk. Uncommunicative meant he would ask me about the progress of my schoolwork and come to the conclusion that I had severe deficits and make me spend the rest of the day answering question papers in mathematics. I did have deficits. Not only in mathematics. But at that age, my existence was a galaxy, and deficits in mathematics were like little stars far away in another galaxy, likely to collide with another star and disappear into yet another galaxy before I even realized it had been a deficient star. But, when one got as old as my father either the galaxy became smaller or the earth larger. I don't know. But my deficits were usually blown proportionately out of place. True, I was not particularly good in mathematics. So what? But since my father's return from the monkey civilization and name change of our mango seed, he was noticing many deficiencies. In the new Sri Lanka and in me.

'Yes Chooti daughter what is it?' He was communicative. I could proceed.

'Thathi what is socialist?'

'Socialist. Socialist… what do you mean socialist?'

'Socialist. Like the Socialist Republic of Sri Lanka.'

'Ah, that socialist.' I did not know there were other socialists.

'Yes, that socialist.'

'Now let me think.' He thought and he thought. The grandfather clock in the dining room struck at least two-quarter hour beats before he replied. 'You said socialist?'

'Yes, socialist.'

'Well it's something like this… there is a thing called capitalist and there is a thing called communist.'

'A thing?'

'Well it is not a thing like a thing you can catch or hold, but more like an idea...'

'An idea?' My ideas varied between a plain red dress and a red dress with yellow flowers for the girl with brown ears standing at the railway track by the English cottage where the train never came in my drawing book.

'Well it is not quite an idea in that sense of the word, how can I put it?' He now stared at the Karapincha tree which stood still. There was no breeze. 'Well the concept of idea is right. Capitalism and communism are ideas. And out of this idea of socialism a philosophy evolved and out of this philosophy a form of government has evolved.'

'A philosophy?' Maybe the idea between the plain red dress and the red dress with yellow flowers would evolve into a sari and become philosophy, which would evolve into a government.

'Like Buddhism. Yes, Buddhism. Now Buddhism is a philosophy.'

'Buddhism is a religion.'

'Well not exactly, Buddhism is more a philosophy than a religion; on the other hand all religions are in actuality philosophies.'

'Okay Thathi,' maybe the yellow flowers on the red dress should have some green leaves.

'Do you understand?'

'Mmm.'

'Now to answer your question. What was it what you wanted to know?'

I had forgotten.

'Chooti, see how bad your concentration is, no wonder you are getting bad marks at school...' I remembered my question.

'I wanted to know the meaning of socialist.'

'Right, that is easy. You know like I said there are two philosophies that are called Communism and Capitalism. Think of it like this: Communism is to the left and Capitalism is to the right. Socialism is something in-between.'

'In-between? Between left and right?'

'Right.'

'That means socialist is in the centre?'

'Not exactly centre, socialism is more to the left of centre than centre.'

'Are there things to the right of centre?'

'I told you they are not things, they are philosophies.'
'I know, like Buddhism.'
'Not exactly like Buddhism, these are philosophies that have been used as a form of government.'
'Is Buddhism not a form of government?'
'Buddhism is a religion.'
'But you said it is a philosophy.'
'It is a philosophy, that is being used as a religion.'
'Thathi, what exactly is a philosophy?'
'It is a way of life.'
'So, socialist is a way of life philosophy to the left of centre?'
'You could put it that way.'
'It is neither to the left, nor to the right. Right?'
'Right.'
'Neither here, nor there?'
My father did not respond. An important thought had entered his mind and he was writing another postcard to Mrs. Bandaranayake.
'Thathi, what is this way of life philosophy, communist and capitalist which is to the left and to the right of the Socialist Republic of Sri Lanka?' My father did not reply. 'Thathi?' I needed to know. Just in case we moved to the left or the right of this 'socialist', I would be able to identify it and rename my new country accordingly. But my father was with his thoughts elsewhere. I repeated my question.
'Oh dear, that is a very complicated question and I don't think you are old enough to understand it. You remind me when you are older.'
'How old?'
'When you understand the meaning of supply and demand.'
I understood supply and demand. After a meal, I would say 'Nenda I would like to eat a chocolate now.' and she would say, 'Chooti the chocolate tin is empty.' The Socialist Republic didn't have any chocolate. That was supply and demand. My demand was not supplied. I understood it, Nenda understood it, and even the servants understood it.
'Thathi I know supply and demand.'
'Well if you know supply and demand I shall write some maths

problems and you can answer it and give it to me before dinnertime.'
That was not supply and demand. I decided to leave my father to his
postcards and retreat. I wrote communism and capitalism under thirty
first December in my diary. I hoped by the end of the year I would be
old enough to understand.

We became a 'neither here nor there' republic. We had neither a
Bolshoi ballet nor a Chinese national circus. We had a few Kandyan
dancers and some Kavadi dancers. When the Bolshoi ballet came,
tickets were sold out. When the Kandyan dancers danced most seats
were empty. I spoke English with my mother; Sinhala with my father.
English with my grandmother; Sinhala with Nenda and the servants.
P language with my friends in school; English with the teachers. Even
the Sinhala teacher spoke in English. We answered our question papers
in Sinhala and received the corrections in English. My father was right.
We were neither here nor there. A philosophy. A religion. An idea.
Perhaps the girl in the red dress should wear a half sari. Ravana's Lanka
had become the British Ceylon. Now Sri Lanka. Had we moved from
the right-side tip of India to the left of centre?

Names changed. Lanka. Ceylon. Sri Lanka. However, the Bank
of Ceylon was still the main bank. Ceylon tea was still the main source
of foreign exchange. Ceylon tyre cooperation still sold tyres for my father's
Hillman. The new Sri Lankan directory listed more telephone numbers
of Ceylon services than Sri Lanka services. My father's definition of
Socialist was right. We were neither here nor there.

The Sinhala newspaper was still called the Lankadeepa. The
island of Lanka. They had remained faithful to king Ravana.

2

House number 186 was large, far larger than house number 58. Everyone had his or her own room. We had a servant area, a boarders area, a dogs area, an office room for my mother, an office room for my father, a newspaper reading room for my grandfather, a radio listening room for Magi and Nenda, a guava tree for me, a room for Lord Buddha, a glass cupboard for the other gods, a shed for a driver, another shed for guest drivers, a family toilet, a guest toilet, a servants' toilet and even a room for the dead. All our beds had their head posts in all directions, except in the room for the dead. In the room for the dead, the bedpost faced west. The dead had to lie with their heads west and the feet east. I was not very happy about the allocation of a dead room, but my opinion was not considered important. When old relatives such as Kandapola siya came to visit, they could die. And if they died there was a dead room to lie.

When Kandapola siya came from Nuwara Eliya, I hung around the Buddha's room and the glass cupboard of gods and prayed that the poor man would die somewhere else but not in my home. He never slept in the visitor's room. He was about a hundred years old and always slept in the dead room. I don't know how he continued to live when people less than hundred were dying. Perhaps that is why he slept in the dead room. Perhaps he thought karma would turn off the switch earlier if he slept with his head towards the west.

Life didn't seem easy for him. He couldn't breathe. He only wheezed. Between every wheeze he coughed and spurted out yellowish-grey phlegm into the bathroom sink which usually got clogged. Then his eyes were so bad that he couldn't read, but he wanted to know the daily news in order to argue with my grandfather about the new republic's political happenings so Achi had to abandon the kitchen and spend time reading the newspapers for him. My poor grandmother entered the line of fire. It was not only Kandapola siya who was nearly blind who listened to the newspaper, but also my grandfather who was not blind. They disagreed with each other about each and every article in the papers. My grandmother was neutral and pragmatic. Between brother and husband she could not choose. And she did not want to choose. Why argue about something one can't change. So, when they got loud, she just went over to the next article.

Every morning I would stick my head through the curtain in Kandapola siya's bedroom to make sure that he wasn't dead. I didn't have to see him, when I heard him wheezing like a dying dinosaur, I would leave the curtain quite relieved. He was not dead! The visitors' toilet was near the dead room and Kandapola siya had a hyper prostate. Or so my mother told me. That was the real reason why he slept in the dead room and not the visitor's room. On the other hand, I wonder why my mother and grandmother did not make the dead room further away from the toilets and the visitors' room closer to the toilets. I had never heard of dead bodies wanting to urinate. In house number 58, I had many encounters with ghosts, but none of them ever wanted to use our toilets.

In our new house the rooms were big and the roof was high. There was no ceiling. Mrs. Adonis's tamarind tree shed its leaves at night and every morning the dainty leaves would make a design upon every available horizontal surface, after making their way between the aged ceylon tiles. Furthermore, every wall in every room had a door. My mother closed off two doors in each room by placing either a cupboard or a chair in front of it. Even then, every room had at least two doors.

Reptiles and rats travelled the ceiling-less tiles, day and night. Rats at night and reptiles during the day. Magi equipped herself with a long pole with a piece of torn rag and each time a reptile travelled above the dining table she dipped the rag in kerosene oil and attacked the reptile. Reptiles don't like the smell of kerosene oil. The rats were worse than the reptiles, but they were clever and stalked the tiles at night, along with the cockroaches.

At night Magi did not use her kerosene oil rag. She said the reptiles caught rats, and therefore supported them at night. At night Ammi filled metal plates with rat nip for the rats and for the mice.

Nenda too contributed by covering all the outlets with a mesh at night. The sink, the toilet, and the drains. That was to prevent cockroach families visiting us when we slept. Occasionally a stench of putrefaction emanated from some corner of the house. We tried to follow our nose. When our noses failed, Podian the driver would come in a bus from Nuwara Eliya and search for the dead animal. He burned the reptiles and buried the mice. For the animals co-existing with us, life was perhaps like Agatha Christie's Mousetrap. Was Ammi, Nenda or Magi the murderer?

House number 186 had a white façade with human face reliefs. I don't know whom they belonged to. They looked like angels. Effeminate and long haired. Like the angels who listened to Lord Buddha when he preached in the Indian forests. Christian angels. 'Mrs. Adonis, what are those faces in front of the house?' I asked as she was discussing Buddhism with my grandfather one Sunday morning.

'What faces?'

'Those faces on the walls.'

'Oh my goodness, I don't know, this house had been built by Tudor's parents before I married him.'

'But didn't you ask whose faces they were?'

'I didn't. To tell you the truth, those faces never interested me. In fact, I hardly noticed them. Let me come with you and see what they look like.' We went outside accompanied by my grandfather and grandmother. Achi did not look at the faces. She plucked limes and Karapincha from the garden.

'Child, I must say I don't know whose faces these are.'

Siya noticed some dog shit and shouted to the servant to come and clear it.

'Are those perhaps faces of the people who died in this house?'

'I don't think so, people don't put dead peoples faces on the walls.'

'Jesus?'

'Jesus doesn't look like that,' said my grandfather who was an authority on Jesus's appearance. Quite rightly; his newspaper reading arm chair in aunty Lydia's house had been directly in front of the picture of a bleeding Jesus on the cross.

'Come to think of it they all have the same face,' Achi had her hands filled with karapincha leaves and limes. She was making a Karapincha sambol for lunch.

'No old girl, the faces are different, here take my glasses and look.' Siya gave Achi his spectacles.

'Aney I don't know, they still look alike to me.'

I was sure that they were the faces of the dead.

Just then Thathi returned after his Sunday morning swim. He smiled cheerfully. My father was a cheerful person when he was not writing post cards to Mrs. Bandaranayake. 'What are you all looking at?'

'We are trying to figure out who's faces are on these walls.'

'Those are not anyone's faces; this was the style of building houses about a hundred years ago. The faces probably resemble the dead parents of the mason who was responsible for building the house. You don't see too many houses like this anymore. But about a hundred years ago most houses looked like this. Unfortunately they have been torn down and more ordinary houses are being built now.'

Not only was I living with Mrs. Adonis's husband's dead relatives, I was also living in a house where the mason's dead parents were fixed on the walls. I didn't think I was going to be very happy in house number 186, for it seemed to have more dead than the Christian section of the Colombo cemetery.

3

I began to explore the surroundings to seek out the living. To the front lived Mrs. Adonis. To the left, Roswitha lived with her daughter. To the right were a black husband, a white wife and two black children. To the back of left was an upstairs house. No one lived there. Like Mrs. Adonis's children, this family had escaped minimization. The house was locked up until minimization ended and the family could return. Mrs. Bandaranayake's minimizations were for house renters, not owners. At the back of house number 186 was the maternity hospital. It had the opposite function of the Colombo cemetery. Or so I thought. To the right of front was a light skinned family consisting of a grandmother, mother, father and two children - a girl and boy. The girl became my friend. Her name was Sharona.

Sharona was also the name of the orange coloured aerated water which most people served when they received visitors. I did not drink aerated water; therefore I had no problems with the name Sharona. I always called her Sharona without mixing it up with Lemonade or Cream soda. But my mother and my brother, who loved sweet aerated waters, had tremendous difficulties remembering her name. TM Mozart usually ended up calling her Portello and my mother varied between Cream soda and Lemonade.

Sharona was nearly my age, and not likely to die. She had a brother who was around TM Mozart's age and was not likely to die either. Her father was older than my father, but he had an extremely loud voice like aunty Seela who had donated gongs to the temple in a previous birth, therefore I did not think he would die for a long time. The mother was as young my mother. She was pretty, my mother was attractive. Fair people were pretty, dark people like my mother were attractive. They were both too young to die. That left the old grandmother. But she lived in the right side of the house while Sharona and her parents lived in the left side. I could not see the right side from the window, so the grandmother whom I had never seen was not a hindrance to my happiness in house number 186.

Sharona visited me daily. We played until shortly before dinnertime. Her brother Asantha visited us during teatime. He was not like TM Mozart. He played neither cricket nor the guitar. He was sociable and played with us. But what he liked the most was chit chatting with Nenda. Asantha never came empty handed. He always had some secretly plucked fruit for Nenda. Sharona came to play daily, but always came empty handed. Nenda didn't like her.

One day, a few weeks after we moved to our new house, Sharona and I were playing 'The Old Curiosity Shop' in the garden. Sharona was the wholesaler, I was the retailer and Asantha was the customer. He had to pay with coins for the goods that we purchased with Karapincha leaves. Ration cards were not a part of our fantasy world. Suddenly, we saw smoke rising behind the back wall. The smoke stank. It stank like the reptiles Kandapola siya's driver burned before burying the ash between the roots of enemy plants. Sharona and I climbed the wall. Asantha stood under the wall and pleaded with us to get down before we were caught climbing walls we were not supposed to climb. We were permitted to climb all walls except the wall between the maternity hospital and our house. They were burning bodies. Of babies who could not enter the statistics of mortality in the Colombo maternity hospital.

'Come down, come down… there Nenda is coming,' Asantha pleaded.

'Murderers, oh Sharona they are murderers!'

'Those are not babies, they are burning something else.'

'What else is there to burn in a maternity home except babies?'

'Snakes.'

'There are no snakes in maternity homes.'

'Maybe some women gave birth to snakes.'

'Women don't give birth to snakes, only snakes give birth to snakes.'

'An elephant entered Mahamaya Devi's stomach,' whispered Asantha, 'now come down; I hear Nenda's voice.'

'That's a dream Aiya,' said Sharona angrily. 'Even though an elephant went into the stomach, Lord Buddha came out of the stomach and it is all unimportant since it was only a dream.' She wished for a brother like TM Mozart. I wished for a brother like Asantha.

'Yes, but Lord Buddha was born from the elephant,' I said defending Asantha even though the burning babies in the maternity hospital and Mahamaya's dream had nothing in common.

'I am glad that I don't live in your house.'

'Why is that?'

'Get down soon.'

'All those dead babies become ghosts and jump over the wall into your garden.'

'Babies don't become ghosts.'

'Of course they do. Everything that is killed before its time to die becomes a ghost.'

'Who told you that nonsense?'

'Aney get down, what do you see?'

'I know, the babies are not killed, they die on their own.'

'They are killed.'

'WHAT ARE THE TWO OF YOU DOING ON THE WALL? COME DOWN AT ONCE!' Ammi.

Sharona was sent home and asked not to come and play for two weeks. She whispered to me about ghosts climbing the walls and left grinning. Asantha left crying. I was punished. I got bread and Mukunuwenna mallung for dinner while the rest of the family ate hoppers.

The next night Podian arrived without Kandapola siya, in the Morris Minor, with two sacks of empty bottles. Magi, Nenda and Karunawathie broke the bottles, while Podian mixed the cement. The next day the wall between our house and the maternity hospital had jagged glass pieces on it.

Like Sharona had predicted, the dead babies became ghosts at night. They climbed over the jagged edges of the wall. They entered the back garden of our house and knocked on the back door when I was just beginning to fall asleep. The back door was next to the toilet. I did not use the toilet at night. I held my bladder instead.

4

The monsoons had delayed. There was a deficit of water. Due to the lack of water there was a deficit of hydro-electricity. The water tanks were depleting and the nights were saturated with darkness like a leaking oil container stranded at the Colombo harbour due to port authority nationalization problems.

It was Mrs. Bandaranayake's fault. Her karma was bad. Her planets and the new Socialist Republic of Sri Lanka's planets were not compatible. The fields were drying, hydro-electricity dwindling, hygiene deteriorating. Buddhist priests filled up in buses and travelled the areas of the hydro-electricity tanks built by the ancient royal relatives of King Parakramabahu the sixth and chanted Buddhist hymns to entice the rains.

I had to write an essay for school. I hated writing essays. My essays were always bad. I never got more than fifty out of hundred for them. I usually changed the fifty into eighty before I showed it to Thathi who still complained that I could easily get a ninety if I tried harder. Ammi said a ninety was not good enough. I should strive to get a hundred. A hundred out of hundred. I wonder what they would have said if they realized that my eighty was not more than a fifty.

The title of the essay was 'The Socialist Republic of Sri Lanka'. How could I write an essay about a country, which was once to the right of centre, now presumed to be left of centre, but in actuality, whose precise location was unclear since the nationalization of the paper industries? I was compelled to write the essay. Excuses were not for students. Excuses were only for ruling bodies. Fault always lay in others. Dudley was at fault. If it wasn't Dudley, it was D.S. If it wasn't D.S. it was the English. If it wasn't the English it was Parakramabahu the sixth. Two thousand five hundred years of Buddhist civilization history had many chapters with many characters who could be blamed for today's uncertainties about left of centre or right of centre. Those ruling bodies that blamed the others were always right themselves. Perhaps in two thousand five hundred years someone like Mrs. Bandaranayake would be re-born to the left of centre who would blame the left of centre of today. But, at this present point of history, the present left of centre was

always right. In fact, they were infallible. Something like the fifty out of
hundred in my essays. In their case they did not change the fifty into an
eighty. They made it directly into a hundred and twenty. I must admit
a hundred and twenty out of hundred was far better that eighty out of
hundred. Perhaps I too should become a socialist? But first, I had to
study two thousand five hundred years of Buddhist civilization and find
someone to blame. That was a lot of reading. And I had not even
finished the minimized David Copperfield, without Uriah Heep, not
to mention the full length David Copperfield my father had brought
from the second hand bookshop. 'Chooti have you finished writing
your essay?' asked Ammi. The new teacher had sneaked my deficits to
Ammi. 'I was just thinking about it.'

'Don't think, WRITE.' Two thousand five hundred years of
Buddhist civilization's historical characters I could have blamed for my
non-fulfilled socialism would have to wait. I had to first write my essay,
without thinking.

It began like this. I was born in Sri Lanka. When I was born, it
was not Sri Lanka it was Ceylon. It was then to the right of centre below
the triangular tip of India. Now it is left of centre and is no longer called
Ceylon, but Sri Lanka. I am not hundred and twenty out of hundred
percent sure if it is now to the left of centre, but I have been told it is
now to the left of centre. The old world map has been removed from
the classroom walls and the new map has not been put in its place. The
classroom wall is now bare. It has not even been whitewashed. There is
a square mark on the wall, which shows that a world map once hung
there. That square is grey and not white like the rest of the wall. There
are four holes on the grey square on the wall. Those four holes were
made by the drawing pins that kept the world map on the wall. The
drawing pins are now rusted. But they are still in my teacher's drawer
and I think they will be reused when we receive a new world map. I am
sure that in the meantime the drawing pins also have been nationalized.
I don't think my new teacher will stand in a queue at the cooperative
store to buy new drawing pins. I don't think she even stands in the dhal
and rice queue, for marshmallow brings her so many pastries every day
that I don't think she will be hungry for anything else thereafter. What
she does not eat, my teacher takes home. (*time for a new paragraph*).

There is a map in our Sinhala textbook. It is neither to the left of centre nor the right of centre. It is a black and white map in the middle of the page and India is not on the map. Therefore, it is impossible to say if the Socialist Republic of Sri Lanka is to the left of centre, or right of centre. It is possible that India has moved and not the Socialist Republic of Sri Lanka, since India is not on the page and Sri Lanka is.

The Socialist Republic no longer looks like a mango seed. It now looks like a teardrop. It is in black and white. The teardrop is white. The mango seed was brown. The colours that were once on the world map on the wall are black and white in my textbook. Straight lines, broken lines and dots indicate mountains and rivers. They are all black and white. The old world map had green fields, brown mountains and blue rivers. Being black and white it is now difficult to differentiate between mountains and rivers.

The Socialist Republic of Sri Lanka was once in the middle of the Indian Ocean. It is an island, surrounded by water. All islands are surrounded by water even in drought. The Buddhist priests chanting hymns trying to entice rains are not only chanting in order to secure hydro-electricity, but also that we will always remain an island. We have always been a self-sufficient island, especially in the times of King Parakramabahu the sixth. If we cease to be an island we will lose our self-sufficiency and become as poor as India.

The Socialist Republic of Sri Lanka has been blessed. With the giant footprints of Lord Shiva, Adam, Lord Buddha, and St. Thomas. Their footprint is on top of the mountain called Adam's peak. This mountain is called Adam's peak for the first man Adam lived on this mountain before the others trod on it. I think it was before Eve came to live with him on the mountain. The Buddha and St. Thomas did not like women, they liked only men. If they had known that a woman lived on the mountain they would not have trod on Adam's peak: perhaps Mount Everest instead. The only person who liked women was Shiva. Of course I am not a hundred percent sure if he liked women, but I know that he has a wife. On the other hand since Lord Shiva is a Hindu god from India, it is possible that he does not like women and married his wife because he could not object to the arranged marriage. Now India is jealous of my country because all these people have trod on our Adam's peak and not on their Mount Everest. They only had a yeti on their mountain. And after the yeti I think the British flag.

Long time ago, the Socialist Republic of Sri Lanka was the kingdom of King Ravana. It was then called Lanka. Ravana turned himself into a deer and stole the Princess Sita from India. Sita's husband Rama sent the monkey Hanuman to Lanka to rescue Sita. Hanuman burned Lanka to ashes and took Sita back to Rama. I think it was very wicked of Hanuman to burn the whole country just to rescue one woman. I think this Prince Rama was very wicked too. He should have either looked after his wife better, taken another queen or remained a bachelor. Everyone in India had more than one wife those days. Even Rama's own father had four. It is not difficult to notice that Hanuman and Rama were not Buddhist people. Buddhist people do not burn other people's property.

Then the Portuguese came and went. They left pol sambol and the Baila dance behind. Then the Dutch came and went. They left mosquito-infested canals behind. Then the English came and planted tea on the earth that Hanuman had burned to cinder. They brought tons of Indian Tamils to work on the tea plantations because the Kandyans who lived in the tea areas were too lazy to work. They called my country Ceylon because people bought tea when it was sold as Ceylon tea. Then The English went and we got independence.

Now we did not have a king or a queen, we had a prime minister. The first prime minister fell off a horse and died. Since then we have no horses. Then lots of things happened which is too long for this essay. Somewhere in-between these lots of things, SWRD was killed by the Buddhist priest. Buddhist priests are supposed to be vegetarian and not kill, but this one killed. Then Mrs. Bandaranayake came and changed our name to Sri Lanka.

She took the 'Sri' from the number plates of the cars and put it in front of Lanka. I don't know why. Perhaps she mistook it for a vehicle. Now, like Sri Jawaharlal Nehru, Dr. Sri Dharan, the priest Sri Sumanathissa and Lord Buddha's Bo tree Sri Mahabodhi, Ravana's Lanka became Sri Lanka. After that, Mrs. Bandaranayake chased the governor general to his Rambutan estate and lived happily ever after. THE END.

I submitted the essay. One week later when the other children received their essays after correction I did not receive mine. My mother had received my essay instead. She did not show me the essay, but just fluttered it about in a crescendo. That very same day I lost my freedom.

Maths tuition was on Mondays, Sinhala tuition on Tuesdays, English on Wednesdays, General science on Thursdays, Buddhism on Fridays and Social studies on Saturdays. On the first day, all the tuition teachers got a copy of my essay. I don't know why? In maths and General Science I did not have to write essays about the Socialist Republic of Sri Lanka. Perhaps Mrs. Bandaranayake had further plans to minimize the syllabus so that new maths and General Science too would be minimized to one essay.

I saw my essay. There was a hundred with a line above it, and on top of the line there was a giant question mark. Was the new socialist note minimized into a question mark? My Sinhala and English tuition teachers who came on Tuesdays and Wednesdays made me re-write my essay. The Sinhala teacher made me write about the nationalities, the three legged lion flag, Buddhism and the water tanks. The English tuition teacher made me write about the landscape, imports, exports, the English tea plantations and English law. A whole paragraph was devoted to Nuwara Eliya and the golf course. The New Maths teacher did not make me write an essay. He only told me what I should have included in my essay. GDP's, UNP's, CTB's, CP's, MP's, JVP's and other percentages. The General Science teacher mentioned something about flora and fauna, the Buddhism teacher wanted more about the Buddha's foot print, the Buddha's tooth relic, the Buddha's Bo-tree and the Buddha's three aerial visits. The Social science teacher could not be bothered. She was more interested in Achi's milk toffee and the milk tea with King Parakramabahu the sixth's condensed milk. My tuition teachers said that they would come back the next week and re-correct my essay.

The monsoons came instead.

5

The chanting of the Buddhists priests had worked. The rains came from all sides, and met. At night, while we all slept Ammi heard dripping. Not outside her bedroom, but inside the house. She assumed it was Kandapola siya's hyper prostate that had missed the toilet. She tried to sleep, but the prostate did not cease to drip. She woke up.

Sitting up in bed, wrapped in the sari of darkness, she contemplated the dilemma of Kandapola siya's hyper prostate. The dripping continued. She jumped out of bed when she finally realized that Kandapola siya was a frail old man whose hyper prostate could not drip so long. Perhaps it was another prostate. Thathi snored next to her in bed. His prostate was dry. Siya's prostate had once been hyper, but now it was gone. TM Mozart did not have a prostate at his age... and the rest of us? No one spoke about our prostates. I don't even know if we had one.

We had a segment called health science in our school syllabus, squashed between pre-vocational one and pre-vocational two. This health science did not mention prostates. Rather, it dwelled on digestive systems, respiratory systems and cardio-vascular systems. The Socialist Republic had created an egalitarian society. Men and women were alike. In Chou En Lai's China they were alike as well. Therefore, the prostate had been eliminated from the health science syllabus. Either, men and women had the same organ, or they had no organ. Minimization was the equal distribution of everything. Even organs. Prostates for all, or prostates for none!

The dripping continued. Ammi wrapped the white bed sheet around her to break the monotony of night, crept out of the mosquito net around her bed and tried to follow her ears towards the drip. She was hardly out of the mosquito net when little waterfalls fell on her head. She looked up into the darkness. The waterfall fell into her eyes. The monsoons had come.

The one moment of elation became the next moment's panic. The rain was supposed to limit itself to the outside, but the Buddhist priest enticed monsoons had invaded our house. She turned on the light switch. Little rivulets of water, streams, waterfalls, springs were making their way thorough the Sinhala tile roof. The Divan, the fan, the laminated photographs of handshakes that decorated the walls were all wet. Ammi rubbed the rainwater deep into her eyes, removed drowsiness and reacted. Hopping between the puddles, she first brought out the backside washing bowls from the toilets, then she brought out the old bathtubs we had used as babies, then she threw out the plastic flowers and used the vases, but the rain continued and the waterfalls increased. Then, as she was about to make it to the kitchen to bring out the pots and pans the monsoons hit the trip switch and hydro-electricity underwent a power cut. My mother, suddenly blinded, slipped on the next puddle and broke her leg.

Thathi stopped snoring and woke up to the noise. He felt for Ammi on the bed. She was gone. Had Ravana sprung though the window and captured her? One Ravana was dead, but many lived. A nation's people who were historically stigmatised as robbers of other's wives would never cease to rob another's wife! That was beyond karma, it was genetics. That slithering de-oxy ribo-nucleic acid chain that had briefly popped up between the digestive tract and the cardio vascular system for health science.

Though we had tried to emulate Vijaya's royalty, we could not avoid Ravana's greed. Genetics continued where mythology stopped. Thathi was no Rama. He had neither a Lakshman, nor a Hanuman. But he had once owned a hunting rifle, which, if he could recollect correctly had been placed behind the Almirah when he returned to Colombo from the monkey civilization. He felt for the torch on his bedside table. It was not there. Without the torch he could not see the rifle. He walked out of the room, with neither a rifle nor a torch. Perhaps he could achieve victory with logic.

Ravana had made one mistake, only one. He had robbed another's wife. Apart from that one mistake Ravana was an honourable man. He had been a great king. He ruled Lanka with pride and glory that hardly a king in India could match. He knew Dharma, he knew karma. The ravishing of Sita was a mistake made by a foolish man. Ravana though a great king, acted like a foolish man.

Thinking out his verbal strategy Thathi left the bedroom and walked though the curtain and into the backside washing toilet bowl.

One foot got stuck inside and the other slipped on the wetness surrounding the bowl. He knocked his head on the piano and forgot Ravana, his missing wife and the stupidity of man.

Siya woke up, turned on the trip switch, found my father muttering about a bandit called Ravana and a gun behind the Almirah, took the gun and went in search of the bandit. He screamed and shouted 'Ado I will catch you, you bugger…you step into this house I will make Maldive fish sambol out of your bones…' Achi woke up to Siya's cacophony. A woman of great wisdom, Achi used her diagnostic logic in detecting infected appendices and tried to persuade Siya to come indoors. 'Henry,' she persuaded 'there is no thief. Thieves are not foolish people. In order to be a thief one needs great dexterity and finesse. Thieves will never rob during monsoons. The rains make even the thief wet and even a thief can catch a cold, and one sneeze, only one sneeze and he is caught. Come inside Henry, there is no thief, you will only catch your death of cold…'

'Ado you bandit bugger… I will catch you. And if I don't catch you, our ferocious Alsatian will catch you and make mince meat out of your intestines.'

Mrs. Adonis had an Alsatian, we had a Valsatian (a Pariah). Valsatians were pedigree-less dogs found by the roadside. They could not catch thieves. In fact they could not even catch the fleas on their own body. Valsatians only hung around by the side of the road in the proximity of cooperative stores and waited for minimization to end. They were even too lazy to scavenge the garbage bins. We did not have one valsatian but three. One had three legs like the Sinhala lion on the Ceylon flag, the other was blind and the third was accidentally born as a dog. It should have been born as a soft toy.

'Now come inside, I can hear you sneeze already.'

'That wasn't me, that was the thief.'

'That was not the thief, that was the dog.'

'It didn't come from the kennel.'

'The dog isn't in the kennel, Magi tied him outside last night because it had vomited.' Siya finally came in when his bronchitis started.

The monsoons were a bad omen. Ammi twisted her ankle, Thathi dented his head, Siya got bronchitis and Nenda became temporarily bed-ridden. The dampness, which had accompanied the monsoons, penetrated the ground, penetrated the space between the ground and the bed and entered Nenda's bones. Her left knee became hydro-electric. Doctors called it rheumatic arthritis.

Kandapola siya's driver Podian who had been sleeping in the shed when the monsoons had started, searched for holes in the roof the next morning. He could not climb the roof since the tiles were still wet. Magi removed the kerosene oil rag from the stick used to scare reptiles and gave it to Podian to move the tiles in order to cover the holes. Podian was a versatile man. But he was short. He jumped up and down and moved the stick in space, but failed to move a single tile. Even Magi who was short, was taller than Podian. But Magi was a woman, and had bad eyes. However, she liked Podian, so she grabbed the pole from him and was about to try:

'Ennappa, no Akkaa!, Aiyo you woman not to repair roof. Only man job,' and he took the pole back and jumped up and down with the pole in space.

'Give that thing here without being an idiot. We are village women; we know how to make roofs.'

'Aiyo, enappa, bad man this Sinhala mans, always letting women do work. Look at Madam Bandaranayake! Workings very hard like man, but aiyo! Look what mess country is in? All this time drought. Now rains! But how! All the monsoons in the world have come here to this country.'

'Give me that pole, I have woven coconut leaves and made roofs that have kept our heads dry, I can manage to get this roof covered too,' said Magi.

'Aiyo no Magi Akka, don't tire yourself. All bad this Sinhala culture. In our estates we men make roofs. So women have dry head.'

'That is why your women pluck tea until they are as black as cinder,' replied Magi.

'That is but alright no Magi Akka. When tourist come and make photographs of tea estates they not want to see black Yindian Tamil man in dirty white vetti plucking tea, they wanting to see nice colourful lady in colourful sari with gold nose ring plucking tea.'

'So that is why your women pluck tea and work like dogs, while your men smoke *suruttu* and waste away the time?'

'Of course, Magi Akka. What else? Tourist industry bringing lot of money to this country. Without tourist with nice camera taking colourful pictures of Tamil woman in coloured sari plucking tea, who he show to other friends in foreign country who say, 'Enappa my friend, so many coloured women in Siri Lanka plucking tea, I go too with my camera to Siri Lanka to make beautiful picture of colourful tea-plucker woman in nice gold nose ring.' If they not come… Enappa Magi Akka! Now problems only becoming bigger! Now with Madam Banaranaike we get only rice and dhal, when foreign tourist not comes, we have nothing. Only *hulang!*'

'Foreigner or no foreigner I don't know how people think that such black women, burned by the sun, like the colour of the black crow are so beautiful.'

'Enappa Magi Akka, you not underistand. Foreigner white, tea-plucking woman black. Different. Foreigner like that what is different. You put white skinned Kandyan hamines to pluck tea in plantation, foreigner not take photos. Same colour not interesting. Foreign people very clever people. They like different things. We here only like same thing. Stupid people we are! Foreigner not like us. He think and think till his head find something different. So foreigner have big nice cars, they have television, they go to the moon… we here stupid people! My people in the tea plantation even more stupid people. Only know what tea estate look like. Not even bothering to come to Colombo to see the sea. I tell them, 'Come with Podian in master's Morris Minor, Master not minding.' They tell, 'Enappa Podian Anna, you mad! That car will fall down mountain in Kadugannawa pass, better you use bull, he know how to cross Kadugannawa pass with Bullock cart without falling down mountain.' See Magi Akka, stupid people! When I come back alive and very happy after eating nice hot chilli food you make, I tell my people 'See, Podian back without falling down the Kadugannawa Mountain.' They tell, 'You lucky man Podian, the Devas been following you all the way to Colombo, you now go to Kovil and thank Devas for not making you fall down Kadugannawa mountain in your car. But next time use bullock cart. Must not tax the Devas too much. Kadugannawa pass is difficult pass, even for the Devas.'

So that was settled. The Ceylon tile roof was too high for Kandapola siya's driver. It was not too high for Magi but if Magi tried to repair the roof, it would end up like Mrs. Bandaranayake's Socialist Republic. More holes than less. Until the monsoons ceased and a suitable man was found for the job either we did not have backside-washing bowls in the toilet or Achi would have had to buy new ones. Ammi and Thathi were disabled. But my grandmother was a thrifty woman. She did not believe in wasting money for new backside washing bowls and insisted that Podian repair the roof from the ground.

'Aiyo madame!' Podian lamented, 'Enappa, how to repair roof from the ground even with ladder? Roof must be repaired from roof. So when water stop falling from sky we repair roof. That way you not offending gods. You only send one post card and Podian come 'pata, pata' by express bus. When that too slow I will come in night train. When master not give money, I come with my own money.'

Podian returned to Nuwara Eliya with Kandapols siya and the Morris Minor. 'I will come with big tall men from estate to repair roof when the raining stops,' he promised, sticking his head out of the window as they drove down the lane. 'Don't forget to come,' Magi shouted behind him. 'You are the only person who knows where the holes are.'

The monsoons wreaked havoc. Thathi got better and returned to the monkey civilization to see his road disappear. It had been a good road, but even a good road could not bear the weight of two monsoons. The road fell down the mountain and buried alive the people who lived under the mountain. Once upon a time there had been no people under the mountain, only monkeys and trees. Then the trees were cut and the road had been built. My father's road. Then the people had begun to come. The few trees that had not been chopped to make the road were now chopped by the people under the mountain. The monkeys left the mountain to the humans. The humans who had taken over from the monkeys now had a road, a mountain, but no trees. Then the two monsoons met on the mountain. Now the road was gone, the mountain was shorter, and the people dead.

The rains did not cease; they filled the streams. The streams became rivers and the rivers became giant pythons and crocodiles, where ferocious river gods hid and swallowed everything that passed. People, animals, trees, houses, children. One gulp. Gone. The python bloated and the riverbed widened. Not just houses, entire villages got sucked into the current. But the rains didn't cease. Minimization had reached a zenith. Those to the left of the left of centre of Mrs. Bandaranayake's policies of minimization gained strength. They forbade the hiring of double decker buses for Buddhist priests. For any purpose. Rather than attempting to minimize chaos created by the monsoons, they minimized the remnants of the cosmos.

Like they had come, they went. While we slept. The south-western monsoon to a terrain in the Indian Ocean and the north-western monsoon back to the Himalyas. The survivors under the mountain chose another mountain and cut the trees and waited for my father to come and build them a road. Ammi's leg got better. She was able to hop around with a walking stick and a piece of chalk and mark with crosses the places where rainwater fell. This was unnecessary as fungus covered the spot, but my mother persevered. She didn't need a reason. Three months of rain had created fungus in our brains. The rice had fungus, the dhal had fungus and the coconuts had fungus. We ate fungus. Food was not a priority, the roof was. Podian the driver was needed.

Ammi made a trunk call to Nuwara Eliya. The lines were out of order. The monsoons had wreaked havoc with the telecommunication system. Minimization delayed repair. Then Ammi dictated a postcard in Sinhala, which Nenda wrote. 'Podian, please come immediately. Monsoon in Colombo is over, roof needs immediate repair.' Nenda had just got out of bed after three months of hydro-electric rheumatic arthritis of her left knee. She knew how to write postcards in Sinhala. My mother who went to missionary school could not. She could only write in English. Podian could read neither Sinhala nor English, but the new postmaster general of the Nuwara Eliya post office could read Sinhala, English and Tamil. He had finished his studies before the advent of minimization. Nenda's knee was no longer swollen, but she now had a trigger finger. During the calamity of the two monsoons the planets had changed. Saturn had entered Nenda's house of health.

Podian did not respond to the postcard. Ammi then sent a telegram. 'Podian come. Urgent.' Nenda and Ammi discussed whether they should use the word immediately between Podian and come. Nenda said use it, Ammi said it was too expensive. But Podian still did not

come. Nenda scolded Ammi for not having used immediately, and
Ammi said it had nothing to do with immediately, and that something
else was wrong. They argued while the fungus on the ground slowly
disappeared.

The sun was beginning to shine through the holes in the roof.
The trauma of the monsoon was becoming a memory. Podian was
desperately needed in case another monsoon came. No one but Podian
knew the exact location of the holes in the roof. But Podian did not
come. Not even after the second telegram.

Ammi then got her Muslim jeweller Niser to send Podian a
telegram, this time in Tamil. Niser the jeweller spoke Tamil fluently. He
was a good businessman. He understood that if he spoke all three
languages, not only the majority Sinhala ladies, but also the minority
Tamil ladies and the minority burgher ladies would buy his gold chains.
Muslim ladies were not a problem. Muslim ladies always bought gold
chains from Muslim jewellers. Muslim ladies understood brotherhood.
Burgher and Tamil ladies, a little brotherhood. Sinhala ladies, no
brotherhood. They were the descendents of Vijaya and Kuveni. Kuveni
betrayed her people and Vijaya betrayed Kuveni. The Sinhala ladies had
double genetic betrayal in their dioxyribonucleicacid chains of re-birth
and karma.

Podian did not come after the Tamil telegram either. My mother
had now realized it was futile to send another telegram in English or in
Tamil. Podian would never come. He never came. None of the Podians
from Nuwara Eliya came. Ever again. Kandapola siya had to find a new
driver. A sinhala driver.

It was called repatriation.

Mrs. Bandaranayake and her left to the left of centre comrades
had continued minimization despite the monsoons. The two monsoons
on top of the mountain were a façade for the further minimization of
minimization. Podian was right. Women did not have the wisdom to
repair roofs or rule countries. Podian was an Indian Tamil. He was born
here, had lived here and was planning to die here. Not yet. One day
after he had seen the river Ganges and the beautiful white Taj Mahal
looking like a white skinned Kandyan hamine. Perhaps he would now
see the river Ganges and the white Taj Mahal, but he could not come

back here, to us, to die. Even if he did not want to die, he could not come back to live. His country had been my country. But now Mrs Bandaranayake was saying that his country was not my country and his country was another country. Podian's mother, his grandmother and her grandmother had plucked the tea that was captured in the picture postcards of Ceylon and the new Socialist Republic. Now suddenly, Podian was told to become a citizen of another country.

Mrs. Bandaranayake and her three children were light skinned Sinhala people. I was one of the dark skinned Sinhala types. I had a Veddha name, they probably had Aryan names. The Aryans were also from India. Like Vijaya, like Rama, like Sita. Perhaps it would be possible to re-patriate them and bring our Podian back? I needed to talk to my father, but like Atlas the giant, he was still holding segments of the road that had not fallen down the mountain.

School recommenced. Most teachers had travelling difficulties since most roads had dissolved. The few teachers who were there distributed essay topics in order to pass the time until the roads were repaired and the other teachers returned to continue normal lessons. We were given a choice of essays. The choice of essay was, 'If I was a boat,' or 'If I was a drop of rain in the Indian ocean'. I chose the third option, 'If I was a prime minister'.

I could not say good-bye to Podian. I wrote the essay, tore the paper out of the book, made a paper boat and kept it in the drain and prayed for another monsoon. Then I re-wrote the essay on another page. I tore it out again. And again. Another paper, another boat. A small flotilla in my drain. I became a good prime minister. Perhaps Mrs. Bandaranayake should make paper boats and keep them in dry drains and await the next monsoon. Perhaps then, she would finally learn to be a prime minister. Not just any prime minister, but a good prime minister.

We were all sad. Magi was the saddest. 'You know baby,' she told me between large teardrops. 'That Podian was a clever man. He told me just before he left; women should do what they are born to do and not rule countries. He was right.' I completed my essay. I did not think Mrs. Bandaranayake could make paper boats... what on earth could she do?

Poor Podian, there was no escaping his karma. He was evicted from a country with one female ruler and was sent to a country with another female ruler. Repatriation or no repatriation, there was no escaping karma.

That night, and many nights after, I dreamt the same dream. Thathi's road had collapsed with the mountain. There was no more road and no more mountain. The mountain looked like a paddy field. Flat. The monkeys in the jungles came out at night and carried the broken mountain to the Indian Ocean and covered the seabed with rubble. They built a road to India. The humans under the mountain were dead. All dead.

Magi, in her anguish became a misogynist.

6

Since she couldn't reach Mrs. Bandaranayake, she blamed Nenda for Podian's repatriation. Magi could have blamed Achi, or Ammi, but she chose Nenda instead. So the battle began again.

When two women fight, the battle between ten headed Ravana and one headed Rama is nothing. When two women become four women, it is like the mighty Shiva getting out of his Nataraja position and bringing his gigantic leg down to destroy the world. Not just the world we live in, but the three worlds of heaven, earth and hell.

Podian's departure was like the abduction of Sita. Both Nenda and Magi loved Podian. But their individual methods of overcoming grief were different. Magi hung on every word Podian had uttered and carried his memory in every molecule of her soul. Nenda on the other hand refused to acknowledge anyone by the name of Podian.

When two people have travelled many karmic rebirths together, consumed by hate, karma, the curious creature doesn't alleviate their suffering by separating them, she just keeps bringing them together to hate and to reconcile and to hate again. Perhaps Nirvana is 'house full' and karma keeps prolonging rebirth as a result.

While Magi was searching for stones in the rice, she found one the size of the Pink Panther.

'Enappa,' she said 'this is but a very big stone.'

Nenda was counting the bed sheets the dhobi had returned after washing.

'Enappa, enappa... what is that you are talking? Have you given up your historically superior language and now become a Tamil?'

'Aney hamu, that Podian always used the word Enappa and always said Enappa Magi Akka. It was like a song when he spoke it.'

'He was a foolish man, only foolish men say Enappa. If he was an intelligent man he would have learned to speak proper Sinhala like we do.'

'His Sinhala was good enough. I understood him.'

'As if you know to speak proper Sinhala, you haven't even been to school in your life!'

'I may have not gone to school, but I am not doing much worse than you, who apparently have gone to school.'

'You think standing in front of an open fire and cooking for the masters while burning your lungs morning, noon and night is a great achievement?'

'And you think washing the babies backsides (meaning TM Mozart and myself) is a much greater achievement?'

'You think taking the dogs to shit down the road and carrying their shit into the dustbins is a greater achievement?'

'I have the spade for the dog shit, you have only hands for the human shit.'

'Humans belong to a higher species with or without a spade.'

Such was our household following Podian's departure. Tragedy and trauma lurked in every corner. If it was not about dogs and humans, they quarrelled about cats and sparrows. If it was not cats and sparrows, it was about Rama and Sita.

Magi nostalgically searched for stones in rice that had recently been imported from India. Maybe there would be a message from Podian in the rice? Maybe he was now working in a rice field? 'I wonder how Podian's life is in India?'

'India, India. Such a dirty fellow that Rama of India was. After destroy-ing our whole country to get his Sita back he didn't even take her back as his bride. If he wasn't planning on taking her back I don't know why he sent that long tailed monkey Hanuman to burn our country. Not an ounce of compassion, that chap! Destroyed us all, because of a woman.'

'How can a man take back a woman who has lived with another man?'

'She didn't live with him, she was captured by him.'

'Yes, but she was with him. And that is that. If I was living with a man and that man, was even accidentally captured by another woman I would never ever take him back. I don't want another woman's used garbage. No I wouldn't take him back even if he prostrated himself on the ground and kissed my feet.'

'No wonder you are without a man.'

'You think you are much better? I at least have a son.'

'And your son's father is the black phantom prince I suppose?'

'My son's father was not a phantom, he was a man.'

'Ravished and left like a servant cleaning dog shit in someone's household!'

...And so their battle continued. When they didn't fight about Rama and Sita, they fought about Vijaya and Kuveni:

'I am sure Podian is from Prince Vijaya's family.'

'That black man is not from a prince. He is as black as a Raksha. He is surely from Kuveni's demonic stock.'

'Apo no Hamu, our Podian was not from that vulgar stock. That Kuveni betrayed her entire family and gave Vijaya their kingdom. Our Podian was not like that; he was the most faithful person I have ever met in my life.'

'Then why did that black man go?'

'He didn't go he was sent. Forced to go.'

'That's because he is a fool. Like Kuveni. Only a foolish person would betray her own family and assist a stranger to rob her father's kingdom.'

'Apo, Podian wasn't like that.'

'Of course he was, that is why he ate and slept here and left without saying a word.'

'He was sent by force. He didn't go on his own.'

'Good thing that Kuveni was killed by her own people. If I had been living in those days I would have killed her with my bare hands.'

Ammi and Achi were irritated by the squabbles but they couldn't find a solution. For Ammi, Nenda was always right. For Achi, Magi was always right. The battle between two women became the battle between four women. Nenda told Achi that the dhobi had not returned her bed sheets and Achi had to sleep on dirty linen. Magi served more stones than dhal during mealtimes. During mealtimes Achi usually bathed, or fertilized the Karapincha tree. When she ate, after we had finished, there were no more stones in the dhal. We had eaten all the stones.

When they didn't fight about Rama and Sita they fought about Sinhabahu and the lion. Sinhabahu and the lion was as important a fighting matter as Rama and Sita or Vijaya and Kuveni. It was another mythological excerpt on Sinhala evolution.

Sinha the lion was a ferocious creature, the unconquered victor of the southern forest who had captured and ravished an Indian Princess - Suppadevi. He loved her and protected her in his cave.

She learned to love her captor and bore him two children. Sinhabahu and Sinhaseevali. The ferocious lion was a wonderful father. He loved his wife and his two children. When he left his cave every morning in search of food, he covered the entrance to the cave with a boulder so that his beloved family would not fall prey to wild beasts.

The children grew up and the roots of suspicion entered the mind of the lion-son Sinhabahu. He exploited his mother's love and forced her to relate to him the tale of the Indian princess captured by the ferocious lion. The son, in the supremacy of human folly, enticed his mother and sister to betray their father and escaped to the kingdom of the north.

Destitute, the lion ravaged the forests. He searched everywhere for the family he had protected in his den. Wildly he searched, tearing the jungle apart. Travellers arrived at the northern kingdom and related the tale of the fearsome lion who terrorised travellers. Sinhabahu the lion-son returned to the forest. He saw a ferocious lion, the king of the forest. He refused to see a father whose broken heart was bleeding with love. With his arrow he shot his good father, the lion through his heart. The ultimate crime was committed. A son had killed his father. We the Sinhala were the descendents of Sinhabahu.

'He was a good man that Podian, ferocious as the lion Sinhabahu,' said Magi.

'You foolish woman, Sinhabahu was not the lion, the lion's son was Sinhabahu.'

'Ah, the ferocious Sinhabahu, like our Podian, if only our Podian had his ferociousness...'

'Don't mention that rascal Sinhabahu's name. It is a shame to say that we are from that dirty fellow who killed his own father. That Podian was like that! He ate and slept in our houses and left without a word. A rascal just like Sinhabahu! I don't even want to hear his name again!'

'He did not go, he was sent.'

'Serves him right! A man who kills his father has no right to live. I hope they hang him!'

Then Thathi fell down the mountain, suffered concussion and was returned to Colombo.

It happened like this. Thathi had managed to pick up a bit of road from the bottom of the plateau that had once been a mountain and re-structured a part of the road that had dissolved when the two monsoons met on top of the mountain. Then he got into his jeep and tried to drive over the mountain. Obviously, it collapsed. The road over the mountain could not remain when the mountain was no more. My father landed on the bottom of the plateau, upside down. His inflatable pillow suffered a puncture. Thus, while they drove him to Colombo thinking he suffered from shock, his head had shaken so much without the inflatable pillow that his memory decided to take a holiday. His assistants took him out of the jeep, placed him on the bed and left. Thathi did not move. Occasionally, like a dream, bits of memory would return, only to disappear again very fast.

I saw him lying there, in his office trousers and the khaki bush shirt. 'Thathi,' I said trying to wake him. He didn't respond. I increased the volume. His mouth opened though the eyes remained closed. 'Will you not get up? Magi is making hoppers for dinner.' I don't know whether my father liked hoppers, but I would have woken up from the dead for hoppers. 'If anyone calls from abroad and asks what we would like to have brought, tell them to bring me an inflatable pillow.' My father had spoken in his sleep.

'A pillow?'

His eyes remained closed.

'A pillow is extremely necessary for the neck. I have lost my pillow. Never forget that we are mis-products of creation. Someone somewhere made a mistake. It was foolish that the primates left all fours and started walking on their hind legs. Our geometry is all wrong to walk on hind legs. We must continue to walk on four legs. But since we have now learned to walk on two legs we can never return to four legs. Our heads are far too heavy for the neck. We must always try to save our heads from falling off our neck. If someone calls from abroad and asks what we need, tell them to bring an inflatable pillow to put around the neck. Maybe two in case one deflates. Tell Ammi not to forget to pay the phone bill in case someone calls from abroad.' Then my father closed his mouth and slept again. I tried to wake him, but he slept. He began to snore. I went for hoppers. Ammi was already eating.

'Ammi, did Sirisangabo in the Jataka tales donate his head because he found it too heavy for his neck?' I asked.

'Have you now completely gone mad, like your father?'

'Thathi was saying that the head is too heavy for the neck.'

'I suppose that is a wonderful reason for your father to sleep all day.'

'He isn't sleeping, he is concussed,' Nenda who entered the dining room was on her usual tour of defending Thathi from Ammi's wrath.

'Concussion is a nicer word for sleep and is used by people who think the people around them are fools.'

'You have a tongue of thorns.'

'Nenda was Sirisangabo's head too heavy, is that why he donated it?'

'Who told you such nonsense?'

'No one. I thought it out myself.'

'Not no one, it is your beloved Tissa Aiya who is putting nonsense in this child's mind in his sleep.'

'Well, if Tissa Aiya said it, there could be some element of truth in what the child says,' and Nenda went into the kitchen to eat her share of hoppers.

'Don't talk nonsense.'

'Thathi was just saying that the human head is too heavy for the neck and we should always try to put an inflatable pillow round the neck.'

'You don't have to listen to all the nonsense he talks.'

'He wants another inflatable pillow.'

'I know.'

'Did you ask someone to bring it?'

'Don't waste time asking silly questions. Just because your father has a head that is bigger than the rest of the human population we can't go begging to people living abroad for things no normal human beings require.'

'His head isn't bigger than the rest of the human population.'

'You haven't looked at him carefully.'

I gobbled the last hopper and ran to examine my father's head. Ammi shouted: 'And don't forget to compare your head as well.'

I took the hand mirror and looked at our heads. My father had the same black ears, the same Jambu fruit run over by the bullock cart nose and the same head that I did. We were both mis-creations of evolution.

When the rain forest became the savannah, the monkey had lost its tail and began its evolutionary journey into man. My father and my forefathers should have remained on the last square millimetre of forest and died of starvation. Allowing my mother's and TM Mozart's forefathers to stand erect on their hind legs. Their heads were smaller than ours.

Having recovered from the initial shock of seeing my sleeping father, Nenda and Magi recommenced their battle. Rama-Sita, Vijaya-Kuveni and Sinhabahu-Lion were over. Now the smaller characters of mythology gained prominence. Thathi slept and slept.

Magi returned to the kitchen, having failed to entice my father into waking to the smell of garlic soup. 'Aney I don't know, the master is sleeping like the giant Kumbhakarana. Will he ever get up?' Nenda was in the kitchen drinking her afternoon plain tea.

'May you go to hell you foolish woman for calling our master Kumbhakarana! Stupid woman, don't you know that the monster Kumbhakarana was a ferocious Raksha with an insatiable appetite who gobbled every creature in sight?'

'How do I know? I wasn't living in those days. I only know that Kumbhakarana slept and slept.'

'Idiotic woman, he slept because the Lord Brahma put him to sleep because he was eating up every animal and human that crossed his path. His stomach was like a giant graveyard. If Brahma had not put him to sleep no creature would be alive on this earth today!'

'How would I know such things?'

'Don't talk about things you know nothing about. Now go and rub some lime on your lips and remove the sin of calling your master the Kumbhakarana.' Magi returned after rubbing lime on her lips.

'Who was Kumbhakarana?' Nenda asked her.

'The Raksha who ate everything in sight.'

'I just told you that you stupid woman. I want to know who's who he was?'

'How do I know, he was no relation of mine.'

'Aney there is no medicine for your foolishness. Of course he was no relation of yours. You are the only woman who lives in this world who does not have a single relation, not even a father for your son.'

'If you know so much then tell.'

'Why should I tell you stories? Do your work.'

'I have finished my work, Enappa.'

'There, there that stupid estate Tamil man's words again. It is a pity that Brahma put Kumbhakarana to sleep before he could eat you up.'

'Will you two stop shouting, you will wake up Tissa.' Achi entered the kitchen amidst the commotion.

'Never mind, let him wake up. It's my ears I am worried about, not that sleeping man. Your squabbling is hurting my ears. I feel like asking Lydia Akka to send me a pre-paid ticket and I will leave your abattoir wailings and go to England.' My mother had entered the fray.

'You are not going anywhere until Tissa Aiya wakes up,' retorted Nenda.

It was no longer two women. Now four women battled about the loss of repatriation. I went to my sleeping father. Perhaps his head had diminished and he was able to get up. I observed my head while passing the mirror. It looked smaller in the wall mirror than in the hand mirror. But, I did not pause to ponder. Pondering may make it grow even bigger. Like Hanuman, who could slither like a worm into Sita's royal dungeons, or inflate like a giant and carry the Himalayas to Lanka when needed.

The bickering of the four women could be heard up to the bedroom. Even if he had Brahma's help, I wondered how my father could sleep through the noise. He sensed my presence, forgot to snore, opened his mouth and said: 'The sea is the sea, the sky is the sky; the sea can be compared only to the sea, and the sky can be compared only to the sky. The battle between Magi and Nenda can only be compared to the battle between Rama and Ravana.'

He snored again.

The battle had not yet reached the final stage. Kumbhakarana need not be woken. Ravana's army was still intact. Rama still battled with Ravana's lesser armies. Until they had been destroyed, Kumbhakarana could continue to sleep. Sita was still captive. And Hanuman rushed back and forth with the Himalayas and their curative herbs each time Rama or his brother Lakshmana were wounded in battle.

7

Saturn which took Podian away brought the hydro-electric knee, the trigger-finger, concussion and bronchitis. That same Saturn even brought Mrs. Bandaranayake. Saturn co-mingled with Venus, exalted woman, sent aunty Lydia to the commonwealth and brought Mrs. Bandaranayake into power. Mrs. Bandaranayake arrived sooner than other Saturnic happenings. But, that is the law of nature. As my grandfather said 'Folly is faster than wisdom.'

It was the age of Venus. And the age of woman.

Man was debilitated. My father had concussion, my grandfather had bronchitis and Podian was repatriated. TM Mozart was neither debilitated, nor quite elevated. Karma obviously could not decide whether he was a man or boy. Since the arrival of the latest period of Saturn, TM Mozart had been unable to bat a hundred-not-out in cricket. He was bowled out with zero, usually with the first ball. Perhaps he too fitted into the category of the debilitated man but his debilitation wasn't that serious. Except for the inability to bat a century, he had no ailments. Venus was being merciful to boys who were not quite men.

Anyway, this Saturn who was responsible for man's and woman's misfortune had visited us a long time ago, even before I had been born under that clock where time stood still at eight, eight. This Saturn had brought Magi and Nenda to our homes. Together. But separate. Like two cow catchered Siamese twins who hated each other and wanted to separate, but without a surgeon in any of the three worlds who was capable of that feat.

Magi was at that time, a young woman. Pregnant. The father unknown.

I don't know who brought Magi to us. When asked, Achi always said 'You don't know her.' After many years I think my grandmother had forgotten herself. But as the story goes, my grandmother had successfully diagnosed that Magi's painful abdomen was not caused by an appendix but was the result of a pregnancy.

Usually, pregnant women have a male counterpart that bears fifty percent blame for the pregnancy. My mother blamed my father for my misdeeds. Aunty Lydia blamed uncle Lionel for their children's misdeeds. But Magi came alone. Jesus Christ's mother Mary did not have a fifty percent either, but that was somewhere in the Arabian Desert where God lived, not in our tropics. In the tropics a pregnancy does not happen without a male. We too had many gods: not Buddhist gods, Hindu gods. Even though they were not blessed with particularly honourable reputations, they certainly did not go around making servants pregnant. But Magi was pregnant, and minus a male.

There had been many who could have been blamed for Magi's pregnancy, but they had not been servants. So, as the story goes, there existed an agreement between my grandmother and the acquaintance who brought Magi for diagnosis, that when a child was born, my grandmother could keep the child but Magi had to be returned to cook.

The child was born. Magi said she would return to cook only if the child could come. But the child looked like the missing fifty percent and due to the risk of divorce of this secret fifty percent the child could not be taken into the house where Magi had once lived and cooked. My grandmother agreed to keep Magi and the child. Achi and her acquaintance made a second agreement. The day my grandmother died, Magi would have to return to the acquaintance's house, but without the child. Ammi would have to continue to care for the child. The pact was signed. Then the acquaintance died. Of starvation. Her stomach had reduced and reduced until it began to look like a transparent *gothamba roti* and then she had died. She could only eat Magi's food. The pact was forgotten and Magi lived happily with us, with her son until…

Nenda came. Nenda had neither an appendix problem nor an inflated abdomen. An old classmate of Achi's brought her to us.

Swinitha, Achi's old friend visited her one Sunday morning and related the dilemma of a relative who had seven daughters. Of the seven daughters five were married, the sixth was bald headed and religious and the seventh, the fairest, prettiest and most learned could not find a man. The planets were blocked and her head was too full of fact.

Achi told her school friend to bring the poor girl to her, until the planets got unblocked and she could find herself a husband. Swinitha returned to the village and came back the next day, with Nenda. Achi took one look at her and lamented, 'Oh my good lord, Swinitha, how on earth can a girl get married, who has a mouth that looks like the castle of Yama, the god of the underworld and death!'

Swinitha agreed to return to Nenda's village and collect enough money to buy her a new set of teeth. Achi in the meantime, ordered the teeth. They waited and waited, but Swinitha did not return. When she eventually returned she had a new set of teeth in her own mouth, but no money for Nenda's teeth. 'Aney Beet darling, I pleaded and pleaded with this poor girl's relatives, but do you think even one of them were willing to spare a single cent? They said, Apo Swinitha Akka you have found her a home in Colombo, she can stay there. It isn't the teeth that prevent her from finding a husband, it's the planets. They are all in her head. Venus hasn't even cast a shadow into her life. You tell her to stay there in your friends' home and do the housework. When she comes here…, oh! Lord Buddha! It is only bad luck! An unmarried woman is only bad luck. Our crops don't grow, the harvest is less, termites attack the grain, coconut trees catch fungus. You keep her in Colombo. In Colombo people don't grow grain and coconuts. They buy everything from the shop.' And so Nenda stayed.

Achi and Ammi got her horoscope read and one astrologer discovered a small slit in the house of marriage where Venus did caste a small ray of hope. Around this time when Venus was casting her shadow I had been born. My birth had distracted my mother and Nenda so much, that finally, when they came out of distraction Thathi had been forced to empty his wallet for the new set of teeth. Swinitha disappeared without trace.

Having got a new set of teeth, Nanda waited for her prince. He did not come. Between my birth and the emptying of the wallet, Venus had taken her leave. Nenda remained unmarried. Like Magi.

With a perfect set of man made teeth she cared for our needs.

The two camps were formed. Magi with Achi, since Achi had made the pact with the acquaintance. Nenda with Ammi since Thathi had paid for the dentures. From this day on, life was like the *Yuddha kanda*, book six of the Ramayana. The fearsome battle between Rama and Ravana had begun.

> *Rama's a lion, you a jackal*
> *He is an ocean, you a rivulet*
> *He is nectar, you stale gruel,*

> *He's gold, you're iron*
> *He's sandalwood, you're mud*
> *He's an elephant, you a cat*
> *He's Garuda, you a crow,*
> *He's a peacock, you a duck*
> *He's a swan, you a vulture"*

We were all around Thathi listening to his ravings. When I was alone with him he spoke, but when others were around he raved. It was a strange illness. 'Mummy listen to this, I think Tissa is going mad.' *'Thuk, thuk, thuk,'* said Nenda spitting on the ground, 'blasphemous woman, thorns will grow out of your mouth!'

> *"Come with me, enjoy celestial pleasures*
> *Forget Rama, he is but a mere mortal*
> *Doomed to die*
> *I passionately desire you*
> *Accept me"*

'Mummy, what are we to do about this man? He has gone stark raving mad!' said Ammi painting her toe nails.

'What to do Mali? It is Saturn. When Saturn departs he will be all right.'

'Can't we do something for Saturn to leave sooner?'

'Apo hamu, like the massive Kumbhakarana, he will sleep for six months without waking,' interrupted Magi.

'Out, out, out of this room before I make sambol out of you,' said Nenda chasing Magi out of the room with Thathi's rubber slipper. Ammi and Achi went out of the room to contemplate how they could evict Saturn sooner than the Karmic date of departure. I sat next to my father on the bed. 'Thathi, why did your road fall with the mountain? Mountains don't usually fall. Look at Adam's peak it is still standing even though Lord Buddha, Shiva, Adam and St. Thomas trod on it with their big feet.'

My father's eyes remained closed but his mouth opened. 'I built the road on the mountain where Sita was held captive by Ravana's demons. Ravana was an intelligent king, but his Raksha assistants were foolish. When they caught Hanuman they swathed his tail in oil and set fire to it. Hanuman escaped, and burned the whole mountain with the fire on his tail.

Who in their senses would set fire to monkey's tail? They should have cut it off! By setting fire to its tail, they set fire to themselves. The mountain could no longer grow trees that held the soil together. So, it collapsed.'

'Why did you build the road on the mountain Hanuman burned?'

'Daughter, when the age of Saturn dawns, there is no one with vision to rule a country, and we government servants have to do what we are ordered to. We are not paid to find the logic of their reason. We are paid to execute their reason without logic. Human folly is mistaken for wisdom.'

Ammi and Achi returned to the room. Thathi's mouth closed. They had found a way to evict Saturn. Preparations had begun. Elisabeth came from the village and made sweetmeats the whole night. Her nephew came with her and removed the cobwebs. Dasa, Magi's son polished the floors.

'Dasa, why are you polishing the floors at night?'

'Apo, you are too small to know what is happening in this house.' Dasa loved to make a mystery out of the simplest of tasks. I approached Elisabeth. 'Elisabeth, why are you making so much *kokis*, is there going to be a party?'

'Aney I don't know baby, I was asked to come, so I came.' I tried Nenda and Magi. They were squabbling as usual. 'If Podian were here we would not need so many people, he would have done the work single handed.'

'Why? You think that black Tamil fellow was Hanuman the monkey who removed the Himalayas and brought them here? If he was capable of such a feat he would not have let those people ship him off to India, he would have first come here and worshipped at our feet and then taken our leave.'

'If he could have, he would have done so. You have already forgotten what a good man he was!'

Ammi and Achi were like whispering hope, they said nothing. Siya was still in a Maldive fish depression and TM Mozart was playing his new composition to Thathi. I found his compositions hideous cacophonies, but my father with his eyes closed was no longer snoring.

I was not jealous of TM Mozart, but he annoyed me. He was always good while I was always bad. He scored a century, I couldn't

even run two feet without panting. He had inherited all the good genes,
I had inherited none. He played the piano and the guitar; I could barely
play the piano though I was the only person who got lessons. Then I
tried to sing. I thought if TM Mozart could compose, karma would
have at least planted a sweet voice in my black frame. Uncle Buddhi's
second son taught me how to press the 'record' and 'play' knobs in the
cassette recorder uncle Buddhi had scavenged from a second hand shop
and given us. I pressed and I sang. Unfortunately, TM Mozart
witnessed this. He called a family conference with our family and uncle
Buddhi's family, pressed 'play' turned the volume up and spent
forty-five minutes cackling with laughter. I didn't press any knob on the
cassette recorder ever again. Perhaps I would do so, one day, when TM
Mozart was evicted from our house, like Saturn. What could I do until
then? I returned to chat with Dasa.

'Dasa, tell me if you know what is happening?'
'I am busy, come back later,' he said polishing the floor.
'I can't come back, I am here now, tell me.'
'It will cost you,' he said travelling on all fours as he rubbed polish on
the ridges between the wall and the floor.
'I'll give you my share of rice.'
He laughed. 'I don't want rice.'
I knew he wouldn't want rice. As Magi's son he got more rice than we
did.
'Chocolates?'
'Foreign?'
'I can't get those.'
'Then forget it.'
'Ten Rupees?'
'Twenty.'
I didn't have money, but Thathi was concussed. I knew where his wallet
was hidden in the Almirah. I returned with the money.
'Now don't tell anyone I told you, but they are doing an exorcising
ceremony.'
'Whom are they exorcising?'
'Mary and Joseph.'
'Mary and Joseph have never been here, they were in the Arabian desert!'

'We also have a Mary and Joseph who are greedy devils that do not let your parents prosper in this house.'

'Aney Dasa don't lie, how would Jesus Christ's parents Mary and Joseph come into our house out of all the houses in Ceylon?'

'They are not Jesus' Mary and Joseph; they are Mrs. Adonis' husband's parents who are unhappy that she sold the house.'

Just then Ammi came into the living room, 'Dasa, don't forget to polish the corners, I will come and check later.'

'Alright Madame,' he said with a cheeky grin.

'They were dead when Mrs. Adonis sold the house.'

'Yes but they died with greed in their minds.'

I was beginning to get goose bumps.

'So?'

'So now they are angry and want to make it impossible for you all to live and prosper in this house.'

'Aney Dasa, don't talk nonsense, I haven't seen any Mary or Joseph doing anything in this house.'

'Not nonsense, your Thathi is concussed, your Ammi broke a leg, Nenda has trigger-finger, my mother has tuberculosis (that was new) and your Siya has bronchitis.'

'That is not Mary and Joseph that is Saturn.'

'They are telling you it is Saturn, because you are always scared. You were even scared of the cemetery near your last house!'

'How do you know?'

'I know,' he grinned like a jackass.

'So why are you polishing the floor?'

'Because the ghost hunters are coming tonight to forcibly remove Mary and Joseph from the house.'

'And is Elisabeth making food for the ghost hunters?'

'Aney, you understand nothing. The food is not for the ghost hunters it is for the ghosts. Ghosts like fried food. When they get the smell of the festive food they will come to the table to eat, and then I will capture them and take them away.'

'*You?*'

'It has all been sorted out. The ghost hunter will entice them to the table and I will carry them out.'

'You with your skin and bone body, as if you can carry two human beings out of this house? That, I would love to see.'

'Bad luck baby. You will not be here tonight.'

'I am here every night.'

'Not tonight.'

'Why not?'

'The ghosts like to gobble small children,' he grinned. 'Now go. I have to finish this fast or else I will be knuckled by your mother.'

Was this true? Or was it another of Dasa's fabrications? The house was being cleaned for a special occasion. As far as I knew there was no special occasion to celebrate. No birthdays, no anniversaries, no funerals. I decided to enter my chameleon skin and be incongruous. I sat in my room and spoke to no one.

Dusk dawned.

Ammi put me into the Hillman and drove me to uncle Buddhi's for the night. I shouted, I yelled, I screamed. My mother was stronger than I.

When I returned the next day the sweetmeats were gone, my father was awake, TM Mozart batted a century and nothing seemed to be different from the day before. Only the cobwebs were gone and the floor was polished. Was it Saturn or Mary and Joseph? I looked at the newspapers. Mrs. Bandaranayake was still there. It was obviously Mary and Joseph.

Not Saturn.

8

Though his eyes were open, my father's head was still too heavy for his neck. The inflatable pillow was on its way. Ammi had not called aunty Lydia for an inflatable pillow, Achi had called her instead. Magi and Nenda battled further into eternity. Thathi lay in bed and wrote postcards to all his relatives informing them that he had recovered from his fall down the mountain. Ammi was irritated. She was beyond childbearing age and could not bear to see Thathi eternally on her bed. 'I think it is time you got out of bed,' she said.

'I can't, my head is still too heavy.'

'Your head has always been too heavy; it has not got any heavier since you rolled down the mountain, if at all, it must have got lighter from the jolt.'

'How would you know? You are not carrying my head on your neck!'

'Well if you insist on staying in bed for the rest of your life, at least do something useful in bed.'

'I am doing something useful. I am writing postcards.'

'Informing your sisters and your relations about your fall is not something useful.'

Thathi did not respond. He began another postcard.

'If you want to be useful, write to your precious government and ask them why they sent Podian away.'

Ammi had not yet forgiven Thathi for painting the green Hillman blue. He was a traitor. He supported Mrs. Bandaranayake who was blue, rather than Dudley, who was green. Dudley was still the lover of the nation. The havoc created by Mrs. Bandaranayake's minimization had increased the number of people who loved Dudley. Now, even men began to love Dudley. Siya began every morning at breakfast, 'When Dudley returns to power Maldive fish will return too.' Even TM Mozart composed a song to Dudley. It was called, 'The green, green grass of Dudley.' Only Thathi remained faithful in his love for my mother and for Mrs. Bandaranayake.

TM Mozart was becoming cleverer. He began to understand the difference between Mrs. Bandaranayake and Dudley. The difference that went beyond gender. I only understood that Dudley was green and

Mrs. Bandaranayake was blue, that she loved Chou En Lai while he loved I don't know whom?

TM Mozart told me that karma had forgotten to give me brain cells and tried to explain to me further differences between Mrs. Bandaranayake and Dudley. Dudley's agriculture versus Mrs. Bandaranayake's left to the left of centre industrialization. Agriculture filled our stomach, not industrialization. The left to the left of centre who rebelled for industrialization and supported Mrs. Bandaranayake were behind bars, and she was now reaping havoc. The havoc she had wreaked.

He said he was going abroad to study. TM Mozart.

'Why on earth would you want to go abroad to study when you can study in your school?' I questioned him. 'When *I* go abroad, I will go to have fun, not to study. Why on earth would a normal thinking human being go abroad to study? Study of all things? I am sure there are far more interesting things to do abroad than study.'

'I really must say, the more I think about it, karma has certainly forgotten to give you a single brain cell. Silly creature, don't you realize that free education is a disaster?'

'Education in itself is a disaster. I don't know why schools were ever invented.'

'Have you never ever craved for knowledge?'

'I have knowledge. I crave for that which I don't have, like platform shoes and chocolates.'

'I think no doctor in the world has a remedy for your foolishness.'

'I don't know why you want to study when you can bat a century again.'

'You will not understand if I tell you.'

He was right, I would not have understood. I did not like school, but I liked my house number 186. I liked playing with Sharona and her brother, and I liked listening to the squabbles between Magi and Nenda. I couldn't think of being separated from them even for a single day. I could never lock myself in my bedroom and strum my guitar like TM Mozart. So it was a good thing I could not play the guitar. Let him go abroad if he wanted. I certainly would not move one step from this island, or this house. Whoever wanted could leave.

'Tissa have you written to the government to check up about what has happened to Podian?'

'What could have happened, he has been sent to India,' my father replied.

'But write and ask why they sent him? That fellow was born and bred here; he does not have a living soul in India.'

'Mali, have you not realized that no one is responsible in this country? I have written and written postcards since the formation of this so called republic of Sri Lanka asking those people who changed Ceylon to Sri Lanka to give me a proper explanation as to why they put this Sri in front of Lanka and guess what?'

'What?'

'No one knows. They did it. But now, no one knows who did it nor why.'

'Don't cry over spilt milk, that is not an issue, no one is concerned if Sri Lanka has a Sri or does not have a Sri, or if it is called Timbuktu, or whatever. What is more important is to know what has happened to Podian.'

'If they don't know why they put a Sri in front of Lanka, they are not likely to know why they sent Podian to another country.'

'Just write and ask.'

I don't know whether Thathi wrote and asked, or not. The topic changed. Podian was forgotten.

The tragedy of tragedies happened.

It was more tragic than Ravana losing Lanka to Rama, worse than Sinhabahu killing the lion, more abominable than Kuveni betraying the Rakshas. This tragedy was the greatest tragedy I had witnessed since my birth; the one that tore the hearts of the Sinhala, the Tamil, the Muslim and the other minority people. The nation wept and wailed. Dudley died.

Nenda and Magi who had been disunited in their sorrow for Podian, united in their sorrow for Dudley. Siya dashed the kitchen furniture on the ground and moved into perpetual slumber. Hope for the rebirth of Maldive fish was dead. Like Dudley. Achi and Ammi joined Magi and Nenda and wailed in a quadruple symphony of sorrow. The boarders joined them in their wailing, and the dogs joined too. Then silence came.

So many words had been used to elaborate the sorrow of the missing Podian that Nenda and Magi had no more words left in their mouth. Dudley having died so soon after Podian's forced departure had not allowed the words to form in their mouths. Dudley's sadness was a quiet sadness. It was a painful sadness. Not only the women, the men were sad too. Everyone in our Socialist Republic was sad.

The milkman cried while he delivered milk. The garbage man dropped half the garbage on the road because his eyes were tearing. The postman wet all the addresses with his tears, so that we received Mrs. Adonis's letters and Mrs. Adonis received our letters. I cut out the stamps and gave the letters to Mrs. Adonis. Mrs. Adonis cried so much about Dudley, about her letters, that she did not notice that the stamps were missing. She lamented with tears rolling down her eyes, 'Child, I am going to die a lonely woman. What would I do without you and your family? When this woman came into power, all my children left. I thought when Dudley comes back they would return. Now Dudley is dead. And I will die too. Alone. All alone…' and she cried her cataracts out of her eyes.

Mrs. Bandaranayake nationalized all the petrol sheds and raised the price of petrol. Dudley's body was left in Independence Square for anyone who was stupid enough to pay the high price of petrol to come and visit the coffin. Mrs. Bandaranayake underestimated the people's love for Dudley. People came from all over the socialist state to see him lying in state. Those who could not afford to buy petrol converted their motors to Diesel. Then Diesel prices rose. The people then converted their motors to kerosene. Then kerosene prices rose and people came with coconut oil. Then the Ceylon Coconut Corporation was unusually rapidly nationalized and coconut oil minimized. Then the people walked.

Thathi got out of bed and walked too. Not because he could not afford the price of petrol; he walked because he wanted to show his solidarity to a man who had been against the Sri in front of Lanka. In the evening he returned from Independence Square which had been built for dead heroes of the state like Dudley, and told us that he had never seen so many people in his life. Not even in Calcutta. Then he took out my abacus from the old toy box and began to calculate a curve of population expansion since independence in nineteen forty-eight. The curve was a diagonal straight line pointing towards heaven.

My father adopted Dudley's agrarian dream. He found a plot of bare land between the dogs' kennel and the Karapincha tree and began to plough. He took a bus to a village in the dry zone and returned with a suitcase of yam. He buried the yam in the ploughed spot and waited for it to grow.

'I shall never ever in my life eat yam,' complained Ammi. 'If there is no rice, that woman should import rice.'

'My dear Mali, I don't think our treasury has enough money to pay for imported rice for all the people I have seen visiting Dudley's cortege.' My mother was a reincarnation of Marie Antoinette. 'I shall eat cake if there is no rice. But I shall never eat yam. That is what bandicoots eat.'

'Don't talk nonsense child,' said Achi angrily. 'You cannot live on cake.'

'I can.' But Ammi got no cake. Achi believed in supporting my father and Dudley's agrarian dream, not my spoiled mother. She refused to make cake. Even those who visited us no longer got cake, but yam. Even as desert.

'I shall ask Lydia Akka for a pre-paid ticket and go to the commonwealth,' complained my mother bitterly. We did not listen to her and ate Thathi's yam. It did not taste like rice and dhal curry, but it was food. One should not forget the fact that even the rice and dhal curry no longer tasted as good as it had tasted before Mrs. Bandaranayake came into power on the gyrating head of Saturn.

Though we lived on the cemetery road the cortege did not pass our house on its way to the cemetery. We went to my mother's friend Dawn's house to watch the cortege. Dawn lived between Independence Square and the Colombo cemetery. Corteges of all dead heroes had to pass Dawn's house to enter the cemetery. My mother decided that eating salmon cutlets and drinking 'Sharona' in Dawn's house while Dudley passed in his cortege was a minimization of the tragedy that had befallen all persons of our Socialist Republic. The women and the men.

We, that is my mother, my father, my grandparents, Nenda, Magi, the servants, the boarders and I went to Dawn's house the day Dudley began his last journey. TM Mozart didn't go. He decided to remain in house number 186 and practice his batting strokes in front of all the full-length mirrors. Since he was now batting centuries again, he felt that an improvement of style was perhaps required. The last photograph of him in the sports page of the national newspaper had him looking like a Kandyan dancer doing the dance of Hanuman. Cricketers do not usually look like Kandyan dancers or monkeys; they look like princes and lords. Therefore, the household departure to wail at Dudley's cortege was a perfect opportunity to work on becoming a lord.

Dawn had invited her other friends and their relatives too. By the time we arrived, all the windows were occupied. My father sat with Dawn's husband, away from the window and discussed his plot of yam between the Karapincha tree and the dog kennel, as well as the population explosion observed with Dudley's death. Ammi and Achi tried to squeeze between Dawn's other friends' armpits and catch a glimpse of Dudley. Nenda cursed Ammi for bringing her to Dawn's, whose windows were already full of people. Magi agreed with her. It was good to see them united. 'I will not creep between people's armpits and try to get a glimpse of our Dudley,' she said to Magi. 'I want a clean memory of him in my head, not the smell of underarm sweat.' Magi agreed.

I hung around near the tray of cutlets and kept popping them into my mouth. Dudley came and went in less than five minutes. Ammi and Achi re-emerged from the armpits and sat with Dawn and her other female friends and discussed Dudley's virtues. 'It's a pity,' they said, 'all good men remain bachelors, and the men who are unsuitable to become husbands and fathers marry and have children.'

'That is what one would call Karma,' Achi said. Dawn agreed.

Thathi, Dawn's husband and the husbands of Dawn's female friends sat at the other end of the living room drinking Arrack and discussed the various kinds of yams available in the dry zone and the population explosion. Sometime between midnight and twelve thirty, we returned home. By that time, the supposed population of fifteen million people that had sky rocketed to perhaps seventeen million had reached the cemetery. The streets were empty as Ammi drove our blue Hillman back.

Thathi slept in the back seat.

9

Seeing Dudley's cortege, Mrs. Bandaranayake panicked. There were more people than anyone could have imagined and the tears they shed were more than the water in the Indian Ocean.

Mrs. Bandaranayake nationalised all the independent newspapers and made them governmental newspapers. When someone died whom the people had loved in life, no government newspaper was permitted to announce his or her obituary without the permission of the government. The snag was that there was no official to grant this permission, and so, people died, went to heaven, hell or nirvana without the public even being aware that they had died. My father took this relatively lightly. 'At least I will save time by not having to attend funerals,' he said. Siya was not so light about it, 'Bloody miserable woman,' he complained, 'there is now nothing to read in the newspapers.'

The one who took it the hardest was Ammi. Not only did the non-independent newspapers now not print obituaries, it no longer advertised classes my mother could attend to satisfy the still roaming head-line on her palm. 'I shall ask Lydia to send me a pre-paid ticket and I shall go to the commonwealth and never come back,' she threatened.

But the people of the Socialist Republic were not as foolish as Mrs. Bandaranayake thought they were. Public meetings took the place of newspapers. Weddings, alms-givings, church services, children's birthdays became meeting places. On my birthday-party relatives and friends of my parents and grandparents arrived and discussed their plots of yam and the population explosion. Most of them forgot to bring me a present. Those who didn't forget, gave me money which I gave Ammi for I didn't know what one could do with money in our Socialist Republic. There was nothing to buy.

The rice and dhal queues in front of co-operative stores lengthened. Now there was a new queue, the bread queue. It was almost as long as the rice and dhal queue, and was growing every day. 'Very soon it will be longer than the rice queue,' said Achi. She was right. Achi was not only an expert on diagnosing infected appendices, she was also an expert on predicting the lengthening of demand and the shortening of supply of socialist queues.

When there were no birthdays, people met at weddings. The same people discussed the same yam plots and the same population explosion.

Then Mrs. Bandaranayake passed a new law. She reduced the quantity of guests permitted to attend weddings. If she could, she would have prohibited weddings altogether, but she could not. She herself was the mother of three unmarried children and despite being the prime minister of a Socialist Republic she was also a mother. Mother love was greater than her love of socialism. Therefore, she only reduced the number of guests and not the weddings. I don't know whether, at the weddings of her children, when they eventually got married, they too had only a handful of guests like at other weddings. I was never invited. The newspapers, being non-independent wrote nothing about the Bandaranayake weddings. Her children probably got married, divorced and re-married with a million guests in attendance, but we knew nothing about it.

Despite minimization of invited guests, the quantity of weddings increased. Everyone in the Socialist Republic was falling in love and getting married. The queues were long; there was nothing to buy. The people had nothing else to do but fall in love. Love thrived.

Even I fell in love. The first person I fell in love with was the captain of TM Mozart's cricket team. He was a beautiful boy, a tall, slim, light skinned, Aryan type. I loved him more than Donny Osmond or Engelbert Humperdinck. But he was Rama and I was Surpunaka, Ravana's sister. Black as night. He held hands with the sister of another cricketer and ignored my black existence like Rama who spurned the love-torn Surpunaka. Then I fell in love again, with the vice-captain, but history repeated itself. I was always Surpunaka.

Then, TM Mozart fell in love with the sister of another batsman and no longer scored a century. Love had created havoc between the bat and the ball and Ammi began her search for more Marys and Josephs. But I knew why he no longer scored a century. Though he still stood in front of the full-length mirror, he no longer stood with the bat; he now posed bare bodied.

Love was everywhere. In our family as well, people fell in love. My grandfather's brother Steven's daughter Mona fell in love with Siya's sister Neela's son Rohan. They married. Fortunately, since it was a single-family marriage, implementing the Bandaranayake minimized guest list was not difficult. Then granduncle Hubert's son Priyantha fell in love with granduncle Hubert's sister in law's daughter Chitra, and they married. Again minimization was relatively easy. Of course, it needs to be mentioned that the family was not happy about cousins marrying cousins, but what could we do? We had to find entertainment to substitute the lack of readable newspapers and Maldive fish.

Love grew and grew. At cricket matches, at almsgivings, at children's birthday parties everywhere. But, since the number of weddings increased, Mrs. Bandaranayake's policy of guest minimization was not as effective as contemplated. So, summarising the reign of the era of new maths, the answer to the mathematical question was the same as in old maths. Mrs. Bandaranayake's method was simply more confusing and not possible to learn, but the answer was the same. The same amount of people who would have attended weddings without the minimization of guests attended weddings. Not together, separate. Everyone got their chance. The plots of yam and the population explosion were discussed more often, but not as loud. The fewer the people the quieter the cacophony.

Then Mrs. Bandaranayake came up with a new idea. Emergency. If she was not a prime minister of a Socialist Republic she could have been as brilliant as Galileo Galilei or Copernicus, for she too was always discovering something new. Emergency had been implemented during the terror of the red fungus. But, they were now in jail, so what was the purpose of emergency now?

Mrs. Bandaranayake had thrown away the jail key. She was an able stateswoman. Throwing away the key was the right decision. When all the rice farmers' and coconut farmers' sons and daughters study art history and philosophy and don't want to work the fields, it was obvious even to a child like me, that they would have nothing to eat. They wanted jobs that did not exist and didn't want jobs that existed.

She understood the gravity of the problem and tucked them into prison cells and fed them. She neither offended karma nor did she give them undue hardship. She minimized their worries. They had a roof over their heads and food to eat. Of course, it could be argued that the food in prisons was not particularly tasty. But I am sure if they came to our house and ate the food that Magi served, they would have happily returned to their prison food. Magi was still sad at Podian's departure and her food, needless to say, was the opposite of culinary delight!

The truth of the matter was that the fear of the red fungus was a façade Mrs. Bandaranayake adopted in order to prevent people like my father, my grandfather and their friends and relatives meeting at weddings, cricket matches and children's birthday parties and discussing the lack of obituaries, the lack of Maldive fish, minimized guest lists, plots of yam and the population explosion witnessed at Dudley's funeral.

With the implementation of emergency, everything nearly came to a stand still. Weddings became registration ceremonies and children's birthday parties were limited to telephone calls and birthday cards. But the cleverest were the cricketers. They discovered the minimization of cricket. Instead of playing the whole weekend, they invented something called 'limited over matches' that fitted into the time span where emergency was lifted. The 'over' was six balls. If the lifted time of emergency was short, the amount of 'overs' were fewer, and vice versa. Within this given amount of 'overs' the team that scored the highest won the game. When the balls were over the game was over.

This was the height of geniality in the midst of minimization. The limited over match brought excitement and action. The draw was eliminated. There was always a winner or a loser. I think this was the moment in the history of the Socialist Republic of Sri Lanka where the seeds of capitalism grew. From cricket. Not from rugger, not from hockey, not from marbles and matchsticks, but from cricket. The cricketers now dropped their girl friends and concentrated on winning the match.

10

Mrs. Bandaranayake began to feel unloved. With or without emergency the people found opportunities to congregate and discuss yams and the other dilemmas facing them.

She launched a new campaign. It was called the institutionalisation of the partial implementation of minimization. It was the non-minimization of a few, versus the minimization of the many. My mother, my grand parents, TM Mozart, Nenda, Magi, the boarders, the servants and I became the minimized many, whereas my father and his pothole discoverers became the non-minimized few.

A letter arrived from Mrs. Bandaranayake, on government stationary with a newly inaugurated stamp in commemoration of SWRD's birthday.

'Dear Mr. Weerasinghe, due to your commendable services the honourable prime minister, Sirimavo Bandaranayake, of the Socialist Republic of Sri Lanka invites you to escort herself and the honourable ministers of the highways department on a government sponsored congressional excursion to the Republic of the Maldives…' Ammi walked out of the room before Thathi could finish the letter. She took me with her.

Nenda packed Thathi's suitcase while Ammi called him a traitor. 'Thathi, why are you going to the Maldives?' I asked my father as he was writing postcards to his sisters informing them that he was leaving the country.

'Because I have been invited to go.'

'Why have *you* been invited?'

'I don't know.'

'Why don't you ask?'

'One should not question the ruler of the nation, one does what one is told.'

'But then you asked about why she changed Ceylon to Sri Lanka no?'

'Well, that is a different type of matter.'

'How different is that matter?'

'That is a matter affecting all people born in this country. It is our civic duty to know why the nation that we have been born in is now being called by a different name.'

'Is it not your civic duty to know why you are going to the Maldives?'

'No. That is not a civic duty, that is an order I have to follow.'

'Is it not the civic duty of Mrs. Bandaranayake to answer your postcard and say why she called Ceylon, Sri Lanka?'

'Well, receiving an explanation would have been commendable, but giving me an answer does not belong to her civic duties.'

'Does she have any civic duties?'

'Running a good government.'

'Is she doing her duty? Siya is always blaguarding her. He says it is because of her that we have no Maldive fish and the pol sambol tastes like tissue paper. Mrs. Adonis is always blaguarding her saying it is because of her that she has to die all alone in her house without any of her children, Ammi is always blaguarding her saying it is because of her that the headline on her palm is not travelling anymore and Magi and Nenda are always blaguarding her that it is because of her that we have no Podian.'

'Well, I cannot say that she is doing a bad job of running a country being a woman who had no experience when she entered the political arena. As you know, she entered politics only after SWRD was killed. As they say, she did not want to enter politics but people in the party forced her to do so.'

'Well she could have said 'No'.' I was always saying 'No' to TM Mozart who was constantly trying to borrow the blue denim shirt that aunty Lydia had sent me from England. Until now my 'NO' had worked. Saying 'no' to running a country was certainly easier than saying 'no' to an annoying brother.

'How could she have said no when the party kept insisting…'

I always say no when TM Mozart insists.

'She is a good speaker and has the people on her side. Of course she has made mistakes, but all humans make mistakes, so why should she be an exception? Secondly, when you run a country it is humanly impossible to satisfy every single citizen. One has to minimize priorities and work towards the general stability of the country, not the individual…'

I realized that my father was on his way to becoming a good socialist. He was beginning to find excuses for people, things and actions, which under non-socialist normal circumstances were inexcusable. Eureka! I was beginning to understand politics. Like TM Mozart's brain cells, mine were beginning to grow too.

'Go, go, go… and don't come back. Bloody turn coat that you are. Now she is putting him in a plane and sending him to the Maldives. Maybe he is holding her hand too in case she feels airsick. Now he is saying she is doing a good job of running the country. A few months ago the story was different. Go! And don't come back! And keep her with you in the Maldives! I am sure I, or Magi or even Mummy would do a better job of running this country than your precious Mrs. Bandaranayake. You are telling your daughter about civic duties! You think you are doing your civic duty? Measuring the length and breadth of potholes and holding onto a mountain that is collapsing or writing to that woman asking a meaning of a name is not a civic duty. You do your civic duty first to your family and then to your bloody country!' My slim waisted, sharp nosed mother gyrated and contorted like a Raksha. Gene manipulated housecoat flapping, cherry blossomed bath cap dripping, she was the personification of the furious demoness Manodhari. Ravana's chief queen and mother of their son Indrajit, railing against him for the insult to her, of having brought Sita to their palace, regardless of his intention.

Thathi grabbed his suitcase and left the house before my mother could dash it on his head. Ammi was certainly suffering from not being included in the exemptions of minimization. I don't know why my father went to the Maldives and I think he didn't know either. Perhaps it was because of the blue Hillman or the potholes on the Colombo Airport road. Or it was simply because Mrs. Bandaranayake needed people to practice the partial implementation of minimization, and my father whose fortune was on the escalating side of karma since my birth accidentally became one of the few. But why the Maldives? The world was full of beautiful countries and historical monuments, but there was nothing in the Maldives!

'If you can't hold her hand then hold onto her *sari pota*!' Ammi was still the demoness Manodhari shouting through the open window as the government vehicle drove down the lane on its way to the airport. 'Don't think I will be here when you return. I am going to Lydia's and I will never come back.'

That is where my mother's resemblance to Manodhari ended. She did not believe in fighting a losing battle. She did not create an epilogue to the Ramayana. My mother created her own story. Her way.

She wrote a long letter to aunty Lydia.

If only Manodhari had been more like my mother! Ravana would never have kidnapped Sita and Hanuman would never have burned our country. Sita would have been just another doe-eyed fair skinned princess in just another kingdom and no one would have bothered to immortalize her beauty in the epic of the Ramayana. At our cost! We were vanquished because she was foolish and ran behind a deer when she should have stayed indoors and written a letter. Like my mother.

A new era in the left to the centre socialism was ushered in. It was the era of nationalization and the institutionalisation of preferential treatment of governmental supporters. The impartial civil service metamorphosed into the partial government service. Government servants, like my father, were partial. People like my mother, could metamorphose into the Raksha Manodhari and shout through the window as the state resource vehicle drove my father to the Bandaranayake International Airport. But her din was not heard. My mother was a dis-partial member of a private service. The pawn in the government's minimized game of chess. The socialist statistic! My grandparents, Nenda, Magi, the servant and I were part of the same statistic.

'Don't shout like that mad woman Manodhari,' hissed Nenda.

'I shall shout how I want; I am not a turncoat like that man.' Nenda, who loved Dudley as much as my father, was at a loss for words. For the first time.

Personally, I don't understand why Mrs. Bandaranayake sent her non-minimized, partial government servants on a holiday to the Maldives. It had nothing of interest. It had living fish and dead fish in the form of Maldive fish. My father was not interested in either. He ate pol sambol without Maldive fish and didn't utter a single word of complaint. Until recently, he thought the goldfish in our tank were tadpoles. How on earth a partial civil servant who was once impartial could mistake a gold goldfish for a tadpole is a mystery in itself. But that was my father. I don't know what advantage Mrs. Bandaranayake would have gained by sending people such as him to the Maldives!

Besides the dead fish and live fish, the Maldives had the sea. But to see the sea, one did not have to go to the Maldives, it was supposed to be somewhere here too. If I was Mrs. Bandaranayake and I wanted to make the impartial government servants into partial government servants, I would have sent them to China, Egypt, or Babylon. I am sure their impartiality would have grown into double partiality if they could have seen the great wall, the pyramids or the hanging gardens. When the world has seven wonders, why on earth would one go to a country which has no wonders at all? Only fish? Even in the midst of socialist minimization, 'fish' was not a wonder. Dead fish were in the market and the live fish in the zoo.

On page four of my second hand atlas 'map of the world', the Maldives was nothing but a stack of barely visible dots. These dots, when put together were even smaller than my teardrop country. If I were prime minister, and had forgotten what the seven wonders of the world were, I would have sent my partial government servants to London, Paris or Japan. London had the Queen and Buckingham Palace. Paris had the Eiffel tower while Japan had Fujiyama. I think I would have insisted on London or Japan. Paris was not that important, I was not particularly hot on towers. But seeing castles and queens was something wonderful.

After all, where did we have castles and queens in our country? King Kashyapa had lived on a rock; all the other kings who had come before and after him built boring Buddhist temples, Stupas and Dagobas but not castles. Kandy, the hill capital had one castle, but there were only bald headed non-glamorous Buddhist monks and the Buddha's decaying tooth in that castle. Mrs. Bandaranayake, I am sure would have certainly loved to have been born a queen, but she wasn't. Hard luck! The British deported the last king we had in 1815 to Vellore in India. And where the king had stood, the English planted their un-creatively coloured and designed Union-jack flag, made us a part of their commonwealth and made us say, 'God save the king,' in English. But we spoke no English at that time. So we learned. Finally, when we said 'God save the king' in English, our king was in Vellore, and another God was saving their king who was wearing a crown full of Ceylon stones.

It was their god. Our gods had gone to Vellore with King Sri Wickrama Rajasinghe. The Buddha had cleverly distanced himself from everything and remained in Nirvana. After we said God save the king, the English planted tea, gave us Jesus Christ in a different form to the Portuguese or the Dutch and linked us with the commonwealth. We were satisfied.

We were no longer that infamous Lanka where the ten-headed kidnapper of Sita had lived and ruled. We were now the proud owners of Ceylon tea and the subjects of a king who wore a crown with our stones. Of course the tea plantations belonged to the British, but the tea grew on our soil. Ceylon tea! The whole world drank it. The Hanuman-scorched earth gave the tea that tinge of perfect bitterness that no other soil possessed.

What did the Maldives have? Nothing, not even tea.

Thathi could have written back to Mrs. Bandaranayake saying, 'Dear Madame, unlike the Maldives, the following countries have architectural monuments worthy of visit, considered wonders of the ancient and modern world. China: the great wall. Egypt: the pyramids. Iraq: the hanging gardens of Babylon. Greece: the Acropolis. India: the Taj Mahal, France: the Eiffel tower. Italy: the leaning tower of Pisa. England: Buckingham Palace. If you need further information please contact me, I shall be delighted to inform you. Yours sincerely, TW Weerasinghe.'

But he didn't. He went to the Maldive islands without writing a word of protest to Mrs. Bandaranayake. Ammi wrote letters to aunty Lydia. Not one, but many. Besides that, she did not tell us what she was doing.

Thathi returned from the Maldive islands with two suitcases. One full of dirty clothes and the other full of Maldive fish. Siya came out of his slumber and invited all his ten brothers for dinner and they played cards and drank arrack the whole night, eating Maldive fish. Even Ammi softened. She was after all Siya's daughter and she had the same culinary preferences as him.

Now I understood why Mrs. Bandaranayake had sent her impartial government servants to the Maldives. Impartiality became express partiality when presented with a suitcase filled with Maldive fish. Buckingham Palace or Fujiyama would not have had the same effect.

The minimization of Maldive fish was still a rigorous precept of the Bandaranayake era. But now its minimization was only applicable to the impartial members of the local population. The citizenry who were partial to Mrs. Bandaranayake did not have to face the crisis of minimized Maldive fish. When the partial members had Maldive fish, so did their impartial families.

We discovered the black market.

This black market was not in the cooperative store. It was everywhere else. As the queues in front of cooperative stores became non-existent, other doors opened and closed, opened and closed, opened and remained open... Mrs. Bandaranayake's socialism had triumphed. There were no more queues in front of cooperative stores. Obviously, the population explosion had enough to eat.

My grandmother started her own black market. She raised the rent for her boarders. She said, 'If you want to eat pol sambol with Maldive fish, you have to pay more for your board and lodging.' Rather than boarders leaving, more joined. The news spread fast that my grandmother was the only boarding mistress in Colombo who served pol sambol with Maldive fish for all three meals. People did not care about cost, they only cared about the quality of food. Achi's business thrived.

11

Mrs. Bandaranayke surpassed Isaac Newton or Galileo Galilei. She came up with another new idea. Non-alignment. It was our new road to discovery. Self-discovery, identity, self-identity, third world identity. Ravana was mythology, Ceylon tea was history, nirvana was hazy. Non-alignment was the present.

She aligned us with other third world leaders who no one else in their right minds would align themselves with and gave us the title of the Non-Aligned Socialist Republic of Sri Lanka.

We aligned ourselves with Muhammad Gadaffi of Libya. A lonely desert nomad who owned vast amounts of sand. Then she allied herself with Marshall Tito of Yugoslavia. He was so humongously fat that when Mrs. Bandaranayake stood beside him for photographs that were published in the non-independent newspapers, even her far from less than emaciated widow's form looked like a Biafra child next to his socialist corpulence. Marshall Tito's wife was even larger, and the photographer's lens being too small to capture her whole, only one of her breasts appeared in the photograph. She was known to us as Marshall Titi.

Mrs. Bandaranayake's alignment went further. She aligned herself with lots of African heads of state. They all looked alike like a bunch of Idi Amins from countries I did not even know existed on the world map. The second hand atlas did not have these countries. The silver fish had eaten most of the pages.

She then aligned herself with leaders of Arab states. They were all dressed alike, and carried the same rosary, but in different colours. I don't know why we wanted to be aligned with them, for they looked like they were aligned only with themselves. Interestingly enough, Mrs. Bandaranayake didn't get the non-independent newspaper to take photographs of her with them. Either they were not photogenic or they did not like to be photographed with women. Soon after they came and left, there was a general commotion at the petrol sheds.

On the other side of non-alignment, the price of Ceylon tea had reached rock bottom and the treasury was empty. If people wanted to go abroad they had to go as paupers for Mrs. Bandaranayake refused to let them take money out. Not even their own money! But all hope was not lost. We got a new and colourful map of the world. It was titled 'The World map of Non-Aligned nations'. We were all multi-coloured. I couldn't understand why anyone in their right minds would want to leave our country when heads of other colourful non-aligned states were coming here.

Gadafi's Libya was green, Marshal Tito's Yugoslavia was red and we were pink. This new non-aligned map had neither rivers nor mountains, neither towers nor palaces. Except for the beautifully coloured non-aligned nations, the countries that were not non-aligned were a dull shade of greyish black. I was proud to be non-aligned. Hanuman's mango seed, which had turned into a teardrop, was now pink. Pink was my favourite colour. I no longer coveted Buckingham Palace or Fujiyama. Those countries were greyish black. We were pink. The future was pink. And bright.

The roads were cleaned, the culverts unblocked, the mosquitoes vanquished, the canals cleared, houses whitewashed, flats built, the potholes covered and Mrs. Bandaranayake's hair dyed.

In that year that we became pink, Mrs. Bandaranayake was elected the president of the non-aligned movement and their summit conference came to our pink country. I don't know much about their movement, but ridding our capital of mosquitoes and unblocking the culverts was a commendable effort.

Sharona and I were elated. While the household had their afternoon siesta, we got onto our bicycles and rode to the Bandaranayake Memorial International Conference Hall where these multicoloured non-aligned heads of state drove in and out of the gates. Sharona stole the Buddhist flag from her grandmother and I stole the Ceylon flag from Nenda. We parked in front of the gates and waved our flags back and forth in pride, as these large bullet proof Mercedes Benzes drove in and out of the gates. Asantha covered up for us.

The next day he joined us. As we pulled out our Buddhist flag and the Ceylon flag, Asantha pulled out his own flag and waved like a hurricane as Marshall Tito and Titi drove in. His flag was pink. Pink! Pink like the new Socialist Republic of Sri Lanka on the new non-aligned map of the world.

Sharona and I returned the stolen flags and returned to the BMICH with our own new flags. In pink.

Our excursions were discovered when Sharona's mother, having woken up earlier from her afternoon siesta, wanted to wear her pink sari and have tea with Mrs. Adonis.

When we finally returned, we were caned. Our bicycles were padlocked and one person in each household had to forgo their afternoon siesta and watch us. Sharona and I sulked and refused to repent. We believed in Mrs. Bandaranayke's non-alignment. Asantha cried. He had not participated in cutting up the pink sari. His pink flag was a white piece of paper that had been coloured pink with the new pink Homerun pas crayon that had appeared with non-alignment.

Sharona's mother had plenty of saris, as did my mother and Achi. Amongst these many saris belonging to the three parties there were many pink saris. I don't know why we were caned and imprisoned because of one pink sari.

It was obvious that these women had no sense of identity. Neither a national nor a third world identity. They were all reincarnations of Sita. Instead of making the best out of her captivity in Ravana's Lanka, she spent her days crying over her spilt milk. Rama.

Magi and Nenda, in their kitchen quarters were like non-alignment's squabbling partners. They were independent, but imprisoned. Nenda needed Ammi and Magi needed Achi. Mrs. Bandaranayake was independent and non-aligned, but she needed Chou En Lai's China for survival even though China was not non-aligned. Ethiopia and Somalia were non-aligned, but they hated each other. So they received money from countries which were not non-aligned and fought with each other between the summits. The Arabs were the cleverest. They aligned themselves with Allah and controlled their own oil. Without oil there was neither non-alignment nor any other alignment. Idi Amin aligned himself with the Arabs, killed his non-aligned opponents and built tons of mosques so Allah would call him to paradise. Vietnam was non-aligned and invaded Cambodia which was non-aligned. But in the jungles of Cambodia and Vietnam every human being was aligned.

Then, Mrs. Bandaranayake got rheumatic arthritis by sitting around in the air-conditioned BMICH. Since she was now president of the non-aligned, she no longer had to stand in queues like the rest of the population explosion to see a rheumatologist who may have remained in our country despite minimization. She just jumped into a plane at the Bandaranayake International Airport and flew to her friend Marshall Tito's Yugoslavia where most of the rheumatologists had gone to escape minimization.

Dagma visited us with granduncle Cecil and their daughter Kusita. I liked Kusita. She always told me, 'Akka I like your colour, you are so nice and fair.' Kusita had a birth defect. She was born without some cells behind the eyeballs that were capable of distinguishing colour. Her eyeballs only distinguished between black and white. 'Be thankful for small mercies!' said Achi as Dagma lamented about Kusita's birth defect, 'She is not blind.'

I wished the rest of the human population was like Kusita. Especially my father's sister Seela, who never failed to mention my ever-increasing blackness. I would pray every night when aunty Seela would leave after visiting us:

'Dear Lord Buddha, may goodness come to all living beings. May they not suffer and may they have enough to eat, but please make aunty Seela live in the same black and white world as Kusita, I think it will do her a lot of good and she will have an easier time entering Nirvana. But if it is not possible to remove the colourful cells behind aunty Seela's eyeballs, I think dear Lord Buddha, you should consider making her dumb. Not deaf, only dumb. For every time she opens her mouth she says something to hurt the feelings of other people and blocks her own path to Nirvana.'

Dagma, granduncle Cecil and Kusita came to visit because Dagma's leg was on its way to becoming the leg of the elephant man again. It had begun at the ankle and risen to the knee. Achi took one glance and diagnosed the same illness as Mrs. Bandaranayake. Dagma had not attended the air-conditioned non-aligned summit at the BMICH, but she too had got Rheumatic Arthritis. Achi sent her straight to hospital. She took a number and stood in a queue in the nationalized hospital in order to consult the rheumatologist. After five hours her number was still not called. Dagma had not made a donation to the clerk who called out the numbers in the free medical service of the Socialist Republic. Dagma returned. By the time she realized that a donation was necessary, the Socialist Republic's free medical service rheumatologist had already left for his private practice.

Achi rubbed some home made oil on Dagma's knee and told her, 'Dagma, what to do? You have to learn to live with it. Avoid eating heaty food and it will not get any worse.' Dagma kissed Achi goodbye and said, 'Sister Beet, avoiding heaty food is certainly not a problem.' Dagma and granduncle Cecil were non partial members of the overpopulation who had no access to the black market. Their diet consisted of rice and dhal. Both unheaty. The goat they had in their garden that gave them heaty milk was slaughtered and sold. In the black market. Goat meat was too heaty for Dagma's consumption. With the money they earned from the slaughter, Dagma consulted the free medical services rheumatologist in his private practice.

Marshall Tito's rheumatologists treated Mrs. Bandaranayake's rheumatic arthritis every year in Yugoslavia. Dagma visited the private practice until the money from the slaughter of the goat was over and thereafter wobbled around. Despite Yugoslavia, Mrs. Bandaranayake wobbled too. So, it was a mystery as to why she wasted so much petrol flying to Yugoslavia, when Dagma who did not go to Yugoslavia continued to wobble just like she did. In the meantime we began to push the blue Hillman. Our country was running out of petrol.

My family did not like non-alignment. They found it extremely expensive and unnecessary. Sharona and I thought the opposite. Non-alignment was something above everything else. It was a compensation for the four holes on the school wall where the world map once had hung. It was compensation for the daily rice and dhal. It was compensation for the yam between the Karapincha tree and the dogs' kennel. It was neither English, nor Sinhala. It was neither history nor geography. It was neither commerce, civics nor moral conduct. It was neither Christianity nor Buddhism. It was international. Sharona and I were pink. And pink was international. We were international. The new emerging women on the wings of Venus.

We were no longer and island.

12

In commemoration of the non-aligned summit, a new postage stamp was released. It was the longest stamp ever. Mrs. Bandaranayake was to the top left and SWRD to the right. The rest of the stamp was occupied by the BMICH. I don't know why these new postage stamps still carried a picture of SWRD. He was long dead. I think our stamp makers should take an example from England. Of course the letters that aunty Lydia and her children sent us had extremely ugly stamps; they were one dull colour and small, with the silhouette of the same queen. But, the queen on our stamp was an alive queen, with a dead SWRD. I was a stamp collector and I hated seeing the face of some dead man on every stamp. Instead of SWRD, I think the new postage stamp should have had Marshall Tito. Of course the stamp may have had to increase in size, but it was also possible to decrease the size of the BMICH.

Thathi received a new job. He was to build a road to the Veddha regions. The elections were nearing and Mrs. Bandaranayake's non-alignment had not brought her the votes she had lost to Dudley's death. Now she wanted to entice the Veddhas into her non-aligned dreams. But first, a road had to built. Thathi began to pack his bag with Nenda's help.

'Where do you think you are going?' asked Ammi.

'Madame has given me a job I have to complete before the elections.'

'So your Madame is more important to you than your own family, am I right?'

'I have to serve my nation.'

'And neglect your family I suppose?'

'A man's duty is to serve his country until he is fifty-five and thereafter, whatever he sees fit.'

'At fifty-five a man cannot serve, he is dead.'

'That is bad luck. But until fifty-five, it is my duty to serve the state.'

'So I suppose you are going to hold on to falling mountains again. And when it finally falls down you will come back here with concussion?'

'I am being sent to an area without mountains.'

'And may I ask what you are doing in this area for your precious Madame?'

'Completing a road before the election.'

'And may I ask why before the election?'

'I did not see fit to question Madame as to why I should complete the road before the election.'

'I suppose blindly serving the state until you are fifty five is also the duty of the man who is serving the state and not serving his family before the age of fifty five.'

'You could it put it that way.'

'I suppose you consider that you have made a right decision?'

'It is not for me to decide.'

'I suppose it is for your Madame to decide?'

'As the representative of the state, Yes.'

'I suppose as a wife I have no right to decide.'

'Not unless you represent the state.'

'So I suppose I have to become a prime minister before you do what I tell you to do?'

'Only until fifty five.' And Thathi got into the highways department vehicle and drove off to the Veddha region; a brown flat land with short bushes, snake holes and a bit of paddy cultivation, with neither mountains nor black faced monkeys.

After Thathi's departure, the card and arrack parties with the Maldive fish increased. Siya's ten brothers came every night. Ammi did not join the parties. She continued her long letters to aunty Lydia. My parents disapproved of cards. Thathi called it a waste of time and Ammi, though she did not say it loud, agreed with him. Nenda called it the kingdom of Ravana. Alcohol, spicy food and womanisers. I would have liked to belong to Ravana's kingdom, not to the pious Rama and the virginal Sita, but no one asked my opinion and automatically included me in the pious portion of my family. I peeped through the curtain enviously. They were having a ball. Karunawathie brought the ice and uncle Hubert's hand had gone from her knee up to her thigh. Even Magi giggled like a young girl when she served the Maldive fish sambol. I don't know why she giggled, I didn't see any of my granduncles touching her thigh. I was sure that no one in their right mind would touch her thigh. She was old, withered, cow catchered, and had thighs bonier than Hansel, before the witch had fattened him. On the other hand, Magi usually served the ice to the other side of the table where granduncle Steven usually sat. I only saw uncle Hubert's hand from my curtain hideout. Not granduncle Steven's.

I was angry. The servants were having a better time than I was. I was stuck in the bedroom forced to listen to sermons by some monotonous Buddhist priest that was broadcast during the same time my granduncles played cards. Nenda and Ammi insisted on me listening to these sermons every night. Ammi pretended to listen, but wrote to aunty Lydia instead. Nenda and I sat next to the radio. Listening? She nodding, me peering through the hole in the curtain.

Every night, night after night. The same card parties, the same people. I began to hate Buddhist priests. The servants' laughter echoed across the house. On nights Mrs. Bandaranayake implemented curfew before the end of the card game, my granduncles would spend the night. Then, there occurred a peculiar phenomenon in our house. The servants who usually slept under the dining table where the card games took place were put into Magi's quarters and the door between the servants' quarters and the masters' quarters was padlocked and the key joined the vast number of keys around my grandmother's waist.

My grandmother loved keys. She did not adorn herself with gold like my mother but decked her ample waist with keys, from the Maldive fish to the Rosenthal crockery chests. Of course, the servants neither stole Maldive fish nor Rosenthal crockery, and none of my granduncles used the floor space under the dining table to sleep on, so it was certainly confusing as to why Achi always increased her load with the added burden of another key when my granduncles decided to spend the night in the visitors' rooms.

'Nenda, why does Achi lock all the servants in the kitchen when the granduncles are here to sleep? She doesn't do so when Kandapola siya comes here to sleep?'

'You are too small to understand.'

'I am not too small, I am as big as you.' The space between Nenda's knees had kept widening. At the beginning of every year, she was shorter than the year before. We were now nearly the same height.

'It is not height that matters, it is the age.'

'When will I be old enough?'

'I have to wait and see'

'Why is Magi not locked in the kitchen quarters like the rest of the servants?' Magi now took Karunawathie's floor space under the dining table.

'She is as ugly as death. Anyone seeing her in the night will only scream in fear.'

'Who is going under the table at night to look at her face?'

'No one. That is why Magi is under the table and not Karunawathie.'

'So that means someone is going under the table when Karunawathie is sleeping there. Am I right?'

'I didn't say so.'

'Then I don't understand what you are trying to say?'

'I told you, you won't understand until you are bigger.' And she went into the bedroom to listen to the Buddhist priest's seven thirty sermon. She didn't ask me to join her that night. I think she had finally realized that I would never become the kind of Buddhist that would enter Nirvana through radio broadcast.

In the middle of this commotion of locking the servants in the night, misplacing the keys between morning and night, and unlocking the servants in the morning, the worst happened. That which my mother said would happen did happen. That which every one else said would not happen and did not want to happen, happened. The impossible happened. My father was missing in the Veddha region, and my mother was about to go missing in the commonwealth. Aunty Lydia finally sent the pre-paid ticket that Ammi had been writing for since the last monsoon.

Uncle Buddhi drove TM Mozart and me to the airport. We could not enter the airport without buying a visitor's ticket. Uncle Buddhi paid twenty rupees and bought one ticket. Only one person was allowed to enter the airport with one travelling passenger. Both TM Mozart and I were too young to come out of the airport alone after Ammi was gone. So, uncle Buddhi locked us up in his car in the car park and escorted Ammi to departure.

'Aiya, why can't we go inside the airport anymore?' I asked TM Mozart.

'Ask Mrs. Bandaranayake,' he replied and stretched his legs on the back seat and closed his eyes.

'Why do we now have to buy a ticket for the airport?' I pestered him.

'Non-alignment is expensive. No one gives us food for nothing,' he replied with his eyes closed.

'Why is uncle Buddhi taking Ammi to the airport and why is Thathi not here?' TM Mozart the first had begun to snore. Who knows how long it would take? Air Ceylon was usually delayed. I wished I could fall asleep as fast as TM Mozart.

TM Mozart and I became post non-aligned orphans. I felt miraculously free. No tuition teachers, no teachers telling tales, no PV1, 2 or Buddhist priest sermons. Welcome cards! I was finally about to learn something that was useful and fun!

I was like a bud about to blossom in the post non-aligned international Socialist Republic of Sri Lanka with its vegetarian façade and Maldive fish black market.

13

Ammi went. Thathi was gone. Chou-en-Lai died. I gave the impression of attending to my homework and awaited the card players as the Buddhist priest started his sermon. Only Nenda was at the radio. But the card players did not come.

Another day came and went. They still did not come.

Yet another day, yet another silence.

The arrack bottle remained untouched and the pol sambol on the dining table no longer had Maldive fish. Siya ate it without a murmur. There was no usual play of choleric. Was the black market over? While Achi slept, I stole her Maldive fish key and opened the teak chest. The Maldive fish was in plenty, beginning to gather fungus. I hid the key between my panties.

Another silent evening. Another meal without Maldive fish in the pol sambol. Achi did not search for the missing key.

Avidly, I searched the newspapers for an explanation for the fungus gathering Maldive fish in the teak chest whose key I still possessed. Mrs. Bandaranayake was not dead, Dudley was not resurrected and SWRD was celebrating another death anniversary with all the Buddhist priests in Sri Lanka wishing him eternal life in Nirvana. Life was the same as it had been always. Thathi sent a post card: 'Keeping fine. No rains. The land is cracked. Aunty Magdalena's servant making delicious dry zone food. Yams available in various forms. If money is required ask Buddhi, I shall reimburse him later. Shall not be coming this weekend. Going to visit my mother. Tissa.'

Thathi was staying with grandaunt Magdalena who lived in the dry zone between the Veddhas and the paddy fields. Grandaunt Magdalena owned paddy fields and a large house with many rooms that were rented out to foreign hippie like people studying behavioural patterns of the Veddhas. Thathi was the first person to live in her house who was building a road to the Veddhas. She liked having my father with her. She could discuss the stupidity of foreigners who had nothing better to do than study the behavioural patterns of Veddhas. She couldn't understand why one human being would study another human being, especially when it was doubtful if this being was human at all! Naked and tree climbing, they seemed to her, closer to monkeys than to humans.

Grandaunt Magdalena was profit-oriented. She wasn't like Mrs. Bandaranayake. She believed it was far more profitable for the foreigners to study paddy cultivation, than Veddha behavioural patterns. At least then, they could return to their countries, plant paddy fields and eat rice. Not that repulsive chewing gum they chewed all day and then dropped on the road after chewing for her unsuspecting servants to tread on. Aunty Magdalena had to buy extra coconut oil to remove the chewed gum from her servant's naked feet.

We received a letter from Ammi. She was eating Cheddar cheese, Cadbury's chocolates and Mc Vites digestive chocolate biscuits. She had got a job at Woolworth's so TM Mozart and I were not to get any clothes sewn. She would buy us all the clothes we needed when this Woolworth had their annual sale. As an employee, she was entitled to a fifty percent discount off the annual sale price.

Life was as normal as ever. So why did the card parties stop like the sudden arrival of the black market and the suitcase of Maldive fish? 'Nenda, why aren't Achi and Siya playing cards any more?'

'SShhhh,' she replied in a whisper. 'Not so loud.' I wasn't even allowed to talk above a certain volume about cards.

Nenda whispered something and left the room carrying the basket of dirty clothes. I tried following her. But she went with the dirty clothes into the bathroom and locked the door saying she was going to bathe. She normally bathed only once a week and I knew that she had bathed yesterday. 'You bathed yesterday,' I shouted through the door and awaited a reply. No reply came. The one-inch wooden door no longer transmitted the sound of words. Only the sound of water.

Whispers echoed in our 186 home. Everyone spoke in whispers, Achi, Siya, Nenda, the servants, even TM Mozart. But one person did not talk at all, and that was Magi.

The monsoon came again; just one monsoon not two. The roof began to leak again. The buckets were kept under the falling rain and nothing was said about calling labourers to repair the roof. It rained and it rained. The buckets were emptied and replaced. In silence, without words or male labourers.

No one walked the dogs down the lane for their shit. They did it in the garden. The shit was then removed with a spade and emptied into a dustbin. Without words. When the dustbin man came Siya tied a handkerchief around his nose and took the bin out for collection. Not the servants.

The front gate got a brand new padlock and a key. The key joined Achi's collection of keys around the waist. The maldive fish key was still under my panties.

Then a mailbox was attached to the gate. The postman no longer rang the bell and hand delivered the letters, he now rang his bicycle bell and put the letters into the mail box. By the time Siya went to collect the letters the postman was gone.

The delivery of fresh milk and the delivery of bread were cancelled. Achi bought yeast and baked her own bread. It did not taste like bought bread. But it was supposed to be good for the teeth, hard like rock.

Then, someone came to collect Dasa. He was to be taken to the village where my other grandmother lived, in order to attend the village school. I don't know why he had to attend school now, when he had never attended school before. I suppose Dasa's lucky streak was coming to an end. All good things come to an end one day. I never had a lucky streak, I always had to attend school. The man who took Dasa away gave us two sack loads of pineapples. One sack with raw pineapples, the other ripe.

First Podian disappeared. That was Mrs. Bandaranayake's fault. Then my father. That too was Mrs. Bandaranayake. Then my mother. Again Mrs. Bandaranayake. But, I could not imagine that Mrs. Bandaranayake had anything to do with Dasa's disappearance. Dasa was a bit older than TM Mozart. If Mrs. Bandaranayake didn't want TM Mozart, she certainly wouldn't want Dasa. TM Mozart was good at cricket. Dasa wasn't even good at floor polishing. He was only good at eating the best pieces of chicken, when the rest of us got the bones. 'Nenda why is Dasa gone?' Nenda went for another bath. Her third in one week. I had by now realized the futility of following Nenda to the bathroom. The wooden door was sound proof.

I went to Magi. Perhaps she could give me an explanation. I liked Dasa. He played with me. Magi was sitting on a stool between the dog kennel and the Karapincha tree eating pineapple. Raw pineapple.

'Magi, why is Dasa gone?'

'Aney I don't know, you have to ask your Achi.'

'You don't know why?'

Magi didn't answer, she ate pineapple instead. Then she vomited the pineapple into the drain near the Karapincha tree. I increased my distance from Magi. I did not like vomit.

'Why are you eating pineapple when you are vomiting?' I asked.

'I don't know, ask your Achi,' she replied, eating more pineapple and vomiting into the drain. It was all very curious. But I no longer had the desire to stay and find out the curious connection between Dasa, the pineapple and Magi's vomit.

I felt like vomiting myself.

14

Russia had launched a sky lab to gather information from space and now they were saying there was something wrong with it and it could crash-land anywhere on this earth. Even in the Socialist Republic of Sri Lanka. Were we on the threshold of losing our non-alignment?

The card parties ceased. The quality of food declined. Achi broke two teeth and Siya broke three. Magi was so busy eating pineapple that she had no time to sift the stones from the rice. Without the usual choleric, Siya ate the food and even found a dentist who hadn't emigrated, and had his teeth fixed. Achi stayed with her broken teeth. She did not want to leave us alone while her teeth were being repaired. 'How to leave these children?' she lamented. 'They have no mother, no father. All are gone. With or without teeth I have to stay here, and one day, when their parents return I shall get my teeth repaired.' Mrs. Adonis hearing her lamentations offered to stay with us. 'No, no, Mrs. Adonis,' she bleated, 'that is too much of a responsibility for you. I promised their mother I will keep an eye on them morning, noon and night. I have to do so until she returns. You know Mrs. Adonis, I am now old. This is a massive responsibility for me. Two growing children. But what to do? Even if my time comes to die, I cannot do so with peace of mind. How can I die when these two children have no mother or father to look after them?'

Achi had never spoken about death, but since Ammi and Thathi's departure she was always dying, and when she was not dying, she was in the exhausting process of deviating the karma of death with Mrs. Adonis' assistance. They had begun praying together.

One was bad enough. But since Achi began talking of death, Mrs. Adonis had decided not to be separated from her good friend in this life or the next. Lo and behold! She left the lovely Roman Catholic religion with their Christmas parties, carol singing sessions and non-vegetarian Poya days and joined my grandmother and grandfather in Buddhist austerity. In the meantime, Magi was getting fatter. Around the stomach.

Thathi sent another postcard. 'Dearest Mummy and Daddy, keeping fine. Land is still cracked. No rains. The sky-lab landed in aunty

Magdalena's roof garden. I did not hear it, but aunty Magdalena and the servants claim it could only be the sky-lab. They claim that no other noise could be so loud. Even smoke had been observed. Aunty Magdalena is extremely upset about what the village people say because the sky-lab has landed in her home out of all the homes on this earth. She believes she has been cursed. She is contemplating beginning a series of Bodhi Pujas in order to deviate the curse. I shall not be coming this weekend. I shall instead visit my mother. Road progressing well. Should be able to complete before elections. If you require money please contact Buddhi. I shall reimburse him later. Regards, Tissa.'

Thathi hadn't visited us since he left. Not that it mattered, both TM Mozart and I were perfectly fine. But Nenda was upset that Thathi was only visiting his mother and not us. 'I shall write and tell Mali that he never comes home since she is gone,' Nenda threatened. 'Why do you want to do that?' I asked, 'We are fine, aren't we?'

'It's not a case of being fine or not fine, but a man has to learn that he has a duty towards his children, not only his mother.'

Without even being aware of it, Nenda had begun to echo Ammi.

Magi's stomach was becoming bigger. The sky-lab, though it had landed in aunty Magdalena's roof garden, was supposedly still out there, somewhere in space. Could it be that the Russians were concealing the fact that there were two sky labs roaming in space?

'Nenda, Magi is getting fat isn't she?' I asked. Nenda picked up the dirty clothes and went for another bath. A new week had begun, it was Tuesday and already her third bath for the week. In the Socialist Republic of Sri Lanka, as in the former Ceylon, people do not usually bathe on Tuesdays. Even the termination of card parties could not induce a human being, who had the desire to live, to bathe on Tuesdays. Bathing on Tuesdays was self sacrifice, suicide and no one who understood Buddhism or the love of self would bathe on that day. Tuesday was the day Mars, the fiery, red and belligerent god of war entered the body. Putting water on Mars inflicted his warrior spirit and debilitated him. If Rama had bathed on a Tuesday and set out to battle Ravana, he would surely have lost and this glorious kingdom of Lanka could have still been ours. Pity he did not!

But curiously, since the end of the card parties and the beginning of Magi's protrusions, Nenda, who dared not bathe on days that Mars was heating her body spent two hours in the bathroom, bathing. My world was losing its population. Dasa was gone. Ammi was gone. Thathi was gone. Podian was gone. Was Mars following Mrs. Bandaranayake's minimizations and leaving the zodiac to non-alignment?

Magi was about to go as well. I felt it in my bones. She was beginning to look like a Bangladeshi victim of famine. All belly and nothing else. If Nenda continued to bathe on Tuesdays she was sure to go as well. If it continued like this, only TM Mozart, Mrs. Bandarnanayake and I would be left on this planet. Alone.

I ventured towards the bathroom for answers. The bathroom door was still sound proof and Nenda was debilitating Mars. The sack of raw pineapple was over. Magi had eaten and vomited the whole sack. She had now begun to devour the sack of ripe pineapples. I shouted through the door. I heard the sound of water, but no one heard me.

Then the calamity happened. A tooth in Nenda's denture broke. The megahertz in house number 186 increased. And, for a moment in the history of post non-alignment we reached a momentary moment of normality. Noise.

'My tooth, my tooth,' Nenda yelled. 'You bloody woman, can't keep your body to yourself? Old hag that you are, now we have to suffer! Right, right, like a great one someone offered to sleep under the table. Aney! In the night, no one knows if it is the devil or the angel under the table. Only the devil under the table thinks it is the angel and doesn't tell the blind man groping under the table that she is the devil and not the angel... Aney, aney! I don't care who fumbles with the devil or the angel, that is of absolutely no importance in my life. But who suffers? WE. I. I, who was happily asleep on my bed, lose my tooth because this devil's hag is busy eating pineapple and has no time to sift the stones from the rice. No, no, she has time only to fumble around under the table when normal people are asleep!'

Before the drama ended I had to leave. It was morning and it was a school day. Sharona's father was horning like a mad man at the top of the lane, waiting to drive us to school.

By the time I returned, post-non-aligned normality was again in the atmosphere. Silence. Magi was still eating pineapple. Achi and Mrs. Adonis were searching for stones in the rice and Nenda was in the bedroom listening to the 2pm sermon by the Buddhist priest.

Her face looked like the moon after being ravaged by a meteorite. 'Nenda, what is the matter?' She did not answer me, instead covered her mouth with her hand. I finished lunch and returned to Nenda after the Buddhist priest had finished preaching. 'What is the matter?'

'What could be the matter? My dentures are with the dentist until the tooth is repaired.'

'Was it so bad?'

'You ask me if it's bad? Of course it's bad. You and Aiya are at our mercy and your parents are happily roaming the world thinking they have nothing better to do than roam the world, leaving the responsibility of you two to us. I can't even die in peace. What will happen to you and your brother when I am dead? Believe me, I don't want to die in greed. I don't want to die thinking about you and Aiya, and I don't want to return to this house after death, like Mary and Joseph, the avatars of greed. I want to go to Nirvana. After all I have sacrificed in my life to look after you and your brother the least compensation I can get is Nirvana.'

'Nenda, If you want to die, please do so. Aiya and I are capable of looking after ourselves. Please don't let us stop you from going to Nirvana. But, I didn't start this conversation because of death or Nirvana, I just wanted to know how your tooth was?"

'My tooth? What tooth? The whole mouth is with the dentist and I have to run around with this hollow until the tooth is repaired.'

'Come to think of it, you don't look too bad.' I grinned cheekily.

'Don't irritate my mouth,' she threatened but could not utter another word. She was a toothless caricature of her former self. I returned to the topic of Magi. Nenda was still angry with her, perhaps I could get some answers. Anger was the pivotal emotion in the quest for truth.

'Nenda, Magi is getting fat isn't she?'

'What do you expect?'

'She is not fat from the pineapple is she?'

'No. Not from pineapple, from the black prince!' A breath of sarcasm entwined with anger. The direction was correct. I was nearing the truth.
'The prince under the table?'

'Princes don't creep under tables to sleep with servant women. Human beings creep under the table to sleep with servant women.'

'Which human beings?'

'Womanising, card playing, intoxicated human beings in trousers.'

'Like our relations?'

'Did I say something like that?'

'No you didn't.' But I had got my answer. Perhaps not clearly defined as I would have liked, but I don't think anyone in our household had clearly defined answers to Magi's stomach. If the beast could be mistaken for the beauty in the night, under the table, then that intoxicated person creeping under the table was equally indefinable. The obvious fact was that this growth in Magi's stomach was the reason for terminating the Maldive fish and card parties. It was the reason for the Maldivefishless pol sambol and it was the reason for the silence. It was the reason why my father did not come, it was the reason why Dasa was gone, but it was not the reason why my mother was in the commonwealth. The 'It' growing in the stomach was karma not attributable to Mrs. Bandaranayake. Karma didn't know the difference between beauty and the beast and the beast sleeping under the table could be impregnated, just as fast as the beauty. Rama had berated Ravana;

> *"Call yourself a hero, abductor of Sita?*
> *Defenceless and alone, what chance had she*
> *Against your brute force? Hero you think yourself -*
> *Molester of women, thief and coward..."*

But in post-Ravana Lanka, in our house number 186, no one could berate anyone. In the blackness of night there was no difference between Rama or Ravana. Rama's Aryan whiteness appeared as dark as Ravana's Dravidian blackness. There was no difference between beauty and the beast. Karunawathie had grown into a beauty. But, she had been locked in the servants quarters the day the beast was fumbled with under the dining table. A dark act in the blackness of night.

Like Lava and Kusha, the twin sons of Sita, who sang the tale of the Ramayana composed by Valmiki - the story of Rama, the incarnation of Vishnu, first born son of the royal sage Dhasharatha, of Sita the daughter of another royal sage Janaka, of Manthara the servant of Dhasharatha's third wife Kaikeyi who planted in Kaikeyi's head the seeds for Rama's exile, of Sita and Lakshmana who followed Rama to exile. And Ravana, the ascetic king of Lanka…

> *And the people sat and listened*
> *Enraptured they listened*
> *Their faces pearled with tears,*
> *Like dew dripping trees in the forest*
> *On a windless morning.*

As Rama rode his horse past Ayodha town he heard the voices of Lava and Kusha reciting the mellifluous words of Valmiki. The Ramayana. The epic of fortitude and compassion. The epic of Rama and Sita. Sita's twin sons, born in exile, were also his sons. Doe eyed replicas of him and the beautiful Sita. Lakshmana, his brother had uttered the words, 'As you ordered, I abandoned the daughter of Janaka on the banks of the river near the beautiful Ashram of Valmiki. Why feel remorse? That is Kaala. Time. What grows, decays; what rises, falls; we meet to separate; we live to die. Separation is inevitable. Be prepared, be detached.'

> *The time is now ripe, to narrate to the world*
> *The epic of wise Rama, of Sumitra's son Lakshmana*
> *Of Sita, and of the Rakshasas*
> *Of Ravana*
> *Who was not unwise.*

The sack of pineapples finished. Magi stood next to the Karapincha tree and became a jumping jack. Her breasts flew in the wind like the pink non-aligned flags Sharona and I waved in celebration of Mrs. Bandaranayake's rheumatic arthritis causing non-alignment, with Marshall Tito and Mrs. Titi.

> *This war, this struggle, was not for your sake, lovely Sita*
> *I did what I did to wipe out the shame, on my family name*
> *And now with rumours, everywhere floating*
> *Regarding your character*
> *Your presence hurts like bright lights to sore eyes.*
> *So go where you will, daughter of Janaka. I give you leave.*

> *I have no more need of you*
> *What man of honour will take back a woman*
> *Who has lived in the house of another,*
> *Just because he loved her once?*

If the pineapples had their way, Magi's child wouldn't be born to relate an epic of fortitude and compassion like the twin sons of Sita. Not knowing the father of the child in Magi's stomach we kept Magi and fed her pineapples. Knowing the father of the sons in Sita's stomach, Rama banished Sita from his life. His wife.

> *"And do you expect, a man of my lineage to accept you again?*
> *I have won the war, my honour is redeemed.*
> *I have no feeling for you.*
> *You can go where you please.*
> *I have made up my mind. My decision is final."*

Lakshmana left her on the doorstep of Valmiki the hermit's humble home and returned to Ayodha, to Rama, the victor of this epic war. Ravana, Kumbhakarana and Indrajit were dead. Lanka was no more. Vibhishana who betrayed his own brother Ravana, ruled the city of ash. Lanka. He died childless. Karma. The severed heads which had once belonged to the great king, rolled on the remains of Lanka, and submerged themselves in ashes and dust. The tale of Lava and Kusha entered the pages of the Ramayana, to gather more dust. It was over.

If exile had been the purpose of this wondrous rescue where Hanuman the simian son of the wind god sprung back and forth across the Palk strait with the Himalayas upon his palms and fire blazing his tail, if exile had been the purpose of Kumbhakarana's death, if exile had been the purpose of Ravana's fearless son Indrajit's death; if exile had been the purpose of Ravana's death, why on earth did Rama's virtuous clan destroy an entire civilization to rescue one woman?

Magi entered the Guinness book of world records as the longest jumping jack.

15

We received another postcard from Thathi. 'Dearest Mummy and Daddy, keeping fine. Still no rain. Aunty Magdalena's servant preparing delicious yams in various variations. I helped in the search for sky-lab. Found pieces of china like material on the roof garden. Origin unknown. No obvious similarity to tiles or rafters. Presumed connected to sky-lab. Directly or indirectly. But, seven thirty PM, world news reported sky-lab still revolving in space. Obviously, china pieces on roof garden not caused by sky-lab. Cannot imagine seven thirty world news giving false information. Perhaps other explanation can be found. Perhaps, speculations on extra terrestrial activity are more than mere speculations. The sky is clearer here than in Colombo. It is possible that extra terrestrial activity is existent. If terrestrial activity is possible on this planet, there is no logical explanation that excludes similar activity on other planets. Shall write further on this topic once research has been completed. The explosion, which was mistaken for the falling of the sky-lab was caused by the gas refrigerator. Road progressing with hindrances. Doubtful if it could be completed before the elections. If money is needed ask Buddhi. I shall reimburse him later. Shall not be coming to Colombo this weekend. Shall be visiting mother instead. Regards to children. Tissa.'

That was the time that Arthur C. Clark, the greatest writer of science fiction (I knew none other), became a naturalised citizen of the Socialist Republic of Sri Lanka. We, as a nation built a bridge of karmic connection, to space.

My grandfather was cross with my father's quest to prove the existence of extra-terrestrial activity. He was cross that Thathi was wasting time on aunty Magdalena's roof top without being on the ground completing his road. He went on a mission choleric, a rocket Apollo mission, vertically up.

'That chap should stop wasting time searching for extra-terrestrial activity and broken sky labs. Who cares if the sky lab is broken or not and who cares if there is extra-terrestrial activity or not? That woman Bandaranayake is doing enough harm with her terrestrial activity... can you imagine Beet, if there are more people like her in outer space? Now we have chaos. But the end of the world is not far away. Tissa should continue with the job of work he was sent to do, and finish it.'

Achi pacified him. 'Tissa would not waste time studying extra-terrestrial activity if it wasn't necessary for our existence. If there is good china on Magdalena's roof garden, perhaps we in this country can learn how to make good china too.'

I understood my father's extra-terrestrial search. It had a direct relationship to Arthur C. Clarks' non-natural resident status in the Socialist Republic of Sri Lanka.

The world had many countries. Many great countries. Countries with kings, queens and world wonders, but Arthur C. Clark made our country his home. Why? People from our country were going to other countries to live because of minimization. Despite minimization Arthur C. Clark had come here to live. Why would a man of such astronomical prominence choose Hanuman's mango seed to live on? I had no answer. I didn't know him.

But, since Arthur C. Clark became a naturalised citizen of our country, my father stopped searching for potholes on the road, looked up into the sky, and found potholes there. Karma prevented my father from becoming a science fiction writer like Arthur C. Clark. My father had no telescope, only binoculars. In the Socialist Republic of Sri Lanka the co-operative store did not sell telescopes. Nor did the blackmarket. My father's connection with Mrs. Bandaranayake gave him access to Maldive fish, but not to telescopes. But my father was a socialist genius. So, he learned to use his binoculars to observe space.

Aunty Magdalena's ladder, now placed on the roof garden, brought my father closer to space with his binoculars. If he had had a telescope he could have observed from the ground and not risked his life climbing ladders. 'The grass is always greener on the other side,' he had told aunty Seela's eldest daughter on her wedding day, 'but you have to be happy with the grass you have.' I suppose the binoculars were like the grass on our side and the telescope was like the grass on the other side. Thus, without pomp and pageantry, standing on the ladder, my father laid the inaugural brick in the quest for extra-terrestrial diversity. If Arthur C. Clark came to live here of his own free will, despite the Maldive fish minimization, we must be closer to space than the rest of the world.

Magi's stomach reached the longest horizontal point and ceased to grow further. It was like the terminator, the dividing line between the illuminated and the non-illuminated parts of the moon. The difference between night and day.

Mrs. Bandaranayake's elected term was coming to an end. Saturn was entering her constellation. The glory of the non-aligned summit with photographs of Marshall Tito and Mrs. Titi was memory. The Arab oil owners fumbling with their rosaries was memory. Even the attractive Muhammad Gaddafi was memory. Minimization was still rampant. The cooperative store was empty. The black market had become too expensive. The people were angrier than ever. They were so angry that they had begun to strike all over the place. The left to the left of centre supporters of Mrs. Bandaranayake were instigating the workers to strike. Even the postman and the garbage collector were on strike. The garbage was collecting outside the gate and mosquitoes were beginning to breed in the coconut husks that had fallen out of the bursting garbage sacks. Fortunately, coconut husks were by-products of the eco system and it was a matter of time before they disintegrated and joined with the earth and the mosquitoes had to seek other homes.

Discussions did not help. The workers refused to return to work. What the workers wanted, Mrs. Bandaranayake refused to give and what Mrs. Bandaranayake offered, the workers refused to take. Then, one wonderfully bright and sunny morning, Mrs. Bandaranayake ceased discussions and used the same tactics she had used in the eradication of the red fungus that was still incarcerated behind bars. The postman returned and the garbage was removed. Their faces were different. But, who cares, no one really looks at the faces of the garbage collector or the postman. My mother's letters did not come. Presumably the postal workers were striking in the commonwealth as well. What the commonwealth needed was a Mrs. Bandaranayake. Not some Tom, Dick or Harry who tried to rule them, and a queen who warmed her backside on a throne. My father's postcard came.

'Dearest Mummy and Daddy, I am well. Aunty Magdalena's servant is preparing delicious food. Yams in all variations. The mystery of the china on the roof garden has been solved. It was neither the sky-lab nor extra terrestrial activity. It was aunty Magdalena's servant who had been breaking the good crockery and hiding the broken bits in the roof garden. The servant has now been sacked. I presume a replacement for the sacked servant would not be difficult. People are having many children in these areas despite the scarcity of food. The people of the dry zone are thriftier than those of the wet zone. Every thatched hut has its own plot of yam in the garden. If you need money ask Buddhi. I shall reimburse him later. The road is more of a hindrance than progress. Details cannot be divulged in postcard. It is unlikely to be completed before the elections. Perhaps the postponement of elections is possible. I shall inform of this possibility once I study the constitution. If the constitution permits, it is advisable for Madame to postpone elections until road is completed. I shall be visiting my mother this weekend. Regards to the children. Tissa. PS: The study of extra-terrestrial activity needs to be postponed until I complete the study of the constitution. Shall keep you informed on progress.'

Siya flew into a rage after reading the postcard. He went into the kitchen and dashed all the clay pots against the wall and broke them. Fortunately it was after breakfast and before lunch. The clay pots were empty. Achi immediately called Mrs. Adonis, who came across with all her clay pots and remained for all three meals for the next few weeks until Kandapola siya's new driver came in the Morris Minor to buy new clay pots. Siya did not fly into a rage because of extra-terrestrial activity, he flew into a rage for the fear of Mrs. Bandaranayake postponing the elections and remaining the prime minister for life.

He dictated a postcard to my grandmother. 'Dear Tissa, Please do not read constitution…' Achi stopped him and suggested beginning the postcard with 'Dear Tissa, How are you?' Siya said it was highly unnecessary to ask my father how he was since he was obviously well, and was going to waste time reading the stupid constitution without finishing the road. But Achi refused to begin the postcard without 'How are you'. Siya went into the kitchen and broke one of Mrs. Adonis's clay pots. Achi called him out of the kitchen and said she would write the postcard without the 'How are you?' Siya began dictating again. 'Dear Tissa, Please do not read the constitution. If you have already done so, kindly forget what you have read. Furthermore, you do not have to tell Mummy or me, what is in constitution, for neither Mummy nor I are interested in what is in it. We only know that if someone like that bloody woman could come into power, it must be a bloody stupid constitution. It's high time she left her office and the country for good. We are sick of her. She is the worst ruler this country has ever seen. Even worse than SWRD. You Tissa, do NOT study sky-labs, constitution or extra-terrestrial activity. Finish the road before the election so we can finally get rid of her. Do NOT give that woman another reason to postpone elections. I may not have a degree like you, but I was born before you, and I have seen better times. We are now sinking into hell. Daddy.'

I don't know if Achi sent the postcard, but I saw her take something white out of her sari jacket and throw it into the kitchen fire. We got one curry less for lunch because of Mrs. Adonis's clay pot which Siya had broken.

16

After the postmen started work again, Mrs. Bandaranayake was without friends. The left to the left of centre former friends were angry with the way she had terminated the strikes and refused to support her further. Alone, from the left of centre, she began to talk about the postponement of elections. But, the talks of postponement alienated her from the rest of her friends who had remained even after the left to the left of centre had moved away. She began the search for new friends. The Tamils. Dudley's supporters.

Magi's stomach reversed direction. It began to decrease. Neither a child cried, nor did a pyre burn, it was as though the stomach had never been. I confided in Sharona and Asantha. As the household had their afternoon nap, Sharona, Asantha and I took spades and kitchen spoons and dug around in the garden for dead bodies.

Mrs. Bandaranayake nullified her Sinhala only policies and tried to entice the Tamils with her rheumatic arthritis and widow's wiles. The Sri Lanka broadcasting services played Tamil music on the Sinhala and English channels and Mrs. Bandaranayake removed her Kandyan sari and spent a few days being photographed in Indian sari. She looked like one of her own repatriation victims. I wondered whether we could have exchanged her for Podian?

Ammi called us. She said that she had no time to write because Woolworth was having their annual sale. She was happy eating Cadbury's chocolates, Mc. Vites digestive biscuits and apples. She asked TM Mozart and me whether we were doing well at school. TM Mozart spoke to her for a long time about his cricket scores. By the time it came to me, the telephone call became too expensive. She promised to call again when the Woolworth annual sale was over, and hung up.

Achi began a desperate search for the key to her chest with Maldive fish. Magi's decreasing stomach enabled her to cut up Maldive fish and put it into the daily pol sambol. The whole house began to search for it. I too. After the lock in the teak chest had been broken open and the Maldive fish was left in the sun to eradicate itself of its fungus, I remembered that the key was still under my panties. I put it into a hole which Sharona, Asantha and I had dug to search for dead children from

Magi's stomach and covered the hole with soil. Since the lock was broken, Achi needed another lock, not the key for the old lock. Gradually, Maldive fish started appearing with the pol sambol on the dining table. Nenda's dentures returned to her mouth. The crater Copernicus which had been the result of the missing dentures now disappeared and her fluency of speech returned.

She stopped bathing on Tuesdays.

Normality returned. We received another note from Thathi. 'My dear Mummy and Daddy, you are right, it isn't my duty to read the constitution. The life of a prime minister is karma, not constitution. I am presently contemplating cosmology and karma, and I think I will reach a conclusion soon. Shall keep you informed. The nights are clear. Mars was evident from aunty Magdalena's visitors' toilet window last night. It was like a red leather cricket ball in the sky. The road will not be finished before the elections. The grapevine informs that road completion is not necessary to elections. The minority Veddhas integrated into the election process after completion of the road will not make a fundamental difference to the votes. If it would have done so, we should have resurrected the indigenous tribes after independence. I hope history's mistakes would be redeemed one day. I shall not be coming this weekend. I shall be visiting my mother instead. If you need money, ask Buddhi. I shall reimburse him later. Regards to children. Tell them to use the subject history, as a mirror to the past. Regards, Tissa. PS: Extra terrestrial activity has not yet been discovered. When I return to Colombo I shall ask Arthur C. Clark what he thinks of the subject when I see him at the Otter Aquatic Club.'

Siya did not fly into a choleric fit after this postcard. But Nenda did. She uprooted all the Bougainvilleas and the Crotons in the garden and yelled that we two children, TM Mozart and I, were far too wonderful to have a karmic father like this. The old song, the same tune, with new lyrics. TM Mozart strummed the tune on his guitar and I designed a dress for my birthday which was coming soon. Off white, off shouldered, transparent, lace, looking like an Aryan princess entering her boudoir on the wedding night. Unfortunately I was still black. Aryan princesses were white. Perhaps there was some truth in Thathi's analogy of the mirror and history. Perhaps I should use the

mirror to understand history, not my karmic blackness. I continued to
design the dress. A maxi. I was a princess in Ravana's kingdom. Full
bodied, black and salacious. Not pale skinned, anaemic or bland.

Nenda re-planted the Crotons and the bougainvilleas and wrote
a long letter to my mother. I don't know what she said, but I believe she
didn't write very well of Thathi. I don't really know what problem she
had with him being away. After all, TM Mozart and I were fine. But I
think the truth of the matter was; Nenda missed Thathi. That was all.
TM Mozart and I understood her problem and were gentle to her
during this time. TM Mozart even played Sinhala songs on his guitar,
while I kept beat with two wooden sticks.

Then, like Asteroid 4923, aunty Lydia and her youngest
daughter came from the commonwealth. They brought with them
Edam cheese, Cadbury's chocolates and a dress from the annual
Woolworth sale which I was supposed to wear for my Birthday.
Goodbye off-the-shoulder, off-white princess from the court of Ravana.
I now looked like queen Victoria's anaemic Asian servant in a rejected
ripple which once belonged to the queen.

The dictionary had no words to describe this dress; neither did it
have words to describe its colours. It was bluish, greyish, creamish,
pinkish, dirtish, ashish, oldish, ripplish, curtainish, horridish. The
neckline rippled itself up to my chin like a paralysed butterfly. The
sleeves were long, rouged and rippled like two masturbating serpents.
The skirt was sole length and resembled the curtains at Donald's photo
studios that rolled up to the ceiling like a double helix of DNA. This
was the most horrific dress ever made. And they expected me to wear it?

It was my first birthday without my mother and it was the first
birthday that I contemplated inviting boys. Of course, these boys didn't
know that they were coming for my birthday since I had no direct
contact to them, but I was going to find a way. But now, with this dress?
My thirty four inch breast, thirty four inch waist and thirty four inch
hips became an all round forty five inches clad in this Woolworth
nightmare...

Before I could implement my sequence of action, Thathi returned
from the dry zone with a notebook on suspected extra-terrestrial
activity and a Fujicolour film roll to take photographs of me in the

Woolworth dress. He thought it was the most wonderful dress he had ever seen and made me wear it and stand under the Karapincha tree for photographs. Posterity, on studying this photograph would realize that the Karapincha tree looked extremely good in it. It was green and brown, with clearly defined dainty leaves that had halted their tropical tango for my father's Fujicolour shot.

I did not celebrate my birthday. Instead, I jumped from the dining table when the household was having their siesta and twisted my ankle. Before the jump I contemplated suicide, but I did not want to be put in a coffin wearing the Woolworth curtain. So I sacrificed my ankle and postponed my birthday party for another year, and prayed that aunty Lydia and her youngest daughter would not return with another Woolworth dress.

The Asteroid 4923 was named the Clark asteroid. Arthur C. Clark was the first Sri Lankan to have an asteroid named after him. Perhaps he was the only person in the world to have an asteroid named after him. And I was perhaps the only girl expected to celebrate the coming of the teens like a dowager Anglo-Saxon queen with Asian pigmentation problems. Forty-five inches all round.

17

Fortunately, aunty Lydia didn't remain long. Uncle Lionel suffered another heart attack during her absence, and she decided to take the next available flight. Before leaving, she cried buckets of tears, and hugged and kissed my grandmother on every single millimetre of her face. I hurriedly disappeared to Sharona's, fearing I would be kissed to death as well. I was no longer overly negative towards the kiss, in fact I dreamt about a kiss. But, this kiss of my dreams was not a kiss from aunty Lydia. My kiss would be from a handsome broad shouldered, slim hipped, male out of a Barbara Cartland novel… And we would live happily ever after. The end.

I barely sipped my 'Orange Barley' at Sharona's, when Mrs. Adonis shouted over the wall asking me to return home immediately. Aunty Lydia was leaving. The kiss was not to be missed. Aunty Lydia looked cross. 'My dear child,' she said in her senior school teacher tone, 'I must tell your mother that you are extremely badly trained. You do not leave the house when relatives are leaving the country? You must stay and bid farewell. Your grandmother and Nenda are spoiling you and not teaching you etiquette. Now look at your brother, before leaving for cricket practices, he kissed Pam and me. Furthermore, he gave this lovely long letter to be given to your mother. Have you written your mother a letter?'

I nodded my head in negation.

'Don't you think you should write her a letter?'

I nodded in affirmation.

'Now hurry up and write it while I finish my farewells to the lovely people in this household.' She went into the kitchen and held an eloquent senior school teacher speech for Nenda, Magi, the servants, the boarders and even the dogs.

When she re-emerged, I handed her the torn page from my exercise book on which I had written a letter to my mother. Aunty Lydia opened and read the letter. I wonder if that was etiquette? 'What is this child?' she said crossly, 'You do not start a letter to your mother with 'Dear Ammi' you must write 'Darling Ammi'.'

I tore another page from my exercise book and began another letter. 'My Darling Ammi, How are you? I am fine. Thank you for the dress you sent for my birthday. It was a lovely dress. I wanted to wear it but I twisted my ankle, I will wear it for my next birthday. So don't worry about sending me a new dress for I will wear this dress on my next birthday. Love, Chooti.'

Aunty Lydia conceded that I had formulated the letter quite well, despite my lack of etiquette, and that my mother would appreciate me thanking her for the dress. She also said it was a lovely gesture not to ask for another dress from my mother who was working very hard at Woolworth's to buy things for us. 'You could have written more,' she said. Fortunately it was time to leave for the airport.

Thathi took aunty Lydia and her daughter to the airport and disappeared back to the dry zone to continue his studies on extra-terrestrial activity. He left on his desk the list questions he had wanted to ask Arthur. C. Clark. His stay in Colombo had been too short for a visit to the Otter Aquatic Club. His first question began like this, 'Mr. Clark, since you have made Sri Lanka your home is it correct to assume that our country is closer to space than the rest of the world?'

First it was Ravana, now it was space.

Ravana had transformed himself into a deer to entice Sita away from her forest home. Once he had captured her, he re-assumed his form as Ravana, the king of Lanka and said;

> "Lovely Lady, may you prosper!
> My name is Ravana, I am ten headed,
> My half brother is Kubera, god of wealth,
> I vanquished him, and he fled,
> He now hides on Kailasa.
> I took his aerial chariot Pushpaka
> Seeing my fearful face,
> The Gods are terrified.
> Where I go, wind calms,
> Sun rays become moon beams,
> Rivers stop flowing,
> Tree leaves cease rustling.

Come with me!
Enjoy celestial pleasures!
Forget Rama:
What is he, but a mere mortal
Doomed to die?
I passionately desire you.
Accept me."

But the foolish woman rejected him. Ravana's eyes glowed, his black skin turned crimson, fire flamed out of his eyeballs, he changed shape, and changed shape again. His one head became ten and his two arms became twenty. He snapped his fingers and his golden aerial chariot materialized from the sky. He grabbed Sita with just one arm, put her into his chariot and flew away.

When my father returned I would tell him why Arthur C. Clark made Sri Lanka his home. Because of Ravana. And because of Ravana's aerial chariot.

While the rest of the world's great civilizations moved on camels and ships and were still trying to invent the wheel, we in Lanka had airborne chariots even before the Wright brothers invented the aeroplane. My father no longer needed to ask Arthur C. Clark whether it was the existence of extra-terrestrial activity that had brought him to Sri Lanka. It was. He had probably read the Ramayana before any of us ever had.

I sang 'Don't cry for me Argentina,' and headed to bed. Evita Peron had invaded Colombo and everyone was singing 'Don't cry for me Argentina.' The age of woman was really beginning to emerge, even for me. Kuveni, Sita, Mrs. Bandaranayake and now Eva Peron. TM Mozart heard my singing and put his head out of the curtain and asked: 'Is someone being sent for execution?' I ignored him, raised my head, flattened my hair twirled my hips and tangoed into my room. I was Eva Peron. My brother, a stupid cricketer.

I prayed to Lord Buddha that night, 'Dear Lord Buddha, when I am dead and I have to be reincarnated, please make sure that I have a beautiful singing voice. I don't want anything else at all.' I added a little PS: 'But please don't make me ugly.'

That night I didn't die. I didn't reincarnate. I crossed.

18

I crossed sometime between night and day.

Crossing did not mean that I crossed the Red Sea like Moses. Nor did I cross the Palk strait like Hanuman. My crossing was into womanhood. A simple, uncomplicated, bloody process. The same blackness, fatness, blackheads and pimples... only, they no longer belonged to a girl, they now belonged to a woman. Another typical Monday morning, I woke up and went straight to the mirror, another Monday morning pimple filled with pus, I took my index fingers and squeezed the pus onto the mirror. The battle against blackness was not over, a battle against pimples had begun.

'*Budu Ammé*!' exclaimed Nenda who was fidgeting around my bed.

'Not *Buduammé*, it's good morning,' I said, discovering another pus filled pimple.

'What is this on your bed?'

I did not look at the bed. I continued with another blackhead.

'*Budu Ammé*! she shouted again. 'And such a thing has to happen when your mother is out of the country. She has an easy life. Now, Achi and I are saddled with all these social problems. I shall book a call and ask your mother to return immediately.'

I turned the radio on. 'Don't cry for me Argentina' was on the air. I returned to the mirror. Except for the miserable pimples that were beginning to cover my face like miniature volcanoes, I did not feel any different to the day before.

'Don't leave the room until I return,' said Nenda, leaving the room with my bed sheet.

'I have to go to the toilet.'

'You can't go to the toilet until the men leave the house.'

'Tell me Nenda, have you been bitten by a rabid dog this Monday morning? And where are you going with my sheet?'

She opened my sheet out and showed me a dirty brown streak, barely evident.

'What is that?' I asked her.

'What do you think this is?'

'Dirt.'

'It is not dirt, you have become a woman.' She locked the door behind me and left the room. I pressed my legs and hoped I would not urinate on the floor. Eva Peron was still singing her heart rending sacrifice for Argentina and I had become a woman because the bed sheet was dirty. I am sure that Evita Peron had better beginnings of womanhood.

I concentrated on other matters to distract my bladder. I had crossed. I was getting fat. I was getting black and now had pimples. Eva Peron was lucky not to have been born an Asian. I decided that day, to take my destiny into my hands. I still did not know how.

Karma and Genetics had failed. My mother's relatives had faces that had more craters than the moon. My father's relatives had faces that were blacker than night. Seela, the only fair skinned sister had got a sudden pigmentation problem after being bitten by a bandicoot that her body did the reverse of what most bodies do. She did not get white, she got black. The iron deposits in her body didn't know where to go and planted themselves on her skin. She abstained from spinach, kankun, mukunuwenna and all iron rich foods, but the bandicoot that bit her leg had done hieroglyphic jugglery with Seela's iron storage, which no doctor could correct. Despite the complete elimination of iron from her diet, Seela became blacker. The pigments piled on top of each other. The iron that was absent in her food, she attracted from the atmosphere. In her proximity all other people became anaemic. Fair skinned Seela was now black. Only her lips were white, like an Albino. Her hair was blonde, like Eva Peron. But, she was as garrulous and obnoxious as ever. I wished the bandicoot had bitten her mouth instead.

Achi came into my room with her knickers in a twist. My bedroom key now joined the keys around her waist. 'Aiyo, child,' she lamented, 'all these thing have to happen when your mother is not here no?'

'Achi, I want to go to the toilet, I can't wait any more.'

'First drink this.' She handed me a tea cup. I swallowed the contents without observing or smelling. If my muscles had not been cramped trying to withhold the urine, I probably would have vomited after Achi's tea cup drink.

'Ugh! What is that? Are you trying to poison me?'

'That is milk coffee with egg.'

'I don't drink coffee.'

'When you grow up you have to. For the next few days, until the astrologer gives an auspicious time for your bath, you will be drinking a coffee every morning with two raw eggs.'

'Achi, I don't eat raw eggs either.'

'I don't care what you do, or do not do. You are my responsibility and I will now do with you, what I did for all the other girls I have brought up.'

'Why eggs?'

'Don't ask unnecessary questions. You are a woman and soon you will be marrying and having children. In order to nourish a child in your womb you have to be healthy, and now itself start nurturing your organs towards childbirth.'

'Okay, I'll drink coffee if I really have to. But with an omelette. Red onions and green chillies.' But, one couldn't make deals with my grandmother. She had brought up many girls who were now married and had many children. I, perhaps the last in line had no choice but to follow.

'Women can't nourish their organs with cooked eggs. They have to be raw.'

'Who said that?'

'Don't try to be too clever for your shoes. Just do what I say. One day when I am dead and gone you will appreciate what I have done for you.' Nenda knocked on my bedroom door. 'There, they have gone. Aiya is in school and Siya has gone to Mrs. Adonis. You can now go to the toilet.'

I spent the next ten days in my room. Coffee and raw eggs, no fried food and no men. Newly crossed, unbathed young women looking at men was detrimental to the existence of man. They had to avoid me and I had to avoid them. Nothing was likely to happen to me, but the existence of the man was jeopardized. The unbathed newly crossed woman was like the devil Surpanaka, Ravana's sister. She entices them, ravages them and causes battle. The end of a civilization. TM Mozart, Siya and Thathi had to be protected from me. Achi tucked the

key back onto her waist and left the room. Nenda put a sheet around
my head, covered me from head to toe and escorted me to the
bathroom.

'Now why are you covering me with a sheet? I thought you said that all
the men were out of the house?'

'That's right, but it is still good to take precautions.'

'Why don't you tie up my eyes as well?'

'Don't joke, you have to now learn to behave like a woman.'

'And how may that be?'

'You cannot go out until you are bathed, and you cannot go out at
night at all.'

'All the women I know go out at night.'

'They shouldn't. Especially if they have not bathed after menstruation
sets in.'

'Nonsense.' I went into the toilet and closed the door without letting
her enter. Nenda continued to shout through the closed toilet door
which no longer seemed to be sound proof.

    'You say nonsense and do what you want, and you know the
result? Have you seen that mad daughter of Roswitha's? She has to be
tied to the bed so that she does not run down the road naked during full
moon. She was once like you. But then she crossed and those people
didn't look after her. She went out to catch her cat in the night and the
black prince raped her. Now she has lost her soul and is stark raving
mad.'

    Roswita had a mad daughter. But no one had yet told me the
reason for her madness. I thought that she had been born mad. During
full moon one did not see her. But on other days she would drape
herself on the balcony and call all the names of the people living down
the road. If we responded to the call, she would say nothing but look at
our faces and laugh. Her laughter was extremely contagious and one
had no choice but to join her. She had a knack of eliminating
depression. I think she was the first psychotherapist the cemetery road
ever had.

    'Alright, alright, I will not let the black prince catch me, but
Nenda please I cannot drink raw eggs every morning, can you make me

an omelette or some fried sprat?'

'See that was another thing Roswitha and them neglected. How do those half burgher people know of our Sinhala customs? They had given the girl fried sprats to eat the night she went out to catch the cat and was raped by the black prince. When you have children don't ever forget that the black prince loves only two things. Newly crossed girls smelling of blood and fried foodstuff.'

Suddenly Siya's voice was heard outside. 'Hello, I am coming into the house.' Nenda quickly wrapped the sheet around me and pushed me back into the bedroom. I spent the next ten days incarcerated. The door was locked, the windows were locked. Kandapola siya's new driver came from Nuwara Eliya to organize the festivities. In the meantime, Mrs. Bandaranayake's elected term was gradually coming to an end. Neither my father, nor any one else seemed to be interested in reading the constitution and giving her a reason for extending her power. Her friendship with the Tamils was not progressing as she had wished. The Tamils were not fickle and of short memory like the Sinhalese. They had not forgiven her for implementing SWRD's 'Sinhala only' policy and repatriation. Friendships had failed with the Muslims too. When 'Sinhala only' came, the Muslims had decided to speak Tamil and continue their jewellery businesses with all communities. Their smattering of the other languages was sufficient for business, and the smattering of Arabic was sufficient for Allah. The Muslim was not like the Sinhala Buddhist followers of Karl Marx or Chairman Mao. They were clever. The son of the Muslim jeweller became a jeweller when his father died. The son of the Sinhala paddy cultivator became a job seeking revolutionary when his father died. Free education seemed to have failed in teaching him that rice filled the stomach, not the revolution.

I spent ten days designing the kit I was going to wear for my coming of age party. Blue denim bell bottoms. A red skinny, blue denim platform shoes. On the radio, Donny Osmond sang straight into my heart.

19

Achi entered my room with coffee eggnog and a notebook to discuss the sequence of events on that tenth auspicious day. I was lying on the bed staring at the Ceylon tiles. 'Get up, I want to discuss something with you.' I sat up.

'So it will begin like this: the dhobi will come at five-thirty am. Kandapola siya's driver will bring her. When she comes, Nenda will wrap you up in a sheet and take you to the bathroom. Then, at five-forty am, Kandapola siya's driver will knock on the door and the dhobi will put the first bucket of water on your body. By six-seventeen you will be finished with the bath. Then you will take the coconut which has been kept in the wash basin and dash it on the ground. You must break it in exactly two halves. Then you will dress in the toilet. Your lucky colour for the day is peach. Mrs. Perera has sewn you a peach coloured half sari...'

'Achi, I hate peach and I want to wear bell bottoms. I cannot enter womanhood in a half sari. That is like going to a temple.'

'It is your father's wish that you wear half sari...'

'Thathi knows about potholes and the milky-way, but he has no idea about fashion, can't you call and ask Ammi? Please?'

'I spoke to your mother and the matter has been settled. You will be wearing a peach half sari. That is it.'

'I want to talk to Ammi.'

'You can't go to the telephone until you have bathed.'

'Once I survive this, I will invent cordless telephones.'

'Good. After you come out of the toilet the first person who will greet you is your aunty Seela.'

'Why aunty Seela? I can't bear her.'

'She is a lucky person and in order to have luck in your life you have to encounter a lucky person immediately after bathing.'

'She is not a lucky person, all the luck she brought with birth has gone away. Look at her face! The beautiful white skin she once had is as black as tar.'

'Don't judge people by appearances. Seela is the only one of your father's sisters who has built her own house, a two storey house at that.'

'But she has seven children, and the last thing I want in life is to have seven children and become as fat and black as her.'

'She is the only one of your father's sisters who gave birth to seven children without a single miscarriage.'

'Achi, I refuse to come out of the toilet if you have Seela Nenda staring at my face.'

'It has been decided, your father has agreed.'

'How would my father know?' My father's village values were certainly different to my Colombo city missionary school values. Since I could not side-track my grandmother, I decided to close my eyes and come out of the toilet. I would rather look at the gecko on the wall than at Seela.

'Thereafter you will go to your room, have your hair combed, wear the jewellery I have kept on the dressing table and come to the dining room. Then you will eat *kiribath* for breakfast and you will remove your half sari and wear the peach cotton dress that Mrs. Perera has sewn for your daytime wear. In the evening you shall wear the peach half sari again and greet the visitors. Remember, when the visitors come, you have to behave like a woman and serve them their cake as soon as they sit down.'

'Why should I do it? Can't Karunawathie do it instead?'

'Has Karunawathie attained age, or you?' Achi left my bedroom with the empty cup of eggnog and the note book. The path to happiness was in the stars. With Achi as its executor.

Evening came. I wore the slippery, sticky butter nylon half sari and ruminated on the morning's happenings. The coffee eggnog had tasted the worst that morning. Five in the morning was more like night and my eyes had trouble opening. My bladder was full. My brain was full of Donny Osmond. I opened the door and went into the bathroom. My grandfather was just leaving the bathroom. I saw him. He didn't see me. My heart beat like Kandapola siya's Morris Minor on the day it had lost its silencer on the Kadugannawa pass. I returned to the bedroom without emptying my bladder. The dhobi came. She wrapped me in the bed sheet. All the men hid. The okay was given. I was taken to the bathroom. The dhobi turned away and I peed. She then tied the sheet onto my body and poured the first bucket of water onto my head. It was like bathing naked in the Alps. My brain forgot

Donny Osmond and became a single goose bump. But, the goose bump did not forget that it had seen its grandfather before its body had been cleansed. Kandapola siya's driver knocked on the door. The time for the coconut had come. The body was still full of soap. The clock was going too fast for the dhobi. With soapy hands I took the coconut, it slipped and fell onto the floor. The coconut did not crack, but a bathroom tile did. I picked up the coconut again and dashed it. Another tile cracked. The coconut remained intact. I picked it up for the third time as the geriatric dhobi told me through her toothless gums: 'You must hold the coconut like this, turn your body like this, and hit it like this, so that this part of the coconut makes contact with the floor.' I did as I was told. The coconut broke into smithereens. I went back to the tub of water to wash the soap off my body. Then I wore the peach half sari and went into the world outside the toilet. I forgot to close my eyes. My thoughts were still with my grandfather. He was old. But not old enough to die. The day outside the toilet was still black. The eyeballs dilated in order to adjust themselves to the darkness and missed Seela's black face in the midst of blackness. I saw only her white sari. And somewhere between the knee and the thigh, a big black spider was making its way up her Corpus hemachromatosis. One inch in diameter. Brown crown. Black legs. Yellow eyes. And a red birthmark on the left side of its torso.

I don't know whether my life as a woman was going to be lucky or unlucky. Astrology interpreted the working of planets on the lives of people, not the workings of spiders on the life of woman. When this was all over I decided to become an arachno-astrologist and predict my own future. I obviously did not belong to the rest of mankind.

Relatives, neighbours, friends, family, all came. My father was the last to arrive. The bus he had been travelling in from the dry zone had driven over an empty bottle of coconut oil lying on the road and had a flat tyre. The spare tyre had been the victim of an older bottle. Finally, when a spare bus arrived with a spare tyre, many hours had passed.

Shortly before dinner was served, Thathi arrived. He said that I looked like the re-incarnation of Princess Viharamaha Devi who had been sacrificed by her father to stop the floods. I wondered whether my father had been spending so much time with extra-terrestrial activity that he was losing touch with terrestrial activity. Viharamaha Devi was white. I was black. She was moulded in white marble in the Viharamahadevi Park. If I was capable of stopping a flood I would probably be carved out of black ebony. Until such time, my father fetched his Made in Japan camera, put in a Fujicolour roll and followed me around the house. I longed for a flood. Preferably before the film roll finished.

The peach butter nylon half sari was the worst Mrs. Perera had ever made. The blouse was tight. The frill too light and the skirt was a slithering skin that got caught between my legs, regardless of which posture I took. On this evening of the party, I used one hand to serve cake and the other to pull the half sari from between my legs. Butter nylon was not an appropriate material for half saris in the tropics.

Sharona's geriatric grandmother wobbled up to me and put ten rupees into my hand, which had just completed a repeat performance of pulling the peach butter nylon from between my legs. 'Daughter, what is this beautiful costume that you are wearing? Now-a-days young girls are not wearing skirts no, they are wearing trousers like men.' I thanked her for the ten rupees, gave her a piece of cake and went to the next guest. Aunt Seela's mother-in law, Anula. 'Ah daughter, give me another piece of cake. Your grandmother makes the most delicious cakes in the world. So, so tell… is this trouser suit you are wearing something which your mother sent from England?' It was time to pull out the butter nylon from between the legs. I gave her a piece of cake and went to uncle Hubert's wife who was waving her arms like a drowning chimpanzee who had fallen off Noah's Ark. 'Give me another piece of cake, darling. I haven't eaten anything the whole day.' It was hard to believe. She not only looked like a chimpanzee, but she looked like a chimpanzee that had eaten the food belonging to all the other chimpanzees before the flood had come. 'Now tell me, I did not bring my glasses, this thing you are wearing, is it a trouser or a skirt? I have been telling Dagma (who was sitting next to her with three pieces of cake that she had helped herself to at the first serving), that I am not sure if it is a trouser or a skirt. She has been telling it is a skirt, but I have been telling her it is a trouser, but sometimes I am not sure, I think it is a skirt. What is it?' Fortunately Kusita came up to me. 'Akka, I love what you are wearing. It is very beautiful. And it has such a beautiful colour. When you don't want it anymore can you give it to me?' Her retina was still oblivious to colour. But I loved her. I gave her the entire tray of cake and told her to eat it all. I went into my room to put gum between my legs to prevent the butter nylon from getting stuck between my thighs.

I re-emerged to serve 'Murukku'. By that time, my costume was history. My mother's absence had become the topic of conversation. Uncle Hubert's wife waved her arms like a dying chimpanzee, over-saturated, about to drown. I went up to her. 'Aney darling, can't you bring a bit more cake after you finish with the Murrukku, but before you go, tell me, when is your mother coming back? I thought she would have at least come back now to see you being a big girl in your trouser suit.' I promised to bring her cake and left. Seela's mother-in-law called me. She was sitting with three of my father's sisters and their mothers-in-law. I offered them Murukku. The bowl was now empty. 'Aney sit with us will you,' said Seela's mother-in-law Anula, patting the corner of her chair. 'I'll come later after I finish serving Murukku.' But they held my hand. I could not leave. 'Tell us daughter, what is your mother doing abroad? She has been gone a very long time hasn't she? Aney, I thought she would return at least now that you have become a woman?'

'Aney... our poor brother,' all my father's sisters lamer.ted together as I took my leave to refill the bowl of Murukku. My mother's departure was a titillating topic of conversation. The titillation caused by my convertible half sari was a previous chapter. I hated my mother for not being there. I hated her for going. I hated her for permitting Achi to dress me up in a peach butter nylon half sari. And I hated her for giving birth to me.

Another chimpanzee was waving her arms. It was uncle Buddhis's mother-in-law. A baboon, not a chimp. Thank God there had only been two of each kind on Noah's ark. I went up to her. I had met her only once before in my life, about a hundred years ago, at uncle Buddhi's mother's funeral. 'You remember me don't you child?' She did not talk. She whimpered. 'Of course I remember you Achi,' I whimpered back. 'Come sit near me and let me look at you properly. Aney, how you have grown. You are really beginning to look like your Seela Nenda. Aney, but daughter, what is wrong with your head? It is as dry as a saucepan on the fire. Doesn't your grandmother put any oil on your head? If Achi forgets to do so you must remember and do so. A woman must have a long head of hair, not a burned parchment on her head. Now where is that mother of yours?' Fortunately Seela and company under the Araliya tree diverted my attention. 'I must go now Achi, I will come back later.' *Bitch*. I did not look like aunty Seela. Certainly not. I would rather look like the black spider which had been on her white sari that morning. I headed towards the kitchen. Perhaps I could put my head into my grandmother's Kenwood machine and get blended into a new constellation of self.

Dagma caught me with her elongated tree climbing chimpanzee arms. Her leg was fattening again, but her arms were still agile. 'Now child, don't look so angry. You should smile. It is a big day for you.' I grimaced.

'So tell me, when is your mother planning to arrive?'

'I don't know.'

She shook her head, looked into my father's potholes in the milky-way and continued, 'She has been gone a long time, hasn't she?'

'I don't know.' More gazing at the milky-way.

'If you want to know, I will ask Thathi to tell you.'

'No need. You sit down and talk to me.' She looked at the sky and I looked at her fattening ankle. In silence.

'Dagma Nenda, can I bring your another piece of cake?'

'No thank you daughter, I had three already. It was very good. Who made it?'

'Magi.'

'Magi, I can't believe it, she has been with your family for so long. Is she still alive?'

'She was alive when she made the cake.'

She looked at the milky-way and laughed heartily. I, on the other hand did not know who had made the cake. The cake was my least concern on this festive day.

'So what is your mother doing in England?'

'She is with aunty Lydia.'

'That I know, but is she working?'

'I don't know. If you want, I will ask Thathi and tell you.'

'No need, you sit with me and talk.' I had been seated next to her for the last twenty minutes. She was talking, I was listening.

'This suit you are wearing, did your mother send it from England?'

'No, Mrs. Perera sewed it.'

'Is she still alive?'

'She was alive when she sewed this.' Another hearty laugh.

'But you still haven't told me if it is supposed to be a trouser or a skirt?'

Once more, I pulled the butter nylon from between my thighs.

'Chooti! CHOOTI! Daughter! CALL! Call. You mother. From ENGLAND.'

I had no choice but to stagger to the telephone. But I was in no mood to speak to her. Not tonight.

My father was bellowing into the receiver.

'HELLO! HELLO! MALI; it's me, TISSA. CAN YOU HEAR ME?'

My father assumed he would be heard clearer in England if he spoke louder into the receiver. 'YES; YES; MALI; WE ARE CELEBRATING. YES, SHE LOOKS VERY NICE. THE WEATHER? HOW IS THE WEATHER? IS IT SNOWING?'

It was April in Sri Lanka, I wondered whether it was a different month in England.

'HOLD ON; SHE IS COMING. HERE IS DADDY. HE WANTS TO TALK TO YOU.'

My grandfather took the receiver. Then he cleared his throat.

'YEEZ; MAELI; WIE ARRE DEWING VAIRY VEELL. YEEZ; YEEZ: GIIVE OURR RAEGARDZ TUE LYDIIA AND LIONEL. YEZ, YEZ THE PAARTIE IZ PROEGREZZING BRILLYIANTLYIE. YEZ, SHEE IZ LOOKIING VEERY MUSCH LAIKE AI LADIE. RIEGARDZ AGAIIN. CHEEIRIO.'

My grandfather tried to speak like the English when he was on international phone calls. It did not sound like the English that the English tourists spoke, but it was not the usual English spoken by us. It was different. Now it was my turn. I heard my mother's voice. Nasal. Far away.

'Chooti, how is the party?'

'Okay.'

'Is it nice what you are wearing?'

'Hm.'

'Why? Don't you like it?'

'Okay.'

'What colour is it?'

'Okay.'

'Have you received lots of presents?'

'Yes.'

'Nice presents?'

'Okay.'

'Do you want me to come back?'

'Okay.'

'Is there anything you have to tell me?'

'Cheerio.' And I hung up.

The party ended, the people left, I opened my presents. I received enough money for a ferry ride to south India. And gold jewellery to fill a trinket box in a doll's house. But I was a woman. Tomorrow, there would be no butter nylon. A new dawn.

Or another sunset? Karma would decide whether Mrs. Bandaranayake extended her term in office or not.

> *"O my dark clouded husband, dressed in golden yellow*
> *Dazzling with armlets, is it blood on your body?*
> *Why don't you answer me? Rise my lord. Rise!"*

Manodari pleaded with him to rise. But he could not. Ravana was dead. Would Mrs. Bandaranayake rise again? I did not know. And I did not care. Since karma could not prevent the election, perhaps the time had come to go. I had other worries. The worry of womanhood.

That night, not only did I take a Barbara Cartland, I also took a Mills & Boon to bed. And experienced the sweetness of 'ever after' with a cognac slugging count upon a black stallion. But before the arrival of 'ever after', he had killed the Australian outback type that had also desired me. (*the end*)

I woke up to Donny Osmond. Nenda was dressing herself in a horrendous green sari that looked like the skin of a tyrannosaurus rex. Nenda did not usually wear dark colours, she only wore pastels. Light skinned people looked good in pastels, it was only the dark skinned types like myself, who had to wear dark colours to alleviate our natural colour.

'Nenda, you look like an alligator. Why are you wearing such an ugly sari?'

'Mrs. Bandaranayake must lose.' It was election-day.

'Did the astrologer tell, that if you wear green and vote, Mrs. Bandaranayake will lose the election?'

'You don't need astrologers for that. Mrs. Bandaranayake is blue, JR is green. We must wear the colour we support in order to bring luck to the party we vote for.' JR was Dudley's replacement. He was not loved like Dudley, but with Dudley dead, Dudley's followers had no choice but to settle for a replacement. In Buddhism, there was no resurrection. Death is death. Of course re-incarnation was there, but reincarnation was not a part of the election process. Nenda believed that Dudley had gone straight to Nirvana. Ammi hoped that he would return through reincarnation. Perhaps by the time I was old enough to vote, Dudley would be a reincarnated candidate for the green party.

Except for my father, the rest of the family including Mrs. Adonis and Roswitha were dressed in green. Siya was in a frog green bush shirt and cow-dung green trousers, Achi in a guava green sari, Magi in a Karapincha green blouse and a crocodile green chintz cloth smelling of kerosene oil. Mrs. Adonis was in a raw-mango green sari with a chunky chain of green jade beads and Roswitha wore a grasshopper green dress, a Mukunuwenna green hat, a spinach green hand bag, blocked culvert green Binco slippers and combat green glass pieces around her neck which she claimed were emeralds. Only my father was neutral. Like Switzerland, in the middle of the green grass of Europe. He wore white. But, on the fourth finger of his left hand he wore a green Peridot ring. Not because he was a supporter of the greens, but the green peridot was supposed to protect him from bad times. Neutrality, astrology and love for green, my family and neighbours walked down the lane to cast their ballot. They looked like a group of green Goblins from Mars.

I hung onto the window and watched them go. They became smaller and smaller in the distance. Then the goblins turned left at the end of the lane and vanished. I ran to the telephone and called Sharona. It was time for mischief. TM Mozart did not understand mischief. He only knew how to play cricket and strum his guitar, and as of late the piano. Sharona came like a green Apollo rocket. She had to wear green for her mother had cried for Dudley too.

It was only once every so many years that we children could have the house to ourselves without adults. Every four years, the constitution claims that an election is due. Every four years, on election day, we children indulge in our creative possibilities and the world belongs to us. I do not like politicians for the simple reason that most of them want to eradicate this luxury. Once they come into power they always strive to postpone elections. I think they have no other interest but to rob us of our childhood and remain in power. Mrs. Bandaranayake stayed for seven years.

Sharona and I began our mischief in Achi's room. Achi had many treasures, for her eyes only. The keys were nowhere to be found. But, Sharona and I were masters of the hairpin trade. We stuck a hairpin into the keyhole and opened the cupboard. Satin sheets full of fungus fell at our feet. It was the wrong cupboard. We went to the second cupboard. Another hairpin. More sheets. This time, butter nylon. I discovered the origin of the peach butter nylon half sari. Another cupboard. All the things aunty Lydia had left when leaving for the commonwealth were there. Her children's report cards, vaccination cards, identity cards, wedding photographs, prize giving photographs, Queen Elizabeth's coronation newspaper cuttings, the Bible. We closed the door. Fortunately house number 186 had a countless number of cupboards. We hoped that the queue in front of the polling booth was countless as well. TM Mozart put his face though the curtain on his way to the toilet.

'I will tell Achi what you both are doing,' he threatened grinning.

'Aney, Aiya please, I promise to give you that new striped T-shirt which aunty Lydia brought.'

'Chee, I don't want to have that ugly thing.'

'The brown belt?'

'Cheekay, boys don't wear such belts.'

'Not goday boys like you, in England they wear these belts.'

'I want the blue denim shirt.'

'But that is my favourite shirt.'

'Okay, I will tell Achi then.' And he moved away from the curtain. Oh Shit! Pity he was not old enough to go to the elections. Another four years, and I would be alone here with Sharona and he would be gone. 'Okay, okay, I'll give you the denim shirt.' I hoped he would get flushed into the toilet bowl. I loved my denim shirt.

The family returned. The polling booth had been empty. I lost my denim shirt and had not found anything of interest in Achi's cupboards. I was depressed.

'Why are you all back so early?'

'People have all been so eager to vote that by eight in the morning most people had finished voting. By the time we went, the polling booth was empty.'

'You should have gone earlier.' I said angrily.

'Why? Don't you want us in the house?' asked Achi.

'No, but if you had gone earlier, you could have then spoken to the people and asked them whom they voted for and at least by now you would know who had won the election.'

'Child, haven't you heard of the secret ballot?'

'Why secret? You all talk about it all the time.'

'Yes, but what we talk here you can't repeat out of this house.'

'My parents are going to vote for JR,' Sharona contributed to the conversation.

'Your parents just left the house to vote.' Sharona and I looked at each other and thought together. During the next appropriate planetary movement we would jump over the wall, into her house, and into their cupboards. But for the moment, we smiled like two well brought up children posing for a Punch and Judy ad, and slithered in the direction of my room.

Siya took a book of Buddhism, sat on the arm chair and began a sermon. He liked having an audience. Roswitha and Mrs. Adonis were new disciples. Siya had never been an authority on Buddhism. He enjoyed beef and Maldive fish far too much to become a good Buddhist, but since we moved into house number 186, and since Mrs. Adonis and Roswitha had become an easy prey for Buddhism, my grandfather had become a Buddhist authority. Karunawathie served them tea. Roswitha and Mrs. Adonis put their tea into the saucer and did fu, fu, and began to drink. Siya began to preach.

'Nirvana is beyond ordinary words or concepts. In Buddha's own words, it is Peace. The Absolute. It is the end of the construction of human personality. The end of every trace that could be reborn. The death of craving.'

Siya's tea became cold in the cup.

'The death of craving is the beginning of detachment.' The tea became undrinkable. Roswitha and Mrs. Adonis had finished theirs. They were still new converts. 'Nirvana is extinction.'

Oh my goodness! I was really going to avoid doing good to end up in Nirvana. Imagine being excavated by palaeontologists searching extinct beings.

'Nirvana is unborn, un-originated, unformed. If the unborn, uncreated, unformed did not exist, escape from the world of the born, created and formed would not be possible.'

Now I thought Siya was talking complete gibberish. Mrs. Adonis and Roswitha looked perplexed. Achi came in with a tray of milk toffees. Siya did not eat, he had eliminated craving. Mrs. Adonis and Roswitha helped themselves.

'Suffering exists, but not the sufferer. The act is done, but there is no doer. Peace exists. But not the one who is at peace. There is a path, but no one walks it.'

The planets moved. Sharona and I catapulted over the wall.

'Your grandfather recites funny poems,' she commented.

'They are not poems, that is Buddhism.'

'In our house we don't have Buddhism like that.'

'What kind of Buddhism do you have?'

'The kind you don't understand.'

'You mean in Pali.'

'Must be.'

We hopped across the wall.

Midday arrived. Sharona's parents arrived. Afternoon arrived. Evening arrived. Then night. No one shouted over the wall for me. I decided to make my way back home in the moonlight. I did not jump the wall, I walked down the lane. Something fluttered above the gate. I rang the bell and ignored the fluttering white flag. Karunawathie came to the gate.

'Did the postman or the garbage collector die at our gate?' Her eyes were streaming with tears. She could not talk. I did not try to make her talk. I walked into the house trying to imagine the faces of the postman and the garbage collector. Someone was dead. If not there would be no white flag. I had to pass the visitors room to go to my room. Siya lay on the bed with his head towards west. A cloth tied around his face to stop his jaw from dropping.

He was dead.

The road
to the Right

JR became prime minister and my country appended another name. It became the Democratic Socialist Republic of Sri Lanka. The postage stamps too, metamorphosed. Instead of SWRD, Mrs Bandaranayake or the BMICH, they carried pictures of indegenous flora, fauna and temples. I think JR would have liked his face on the postage stamps, but with his seventy something years, no longer had a face that looked good enough to attract the foreign tourists to fill up the coffers depleted by minimization. The tourists streamed in to see Asian animals before extinction and Asian temples before erosion. For those tourists who liked neither flora, fauna nor history, but wanted to lie in the sun and become as black as Asians, some stamps carried beaches and coconut trees.

JR ascended to utmost importance. The mango seed at the edge of the Palk strait began to blossom. Then he changed the constitution, became president and gained more importance. The roaring majority he had received at the election made him the new Asian superman. We hoped our superman would live for a long time even though he was already seventy something years old. We liked having an executive president like the United States of America. It was nearly as important as non-alignment.

JR was no ordinary president. He was a 'Dharmishta' president. That is, a president who follows the teachings of the Buddha. Before JR became president, he was not even a dharmishta person, but now, he straight away became a dharmishta president. A new word entered our vocabulary. 'Dharmishta': a person who follows the dharma.

Of course, 'dharmishtaness' alone did not suffice and by itself, had no direction. The Democratic Socialist Republic needed direction. Mrs. Bandaranayake had made us go left. Since JR was the diametrical opposite to her, he put us on the road to the right. A dharmishta road to the right.

It had been said, that after the death of Prince Siddhartha who was known to the world as the Gautama Buddha (that was our Buddha who had left his foot print on the mountain), another Buddha would come. The Maithriya Buddha. The Gautama Buddha predicted his coming. But, did not say when. Perhaps the Maithriya Buddha was on his way, but, nearly two thousand five hundred years after Gautama Buddha, he was still nowhere in sight.

India, the land of the Buddha's birth had entered democracy in a blood bath and was now divided. She gave birth to an Islamic Pakistan and

Pakistan gave birth to an Islamic Bangladesh. Millions died. The Chinese invaded Tibet; the Dalai Lama fled, preaching non-violence, letting the Chinese practice occupation. Burma could not decide whether to be Buddhist or militant, Thailand could not decide between sex and Buddhism, Cambodia could not choose between communism and Buddhism. The left and the right were divided. In Sri Lanka, the Sinhala and Tamils were getting divided... but the Maithriya Buddha was still nowhere to be seen. Then, along came JR.

He came with seventy odd years and his tactical political history, and took the oath of dharmishtaness. In this new era of the non-ferocious dharmishta lion, everyone was to get what they wanted. All the colours of the national lion flag were about to glitter with self satisfaction. Every group represented in the flag would have their moment of hereditary glory. It was the era of dharmishtaness.

Not far away, the Gautama Buddha's decaying tooth in its golden casket began to rejuvenate. The yellow colour in the lion flag would become golden as the old tooth rocked on the back of the temple tusker as it meandered along this illuminated, televised, dharmishta road to the right.

JR went wild with dharmishta enthusiasm and began to perform one dharmishta act after the other. First, he released the red chimpanzees from jail. Then he gave the stateless Indian Tamils working in the tea plantations the same civic rights that were granted to citizens by birth. He eliminated the blackmarket and introduced the free market. He reduced the independent authority of the judiciary. He gave rights to minorities. Finally, his dharmishta presidential commission of inquiry found Mrs. Bandaranayake guilty of 'abuse of power' and expelled her from parliament, stripping her of her civic rights. He could now rule over Ravana's former kingdom like a king of dharma. There was no opposition. Dharmishtaness faltered.

Many years before he became dharmishta, JR had walked seventy two miles up the mountain, to the Kandyan hill capital, in a protest march to abrogate the Bandaranayake-Chelvanayagam pact, which would have given the Tamils more autonomy and self rule. But at that time, JR was not a Dharmishta president. He was not even in power. SWRD was in power. 'History will not thank me for what I am about to do,' SWRD is supposed to have said before tearing up the pact that no one had ever seen. He was right. *History did not thank him. However, SWRD only tore up the pact, JR led the march that demanded the tearing up of the pact. SWRD was a non-dharmishta prime minister who contemplated giving too much power to the Tamils; JR was good at rousing the masses.*

That was then. Now JR was dharmishta. He was in power. He was ready to be gracious. He was our own dharmishta president who amnestied the red chimpanzees and removed Mrs. Bandaranayake's civic rights. Now he was ready to re-create the Buddha from his two thousand five hundred year old tooth and the footprint on the mountain.

My father returned from the dry zone in a private bus. They were quick and had spare tyres. Even if the spare tyre was missing there was no fear of a tyre becoming deflated by a broken bottle. Plastic had invaded the nation. Coconut oil was sold in plastic bottles, and where plastic bottles were not available, plastic bags did the rest. My father was laden with plastic 'siri siri' bags full of imported apples, imported grapes, imported carrots and even imported onions. The imported apple did not taste as good as the local mango. But, the 'siri-siri bags' were of progressive value. They did not tear like paper bags. Achi folded the siri siri bags and preserved them under her mattress.

My father had not completed his road. The new minister of the highways department who had taken over the old ministry was undecided as to which company in which country he should grant the tender for the completion of the road. The world maps re-emerged. No longer pink and blue, but normal. Rivers, mountains, deserts… the usual. The new minister, no longer an Oxford or a Cambridge graduate, if he was a graduate at all, was confused by so many countries with so many different currencies that he had to study the currencies and countries before deciding who should build the road with which currency. My father was not informed of currency matters. Such matters were the sole responsibility of the minister, or his wife. Thus, as my father was whiling away his time, looking at potholes no one else looked at, the planet that had favoured him since my birth, brought him to the ministry of canal and canal development. He was appointed the chief executor for the clearing of Dutch canals in Colombo. Needless to say, the minister was responsible for fiscal matters while my father was responsible only for the algae.

My mother returned from the commonwealth. She brought a television set from the new duty free shop at the Colombo International airport which had been the former Bandaranayake International Airport. For the first time we had television in our country.

I liked JR. The dharmishta part did not particularly interest me even though I had become a vegetarian. Actually, I had become a vegetarian in order to lose weight. But, since everyone in the democratic Socialist Republic was having their moment of dharmishtaness I decided to contribute my vegetarianism to dharmishtaness rather than to weight. It was my way of saying 'I do'. Not in the sense of marriage, but more in a sense of 'I do agree'. JR, you are the superman.

The road to the right progressed with great enthusiasm. We became a proud nation of factory rejects. All those wonderful foreign clothes that were draped on the super models in the magazines aunty Lydia's youngest daughter sent me, were manufactured in our own country, and then sent abroad to clothe those emaciated creatures. Of course, they were not permitted to be sold here because they were produced in factories in the free trade zone which were something like foreign embassies on our soil. But, like everything in our country, there were enough people who were capable of stealing some of these wonderful clothes from these factory embassies and selling them on the local market. We began to look beautiful and foreign.

JR found out that many of these factory embassy products were being stolen and sold on the open market. He could not prevent it. We were on the road to the right. We were sick of looking like indigenous island inhabitants. He permitted the sale of 'rejects'. Legalised and dharmishta. A broken zip, a missing button, a cut out label… who cared? Disney, Dior, Armani… made us a content nation of factory rejects on their own road to the right. The man selling the rejects became rich and the minister who cut the ribbon at the opening ceremony of the factory embassy, even richer.

In the meantime, PV one and PV two dropped out of the syllabus and we returned to the commonwealth system of education. The written material within the subject was not commonwealth material, but the subject had a commonwealth title. So, if we passed all our exams with the commonwealth title and still did not manage to enter local university due to the regional basis of university entrance implemented by Mrs. Bandaranayake, it was not a huge problem. The commonwealth was deceived by our titles and accepted us to their universities. This education was not free. But, it was free economy and garment factory-embassy politics. The moment in history had come, when everyone could aspire to reach the greatness of Ravana. Wealth. Dignity. Dharma. And perhaps a kingdom…

JR substantially reduced free education and eliminated the standardised entrance into universities on a regional basis. He opened commonwealth universities and schools in our country. They were not free. But they claimed to be international. Where the word international shone like a beacon, a man would beg, borrow or steal to send his child to school.

It was like the Ceylon fisheries co-operation. When it was called Ceylon fisheries, they sold Ceylon fish and Ceylon prawn caught by the Ceylon fisherman. When Ceylon ended and the Ceylon fisheries became the Sri Lankan fisheries, the Sri Lankan fisherman did not catch Sri Lankan fish or Sri Lankan prawn for we were in the heart of Mrs. Bandaranayake's minimization. When the Ceylon fisheries became the International fisheries, they no longer needed fishermen to catch the fish or prawn. International experts, not fishermen, practiced longevity with antibiotics on these fish and sold it on the local market as International fish for ten times the price, and on the foreign market as Ceylon fish for hundred times the price.

The antibiotics that enabled aquatic longevity was international. Foreign shit was better than local cow dung. Antibiotics became as fashionable as factory rejects.

1

Everything happened at the same time. JR, my father's return, my mother's return and the monsoons. Ammi placed the duty free television set in an auspicious corner of the house and looked at the roof as the first sound of thunder roared across the sky. 'Plomp, floosh.' Rain water fell into her eyes like Optrex eye cleanser. She cursed Thathi for not having the roof fixed during her absence and moved the television to the only room in the house which had a ceiling. The ten foot by four foot section between the kitchen and the dining room, which we called the pantry. Kandapola siya's new driver removed the pantry cupboards and we learned to call the pantry 'the television room'. After the electrician came, installed the TV and went, Thathi switched it on, sat down and observed the coloured stripes that look liked a national television flag. 'Stop wasting your time staring at the screen and kindly tell me why this roof has not been repaired?' questioned Ammi. Thathi did not answer, he was hypnotised by the stripes. Occasionally the stripes would go and the screen would become blue, with white lights flickering upon it like stars within Arthur C. Clark's milky-way. Nenda whispered into Ammi's ear, 'How can he repair the roof? He didn't even come to Colombo since you left.' Ammi became crimson with anger.

'Tissa, how often did you come to Colombo to see your family while I was gone?'
'The family? I saw my mother and sisters many times.'
'I didn't ask about your mother and sisters, I asked you... how often you came to see your children? That too is family.'
'I came.'
'How often?'
'Let me think...' He stared at the flickering stars on the television, and then pulled his chair closer to the screen. I think he had just discovered the great bear in the new duty free TV set.

'Let me make it easier for you to think. I was gone for more than a year, a year has fifty two weekends; on how many of those weekends did you visit your children?'
'You must understand Mali, I was under heavy pressure to complete the road before the elections.'

'Don't change the subject. Out of fifty two weekends, how many weekends did you spend with your children?'

'Nanda (that was Nenda's real name), I came to Colombo no?'

Nenda nodded her head silently. It was a rare moment. Nenda was normally never without words.

'NANDA...,' Ammi glared at her.

'Now I remember, I came when Lydia and Pam were here, then I came when Chooti became a big girl and then I, and then I...'

'And then you what?'

'Then I came...'

'Tissa. Don't lie. Then you did not come. You came only two times in a total of fifty two weekends. You should be ashamed to call yourself a father.'

'Time really flies doesn't it? It doesn't seem like fifty two weekends that you have been away. I remember dropping you at the airport like it was yesterday.'

'I don't know if you dropped another woman at the airport, Tissa Weerasinghe, for you did NOT drop me at the airport, your cousin Buddhi took me.'

'Ah, really? I must have mistaken Lydia for you.' Ammi snorted like an angry rhinoceros. Wordless. The erupting volcano of her soul had gorged the words. 'Now let me think, why was it that I could not drop you that day at the airport?'

'Tissa Weerasinghe, I'm not interested in why you didn't drop me at the airport. I'm interested in knowing what business could have been more important than visiting your children during my absence. But knowing you, I know I will not get an answer. You will beat around the bush and wait until I forget the question. So, I will not waste time asking or expecting an answer. But Tissa Weerasinghe, don't think I will forget it and don't think I'm not angry. I'm absolutely furious and when I meet your mother I will tell her what I think of her son! What I want to know for the moment is, when you are thinking about getting this roof repaired? You no longer have an excuse to go to the dry zone to complete roads. You are here and thank God all the canals the Dutch built, they built in Colombo. The canals cannot be used as excuses for the roof. So I ask you, for the last time. When?'

'When the monsoon stops.'

'This thing falling through the holes in the roof is not the monsoon, it is rain. It will last a day and then will be over.'

'Okay, I'll call the labourers when the rains are over.'

'Tissa, don't wait until the rains are over, call them now and tell them to wait here until the rain ceases.'

'Why? That's too expensive.'

'I don't care if it's expensive, I know you. Once the rains are over you will look into the sky and discover another milky-way and perhaps even people waving to you from there, and you will forget the roof.'

For the first time in the course of this conversation, Thathi diverted his eyes from the televison set in the joy of explaining extra-terrestrial activity to Ammi. 'Mali, it's incredibe. You won't believe it. Our galaxy is not the only existing galaxy. There are other galaxies with their own planetary systems. And, can you believe that people may perhaps live on those planets, people who look like us, eat like us, speak like us.'

'Tissa, where is everybody? If there are people living on other planets, why haven't they come to earth? We have been colonised by the Portuguese, the Dutch and the English. If as you say there are people living on other planets why haven't they come and colonised us? Where are they?' And she turned her face up and stared through the hole in the roof, into the sky which was beginning to clear up. Thathi jumped out of the chair like he had been bitten by a bug, kissed Ammi, jumped onto his bicycle and left.

As he tied his trouser leg with an elastic to prevent it from getting caught in the chain he told me, 'Don't ever underestimate you mother. Without having a clue about astronomy, she just stated the Fermi Paradox.' My father was a paradox himself. I didn't know any Fermi, I knew Arthur C. Clark. 'Do you know that Enrico Fermi was a physicist who asked his colleagues the famous question your mother asked me; 'Where is everybody?' And he cycled down the lane in his raincoat to meet Arthur C. Clark at the Otter Aquatic Club.

We were alone with Fermi's paradox. Where was everybody? We watched 'Sesame Street' as the rain gave way to sun.

2

Mrs. Bandaranayake had walked a tight rope between survival and extinction. The left to the left of centre was like the Mukunuwenna sandwich behind the Crotons in the school garden. They were scattered and disunited. There was no opposition. No Sinhala opposition. But there was a Tamil opposition.

JR had been voted into power from the Sinhalese areas; the Tamils parties had been voted in the Tamil areas of the north and the tea plantation areas in the mountains. Of course these were two different kinds of Tamil parties with separate interests and separate dialects. But to the casual observer, they were both Tamil. Those of the north were Sri Lankan Tamils, descendants supposedly of Tamil trade and conquest and those in the plantations were Indian Tamils caught between repatriation and non-repatriation. The supposed manpower of British colonialization and tea trade.

The Tamils had a history of grievances. The Bandaranayake-Chelvanayagam pact which would have brought them benefits, had been abrogated before being implemented. Again, this pact was mainly for Sri Lankan Jaffna Tamils and not for the Indian plantation Tamils. Now JR, upon his new dharmishta road to the right, tried to neaten up history to whose confusion he too had lent a helping hand before becoming President.

In his bid for power in the battle against Mrs. Bandaranayake, who had ignored the Tamil grievances, he stated: 'My party accepts the position that there are numerous problems confronting the Tamil speaking people.' The orange stripe next to the green stripe on the Ceylon flag had now got a voice in parliament. JR stated: 'The lack of a solution to their problems has made the Tamil speaking people support even a movement for the creation of a Tamil state.' He further stated: 'My party, when it comes to power, will take all possible steps to remedy the grievances of the Tamil people. Education, colonisation, Tamil language, employment.' JR won the election and ceased to understand why the Tamils would want a Tamil state.

The equivalent of the red chimpanzees was gaining momentum in the northern Tamil areas. They were not as unkempt as the chimpanzees. No facial hair, only a moustache, Kalashnikov and cyanide capsule. They were known as 'the Boys'.

The antiquated grievances of the Tamil people in the north were now represented by the Boys. The Boys wanted nothing less than a separate state called Eelam. Mahatma Gandhi's story of 'non-violence', the great heritage of the Asian sub-continent, was made into a massive screen epic by Sir Richard Attenborough and sold as videos in the newly constructed supermarkets in the country. Blood splattered the streets of the north. The Boys embarked on their journey to the separation called Eelam.

People bought duty-free video recorders and watched Sir Richard Attenborough's 'Gandhi', in the south. Ben Kingsley, who played the leading role, was catapulted to film stardom.

The Tamil representative to parliament called it 'non-violent agitation which would probably have to be fought out one day.' The day did not take long to come. Mahatma Gandhi was dead. The Maithriya Buddha had not set foot. Non-violence was gradually removing itself from one of its last bastions on the sub-continent.

Uncle Buddhi became diabetic. First he started losing weight; then he began urinating like an endless monsoon. It was a peculiar phenomenon. Everyone else in the Democratic Socialist Republic was gaining weight but he was becoming like a toothpick. Ammi asked him to go to a doctor. He said 'I'm fine,' and did not go. Nenda blamed uncle Buddhi's wife who had got used to hamburgers and was refusing to return even though money could now be made in our country. Without a wife, uncle Buddhi did not get proper food, so, he was losing weight. That was a logical conclusion to a man's misery even though hired cooks cook in our country and not wives. But when a husband loses weight when his wife is away, it is not the cook's fault, it is the wife's. Nenda told Ammi to tell Magi to prepare extra food so that uncle Buddhi could eat with us and gain weight.

In the Tamil speaking north, Sinhala policemen stopped a cyclist. The cyclist took a revolver from a 'siri siri' bag and shot the policemen. The next day the police shot double the amount of Tamil civilians than the cyclist with the 'siri siri' bag. JR sent the army to the Tamil speaking areas of the north and they quadrupled the double and opened fire at the old market place in Jaffna town and shot the Tamils dead. An eye for and eye, a tooth for a tooth became a head for an eye and a body for a tooth. Then the Sinhala mobs suffering a moment of dharmishta amnesia went on a rampage and attacked Tamils in the north-east. The Sinhala mobs felt safe on their rampage for the Sinhala security forces were near. The fearsome boys were in the north, not in the north-east. The Sinhala mobs attacked Hindu temples, forgetting that these same gods decorated their own Buddhist temples. When that was over they attacked the estate Tamils in the mountains. Those Tamils did not even know what the fighting was all about. They just happened to speak the same language.

Uncle Buddhi was diagnosed as having sugar. 'Apo,' said Nenda, 'saying he does not eat, he must be slowly buying chocolates and eating, or he must be eating all alone what his wife sends from abroad.' She told Ammi to stop telling Magi to prepare food for him. 'Aney Nanda, what are you talking?' said Thathi, 'though they call it sugar it is a malfunction of the pancreas. It is not because Buddhi is eating chocolates on the sly.'

'That pancrea must be malfunctioning because he has eaten too many chocolates!'

'The Pancreas do not malfunction because of chocolates.'

'Then how is it that none of us have sugar?' asked Nenda.

'How is it that some people get heart attacks and not others?' Thathi had become paradoxical since Ammi quoted the Fermi paradox.

'That is different,' said Nenda.

'How is that different?'

'People who have blood sugar, are people who have stolen and eaten other people's food in their previous birth. That is, if they are not doing it in this birth too.'

'And people who get heart attacks, what have they done in their previous births?'

'That has nothing to do with previous births, that is this birth.' The conversation was over. Nenda had discovered the reason for uncle Buddhi's diabetes.

No Sinhalese living in the Tamil speaking north had come under attack from either the Boys, or Tamil mobs. In the north and the east,

Tamil speaking people lost their homes through the Sinhala mobs and were given refugee status in the north and in the south. JR's army that had fired the market place was not around in the north-east to prevent the Sinhala mobs from attacking people just because they spoke the wrong language. The north-east was occupied by the Sinhalese, Muslims and Tamils. Not only the Tamils, but the Muslims spoke Tamil as well. Of course the Muslims had a different accent to the Tamils, but, when a Sinhalese does not speak Tamil, he cannot differentiate accents. So the Muslims became the victims of Sinhala fervour, not because they were Tamil but because they spoke Tamil which the Sinhalese had been too lazy to learn due to Majority status.

Uncle Buddhi, the experimental genius, experimented with old hospital syringes and batteries on himself to eliminate sugar from his blood. The battery connected to a new digital clock that peeped when the food he had consumed completed digestion. Then he took a skipping rope and skipped until the urge to urinate was over. When the urge had passed, uncle Buddhi had received the evidence that his muscles had utilised the sugar that had been broken down from the food he had consumed. Then he took a syringe and ejected a droplet of blood from one of his finger tips, put it onto his tongue and claimed there was no sugar. If we were around during this process, he would say, 'Eureka, in this fleeting moment I am free of sugar.' Uncle Buddhi was not only diabetic, he was also a good Buddhist. Everything in life was for him, something which was fleeting. When it was there, it was there, when it was gone, it was gone. Like his wife.

It looked like uncle Buddhi was able to conquer diabetes through his knowledge of physics. Thathi was not convinced. He would sit for hours with uncle Buddhi as he skipped with his rope and say, 'Buddhi, you have to take medicines to overcome diabetes.' But uncle Buddhi would reply, 'Tissa, diabetes is physics, medicine is chemistry. Chemistry cannot cure diabetes, only physics can.'

'Buddhi, I am not convinced. Diabetes is not a physical problem, it is chemical. Think of the chemical components that are lacking in your body that are necessary to take the blood sugar into the cells.'

'That isn't the primary problem Tissa, that's the secondary problem. Chemistry is always secondary, physics is primary.' Uncle Buddhi had studied physics to build the bridge on the river Kwai. For him, everything in life had a physical solution.

'Tissa, everything in life has its origin in physics,' he repeated.
'I disagree. Look at evolution and the origin of species. Evolution is chemistry, not physics.'
'Tissa, what you seem to have overlooked is this, there would have been no evolution without the theory of the big bang. And the big bang was a physical phenomenon, not a chemical one.'

My father's knowledge of chemistry was not sufficient to discuss the chemical components that caused the big bang that created mice and men, Tamils and Sinhalese.

JR implemented island-wide curfew. Sinhala mobs ignored the curfew and executed their anger against a language. The Sinhala forces chose temporary blindness and ignored their crimes.

The international press did not speak creditably about JR's forces. It made him furious for he needed foreign investment for the journey to the right, free economy and dharmishtaness. In parliament he bombasted the leader of the Tamil opposition, 'If you want to fight, let there be a fight. If it is peace, let there be peace. It is not what I am saying. The people of Sri Lanka say that.'

Most Tamil speaking people did not want an independent Tamil speaking state of Eelam. But, the Boys, like the red chimpanzees, could not be deterred. Once a revolution was born, it did not die. The Tamil leader of the opposition retorted, 'We tried our best to live in a united Sri Lanka like brothers, but failed. We are still prepared to explore a peaceful solution.' He was, but not the Boys.

The Boys were not in parliament. Although the Tamil speaking people did not want an independent Tamil speaking state of Eelam, if one was created, they would certainly live in it. The Tamil leader of the opposition played a double game. He said one thing to JR and another thing to the Boys. It was understandable. He had to survive. The Boys had their Kalashnikovs at hand. To be used against traitors to the cause of Eelam.

It did not look as though uncle Buddhi was losing his battle against diabetes, nor did it look as though he was winning. But diabetes was no longer the topic of conversation between my father and uncle

Buddhi. Diabetes was secondary, they had now reduced themselves to primary matter. Physics and chemistry.

I sat in a corner of uncle Buddhi's living room with the new Woolworth crayons my mother had brought and decided to become a painter. I began with the experimentation of primary colours. Uncle Buddhi had discovered Homeopathy. My father considered homeopathy to be chemistry, but uncle Buddhi called it physics. They argued endlessly. I concentrated on my drawing. When I looked up, uncle Buddhi was saying: '…but the symptoms, the symptoms are what creates the disease. It is like the sun. When there is no sun, there is no shadow. I'm not saying that the substance is nothing in homeopathy, what I am trying to tell you is that substance is secondary, the dose is primary.' My father did not argue further. He said he would think and return.

On our way back home in the recently green painted Hillman, my father did not talk to me. I tried to show him my artwork of primary colours and the resulting differences when I added minute doses of other colours. But he was distracted. His physics and chemistry did not extend to the world of art. Mine did. Mistaking the red traffic light for the green traffic light, my father created chaos in the city of Colombo as we returned home to his soliloquy of, 'It cannot be…it cannot be, there is certainly something I have overlooked… it cannot be…' Karma had followed us in our green Hillman that day. Perhaps she was in the back seat like uncle Buddhi's diabetes and the shadow that disappeared with the sun.

The leader of the Tamil opposition spoke of federalism with JR, and of Eelam with the Boys. They shouted at each other in parliament while the Boys gained power and the recently released chimpanzees began to gather on another spree to protect the homeland from what they conceived was non-traditional, non-Sinhala, non-Buddhist, non-grass root, non-rice eating, non-ethnic. Non. The Sinhala Budhist Karl Marx was still beating in their hearts like Kandapola siya's Morris Minor that had lost its silencer.

Then, four young men robbed a Morris Minor, strolled into a bank and stole twenty-six thousand rupees. The Morris Minor was blue, like Kandapola siya's car. Fortunately, Kandapola siya's new driver was Sinhala. The boys who had stolen the twenty six thousand rupees were not Sinhala, they had spoken Tamil. Four days later twenty policemen caught the four boys and recovered twenty-eight thousand rupees. These boys were not the same boys who had stolen the twenty-six thousand. But they, like the other boys, spoke Tamil.

It was obvious that the glorious cause for the founding of the Tamil speaking nation of Eelam was contagious. The new concept of Eelam now had many versions. And many propagators. The Tamil representative in Colombo who could not be bothered listening to so many Tamil Boys in the same Tamil dialect saying different things but wanting the same thing, switched sides and joined JR. Two of the Boys then came to Colombo and shot him. He died.

Eelam was beginning to reach us in Colombo. It was an eye for and eye, a tooth for a tooth. In Jaffna, the Tamil speaking north, a star was born. The fearsome, fearless, roaring tiger. The symbol of the Boys. 'To Whom it may concern,' wrote the Boys, on their letterhead with their tiger emblem glaring from above, 'No other groups, organisations or Individuals can claim these deaths. Serious action will be taken against those who claim to have done the deeds other than the Tigers in Ceylon, or abroad. We, the Tigers are also not responsible for past robberies of any kind. Sincerely, The liberation Tigers of Tamil Eelam.' In other words, the Tigers were zealous revolutionaries in the quest for a homeland. They were not robbers. Robbing a mother of her son was not robbery. Nor was robbing a wife of her husband or a sister of her brother. It was revolution. Losing a life in the name of the revolution was heroic. When the mother lost her son to the cause she was not expected to feel sorrow. It was bravado. It was the struggle for Eelam. JR got angry. He proscribed the Liberation Tigers of Tamil Eelam and all other organisations asking for Eelam.

A few days later, my father returned to uncle Buddhi. He had a peaceful expression on his face as though he had reached enlightenment. He held uncle Buddhi's hand and said, 'Buddhi, everything we have been discussing until now may be right, or it may be wrong. It is relative. The world is circular, there is no beginning and no end. On the other hand the world may not be circular and there may not be a beginning or an end. That too is relative. Everything we discuss has to be judged by its own value. Its own moment of truth. Then again truth is relative.

You are you, I am me, Chooti over there with her pencil colours is she. What we say to each other may appear empirical in our eyes. But two years later this knowledge may not seem to be as empirical at it seems now. Your eye is different to my eye and the space you occupy in this room is different to the space I occupy. But since we, that is you and I, have had nearly the same background, nearly the same education, nearly the same values, our points of relativity are not too divergent. But to Chooti, who was born at another time, with another set of values, another political history, our conversation regarding the boundaries of relativity has no meaning. Or else, is extremely trivialized. Nothing more. Let me now demonstrate by example,' he then called out to me.

'Chooti, you have been sitting there since I began talking to uncle Buddhi, tell us what we have been talking about?'
'Albert Einstein.' I said proudly. I had just learned that a man named Einstein had spoken about a thing called relativity. They looked at each other in affirmation. I had just concluded my father's hypothesis.
'Alright, now you have been here during our last conversation. Do you remember what we were talking about?'

So much had happened to me in my life during the last week. The Royal-Thomian cricket match souvenir had come out and my name had been written in the thought bubble connecting to the head of their most famous bowler. I think it was me. No other girl in this world would have such a stupid name. I was in the seventh heaven of delight. In love.

'Thathi, I can't quite remember, but I think you and uncle Buddhi spoke about primary colours.' I had just drawn a big red heart in my drawing book. My favourite primary colour.
My father and uncle Buddhi glanced at each other again. I felt like a laboratory mouse.
'Do you remember anything else?' my father asked.
'Yes. Charles Darwin.'
'You see what I mean Buddhi, it is relative. That what we have been discussing, physics, chemistry or the theory of the big-bang is unimportant to your blood sugar. We have to observe diabetes for itself, not as a process of the evolutionary process. And now, I have come to a conclusion. Diabetes is nothing but the theory of stagnation in the midst of plenty.'

My father was right. I should not hang on the five primary colours, I should use the entire twenty four colours in the new Woolworth pencil box. Why use only the five colours when the box had twenty four? Uncle Buddhi was silent. Thinking.

'You understand what I mean Buddhi? Stagnation in the midst of plenty. Your blood has enough sugar to supply energy to your muscles. But for some reason the mechanism is blocked that takes this sugar to the muscles.'

Stagnation in the midst of plenty. It was like the project for the development of the Mahaveli river basin. JR's minister in charge of the Mahaveli development project received plenty of funding and plenty of rain to deviate not only the Mahaveli, but even the Nile into our dry zone for cultivation. But, except for the fact that the minister moved out of his two roomed annex into a massive mansion, there had been no change to the Mahaveli basin. Neither the cultivator saw water, nor did the dry zone. Monies donated and allocated for deviation and development of the Mahaveli river basin stagnated in the minister's bank account, abroad.

'Tissa, I think I understand. It is not the sugar that is the problem, it is the stagnation of the sugar that is the problem. Stagnation in the midst of plenty! Yes. You are right, *that* is the problem we have to solve.'

In this sweet land beyond the Palk strait with its mangoes, bananas, sugar cane and guavas, there was enough space for all of us to live. Enough mouths to speak whatever language they desired. We were not going to fall into the Indian Ocean and drown if someone spoke another language. Nor was the Buddha going to get angry and remove his footprint or his old tooth if someone spoke a different language. But somehow, we were stagnating like uncle Buddhi's sugar that was refusing to leave his blood stream.

3

Then my mother began dying. She walked around the house singing and telling everyone that she was dying. 'You are not dying,' said my father, 'dying people are not cheerful.'

'I am cheerful because, what is the point of being uncheerful? Sooner or later death comes. It is better to go with a song and a dance than go in tears. Believe me Tissa Weerasinghe, to finally lead a life without having the heartache of living with you, is a pleasure, not a tragedy!'

My mother had never forgiven my father for hanging onto falling mountains and Fermi paradoxes while the roof continued to leak. 'You sing and dance, I will wail and cry and pray that I will be together with you in my next life,' said my father laughing. I think my father could not have held onto the falling mountain, or re-discovered the Fermi paradox without my mother's nagging. Her nagging was his incentive to search for the unknown, or attempt the impossible. Covering up potholes in the tropics was certainly not to be underestimated.

'Apo, please don't ask for me again. I certainly don't want to be your wife in the next birth.'

'I will never let you marry another man in another life, I will come and break the marriage,' replied my father. Ammi laughed heartily.

'You think I will be as foolish in my next birth? You think I will make the same mistake twice? I will not marry.'

'I will serenade you the whole day; you will want nothing else but to marry me.'

'If you serenade me with those ancient Sinhala songs you sing in the toilet, I will kill myself and escape into another birth.'

The impending death did not yet have the element of tragedy. I wondered if it ever would! There was always rebirth to continue that which one was doing in this birth. Neither of my parents seemed to be overly eager to eliminate the desire to live and enter Nirvana. I was glad. I needed a pair of parents in order to be reborn myself. And these two, despite all their faults, were the only parents I knew.

Nenda, who had been listening to the conversation from the non-sound proof curtain, berated Ammi for being so nonchalant about the great gift she had received in life. Namely, having my father for a husband.

'Aney, if you think so highly about him, why don't you marry him?' And she jumped into the green Hillman and drove to the supermarket that had come up in a new multi-storey building with a shopping mall.

In this democratic, socialist, dharmishta era of JR's, we the people no longer went to the beach for recreation. We went to shopping malls, supermarkets and factory reject stores. Recreation was far more pleasurable in air-conditioned buildings than in the tropical heat. Ammi drove the green Hillman to the supermarket even when she did not need to buy anything, only to see if it had anything extraordinary that the street markets did not have. Once she was saturated with the supermarket she went into the factory reject stores and searched the piles of rejects for rejects that none other may have. If that factory reject store did not have the right reject, she went on to the next. It was like rebirth, there was never an end to factory rejects.

But when the shops finally closed for the night, death returned. Ammi sang while everyone else looked extremely disturbed. I pretended to neither see nor hear. I was not ready for death.
'Mali, why don't you go to a doctor?' Achi asked.
'What Doctor? Dr. Wijedasa is dead no?'
'Hangs on the phone and talks tons of gossip to every Tom, Dick and Harry who has time to waste, but hasn't had time to find a family doctor since Dr. Wijedasa died more that fifteen years ago.' Nenda was entering the warpath, subject in third person.
'Then go and see Dr. Attygala.' Dr. Attygala lived at the top of Cemetery Road and had been responsible for the watermelon-hearts of my grandfather and grandmother, and all other people with watermelon hearts.
'He knows nothing about my condition,' replied Ammi cheerfully.
'If she opens her mouth, foolishness drops out,' said Nenda angrily. 'Doesn't know a thing about anything, but talks like a great sage.'
'Yes, Mali, but at least Dr. Attygala can tell what is wrong with you.'
'Mummy, how can he tell when he doesn't know?'
'I suppose you are the expert who knows what he knows and what he does not know?' said Nenda angrily. Ammi nodded in agreement.

'I am sick of your foolishness, I am going to bed,' and Nenda wobbled away. Achi looked worried and stared into her Buddhist book without turning a single page. Ammi got into the Hillman to tell her friends about her impending death.

I don't know why she was dying. I didn't ask. I didn't want to become half an orphan. I remained quiet and decided to give Karma a boost. I decided to become a vegetarian again. I had become a vegetarian once before, but had given up. Too many delicious sausages were being sold in the air-conditioned supermarkets. Now I decided to become a double vegetarian and abstain from eggs as well... I loved omelettes.

My birthday was nearing. I was planning on having a party, with boys. If I abstained from having a birthday party would my mother's chances of life improve? I decided to abstain not only from eggs and sausages, but sprats as well. That was more than a double sacrifice, it was a triple sacrifice. I hoped it would suffice. I certainly would have liked to celebrate my birthday party without my mother having to die.

I tried to talk to my mother about my birthday party. She had forgotten that I was becoming a year older. 'Do what you want,' she told me. 'I don't know if I will be alive to see it all.'

'Don't talk in front of the child like that, are you completely off your head?' Nenda scolded.

'She is old enough to know what is happening.'

'How can you tell her what is happening, when you yourself don't know?'

'I am dying, that's what is happening.'

'People don't die when they don't get periods for two months.'

Eureka! I now knew why she was dying. I hadn't learned for health science in school that death comes through the lack of menstruation blood. Perhaps they had not told us everything. When JR came, the pre-vocational one that covered health science, disappeared into the commonwealth syllabus titles. The new commonwealth syllabus title did not teach the pathology of menstruation, in fact it had no menstruation in its syllabus.

'It could be a cancer.'

'Thuh, thuh, thuh,' said Nenda spitting three times on the ground in order to deviate my mother's words of ill omen. 'Don't say such foul things.'

'What do you want me to say?'

'When people get older their periods stop, haven't you heard that?'

'Not at my age. When it stops at my age, it means that something seriously is wrong.'

'Don't talk such ignorance through that God given mouth of yours. Why can't your periods stop? You are no longer the youngest, no?'

'I'm thirty nine.'

'Thirty nine my foot!' replied Nenda angrily. 'I am forty three this year and you are only one year younger than I am.' How can one forget his or her age? That was, for me, a far greater riddle than the riddle of death. But first, I had to sort out the riddle of my impending birthday party. Could I have one or not? Would I be permitted to have one or not? With boys. On the other hand my report this last term had been light years away from the expected brilliance. TM Mozart had the brilliance. I was something beyond the absolute opposite. Perhaps the black hole in the milky-way where knowledge got suctioned into the yonder beyond, never to re-emerge.

That evening as Ammi got into the green Hillman and drove off to tell more friends of her impending death, I approached Thathi who had recently diverted himself from the milky-way and was standing on his head, having discovered yoga. Perhaps he had switched his interest from the milky-way to the magma chamber at the earth's core.

I hoped for the best and approached him as his legs swayed above his head in the living room. It was a good moment for me to talk and for him to listen. 'Thathi, I want to have a party for my birthday and some of my friends were asking me if they could bring their brothers. I think it's a good idea for otherwise Aiya will be bored with only girls. That way I can have a nice time with my girlfriends and Aiya can talk about cricket with the boys.'

'What do you want to do with girls and boys at the party?' It was possible for my father to talk while standing on his head.

'I don't know. Nothing.' We were certainly not going to play carom. I was planning on playing all the Jim Reeves and the Englebert Humperdick songs and dance, cheek to cheek, with that bowler in the cricket souvenir. I had not spoken to him as yet, but I had fallen in love with him since my name had appeared in his thought bubble. Though

I had to lie to my father that I had nothing planned with the boys, my future was planned. With my bowler. I was going to hold his hand that night, then I was going to permit him to kiss me. And then, when Venus showed her face in my horoscope I would marry him and have a house full of children and dogs and live happily ever after. But everything had to begin at a beginning. This was my begining. The birthday.

'Chooti, I have a better idea. Why don't you invite your friends to spend the day and we can go in the motor boat in the canal I just dredged. It eventually ends up in the lagoon and is an interesting trip. You can see how the people in the fishing villages live. I'm sure your friends have never been in a motor boat in their lives.' It was obvious that my father still lived within Fermi's paradox. He had lost all concept of reality. A boat ride instead of a holding hands Jim Reeves party! I had to lie fast.

'Thathi, that is an excellent idea, but unfortunately it isn't possible. Even though I must say I would have loved to do that instead of having a party with boring brothers. But Deepa has broken her leg (a lie) and Madhubakshini (Marshmallow) gets sea sick at the sight of water,' (another lie.)

'Ah then, we have to think about something else.'

'That is why I was saying…'

'I know! We will take all your friends to a Tower hall play.' My father seemed to be full of ideas since his head was being stimulated by the weight of his legs.

'A tower hall play? A *Sinhala* play?'

'Yes. Like the one we saw last week.'

I had been going for Tower hall plays every weekend since the dawn of the JR era. JR's new prime minister was on a fanatical quest to resurrect Sinhala theatre and Sinhala culture. I had seen the lives of nearly all the kings and queens of Ceylon performed on the Tower hall stage since the Aryan Vijaya's landing. But, if I took my English speaking missionary school friends for a Tower hall play, I probably would have to look for new friends. I had to convince my father that his idea was not right without him thinking I had no pride in the indigenous. But my brain was traveling slower than that of my father's. I had no excuses.

'Yes. That's a brilliant idea,' continued my father. 'We can park the car near the Maradana cinema and we can take your friends on the new overhead bridge for pedestrians,' (The new overhead bridge was built by the same prime minister of JR's. He dredged canals, resurrected Sinhala culture and raised Sinhala mortality by building an over-head pedestrian bridge) 'which goes nearly straight into the theatre. It is much safer than crossing the road. And I am sure your friends have never climbed a pedestrian bridge in their lives.'

Thathi was temporarily without potholes. He was now a devout follower of JR's minister who had become the prime minister and was getting my father to dredge the Dutch canals and aid him in building orange coloured over-head bridges for pedestrians crossing roads. He seemed to be the only minister of JR's to be doing some work, without only contributing to the stagnation of finances, like the Mahaveli minister.

'I was on that bridge last evening. We can drive there tonight after dinner. It's a great feeling to see the cars traveling under you. I don't know why more people don't use it. After all, it is much safer than crossing the road.' More people did not use it for the simple fact that one had to walk more when one climbed the bridge rather than when one jumped the road between cars. People in the tropics walked only in air-conditioned malls, they did not walk on non-air conditioned bridges to avoid traffic. In the life of the tropical being karma increased mortality, not a minister's bridge.

'Alright Thathi,' and I left.

I skipped dinner that night. Hopefully karma appreciated the sacrifices I made.

4

Dagma arrived. Many tragedies had struck together. Dagma's Filaria had returned. She did not yet look like the elephant man, but it was a matter of time before she would. The Buddhist priest who had given her oils and told her to kill mosquitoes had made a mistake. Mosquitoes alone were not responsible for Dagma's Filaria. The mosquitoes were dead, but the Filaria in Dagma's body was still alive. There was an occult element that the Buddhist priest with his oils had overlooked. 'Not to worry sister Beet, with the president making the new hospital with so much foreign funding, it's only a matter of time before illness is eliminated for good.'

JR was on a road to the right to immortality. He was building the greatest hospital south-east Asia had ever seen. The Sri Jayawardanepura hospital in Sri Jayawardanepura, which was once called Kotte, situated past the cemetery and the maternity hospital on Cemetery Rd. Kotte was a once upon a time kingdom of the Kotte kings whose place JR had now taken and re-christened Sri Jayawardanepura Kotte, after himself. JR's surname Jayawardane, appended to 'pura' meaning town and the Sri from the same old Sri as the automobile number plates. JR was now like Sri Jawaharlal Nehru, Dr. Sri Dharan, the priest Sri Sumanatissa, the Bo tree Sri Mahabodhi and Sri Lanka.

'Aney Dagma, let us wait until the parliament is completed to see if this hospital ever happens,' said Achi pessimistically. JR was not only building the Sri Jayawardanepura hospital, he was also building the Sri Jayawardanepura parliament. The old parliament would remain a historical monument of the colonial era while JR and his ministers would travel in Mercedes Benzes with their body guards in green Pajeros, two in front and three at the back, to the new parliament.

The cemetery road was being widened. Roswitha lost her front garden. Sharona lost the front garden and the veranda. Mrs. Adonis lost her Daschund Cleopatra to a steam roller that steamed down Cemetery road eliminating everything in sight to make room for the ministers and their bodyguards traveling to the new parliament. In the meantime, JR's minister for the widening of roads, built three houses. Two in

Colombo, one in London. He had three legitimate children. A fourth house was being built. We did not know where.

'Aney aunty you are in a bad mood. I am sure the president's new hospital will be the best the world has ever seen. Look at the beautiful tall shopping malls that have come up. If this government can get something like that off the ground, what is a hospital?' and she popped three multi-coloured tablets into her mouth.

'What are you swallowing Dagma?'

'Tablets.'

'I can see that,' replied Achi, 'But what kind of tablets?'

'Aney I don't know, the doctor said to take it and I am taking it.'

'Foolish woman, you can't take tablets without knowing what they are for.'

'He said something…'

'What?'

'Sister Beet, wait, let me think.' Dagma thought slowly. In the meantime the clock struck twelve. It looked as though Dagma was staying for lunch. The age of the tablet had arrived. The doctors who had left the country during the Socialist Republic times had now returned with antibiotics and vaccines for every ailment.

'I know sister Beet! I remember now. The pink tablet and the blue tablet are for the filaria, the orange tablet is for dengue.'

'Dengue? You don't have dengue?'

'I don't have dengue, but I can get dengue like I got Filaria. Aney sister Beet since the new international school opened next to our house, the roadside is full of siri-siri bags and plastic bottles, so I have to take medication to prevent dengue breeding in the bottles.' Dagma liked to talk a lot, but she did not know her facts. I knew them.

Aunty Lydia had sent my grandmother a new book on disease. 'Siri siri' bags did not breed dengue. 'Siri siri' bags bred the mosquito that spread the dengue. A new sickness had come since our left to the centre republic started its walk to the right. The glass bottle on the road had been run over by a lorry and was broken. The plastic bottle on the road was run over by a lorry, but survived. Then the rains came and water happily collected within the luxury of plastic. Mosquitoes, the clever creatures, got a new modern home. It was different to the coconut.

Breeding possibilities were there in the coconut husk, but the eco system embraced the coconut with time, though it never embraced the plastic. Mosquitoes were the winners in JR's road to the right, even though we humans thought we were the winners by consuming everything plastic.

'Aney sister Beet, that is near our house, but down the other road there is this massive tuition class for children of non-international schools. There you find more siri siri bags and plastic bottles than down our road. At least down our road it is an international school, they don't make as much dirt as the local tuition class. And you won't believe sister Beet, down that road I have a friend, Mabel, her husband died no! Of dengue! They got a different type of dengue than what you get down our road with the international school.'

True. There was a difference in dengue though there was no difference in dirt. But, when the word international came in front of any institution their dirt was cleaner than other dirt. Worse than the dengue or the dirt was the fact that when 'international' was placed in front of a school name, not only did men beg, borrow or steal to send their children there, but all the teachers in normal local schools joined them for better pay. The children of those who could not beg, borrow or steal, went to a normal free education school during the morning, and paid heavily for tuition classes in the afternoon. The tuition class was not a part of the free education system. It became the logical result of the competition between free education and paid 'international school' education.

'Aney Dagma don't talk nonsense,' scolded Achi.

I personally thought that the Filaria had become dementia in Dagma's brain.

'Truly sister Beet, I am not talking nonsense. That is what the doctor said.'

'What doctor?'

'A new doctor down our road who just returned from abroad.'

'Dagma, doctors who come from abroad know nothing about dengue. You don't get it in those countries.'

'Are you sure sister Beet?'

'I am sure.'

'Aney sister Beet, what am I to do now?'

'First, throw your tablets away.'

'Aney but they cost money no?'

'Is money more important to you than your health?'

'Aney no sister Beet.'

'Then! What are you waiting for?'

'Okay, I will throw them away when I am home. Ah! But the Filaria tablet, I should take that one no?'

'Before you take it you should consult another doctor who has been living here and treating patients for diseases caused by mosquitoes.'

'Aney but sister Beet, it is now said that Filaria is not caused by mosquitoes, it is caused by worms. I have given Cecil and Kusita 'Wormex' every day for the past two weeks.' Achi rolled her eyeballs and left Dagma to ponder the difference between mosquitoes and worms, and brought from her bedroom the heavy book of disease sent by aunty Lydia.

'Dagma, put on your glasses and read.' Achi turned to 'F: Filarasis.' Dagma put on her glasses and began to read.

'The diurnally sub periodic form in the Pacific is transmitted by day biting mosquitoes…' Achi stopped her. 'Dagma what are you reading?

'Sister Beet I am reading what you told me to read.'

'What did you just read?'

'I read that the diurnally sub period form in the Pacific…'

'Dagma, is the Pacific of any importance to us?'

Dagma grinned like a woodpecker that had just finished its peck, 'You are right sister Beet, we are not in the Pacific, sometimes I wonder where my head is!' I wondered too. She continued. 'Filaria is transmitted by female mosquitoes Aedes aegypti, Culex and Anopheles where presence of Nematod worm Wuchereria bancrofti is transmitted to patient. Wuchereria bancrofti is a slender elongated filarial worm where the male form resembles a corksrew like tail and the female form has a tapering anterior and a rounded swelling. Apo! Listen to this! The filaria worm remains in lymphatic system for ten to eighteen years and dies a natural death if male and female worms do not encounter each other in lymphatic system.' Dagma stared at my grandmother totally perturbed, 'Aney sister Beet, I am sure the male and the female have not yet got together in my body, I have to stop them from meeting. I have had this leg for the last ten years, I do not want to have it for the rest of my life!'

'Good. Now you have understood. Swallowing coloured tablets will not help you.'

She stared at my grandmother with her mouth wide open. All her lipstick had rubbed onto her teeth.

'What else have you learned from this book?' asked Achi.

'Aiyo, that these ugly twirling worms are in my body. I think it is this one,' she said pointing to the black and white picture of the female worm in Achi's book on disease. 'See, see sister Beet, here, here is that worm!' and she tried to convince Achi that the stretch marks on her fat thigh were Nematod worms.

'Dagma, that is not what I asked, I asked you what you learned? In regard to mosquitoes.'

'The female mosquitoes are vicious.'

'That is not all that you have learned. You have learned, that whatever treatment you get, you have to protect yourself from mosquitoes. It is the mosquito that transmits Malaria, Filaria and dengue. Some attack at night, some during the day, some during both night and day. So during the evenings, never stay without mosquito coils, and during the day kill them when they come.'

'Alright sister Beet, alright.' and she went down on her knees and kissed my grandmother's feet.

'Now let's have lunch. When you are finished, you tell Mali to take you to the doctor. If she refuses, plead with her. Then, when you are at the doctors' take Mali into the practice and tell the doctor that she has not had her menstruation for the last three months and he should examine her. Thereafter you tell the doctor what your problem is and tell him to recommend a specialist to whom you could go to.'

My grandmother was clever. The entire treatise about worms and mosquitoes was not for Dagma, it was to see if my mother's moment of death and reincarnation had arrived. Perhaps the blue tablets for Filaria had been necessary after all.

5

The dengue lessened like magic.

The same prime minister who dredged the canal and built the orange overhead bridge eradicated dengue. It had been easier than building bridges or dredging canals. He only had to smile at the municipal workers and they cleaned the garbage. Without garbage, there was no dengue. None of the previous prime ministers had smiled at municipal workers, but this one did. He brought our mango in the ocean to an era of cleanliness that had only existed in the times of the great Ravana.

My mother was not dying. She was with child. Of course, before *I* found out the details, everyone else in the household knew about it and were whispering and laughing without conveying a word to me. I don't know why. Ammi's pregnancy was the least of my concerns. I was more concerned about how to not only have a birthday party, but to have a party where that bowler was a part of my guest list. My mother pregnant! Other children's mothers and fathers hold hands and walk on the beach or down the road in the evenings, my parents don't hold hands but become directly hardcore. They produce babies when TM Mozart and I are nearly ready to produce babies ourselves. Okay, I still had to find a person with whom I could produce babies. Having my name in the school cricket souvenir thought bubble was not sufficient to produce babies. But TM Mozart, for all I know could already have produced babies. He had one girlfriend after another. In the nights strange stray girls would wander into the house when my parents slept in their beds, and the dogs in their kennels. I knew the girls, most of them were older girls from my school. I looked them in the eyes and pretended the night was too dark to recognise them. TM Mozart would take them to his room and I would sit outside and read the telephone directory until the girl left. By the time she left I had memorised all the telephone numbers of the boys in TM Mozart's cricket team. I don't know what happened in the room. Perhaps he played the guitar? I couldn't imagine TM Mozart becoming hardcore like my parents. On the other hand neither could I have imagined my parents becoming hardcore until the Filaria doctor diagnosed my mother's imminent death as pregnancy.

Life was not particularly pleasant thereafter. I didn't like my mother becoming pregnant. And I didn't like seeing my parents behaving like young lovers. When they were in the house, which was quite often now, I never knew where to focus my eyes. This constant play of love was a sheer embarrassment. To me. TM Mozart didn't seem to be bothered. He even played his guitar to the child in my mother's stomach.

Personally I didn't care what gender the child in the stomach would have. But I was going to commit suicide if it was a girl. On the other hand, life had so much to offer. Why kill myself? What if that bowler came to my hypothetical birthday party and fell in love with my questionable dark beauty, proposed to me and married me? Immediately. Perhaps I could go to the commonwealth and live with aunty Lydia. There was certainly no possibility of aunty Lydia getting pregnant. Between her age and uncle Lionel's heart condition, the possibility of pregnancy was like the arrival of the Maithriya Buddha. But, I could not leave my bowler and go to the commonwealth. If that bowler didn't work out, perhaps there would be another bowler whose bowling had that element of masculinity that appealed to me. I had never seen my bowler bowling live. I had only seen his black and white picture on the sports page. I liked the pictures. The rest I could imagine… the rubbing of the red leather ball on his right thigh, the swirl of his arm, the element of tragedy that emanated from his soul when the batsman scored a 'sixer'. His passionate anger when his school lost the match.

My mother's stomach began to make its self obvious. I couldn't keep it a secret any more, my friends were beginning to notice her protrusion. I wished I could turn the clock back to a time before this pregnancy. 'Makuna,' said Marshmallow staring at my mother who was talking to another teacher in school, 'is your mother pregnant or something?' I changed the subject. 'Madhubakshini, haven't you got some prawn pies in your lunch box?' I hadn't eaten her prawn pies for years. 'Don't try to change the subject, I think she's having a baby.' I tried to catch a butterfly on the Croton tree. 'Come here,' Marshmallow called my other friends. 'Look at Makuna's mother, doesn't she look like she is having a baby?' Two friends became four, four became eight. 'She's definitely pregnant.' They arrived at a unified conclusion. 'Is she?'

'I don't know, ask her,' I replied angrily. I had by this time killed the butterfly. 'She is, isn't she?' I nodded and began making my pigtail into a plait. They looked at my mother, then at me and laughed their guts out. I don't know why they laughed, I wanted to cry. I decided that I would go and live with aunty Lydia in the commonwealth.

But, between the commonwealth and the pregnancy I needed a place to stay. Sharona was no longer my friend. She was still interested in climbing trees and walls, whereas I had changed my interests to bowlers and batsmen. Asantha was no longer my friend either. He would spend his spare time with my mother observing the movements of the 'it' inside her stomach. TM Mozart was the same. He had added a mouth-organ to his repertoire and composed embryonic and foetal songs for the 'it'. I spent my spare time with Mrs. Adonis. Only Mrs. Adonis didn't seem to make a drama out of this pregnancy and mourned the death of her dachshund Cleopatra.

Since the creation of the Democratic Socialist Republic, three of Mrs. Adonis's children had returned from abroad. Wealthy, polished and ready to make money. But no child could eradicate Cleopatra's loss. Cleopatra had accompanied her through minimisation when her children had left. It was a greater tragedy than the fall of the Egyptian empire. Perhaps it was greater than Dudley's death! We spent hours staring at the flower pots where Cleopatra had raised her short legs and pissed. Mrs. Adonis mourned for the past. I mourned for the future.

'Your mother is getting a child?'
'Mm.' I murmured.
'You are happy to get a brother?'
'Mm.' I murmured. I did not know that the 'it' in my mother's womb had a gender.
'He will be born in January,' she continued.
'Mm.' I murmured. I would not have cared if 'it' was never born.
'Life leads to death, death leads to life. Life is death, death is life. A circle. We go round and round until we learn to escape the vicious circle of life and death.'
I said nothing. She continued.
'January is the month where the *Duruthu* full moon Poya comes. Did you know that?'

'Yes.'

'It is an important month. People born in this month are good people. They are fortunate people. Do you know why?'

'No.'

'*Duruthu* is the first month of the year for the Sinhala people. It is an auspicious month. It was on a *Duruthu poya* day that Lord Buddha came to Ceylon for the third and last time, shortly before his death. Did you know that?'

'I knew he came three times, but I didn't know it was during the month of January.'

I personally didn't care. Everyone in this country knew he had come three times but no one had seen him, nor had these nobodies met anyone who had seen him. Except for a footprint which could have been anyone's and a decaying tooth which again could have been anyone's, there was nothing left of him. To add to it, I had never seen the rotting tooth. Nor had anyone I knew seen it. I had seen the expensive golden casket with its precious stones in which the tooth was supposed to be concealed, but never the tooth. To be truthful about the matter, I wasn't sure if we were humbugged into believing there was a tooth at all. But the truth of the matter was, if I was a robber and I had a choice of a tooth or the gold casket that concealed the tooth, I would rather steal the casket than the tooth.

'Do you know why he came?'

'No.'

'He came to sort a dispute between the two brothers Chulodara and Mahodara.'

'Was there no one in this country capable of sorting out the dispute?'

'Perhaps. But no one like the Buddha.'

I remained silent. We had been foolish even then.

'Do you know what the dispute was all about?'

'No.'

'It was over a gem-studded throne. The two brothers could not decide which brother should have it.'

'And who got it finally?' Not that it mattered to me, I didn't know either of the brothers nor did I know anyone who knew them.

'After the Buddha came, neither of the brothers wanted the throne. They tried to give the Buddha the throne. He refused it.'

'Where is the throne now?' Rather than going to see a decaying tooth on another boring school trip, perhaps I could suggest visiting the gem studded throne.

'It is enshrined in the Kelaniya Temple in remembrance of the Lord Buddha's third visit.'

'Have you seen it?'

'No. Your grandfather wanted to take me there, but he died.'

'Maybe one of your sons can take you.'

'They are busy getting rich.'

'But I'm sure they have a day off?'

'I have seen what I have to see in life. But you have a lot more to see. Don't waste your life closing your eyes.'

'Mm.'

'Can you play chess?'

'No.'

'Go into my bedroom and you will find a chess board with its pieces at the bottom of the Almirah on the right side. Bring it. I will teach you to play chess.'

I brought it. She arranged the pieces on the board.

When your brother is born in January, tell your father to take you to the Kelani temple for the *Duruthu Poya* pageant. If you are fortunate you will see the gem studded throne.'

'Mm.'

'These are the pawns. They are there for the protection of the king. And they are the first to be sacrificed to protect the king, or the queen. Now arrange your pawns on the board like I have arranged mine.'

I started placing my black pawns on the board.

'When king Ravana died, his brother Vibhashana ruled what was left of Lanka from Kelaniya. Did you know that?'

'No.'

'The whole purpose of the game of chess is to destroy the other king. If you are not capable of eliminating the other king, your fundamental attention should be towards protecting your king. If you lose the king, you have lost.'

It was like the battle between JR and Mrs. Bandaranayake; Chulodara and Mahodara. Perhaps the game of chess should have a Buddha figure.

'Now arrange your pieces the way I have arranged mine.'

I proceeded to do so.

'Did you know that a hideous crime happened in Kelaniya long after the Buddha came and went?'

'No.'

'See you have the castles at the ends of the board. They move straight: horizontally and vertically. The bishops next to them move diagonally. The white bishop on the white squares, the black bishops on the black squares. The bishop is the only piece in the game of chess that cannot cross over to another colour. Once black always black. Once white always white. Now I will keep my pawn here. Show me how you will get rid of it with your bishop.'

I put my thinking cap on.

'It happened when King Kelani Tissa was king of Kelaniya. The king found the young monk who was supposed to teach the queen, carrying a love letter from the king's own brother to her. Instead of punishing his brother or the young monk, the king punished the teacher of the monk. The teacher, unlike his student had attained sainthood and was not responsible for the actions of either the young monk or the king's brother.'

I captured Mrs. Adonis' pawn. The first trophy in my collection.

'I know you did that move because I asked you to do it, but you should not have done it. You see the pawn standing here? The pawn can now take your bishop. It was not worth the price. It is not worth sacrificing a bishop for a pawn. You should not have done what I said, even if I told you to do so. You must first think.'

She kept my bishop back on the board and asked me to think up another strategy to eliminate her pawn without losing my bishop.

'King Kelani Tissa put the sainted monk in a cauldron of boiling oil. Now, the knight you can move in the shape of an L. Use it as a secret weapon. Due to its L shaped movement, usually opponents cannot predict the knight. In a game of chess most people have the tendency to overlook the knight. Keep him in mind and use him.'

I moved the bishop back to a safe position. I didn't want to lose a single piece. I waited for her next move.

'Then the gods got angry with King Kelani Tissa and they sent a massive flood that was so rough and violent that it threatened to destroy the kingdom of Kelaniya.' She moved her queen. There was one pawn between my king and her queen.

I moved my pawn towards her queen. In the next move I would capture her queen with the knight that was lurking in the corner.

'The people were angry with the king. They blamed him for causing the flood by his wicked deed towards the monk. There was only one way the king could escape their anger and remain king. He had to sacrifice his daughter Viharamahadevi.' That was the same Viharamahadevi who stood carved in marble in the Viharamahadevi Park in Colombo.

'Check.' I had paid all the attention to the queen, forgetting the person that needed to be protected was the king.

I put on my thinking cap again.

'The month of *Duruthu* is an important month. It is a fortunate month. Your brother will be born in that month. Keep your eyes open, you are too young to be blind.'

I moved my castle in front of the king. Mrs. Adonis' queen now had to retreat. 'You are learning,' she said. It was no longer check. I relocated my knights.

She relocated her queen, the bishop and the castle. My king was cornered. 'Checkmate.' I lost that game. I lost the next game as well. We played another game. I lost that one too. Then we began yet another game. It was a stalemate. I arranged the pieces to play another game. The half moon was glistening in the sky and the mosquitoes were trying to transmit Malaria, Filaria and Dagma's dengue onto my legs. But I didn't want to stop. I had nowhere to go.

This time around I was white.

'How is school?' Mrs. Adonis asked.

'Okay.' I moved the white pawn.

'And how is your work?' she moved the black.

'Okay.' I lied. I was the worst student in my class. Even worse than Marshmallow. I moved another pawn.

'You like school?' She moved another pawn.

'Yes.' A half lie. I liked the intervals, not the classes. Since I was so bad in nearly every subject it didn't seem worth listening in class. I didn't know what was happening when I listened, so I decided not to upset myself too much by bothering to listen. It was better to be deaf and think about something I understood. Like the bowler in the college souvenir. I moved my pawn. In the next move it was her pawn or mine.

'It is your birthday soon, no?' Mrs. Adonis made a foolish move with her pawn.

'Are you planning on having a birthday party?' I captured her pawn. Her king was exposed on one side.

'I want to have a party, but no one else seems to be interested in what I want. They are busy with the stomach.' She was still thinking about her next move.

'Did you tell them you want to have a party?'

'I mentioned it somewhat. Thathi was on his head and didn't listen. He only spoke.'

'And your mother?' Mrs. Adonis moved her queen away from her king.

'She is not very happy with me right now. Whatever I tell her, it is NO and NOT.'

'Why?'

'Some of the teachers in school are running and sneaking to her about different things and she always believes them. Everything I do is not right or it is bad.' I sacrificed a pawn and opened the road for my castle.

'What exactly did your mother tell you about the party you want to have?' Mrs. Adonis sacrificed her queen for no reason at all. There was no flood. Nor was the king in danger. She looked like she was practising JR's politics on her chess board. Without Mrs. Bandaranayake there was no opposition.

'Ammi told me: whatever you ask for, it is no.'

'That's all?'

'That's all.' I sacrificed another pawn to reach her king.

'I will tell you a story. Listen to it carefully and do what you think is right.' I froze my move and listened.

'You know Andaré don't you?'

'Yes.' Everyone in the country knew Andaré. Andaré was the most celebrated court jester this country had ever had. No one had seen him, like no one had seen the Lord Buddha or Chulodara and Mahodara, but there was no one who didn't know of his antics. Mrs. Adonis began.

     'Andaré's brother in law was once in the palace grounds trying to steal something and was caught by the king's guards. The king ordered

him to be punished. The ministers and other governmental persons
tried to save him, but the king was angry and refused mercy. Punishment
was going to be enacted and that was the king's last word. When Andaré
heard about the matter he decided to plead with the king. The ministers
told him it is of no use, but Andaré was not deterred. He went to the
palace seeking an audience with the king. On seeing Andaré the king
spoke before Andaré could speak to him. The king said: 'Andaré, no
matter what you say I will not do what you want me to do.' Andaré
heard this, scratched his head and thought awhile. Then he said, 'Your
majesty, my brother in law is a good-for-nothing man. He spends his
time getting drunk and he goes about stealing. He is a bad man. Your
Majesty, I came to ask you to punish him.' And he prostrated himself in
front of the king. Andaré had got the better of the king. The brother in
law was set free.'

Mrs. Adonis's white king was surrounded from three sides.
Checkmate. It was the worst game of chess she had ever played. I won.
Having another brother besides TM Mozart was perhaps not too bad
after all. Perhaps a brother and a party were both possible?

I returned through the gate. Ammi, Achi and Nenda were sitting
in the television room. The television was on. Loud. The Buddhist priest
had now moved from the radio to the duty free television set and was
relating a sermon about '*Dukka*'. Suffering. The Buddhist priest was an
incarnation of suffering. Skin and eyes the colour of jaundice, beetle
juice stained teeth, two Copernicus craters upon his cheeks, and a
bubbling eruption of a mouth that was permanently spraying microbiotic
lava from the depths of his phlegmy trachea.

Suffering was on top of the Buddhist list of elimination priorities
in order to reach the realm of extinction. Nirvana. Nirvana was the
elimination of Dukka. The Buddhist priest was citing examples of
Dukka. The girl who lost her lover, the prime minister who lost her
civic rights, the Sinhala educated youth who got no jobs. Dukka was
more than suffering. It seemed to be everything. Unsatisfactory-ness
was Dukka, inconclusiveness was Dukka, incoherence was Dukka and
to add to the melting pot of suffering, the entire human experience was
Dukka. The Buddhist priest was trying to tell his listeners over the
televison that sitting and watching the television on the saucer chairs

within the comfort of the television room was Dukka. I decided to intervene.

I went to my room put batteries into the cassette recorder and brought it into the television room and pressed the play button. '*Oh..oh ..oh..oh..oh play that funky music till you die, till you die…till you die…*' roared above the Buddhist priest's Dukka. I kept the cassette player on my mothers lap with the speakers turned to my brother. If they all wanted their Dukka they could have it. But I didn't think that the brother in my mother's stomach would have much fun coming into a world preaching Dukka. My mother's feet moved to the beat,
'*oh… oh… oh… oh… oh, play that funky music till you die.*'

6

I got my party. It wasn't quite the same as Andaré the court jester, and the king. But I got what I wanted and my mother got what she said. We were both happy.

But such harmony did not reign in the whole country. JR's dharmishta journey to the right moved to the right, but was losing its dharmishtaness. The yellow borders and the yellow Bo leaves, symbolising Buddhism in the lion flag was turning a grotesque shade of yellow. The lion, already handicapped on three legs, was now trying to rid itself of the sword and stand with a gun. Lions were everywhere, not only on the flag. Now, besides the lion, the country was getting another predator. The Tiger.

The plain orange stripe next to the green stripe on the lion flag wanted its own predator. The Boys were no longer satisfied with a faceless orange stripe.

But JR had other ideas. He battled in parliament with the representative of the orange stripe and refused to comprehend the ferocity of the tiger. The tiger didn't have three legs. He had no legs. But he was like the hundred headed King Ravana. When legs were needed, they grew.

Rama fitted a snake arrow to his bow and severed Ravana's jewelled head. Instantly another head sprung upon the great king's neck. Rama aimed another arrow. The second head fell. A third head rose. It fell too. Rama aimed again. Again and again. And a hundred heads appeared one after another.

Ravana had only one hundred heads, while Rama had an infinite number of arrows. Rama was Lord Vishnu's incarnation while Ravana was Lord Brahma's grandson. JR, as far as I knew, was no one's incarnation, he had mere mortal beginnings. Like myself and the bowler I loved in the souvenir. There was no infinity, neither for JR nor myself.

He came. I was wearing a strappy black batik dress with green flowers and gold chain stitch around the petals. I had shaved my legs for the first time and found my way into my mother's locked dressing table cupboard for a whiff of Chanel number five. Kajaled, lipsticked and rouged, I metamorphosed.

My shaved legs were beginning to itch. But my heart was beating like a double-decker bus on its way up the hill country, using up so much fuel that my extremities were too feeble to scratch my freshly shaved legs.

He came with Marshmallow's cousin. Marshmallow's cousin, who had a non-cousin like interest in Marshmallow, happened to be my bowler's neighbour. I don't know what reasons had been given for him to come to my party, but he was there. I didn't know what to say to him. I stuttered to TM Mozart that he should talk to him until I managed to fix up the music for us to dance, but, TM Mozart was not very good at conversation. Not with boys. He sat in the midst of my girlfriends and sang between playing his guitar and mouth organ. I think *he* ought to be reincarnated as Ravana. With his many faceted musicality, one mouth and two pairs of hands was not enough. Not for him.

'Aiya talk to him, he is standing outside alone,' I pleaded with TM Mozart.
'He must be a fool if he is standing outside alone, when he can come inside and listen to my music.'
'Maybe he is shy.'
'I am also shy, that is why I play music.'
'Maybe he doesn't understand music?'
'Then he must be a bigger mutt than I thought he was.'
'Can't you talk about cricket?'
'Only the greatest fools on earth talk about cricket.'
'Then you are one of them.'
'I don't talk about cricket. I only play cricket.'
TM Mozart was of no use. If he had been Ravana, at least we would still have had our glorious Lanka. I then tried to tell Marshmallow's cousin to talk to him. But he replied,
'Aney let him be, he doesn't talk much.'
'But he must be bored. He has been staring at the bougainvilleas since he arrived.'
'He likes bougainvilleas,' he grinned. He was busy feeling Marshmallow's naturally beautiful unshaved leg under the Laura Ashley looking shower curtain she was wearing. 'Why don't you talk to him?' he asked me as I was leaving them in exasperation. 'I will,' I replied. But I couldn't. I had nothing to say.

In the meantime, the girls in the living room were having an inspired conversation since TM Mozart had left for a short moment, either to empty his bladder, or to practice a batting stroke in front of the mirror. I could perhaps ask one of them to talk. But I was afraid that their name would come in the souvenir the next year and not mine.

'Cheekay, how can you have an affair with a Muslim?' my friend Harini was asking Sohani. Harini was always the first in class.

'I am not having an affair with him, what can I do if he is sending me letters?'

Sohani had just received three letters from the Muslim boy who lived on the other side of the canal.

'Can he write proper English?' Harini was also an intellectual snob.

'I didn't check the spelling that closely, but it was so sweet, what he had written,' replied Sohani.

It was like my souvenir. Sohani, like myself, was reciprocating love.

'Have you at least looked at his face properly?' Harini was being difficult. She had not received an opportunity of reciprocating love.

'I see him seated on a chair on the other side of the canal every evening,' she replied.

'Yes, but it is too far to see properly in the evenings and you don't even have the best eye-sight.' Sohani was the only one of us who wore spectacles.

'Of course she has seen him,' butted in Deepa, 'Can't you remember he gave her the first letter at her grandfather's funeral?'

That was true. Sohani's grandfather's arteries had suddenly blocked-up, and he had died. The blockage had been due to the imperative desire to shoot a man who sat on the other side of the canal and stared at his granddaughters, every day, every evening and every night. In exasperation, he had pulled out his shot-gun, loaded a cartridge and aimed it across the canal. In the middle of the shooting episode, while he was pulling the trigger, his artery blocked and he fell down dead. A black crow, flying overhead, fell down dead next to him.

While the grandfather's body lay in cortege in the family living room, a Muslim boy had come with his mother to sympathise with Sohani's family. The mother had sympathised. The boy hadn't said a single word. He had gone straight to Sohani who was mixing iced coffee in the kitchen and given her a big tray of Wattalappam as a part of the funeral feast contributed by the neighbours of the deceased. Between the cloth covering the Wattalappam dish and the Wattalappam, there had been a sweet scented love letter in a 'siri siri' bag.

That was the first love letter a girl from our class had ever received. We were naturally rather envious. 'Cheekay, giving love letters at a funeral!' contributed Harini. But Harini's frustration was not contagious. The girls were elated. A love letter at a funeral was better than no love letter at all. 'So if you marry him, don't convert. Always remain faithful to your religion.' Both Harini and Sohani were Christmas celebrating Christians. 'Of course I will not convert,' assured Sohani. Harini was pacified. At least in one small thing Sohani had listened to her.

TM Mozart returned. Deepa sat at his feet and the rest surrounded her. '*Please release me let me go… for I don't love you anymore…*,' crooned TM Mozart. The girls stared into his eyes and decided never to let him go. Even though they did not 'have him' to let him go. Sohani's eyes kept leaping to the window. She had invited the Muslim love letter writer to the party. I hoped Magi had not cooked pork for dinner.

The Muslim love letter writer came on a motor cycle. He brought a friend. The friend was not my type. He had curly hair. My type of man had straight hair. Sohani refused to go out and speak to the Muslim love letter writer. 'I can't go out, what can I tell him?' And she stood listening to TM Mozart's song, wringing her hands.

Those were the times when we were in love with love. Love letters, a tender glance, an accidental touch was more than a thousand words. Then, Englebert Humperdinck came to our rescue. Not in the form of TM Mozart, but in the form of Dasa.

Dasa had returned from the village to be my DJ. I had told him not to look at the people dancing, just to play the music I gave him. Cassette number one, cassette number two, etcetera. 'What happens when I see something I should not see?' he had asked cheekily. 'Put your head in a cooking pot and burn it,' I retorted. 'It will cost you two imported chocolates,' he replied grinning. I had no choice but to steal money from Ammi and buy him two imported chocolates. TM Mozart was useless in the elementary functions of life. And I had no one else who was deaf and blind, and would still do what I say, except Dasa. I was happy that the black prince had impregnated Magi.

'*Please release me let me go... for I don't love you any more...*' The bougainvillea examining boys came inside. They knew the rules of the game. The Muslim love letter writer went up to Sohani, the bowler came to me and the curly haired boy had the choice of anybody. TM Mozart grabbed Deepa and whispered sweet nothings into her ear. Probably the lyrics; I don't think he knew anything else. Between their two bodies there was no space. Between the rest of us there was the space of a six-inch foot ruler. The bowler was short. He was not short like a dwarf, but was too short for my platform shoes. I had no choice but to remove the Boot manufactured platform shoes specially created by Percy the shoe maker for my birthday. As Englebert Humperdick sang '*Sooo... release me and let me love again...*' I moved away from my bowler, removed my three-inch platform shoes and returned to his arms, with the correct height. The six-inch foot ruler between us was now three inches. The same height as the platform shoes in the corner of the living room.

As Englebert sang, the space between us shrank. The three inches became one inch. He did not talk. He tried to hum. His bowling was better than his humming. He smelled of smoke. I liked men who smoked. I liked their smell. They were more manly than men who didn't smoke. I made the one inch into no inch. I hoped he wouldn't notice. It was our first date, I did not want him to think I was fast. I felt his breath on my left ear. Englebert had left the cassette and Jim Reeves was singing '*See the pyramids along the Nile, watch the sunrise on a clouded night...*' I pictured us walking, hand in hand up the Sigiriya rock. He was smoking a cigarette, I was pregnant. He stepped on my foot. There was no pain, just pleasure. He buried his nose in my hair. The no inch closed, we were together. Spaceless.

The lights came on. 'Click.' Thathi looked through his Made in Japan camera and clicked. He told us not to be distracted by him. He was only taking some photographs for the family album. Another click. The magic was broken, the lights were on. I tried to switch off the lights. Thathi wanted them on, his flash was broken. 'Don't even look

at me, y'all keep on dancing, I will only take some photographs and go.'
The no inches between us became a foot ruler again. His head removed
itself from my hair. TM Mozart left Deepa and returned to his bat. The
Muslim love letter writer and his friend went out for a cigarette. My
father continued to click. He then recognised the bowler. He spoke to
him and said that he did not realise that the bowler was a friend of his
son's. The bowler didn't correct him. Thathi proceeded to congratulate
him for all the batsmen he had bowled out that season. The season had
begun in January, it was August.

The bowler was now lit. He had black smoky lips, a shy pleasant
face. Not the type I had dreamed about, but a type I could live with.
But if my father continued like this, I think our life together would be
over before it could even begin. Then Dasa took the reins. He was cleverer
than I thought. He changed the Cassette. Jim Reeves gave way to Baila.
Baila was for old lovers, not for young lovers like us. Dasa said, 'You all
continue dancing, don't stop. I have a serious business matter to attend
to for the moment, when that is completed I will come and change the
cassette.' He came up to my father and said, 'Master sir, come now
soon, I have something important to tell you. Now. But not here.' He
took my father with his camera and left the living room. The bowler
went to the cassette player and changed the Baila back to Jim Reeves.
Obviously he liked me. I switched off the lights. The others returned
from their smokes and TM Mozart from his bat. I was happy. He had a
pleasant smoky smell. He was not a magnificent dancer, but since he
was a bowler he didn't have to dance.

Dasa returned and took the DJ position behind the cassette player.
My father didn't return. When I went into the room between cassette
changes for a dash of perfume and lipstick, I saw him taking photographs
of my unborn brother. With his mother, with his grandmother, with
Nenda, with Magi, with the servants, with Kandapola siya's new driver
and finally the boarders.

Love upon the living room floor had to stop for dinner. The girls
served and ate inside. The boys served and ate outside. I could not eat.
I was in love. Only TM Mozart ate inside with the girls. They were
more interested in watching him eat than asking me about my love
story. 'Aiya, why don't you eat with the boys, outside?'

'Why should I?' he replied. 'For one thing, all of you, except my sister, look better than the boys.' (Giggle, giggle). 'Secondly, they are so stupid they have nothing to talk about except cricket.'

'Aney but you also play cricket no?' said Deepa with her faded lipsticked mouth.

'But did I talk to any of you about cricket? I only play cricket, not talk about it. There are far more interesting things in this world to talk about than cricket.'

'That is true. You are not boring like them,' she replied honoured to have been dancing with such an intellect. Intellect my foot! His intellect appeared only in the presence of girls. With the family, he only spoke about the angle of his bat and his scores. I decided to be daring and go to the boys. Let TM Mozart talk about intellect to giggling girls. I ventured outside. I hoped my mother, father and the rest of adulthood was either in bed or blinded by the flash in my father's camera that hopefully functioned again.

'Come and sit with us,' said Marshmallow's cousin.

'Yes, yes come,' echoed the Muslim love letter writer.

'Come and sit, nice party,' donated his friend.

Only my bowler said nothing and continued to blow smoke rings from between his lips. They made room for me between the bowler's neighbour and the bowler. I sat, my heart beating like a double-decker bus which had lost its silencer. 'So when are the two of you going to meet again?' asked the neighbour. I stared at my bowler's smoke rings. He smiled shyly and held my hand. My heart now sounded like a triple-decker bus without a silencer. 'Tell the other girls to come out will you?' pleaded the Muslim love letter writer.

'Aney they are still eating.' I replied.

'But they can come here and eat no?'

'Wait, I will call them,' and was nearly about to get up when my bowler said, 'No, don't go.' He had spoken! He had the voice of Englebert Humperdick, only better! I was dumb struck. The boys smoked and admired each other's smoke rings. I could neither smoke, nor did I know much about cricket and none of my numerous tuition teachers had told me what one should talk about when one met a boy for the first time. 'Have you all eaten?' I asked. I know it was a stupid question, but nothing else came into my head. 'Yes.'

'You all ate enough?'

'Yes.'

'Ah! I hope you didn't eat the pork curry?' I asked the Muslim love letter writer.

'Pork, what pork?' he asked.

'This bugger ate everything on the table,' grinned his friend.

'Never mind *machang*,' replied the Muslim love letter writer. 'Fortunately I ate under this tree. Allah doesn't look under trees for pork-eaters, he looks for them in the desert. Even if he happened to look under the tree, which I doubt, he would not have seen me eating pork in the dark. That is why, when Allah planted some of us Muslims away from the Arabian desert, he was clever enough to make us black. That way he has less trouble and less worry. Only what he sees bothers him, not what he cannot see!'

'Oh, I'm sorry, I forgot to mention to you that there was pork served.' I was more concerned than amused that night.

'Don't worry girl, if I don't know, and Allah doesn't know, there is nothing to worry about.' I like the Muslim love letter writer. I wished my bowler had his sense of humour.

Dasa came out to get the lovers onto the dance floor. 'Come, come enough talkings. Musik beginning. Time to do dancings.' As my bowler and I kind of held hands and walked into the living room, I hissed into Dasa's ear. 'You don't have to talk your broken English. I told you only to do the music, nothing else.' He grinned back at me cheekily, 'My name is Dasa. I am from village school. I study English. I see house baby holding hand with mans when house lady and house master not looking.' I ignored him. My bowler and I returned to the dance floor and danced without space. It did not matter who sang from the cassette player, I only heard my bowler's heart beat and his breath on my ear. Then he burped. And he stank. And my love ended.

Hello and goodbye. It was twelve thirty. Ammi turned on the lights and asked the people to leave. She had agreed with the parents of my friends that midnight was the end-of-party time. It was half an hour beyond. The boys thanked her and asked her about her date for delivery. She asked them who's who they were. Meaning, who their mothers were, who their fathers were and who their uncles and aunts were. She discovered many known people in the family circles. Then Thathi packed the girls in his car, Kandapola siya's driver packed another set in his car and they were driven to their homes.

Only I remained, depressed, loveless. I should have left my bowler within the pages of the souvenir. At least then, my love would have thrived. Now it was no more. Shakespeare said, 'It is better to have loved and lost than never loved at all,' I was not Shakespeare. I was too young to have lost this love which was like a fleeting shadow in my long and tiresome life. Dasa turned on the Baila and moved along the floor as if he was electrocuted. He was irritating me with his happiness. 'Dasa,' I shouted. 'Will you stop that noise!' He gyrated further. 'Now it is noise, but before it was butterflies and fragrant Jasmine flowers.' I did not respond. 'You owe me three chocolates,' he said continuing to gyrate with the cassette player on his shoulder. 'Why three? We agreed on two.'

'When we agreed on two, the situation was different. Then there was no chain smoking bowler in the picture.' Dasa was clever. I had to pay for his silence. I did not care. If I had the money I would buy him a chocolate factory. My life was without worth. There was no more bowler on the horizon.

'Your friends told me I should come as a DJ to their parties.'
'Don't talk nonsense, as if they would ask you to come to their parties? You can't even talk English.'
'My name is Dasa. I go to village school. I live in village big house where Mister Tissa's mother living. I am...'
'Not like that. You don't speak English like a person from a Colombo school.' Dasa looked hurt.
'Okay, your English is good, but it is different to ours,' I tried to pacify him. I realised that what I had said wasn't very nice. We English speaking people had a sense of linguistic superiority. It was an idiotic sense of superiority, but it was hard to eliminate.

'Since when does one need English to be a music DJ?'
'Okay go. But you tell me when you go to my friend's parties, for I certainly will not be going to them when you are there!'
'That is your problem, not mine,' he grinned cheekily. 'That Miss Ruwani even gave me her address and drew a picture how to get there.'

He pulled something out of his pocket and fluttered it in front of my face.

'She! She has the most boring parties in town. But tell me Dasa, how did you manage to get Thathi to disappear with his camera?'

He grinned. 'That will cost you another chocolate.'

'Then I don't want to know.'

'Whether you want to know or not you have to give me a chocolate. I got your father and his camera from you and your bowler - hugging each other's bodies on the dance floor.'

I was tired, but I couldn't sleep. I might as well spend the night listening to Dasa's stories. 'Okay, tell.'

'I told your father the story of the star gazer.'

'What star gazer?'

'Aney I don't know what you learn in these Colombo schools. Everyone in other parts of the country knows the story of the star gazer.'

'Are you talking about Arthur C. Clark?'

'I am not talking about someone seeing a clerk, I am talking about a star gazer.'

'Tell, tell.'

'Okay this is how it began. I told your father to come with me...'

'I know that part, tell me about the star gazer.'

'Don't disturb me when I am trying to tell you something.'

My mouth was shut.

'When your father came out with me I told him: 'Master Sir, do you remember the story of the star gazer?' He smiled at me and said, 'Dasa repeat it, I haven't heard it in a long time.' So I began. Once upon a time there lived a man who knew a great deal about stars. This man spent all his time watching the heavens, trying to find out more about them. All day long he thought of nothing else but the stars and all night long he watched the stars in the sky. That is why the people called him the star gazer. One night, the sky was full of a million stars. The star gazer went walking that night with his face turned towards the sky. Suddenly he fell into a ditch. He tried climbing out, but could not. 'Help! Help!' he cried until a passerby heard his voice and lifted him out of the ditch. The star gazer thanked him. But the person who helped him out of the ditch looked at the dirty star gazer and told him, 'Good

sir, you are always watching stars. Why don't you watch the ditches too?
You clever men know a great deal about remarkable things, but know
nothing about the simple things in life.'

Dasa with his village education was cleverer than I thought. From
that moment on I decided to stop calling the red chimpanzees the
chimpanzees. They were unemployed youth from the grass roots who
wanted their share of Ravana's former kingdom. Since JR's dharmishta
amnesty freed them from jail, they were back in action demanding their
rights. Theirs was the voice of the grass root population. How was it
that JR's ministers were getting richer, but they were still poor? Had JR
not said that everyone would have their moment of glory upon the new
dharmishta road to the right? They were now clean shaven. The Sinhala
equivalent of 'the boys'. The Sinhala boys.

JR was going right, but they wanted to go left. Globally, the left
was dying out. Leftist remnants were immolated and poor as church
mice. Only the smoke of pollution was left with poverty in its wake.
The industrial smog was long gone and existence was as stagnant as the
Mahaveli development and uncle Buddhi's diabetes. God, their God,
who was supposedly killed in the October revolution of 1917 was coming
back to life in Sri Lanka.

Communism was no substitute for God. In a stagnated existence
where nothing was left, only God could be resurrected. He needed no
food, no clothes and no roof above his head. The Sinhala boys were
trying to resurrect the Lord Buddha from his footprint on Adam's peak.
We were stagnating too.

I removed my party dress. The bowler had made a gaping hole
in the skirt with his burning cigarette. I understood love. It was that
gaping hole. As Shakespeare is supposed to have said: 'tis is better to
have loved and lost than never loved at all,' I decided never to have that
hole darned.

It was my hole. My love. My loss.

7

My mother entered the maternity hospital when Achi told her the time was right. Achi knew the time was right because the astrologer told her the time was right. Achi borrowed Ammi's watch and Nenda's watch and wore one on the left hand and the other on the right hand. She did not want to risk a repetition of the fiasco that occurred during my birth.

Ammi and Achi were already in the car ready to leave, while Thathi was still covered in dust looking for Dr. Spock's Guide to Raising Infants. Ammi pressed the horn. Thathi refused to drive until the book was found. Ammi cursed. Achi asked her not to use vile words against the father of her unborn child. But Ammi continued to curse. He finally found the book. Covered in dust, silverfish beginning to bite the edges. Ammi sat in the car and refused to release the horn. Without cleaning the cobwebs, Thathi brought the dusty Dr. Spock's guide to infants. Ammi broke into a fit of sneezing. She was allergic to dust. Then her water sack exploded. The astrologer was right, that was the day my brother was to be born.

Achi went into the labour room with Ammi, while Thathi stayed outside reading Dr. Spock. He continued from the page he had stopped at when I was born. I don't know why he read such books for he neither brought us up nor did he give the servants advice as to how they should bring us up. Thathi remembered Dr. Spock only when Ammi delivered. I think if she had another seven children, he would finally be able to finish the entire three hundred and fifty six pages of Dr. Spock.

In the meantime I invited Sharona for a chat and kept watch over the wall to the maternity hospital in case they burnt infants while my mother was in delivery. It was a smokeless morning. Sharona chattered about the hockey player she had met during an inter-school hockey match. She didn't know his name. But he was an excellent hockey player and he was cute. I liked bowlers. She liked hockey players. I was still looking for a new bowler. They were scarce. I was not willing to settle for any bowler, I wanted a good bowler, preferably from Royal College.

Thathi returned, excited, with Dr. Spock in his hand. 'Chooti.' he shouted into my ear. 'You have a brother!' I don't think he could have read much of Dr. Spock. My brother had emerged too fast. Then he went looking for Nenda. 'Nanda, Nanda,' he shouted walking through the house. 'Mali has got a son.'

'May the triple-gem bless him,' Nenda shouted in return. I don't know where the triple gem was, but even if it was in the moon I think it would have heard Nenda's cry.

'So, you have another brother.' Sharona stated the obvious.

'Yes I do. I hope he does things other than music and cricket, unlike TM Mozart.'

'Hm…' said Sharona and furrowed her forehead. 'I hope it has occurred to you that people are likely to mistake you for his mother?'

'Who's mother?' I asked.

'Your new brother's mother.'

'Why?'

'Your mother is having children when you are old enough to have children yourself.'

'Nonsense,' I replied angrily.

'Not nonsense! In Pakistan, I read, a girl got a child at thirteen. In India they are all the time getting children when they are fourteen and even in America, by the time girls are fifteen they are mothers.'

She was right. I was old enough to have a child myself, and my mother was getting children instead. Uncle Buddhi had just become a grandfather though he was four years younger than my father. Thathi had just become a father, again.

I locked up my halter tops, strapless dresses and platform shoes and got into heel-less shoes and baby doll dresses. I tied my hair in pigtails with pink ribbons. The bowler would have to wait until I saw my brother and he didn't mistake me for his mother. But, I hoped he would mistake TM Mozart for his father.

Dr. Spock returned to the dusty bookshelf and Thathi returned to us with his note pad and car keys. Nenda came with him in a new white sari. 'We are going to the Kelani temple and to the astrologers. When we return, I will take you, Magi and the servants to see Ammi.' They left together in the green Hillman.

'Why are they going to the Kelaniya temple? We have a temple across the street?' Sharona asked.

'They are going there because of Chulodara and Mahodara and the gem studded throne.'

'Ah?' Sharona was confused.

'Aney what do you know about life? Chulodara and Mahodara fought over the gem studded throne and Lord Buddha came to sort the dispute,' I answered her crossly trying to get even with her for assuming that my new born brother would mistake me for his mother.

'So what does it have to do with your brother?'

'They fought over the gem studded throne in January and the Lord Buddha came in January.'

'So?'

'So what month is this?'

'January.'

'What day is this?'

'Monday.'

'Besides Monday, what other day is this?' I asked her with exasperation.

'Poya day.'

'Right. Nenda prayed and prayed for the baby to be born on the Duruthu poya day because it was the last time the Lord Buddha came to this country. Now, since the baby has been born on Duruthu poya day, she has to fulfill her vows to the Kelani temple.'

'Aney I still don't understand. We have twelve poyas for a year and I am sure that the other two times the Lord Buddha came were on poya days too, so what is the big thing about this poya day?'

'Sharona, if I knew that, I would not be here with you, I would be on the gem studded throne myself,' I replied.

She thought further. 'I don't know if I was born on a poya day or not?'

'I don't either.'

'You think we are handicapped because we were not born on a poya day?'

'I don't know. And I don't care.' We returned to the conversation about the bowler and the hockey player. It was easier to comprehend than the connection between Chulodara, Mahodara, the gem studded throne and my brother. Not to mention the Buddha.

JR's dharmishtaness was no longer universal. It had become selective! He was not dharmishta towards Mrs. Bandaranayake who was deprived of civic rights, but he was dharmishta toward his ministers who were amassing great quantities of wealth and gathering gun-toting private armies for self-protection. Following the ministers' pledge of dharmishta affiliation to JR, they were now beyond the law. Those who did not pledge their dharmishta allegiance to JR were victims of the law. Like Mrs. Bandaranayake, who lost her civic rights. The villain was promoted to the highest office for the enactment of JR's justice. Selective dharmishta justice.

Some ministers did not say much, they did. Of course the results of their doings were not visible to the naked eye. Rather, what they did, they did for their eyes. For example the Mahaveli development minister developed faster than the Mahaveli. It was as though the only plentiful subsidiary of the Mahaveli went straight for the harvesting of his property. Even in drought. Others ministers did not do so much, they said. It was hard to tell which was worse. JR's dharmishtaness had created a new species of enlightened beings. Sinhalese, Buddhists, Patriots and Priests - blinded by culture and a new interpretation of the dharma.

One of JR's ministers woke up one morning and felt he had to say something different. Without rhyme or reason perhaps, but different. Just for the sake of difference. So, he opened his mouth and stated, '*It is obviously evident that the Tamil examiners have cheated by awarding excessively high marks to Tamil Advanced level candidates.*'

The Sinhalese who neither spoke nor understood Tamil, nor had ever tried to understand Tamil, found the minister's speculations extremely convincing. Two thousand five hundred years of Buddhist civilisation had re-discovered a scapegoat for their deficits. The sub-standard education of the rural Sinhala youth was conveniently pushed aside. The Tamil who lived in the north was to blame for the Sinhalese drop outs.

The minister caused a domino effect and JR re-introduced standardisation. University entrances were again regionally allocated. Somewhere along this regional allocation, merit had ceased to be important. But who cared? The Sinhala Buddhist got a temporary feeling of satisfaction. The Sinhala boys shut up for the moment. And the minister with the big mouth changed the subject. The Buddha's footprint atop Adam's peak got a gilted balustrade for pilgrims to hang upon and venerate the giant footprint with pride. There were many countries in the world, but the Buddha had decided to place his foot print in our country.

When I went to hospital with TM Mozart, Nenda, Magi, the servants and the boarders, my mother was angry. She was angry with JR's minister whose big mouth had re-introduced standardisation. She was more than angry, she was furious. She did not let TM Mozart look at the baby. She made him sit on the bed and told him that the country we were born in was a hopelessly miserable fleck in the ocean that should be wiped off the world map. I looked at my little brother. His ears were blacker than the rest of him and he looked like a cross between a gecko and a human being. Red and scrunched like a piece of crêpe paper that had got wet in the monsoon. He made bubbly sounds from all his cavities and tried to eat both his fists at the same time.

'Don't wait till tomorrow,' my mother told TM Mozart, 'You go today itself to the American Centre and register yourself for whatever exam you have to do in order to enter an American university. Then, without coming home, you go to the American Embassy library and make a list of all the universities in America and apply to each and every one of them.'

'I have cricket practices this evening.'

'You had better forget cricket now and start studying for the qualifying exams for American universities.'

'I don't want to go to America Ammi, I want to stay here and study.'

'You have a fat hope of studying in this country with their wretched standardisation.'

People schooling in Colombo had fat chances of entering university with standardization. The Tamils had fat chances of entering university.

'I can go to Thathi's village and apply for university.'

'You are not going to any village, you are going to America.'

'But cricket?'

'You can forget your cricket.' When my mother decided, she decided. Nothing in this world could make her change her mind.

'But American universities are so expensive.'

'That is why you have to stop cricket from today, get top marks at the exams and ask for a scholarship.' The chapter was closed. TM Mozart barely had time to look at his brother, my mother chased him away to

the American Centre. I was glad that I was too young for university. I
didn't want to go to university, not here and not in America. I looked at
my brother. Every passing second he was ceasing to look a gecko and
becoming more human. I put my hand into his cot. He tried to eat my
hand. I think he had been starving in my mother's stomach.

'*Ni*, should be the fist letter of his name, said my father entering
that hospital room. He came straight from the astrologer with a large
piece of paper with letters and names. 'I have jotted down some names
that came into my head as I was coming here. Niranjan, Nirantha, Nihal,
Nimal, Nissanka, Nimaltha, Nishmal, Nilantha, Nilan.' Ammi asked
him to throw the piece of paper into the dustbin, she did not like any of
the names.

'What does his horoscope say?' She asked him impatiently.
Knowledge of the future was more important than a name. If the
astrologer had said that the child had not brought sufficient life karma
to live in this planet, there was no point wasting time looking for a
name. 'I don't know. As soon as I got the letters for the name I came
here,' Thathi replied, putting into place his few strands of hair, as he
looked at his new born son. 'You don't have to comb your baldness,'
said Ammi, 'Go back to the astrologer and return only after you find
out what is in store for this child for the next twenty years.' My father
left the room. Before leaving, he gave me the piece of paper with the
letters and asked me to think of more names.

'Ni' was not the only suitable Sinhala letter. 'Ra' was as good as
'Ni'. I decided to call my brother Rasitha. I liked the name. It was not
stupid like my Aboriginal name between manufacturer and
manumission. Rasitha meant something tasty. Ra was the Egyptian falcon
god. Ra was a nickname for Ravana. And Rasitha was the masculinized
diphthong that connected Ravana and Sita. Rasitha, my brother.

I decided to become an etymologist. I had the first word. Rasitha:
Male child born to Ravana and Sita, the legitimate king of Lanka. Perhaps
it was time for a sequel to the Ramayana. I had enough of JR's dharmishta
Mercedes-Benz Buddhism on its televised trips to Nirvana.

Lava and Kusha, whom had they resembled? Pity my father had
not been around with his Made in Japan camera and the Fujicolour
film roll when Lava and Kusha had been born to Sita.

8

Dagma visited baby Rasitha. Dagma now had asthma. When she did not have asthma she had eczema. But everything was under control. The dharmishta dermatologist had a large supply of cortisone in tubes which did not carry expiry dates. Dagma preferred asthma to eczema. After the cortisone tubes had cured the eczema, the asthma re-started, following the over-consumption of ice cream. Dagma's ailments were compartmentalized. She had a doctor for each disease.

Since JR put us on the road to the right, the new multi-storey air-conditioned supermarkets were full of ice cream. From New Zealand, Australia, England, Denmark and Sri Lanka. Chocolate, chocolate-chip, chocolate-ripple, chocolate-delight, chocolate-nut, fruit and nut, nut and nut, mango and nut, water melon and nut, everything. Dagma loved ice cream. She could eat endless servings of it. But, since the appearance of her asthma, three helpings were the limit.

Dagma had gained weight. The weight was not caused by ice-cream, it was caused by the cortisone cream. A life of suffering on the newly cut road to the right! Who would have thought that could happen? Dagma could not walk the road in order to exercise the cortisone cream. The Elephantine leg caused by the filarial-worm-carrying mosquito could only carry her weight in a private air-conditioned taxi. Her legs were no longer capable of carrying her weight. At the end of the day, the fault lay in that Latin worm. It was not JR, it was not the road to the right, and it was not Dagma.

'You are right sister Beet,' Dagma agreed with Achi. 'You once told me, 'Dagma, mosquitoes are the greatest curse on earth.' You were right. Now, when I see or hear a mosquito, I don't think of Buddhism. I kill. It is a question of their survival or our survival. I think the Lord Buddha would not have told us Buddhists not to kill if he had been exposed to mosquitoes! Really sister Beet, this dharmishta government should put an asterix mark on all the Buddhist texts and say, 'killing mosquitoes does not make a Buddhist, non-Buddhist'.'

'The government has other things to sort out before it starts putting asterixes on Buddhist books,' said Achi and served Dagma another helping of chicken curry. They were having a late lunch after putting my brother Rasitha to sleep.

The Tamils were proud of their Boys. They were taking over where democracy and words had failed. Even the unemployed Sinhala educated youth had to admit that the Tamil Boys in their battle for Eelam had begun to rock the cradle of future revolution. The rural Sinhala youth were not free like the Tamil Boys. They were still in foreign bondage. Marxs, Lenins and Maos were still their heroes. The Boys in their quest for Eelam had no foreign heroes. Their Tamil leader was their hero. He was not dead in some foreign country, he was here, with them, fighting. For their Tamil speaking promised land.

The Colombo based Tamil businessmen were a source of irritation to the Boys. They did large favours for JR's dharmishta government, but did not invest in the Tamil homeland. Tamils who went abroad, spent their money on gold jewellery or building bungalows in Colombo. The heart of the Tamil homeland in the North remained a Palmyrah tree bearing barren land. The Tamil representatives in parliament tried to pacify the Boys. But the Boys had lost faith in their representatives to parliament.

Two neutral Tamils with foreign degrees and foreign education, supportive of the road to the right, tried to negotiate on behalf of the Tamil homeland with JR's dharmishta government. The Tamil homeland wanted to move to the right, along with their Palmyrah tree, like we in Colombo were doing with our coconut tree.

So, JR studied up a new word beginning with D, (besides Dharmishata), and came up with devolution. Devolution: transference (as of rights or powers) from one individual to another. (Medieval Latin: devolutio, from Latin, devolvere: to roll down). JR then sent his favourite ministers to the Tamil capital to ensure the smooth fluidity of the district development council election that would implement the non-discriminatory devolution that would enable the independent development of the Tamil homeland without its life long bondage to Colombo.

But, JR did not tell his ministers the English meaning of devolution. He told them only the Latin meaning. To roll down.

JR's dharmishta ministers rolled down. By the time they returned to Colombo after a district development council election which was to have ensured devolution, the monumental public library of the Tamil capital Jaffna, had rolled down its massive edifice. To excessive heat. Thousands of Tamil books and rare manuscripts turned to ash. The written Tamil legacy in the North of Lanka was gone. First in flames, then in ash that blew with the wind and sunk into the Indian ocean. Like devolution. There was no culprit. Hanuman had not come to Lanka this time around.

Between the Sanskrit and Pali dictionaries there was a Latin dictionary on JR's book shelf. Perhaps he studied it, perhaps not. Perhaps his Mahaveli stagnation minister or the big mouthed minister glanced at it during the tea-break before going to Jaffna. Devolvere, devolvi, devolvitum: To roll down, fall, spin off. But, below devolvere there was another word. Devoro, devorare, devoratum: To swallow, gulp, engulf, devour. Devolution and devour were not too far apart. JR spoke of devolution, but his ministers enacted devour. Perhaps the time had come for the legacy of the minority to be devoured by the legacy of the majority. Perhaps JR's devouring ministers thought that Hanuman's mango seed had no room for two historic legacies. One would never know. Dharmishtaness had many assets, but truth was not one of them.

JR did many great things for my country. He created the free market road to the right. He created dharmishta out of the aged dharma. He amnestied the jailed. He created the presidency out of the constitution and the multi-functional air-conditioned super market where one could buy anything from anywhere in the world, at all times. If JR could have only extended the day's twenty-four hours, he could even have written a new dictionary.

C. Constitution: The physical make up of individual and basic principles and law of Nation State, created by individual representing state. JR.

D. Devolution: Roll over.

D. Dharmishta: also roll over. (origin: Sinhala: roll over and rule. Etymology traced to JR of Lanka. No further room for analysis or interpretation). In my book of etymology I too would be creative, like JR.

D. Devolution: destroy and dominate. (origin: JR of Lanka. Two thousand five hundred years after the birth of the Gautama Buddha. Cultural immolation of minority legacy. Meaning literal.

Synonym: Dharmishta. Pre-JR times dharmishta used as antonym).

'Aney sister Beet, I didn't come to talk about mosquitoes. I have another problem,' lamented Dagma. She had taken the third serving of Caramel pudding. 'Sister Beet you won't believe what a relief it is being able to eat something knowing that I would not suffer another attack of asthma.'

'Hm,' said Achi, warming the king coconut water in a bowl of hot water for my brother Rasitha to drink upon waking.

'It is Cecil.'

'What's wrong with Cecil?' Achi asked.

'We have to take him to Apollo.'

'The rocket?' asked Achi perturbed. There were moments in Dagma's conversation where I seriously wondered if the filarial worms were perhaps crawling in her brain and not in her leg.

'Aney sister Beet, you are so hilarious!' and she laughed like a bubbling crater. 'Not the rocket, we have to take him to Apollo in India to do a bypass.'

'What bypass?' Achi's lexicon of medicine was old. It did not have a bypass. Instead, the map of Sri Lanka had an Elephant Pass. I wondered if Dagma had got the wrong end of the stick again.

'A bypass for his heart.'

'Who told you to do that? I didn't feel he had anything wrong with his heart when I last saw him.'

'Apo sister Beet! Cecil has been having a bad heart for years.'

'Who told you that?'

'The new doctor.'

'What new doctor?'

'There is a new Indian doctor from Apollo hospital who comes for a few months a year to see patients here.'

'Why does he come here to see patients? Aren't there patients in India?'

'Apo! There are lots of patients in India, but he comes here to see patients here.'

'And he has told you that Cecil needs a new heart?'

'Apo, not a new heart sister Beet, Cecil needs a bypass.'

Obviously Dagma was not referring to the Elephant Pass. This pass was different.

'Dagma, do you know what a bypass is?'

'Aney, I don't know sister Beet, but I heard some ladies in the supermarket discussing a man with a weak heart who had gone to Apollo for a bypass and returned twenty years younger. Then I asked them to describe this gentleman before the bypass. Apo, sister Beet you would not believe it! This gentleman sounded just like my Cecil. So I asked the ladies where I could consult this doctor and they told me where.'

'So I suppose you have been there?'

'Of course I didn't waste any time. I went the next day. No queue, no nothing. Nice air conditioned place! The doctor did some examinations and said the bypass was the only answer.'

'Answer to what?'

'What then? Answer to life of course sister Beet.'

It was obvious that times had changed. JR's road to the right was not like the times when my grandfather and uncle Lionel had heart attacks. Those days they gave up cigarettes and stopped climbing stairs to give the heart a rest. Today, people were going in rockets to get their hearts repaired in India. Pity JR did not come into power earlier, perhaps my grandfather would have still been alive then.

'Aney, I don't know Dagma, I think you should consult another doctor before you make such decisions.'

'No time now sister Beet, we are flying next week for the bypass,' and she laughed gleefully that she was going to get her Cecil back, twenty years younger. 'But that is not the problem sister Beet, Kusita is the problem. Can you keep her here until Cecil and I come back?'

'Why here? Her school is near your house no?'

'Not any more, she is now at the international school which is close to your house.'

'Apo! Why did you put that child in the international school? All our children are going to local schools no?' asked Achi.

'Yes, but the local schools are not good like the international schools. International schools are much better. And when you are qualified from international schools you can go to university abroad.'

'Nonsense Dagma, there, Mali's son has got three university offers for America, with scholarships too.'

I don't know how, but my brother wasn't offered just one scholarship, he was offered three. He now strutted around the house like a proud peacock. The bat was no longer on the ground, it was on his head!

'Aney sister Beet, that is your grandson no! When those universities hear that the boy has got a grandmother like you they will just give scholarship after scholarship. And that is not all, the child has such an intelligent man like Tissa for a father. The other day Tissa told me all about the stars in the sky. Now when I step out of the house at night I always look at the sky, and then only I go where I have to go. Tissa told me I will learn a lot if I only take the time to look at the sky, so I'm following his advice and doing so. But what does my Kusita have? My poor mother is dead and Cecil's mother is as insane as a hurricane. There, she was screaming at all the servants down the road for stealing jam fruits from the jam tree when I was leaving the house to come and see you. Last week, she ran to temple in her underskirt to ask the monk if he would like to have some chicken curry for lunch. I had to lock her up in her room. Imagine going to temple only in an underskirt! I wonder what sin I have done to get a mother-in-law like her?'

The king coconut water was warm. Achi sat next to Dagma in the armchair in which my grandfather had died. 'Of course those things are the sins of previous births, but tell me how can you afford the international school? Cecil is not even working anymore?'

'We sold our land.'

'Dagma! You don't mean to tell me you are sending this child to an expensive international school with the money you got from the sale of land. That was all you had to give that child for a dowry.'

'Sister Beet. We have only one child. We must invest in her future. Aney sister Beet, Kusita will be coming here now, just look at her, she has become a nice posh lady, speaking only English.'

My brother Rasitha woke up. I carried him over to Achi who fed him the king coconut water. Fortunately he was in a good mood. He drank without burping, farting or shouting. Dagma smiled at him through her lipsticked cow-catcher and my brother seemed to be fascinated with her appearance. Then the bell rang. 'Aney that must be Kusita,' shouted Dagma shocking my peacefully drinking brother. Kusita entered the house.

'Good afternoon aunty Beet, Manuka, Mummy. How are you?' She sounded like Eliza Doolitle in 'My fair lady'.

'Aney we are fine darling, did you have a good class? Aney sister Beet, they had a history lesson this afternoon. It is so interesting, they just finished Queen Elizabeth the First and now they are studying George the First.'

Mummy, you are extremely forgetful! We spent one day speaking about Mary Queen of Scotland before beginning with James the Sixth of Scotland who was later known as George the First of Great Britain.'

Dagma glowed like a freshly ignited joss stick.

'See sister Beet, what did I tell?' Pride emanated from Dagma's soul.

'Aney, I don't know Dagma if those English kings and queens are of any use to us?'

'And Scottish sister Beet, don't forget the Scottish James,' answered Dagma.

'Manuka what are you studying in school?'

Kusita no longer called me Akka as she had done prior to becoming a student at the international school.

'Well, right now we are in the middle of term tests.' I replied. 'Then we are going for a three day trip to Sigiriya.'

'Ah, that is that rock with the Buddha's footprint isn't it?'

I didn't reply. I went to my bedroom and laughed my guts out. Kusita had been in the international school for six months and no longer knew that the Buddha's footprint was on a mountain, not a rock. The rock had too many frescoes of bare breasted ladies; the Buddha would certainly not put his footprint there. But, for a child of an international school, and for its mother, the Buddha could put his footprints wherever he chose, it was unimportant. But, the correct chronological order of Elizabeths, Marys and Georges was of primordial value.

JR located international schools which subsequently sprouted like fungus, on his dharmishta road to the right. His ministers with school going children were the first to send their children to them. Then the likes of Dagma. I too would not have minded going to an international school, but my father did not make enough money dredging canals. I don't know if JR's ministers received special discounts since they were important ministers, but the rest of mankind had to pay horrendous prices. My father perhaps could have used his connections and got a discount, but he refused to contribute to the system. He had some strange archaic notion that I should first learn the history of kings before and after Parakramabahu the sixth before beginning with the Georges and Henrys of England.

Kusita stayed with us while Dagma and granduncle Cecil went for the bypass. Dagma was so euphoric about the bypass that I was unsure she would not get a bypass herself. The condition of the heart was the least of her concerns.

One could not deny that we were on a wonderful road to the right. The government had their mosquitoes with human faces, Dagma got a Valentine's day heart, JR headed a televised trip to Nirvana, Kusita learned of Marys and Georges and TM Mozart got three scholarships to America.

The Buddha's sermons of compassion began to fossilize like his foot-print.

9

The following Sunday, the new astrologer who cast my new brother's horoscope came for lunch. He was young, vegetarian and a teetotaller. Achi, assuming all astrologers were like Pathiraja, prepared chicken curry, sausage curry, wild boar curry, and beef curry. Lalith the astrologer ate only vegetables. Hurriedly, Kandapola siya's driver got onto my father's bicycle and went to the vegetarian restaurant at the cemetery road junction and bought all the vegetarian food he, the driver liked.

The new astrologer's vocal chords squeaked. He squeaked us into sitting around him and listening carefully. If we had questions we should please wait until he finished his reading. He began: 'This male child has been born into the Makara lagne (Capricorn), when the sun is in the two hundred and seventieth degree counted from the vernal equinox. Exactly half a day is over for the people in the south-pole, and for the people of the north-pole it is exactly midnight. Capricorn - Makara is the tenth sign of the zodiac. It is the first sign governed by Saturn. It is movable, cardinal, tropical, negative, feminine, earthy, dry, cold, quadrupedal, persevering, despondent and of short ascension. Mars gets exalted in this sign governed by Saturn, though Saturn gets debilitated in a sign owned by Mars. Jupiter is debilitated. When Capricorn is occupied by both luminaries the sun and the moon, they are in enemy camp. Venus and Mercury are on friendly terms when they are in Capricorn. Capricorn is the sign of sacrifice. When Jesus Christ was born, the sun entered Capricorn, which is a sign of resurrection. The goat is the sacrificial animal for the Capricorn. Therefore it is advisable to sacrifice a goat when a Capricorn is born.' Achi looked at Ammi. Ammi looked at Achi. Achi quickly got the servant Karunawathie to bring Lalith a cup of tea and went to the kitchen to Kandapola siya's driver and gave him money for a goat to be sacrificed at the Hindu Kovil. He refused. He was an orthodox vegetarian. Achi threatened to sack him even though she had no authority to do so. He still refused. He did not want to accumulate negative karma by authorising the killing of goats. He preferred to kill Tamils instead. Achi then lied. She said it was a sacrifice that had to be made for the Sinhala race, if we were to be resurrected. Like Jesus Christ. The driver took the money and went. Smiling.

Lalith continued, 'Saturn, the lord of the sign shows that the person born under this sign will be emaciated, weak and grow slowly. The body will be thin. Height will be acquired after the age of sixteen. The hair is coarse. In the first five years of this male child, Saturn is badly placed. Since Saturn governs the bones of the body, it is advisable to protect the child from falls and injury. Tuberculosis of the bones is indicated in the first five years. It is advisable to put a white sapphire on the child, though that alone will not protect him from injury to the osseous system. Extreme care and caution need to be observed. Following the sacrifice of the goat, it is advisable to do a Bodhi puja every Tuesday until the child reaches its fifth year. It is further advisable to tie on the child's hand a blessed Pirith thread which should be worn until the fifth year. That should protect him for the first five years, if it is not possible to make him cross water during that period.' Ammi was hyper-ventilating. Nenda had contracted pupils, Achi's wrinkles had deepened like the Mariana crater upon the sea bed. Their mouths were open to question, but Lalith raised his hand and made them remain quiet.

'Capricorn is an earthy sign. Therefore, this child, if it survives the fifth year will be prudent and practical minded. Patient, calculative and business minded. He will have organising capabilities and a steady nature which attracts many friends. But he will not make friends easily. He will value and evaluate before making a friend or a decision. But when it is made it is a friend for life or a wise decision. Since Saturn owns the sign he will be fond of music, drama and cinema. Since moon owns the seventh house he will always have company. Saturn also makes him tactful, cunning and diplomatic. This child will study and do well in life. The Makara sign is favourable towards the parents. But it is exceptionally favourable towards elder brothers. The elder brother of the Makara born will have special benefits and glories after the birth of this child.' TM Mozart grinned in ecstasy. I did too. I whispered in his ear: 'It was not your talent that gave you three scholarships. Your brother brought you luck.' He whispered back into my ear, 'You are jealous! Not only are you black, you don't even have luck!' Black, luckless, talentless. That was me. Not to mention the many things I couldn't do, there wasn't even a bowler on the horizon.

The reading was over. Lalith had received his second cup of tea and the question answer time had begun. '*Mae, Lalith*,' Ammi began, 'if we go abroad with this child is there a possibility of escaping his bad times?'

'Don't waste time asking things that are not likely to happen, ask Lalith how to protect him in this country for the first five years of his life. And write it down,' retorted Nenda.

'Nanda, don't you tell me what is going to happen or not going to happen, let me do it my way,' shot back Ammi.

TM Mozart began to hum Frank Sinatra's 'My Way' and everyone glared at him furiously.

Lalith looked back and forth not knowing whom to answer. He smiled. 'Yes. Leaving the country is better,' he replied.

'And if they can't leave the country? One cannot get into a plane and go somewhere, one has to have a house and a job to go to,' said Nenda angrily.

Lalith smiled again. 'Yes, when that is the case, you have to do the Bodhi Pujas like I told you.'

Just then Kandapola siya's driver arived with the goat. No, the goat arrived with Kandapola siya's driver. His sarong falling and beetle juice spurting from his mouth. 'Bloody curse of an animal!' shouted the driver. 'Ah, what a pleasure it is to bring it to slaughter.'

'Not slaughter, sacrifice!' Achi corrected him. The goat ran up to my grandmother with little black marbles of shit falling out of his anal cavity. Karunawathie, Magi and the driver caught the animal and pushed him into the dickey of the car. Achi sat in the back seat and they drove to the Kovil in the Morris Minor. There was no need to delay the sacrifice. The rest of us sat down for lunch.

TM Mozart glowed during lunch, I sulked. My mother gives birth to a child, and only TM Mozart reaps the benefits. I had nothing. I decided to ignore my new brother. Let TM Mozart take care of him. 'Lalith, don't you see in the horoscope that we should go abroad?' Ammi always dreamed about going abroad. She had loved her time at Woolworth and always dreamed of going abroad again. The sales in the modern twenty-four hour air-conditioned supermarkets in our democratic Socialist Republic road to the right were not the same as Woolworth. Colombo ladies did not work in Colombo supermarkets. If they did work, it was only in English supermarkets, in England. 'Well, for me to see if you all will be going abroad, I have to look at all the horoscopes,' said Lalith. Ammi stopped eating lunch, washed her hands and went in search of the horoscopes. Going abroad was a greater priority than having lunch. 'Lalith, the child has no *Maaraka* (death prophesies) no?' asked Nenda fearfully. I think she loved my brother the most. 'Well one has to take precautions,' replied Lalith. He was as diplomatic as a Capricorn. He did not say yes or no like Pathiraja had done, his astrology was more like 'if there is a will there is a way'. There was more room for interpretation.

'Lalith, tell me,' Nenda whispered sitting closer to him, 'don't tell this to anybody, but the baby son has a birthmark on the back of his neck. You know Mali's father had the same birthmark, could it be that he has been reincarnated as this baby boy?' Lalith whispered back to her, 'That is possible, but didn't the family do the proper death rituals, like *Danas* (inviting the Buddhist priests for lunch and preaching in order to ensure the deceased's direct flight to Nirvana) and stuff?' 'We did. We did all the necessary stuff,' she replied.
'Yes, but you never know the Buddhist priests now-a-days no?' said Lalith, 'They are no longer virtuous vegetarians like they used to be. I have heard from many sources that when they are invited to Danas one has to pick them up in cars and if there is no chicken curry they do not come at all.'
'But that is true,' said Nenda, 'Three cars went to pick them up and we served chicken curry.' Lalith smiled in understanding. 'And now you ask me if Mrs. Weerasinghe's father has been re-born? When Buddhist priests eat meat and try to send the dead to Nirvana, the dead do not go to Nirvana they return because they are incorporated into the greed of the Buddhist priests. You cannot tarnish yourself and ask for Nirvana. That does not happen. You have to be pure in order to go to Nirvana. That is why I never go to temple any more, if I feel like giving a Dana, I give a Dana to the beggars or to the orphanage.'

'You are right,' said Nenda. My brother Rasitha screamed from the bedroom. He had just woken up. Nenda pushed her chair away and ran to the room, her bow legs nearly knotting and pulling her to the ground, 'Aney uncle, aney uncle I am coming, I am coming don't cry so loud…' My grandfather was back.

Ammi returned with a stack of horoscopes. The rolled palm leaves, unrolling themselves and following her like a curled sari pota. She gave them to Lalith and continued her lunch. 'Don't hurry, look at them carefully. Remember, the first priority is to save this child's life.' Lalith brought system to the scrolls and opened each scroll to the present. Ammi's, Thathi's, TM Mozart's and mine. 'What do you see?'

'Will you stop disturbing Lalith,' Nenda scolded her. She had returned with the baby. Lalith studied the scrolls, drew some charts and spent about an hour in silence. My mother finished the entire dish of rice, the sausage curry, the chicken curry and the beef curry. Perhaps she was sure that she was going abroad to save my brother's life and she had a last supper – of curry.

'Haven't you left food for Tissa Aiya?' asked Nenda angrily.

'If he isn't here it's his own fault,' said Ammi; washed her hands and re-located in front of Lalith.

'It is not clear,' began Lalith slowly. 'There are trips indicated, but they will not fall into the lap. You have to fight for them.'

'What do you mean fight?'

'What I mean is, you have to apply for jobs abroad in order for you to get them. If you just stay in the house and expect someone to call and offer a job abroad it will not happen. '*Unanduwa*', or perseverance is required."

'Did you see it in my horoscope?' asked Ammi eagerly. It had always been her greatest love to follow her head line to Minnesota where uncle Buddhi's wife was a Montessori teacher. But my mother's head line did not go to a Montessori in Minnesota, rather into a Montessori in Colombo.

'No. Not in your horoscope.' Ammi's eagerness evaporated like a drop of water in the desert. 'You can apply as much as you want, but your horoscope will not make you budge. The only way you can leave this country is through Mr. Weerasinghe's horoscope. If he applies to go abroad, he will get the job and then the rest of the family can go with him.'

'Aney are you sure Lalith? Look again and see…'

'I can look a hundred times, I see the same thing.'

'You have no choice but to protect the child here,' said Achi comforting her. She had just returned after the drama with the goat. 'Tissa will never leave the country as long as his mother is living.'

'That is correct,' echoed Nenda.

'Are you sure we can leave as a family?' Ammi asked Lalith again.

'That, I am sure.'

My mother began her holy war. 'Mummy, Nanda, I didn't waste nine months of my life throwing up and feeling nauseous to escort this child to the cemetery. Tissa has to now decide between his family and his mother,' said Ammi adamantly. I made a silent note to leave the house when this confrontation arose. When my mother and father fought, Ammi was like an erupting Vesuvius, and Thathi like Pompeii buried in ash. 'But Mali, you can't make him do a thing like that?' said Achi.

It was not only my father's mother they would be leaving behind, my grandmother would be left behind as well. 'I can. And if I fail I will speak to his mother about the dilemma. She is a mother, she will understand me and make her son take the right decision, for his family. For the future.' I knew she was right. My father's mother was a woman to be venerated. She was the living incarnation of Buddha's compassion and detachment. Not as a façade, but a practicing reality. She would make the right decision according to the situation, but I wonder if the right decision for the moment would be the right decision for the future? But who was I to tell? I was the least influenced in this tragi-comedy of planets.

Just then Thathi entered the house after a mid-morning swim and a chat with Arthur C. Clark about the dialectical difference between astrology and astronomy. 'Ah Lalith, how are you?' he asked entering with his wet towel and wet swimming trunks. 'I just spoke to Mr. Arthur C. Clark, and you know, he said that astrology has absolutely no relevance to astronomy. He is even doubtful about the verity of astrology and the role of man based on prediction.'

'Tissa, I'm personally disinterested in what your Arthur C. Clark says, Lalith says we have to leave the country to save my small boy's life.'

'Ah, really?' said Thathi serving rice onto his plate, the crumbs my mother had left him. 'But how can we do such a thing? The minister has just appointed me the chief engineer of the canal development project and I have also promised to help the Mahaveli minister draw up a new system of irrigation for the dry zone.'

'I don't care about your promises to ministers, think about your promises to me.'

'I promised you something?' he asked patiently mixing a spoonful of rice with a bit of gravy.

'You remember marrying me, I hope?'

'Mali, that was donkeys years ago! How can I remember what I said then, when I don't even remember what Arthur C. Clark told me two weeks ago?'

'Lalith tell him.' It was becoming unpleasant. I went to my room and listened through the hole in the curtain.

'It is like this,' began Lalith, 'It's better for the child...' Ammi interrupted. 'Lalith, tell him how you told me. It is not better for the child, it is of absolute importance to the child.'

Lalith began again. 'It's like this Tissa sir, the child is born under an *Eyrashtaka*, Saturn the governing planet is badly placed for the first five years of his life. In order to ensure his survival it is advisable...'

'Not advisable, vital,' cut in Ammi.

'...that you all cross water with him.'

'How can that be Lalith? My mother gave birth to five healthy children and they are all married with their own healthy children and they never had to cross water in order to live. How do you want me to do that? Am I supposed to get into a plane and leave, and hope someone on the other side of the water will give me a job at my age? Lalith, I'm over fifty. All my friends are becoming grandfathers, I have just become a father. Don't tell me to leave the country. I cannot do so. I have a job here. And I have my mother here.'

'Well then,' said Lalith meekly, 'then we have to think of the other means.'

In the meantime, Ammi started to erupt, like a volcano spewing the first sparks of magma from her centre. 'Tissa, I don't want to hear your bullshit. I don't want to hear about your job and I don't want to hear about your friends becoming grandfathers. If you acted your bloody age we would not have had another child. But you did not act your bloody age! You were prancing around like a dandy when your friends started using walking sticks. Is it my fault? NO. It's your fault! If you could do a thing which is not in accordance with your bloody age you have to bear the consequences. Your first priority is towards your family, everything else is secondary. And I do NOT care if you have to beg, borrow or steal, we are taking our son out of this country for the first five years. I don't care where, but out of here. If you do not do so, believe me, you and I can see each other in divorce courts. Now go! And don't return until you have found a job abroad!'

Achi pleaded with Ammi to let Thathi finish his meal before going in search for a job across the water. She gave him a moment to satisfy his stomach. He ate his lunch in near silence, exchanging an occasional word with Lalith on a neutral subject, but no word with my mother. I escaped over the wall to Sharona. Thank God her father was too old to prance on her mother and give birth to unnecessary children that disrupt one's life. For the time being I decided not to have children if another bowler entered my life. I was not in the mood to cross water.

10

Africa. My father got a job in Africa. Of all the continents in the world, he got a job in Africa. Ammi blew up like the recently exploded Mount St. Helen in America, close to TM Mozart's chosen university. 'Out of all the places in the world, you don't mean to tell me you signed a contract for a job in Africa! Are you completely off your mind? Why couldn't you sign a contract for a job in America or Europe? Why Africa?'

Thathi replied patiently. 'America and Europe do not need people of my age to build roads, they already have roads. Africa has no roads, so either I go to Africa to build roads or I stay here and dredge canals.'

'I refuse to go to Africa.'

'Good,' said my father glowing with inner-happiness that the quest for crossing water would be de-quested before it began. 'If you don't want to go, I don't want to go either. I will cancel the contract and the matter is settled.' But a mother's instinct got the better of her. She put on her buccaneer boots and the pioneering clothes and planned their departure.

TM Mozart went first. My father could not take him to the airport, he was at a re-opening ceremony for a newly dredged canal with JR's minister who had a dream similar to the twenty-four hour supermarkets where everything was available from a video to a bypass. This minister had an indigenous dream where everything indigenous was available in the re-created indigenous market place where native vendors sold indigenous products under orange lights. This was the same minister who built the orange overhead bridges which were now great orange skeletons above the highways. People crossing the roads had broken the fences and were now crawling again between the cars to cross the roads. In our country, no minister could build overhead bridges and expect indigenous citizens to cross the road on the overhead bridge in the hot blazing son. Only non-indigenous tourists did so. First, tourists had a masochistic delight in being exposed to our blazing sun and secondly, they did not have faith in karma, as we did. Crossing the road in the midst of rush hour traffic meant death to the tourist. But to the indigenous, karma brought on death, not the traffic.

TM Mozart had one suitcase. The rest was the guitar, the mouth organ and the new accordion. If he could have taken the piano he would have done so. Uncle Buddhi took my mother and me to the airport. Uncle Buddhi had discarded his trousers since the diabetes and was wearing indigenous clothes bought at orange-lit night bazaars. He had also stopped swallowing homeopathy molecules, and was now inserting strange needles all over his body to halt the diabetes. He said it worked. It was more physical than the homeopathy, which was belatedly discovered to be a partial balance between physics and chemistry. Uncle Buddhi still believed in physics causing the big bang that created mice and men with diabetes.

On the way to the airport uncle Budddhi told my mother about his needles. He had learned to stick his own needles. He told my mother she should learn to stick needles too. He told my brother that there were needles for learning, for concentration and sufficient sleep. The needle was the future. He tried to tell us the fundamentals of needling and held a sermon which sounded more Chinese or Japanese than English or Sinhala.

'The Chee,' he said, is the vital element of life. 'When the Chee travels smoothly good health is inevitable.' I understood the Chee. We indigenous people said, 'Chee, you are urinating with the toilet door open!' Or we said, 'Chee, don't dig your back!' In other words, everything that was not okay and had to be corrected to fit into the norms of etiquette was Chee. It never struck me that uncle Buddhi's Chee was different to my Chee. In his new second hand convertible Volkswagen with the wind blowing in my ears, his chee sounded the same as mine.

Again, the tickets were bought for the airport visitors' lounge. They had increased in price. We were on the road to the right and the Bandaranayake International Airport had been re-named the Colombo International Airport. Fortunately, since JR named the new parliament area of the old kingdom after him, he did not have the desire to name the airport after himself. His megalomania had its roots in Buddhism. It was a case of re-christening with moderation.

As TM Mozart got out of the car, he grinned and told me, 'Be careful, in Africa the cannibals like to eat black skinned, flat nosed teenage girls! Wear a veil or something that they don't see your ugliness!'

I could not be bothered telling him that I was not planning on going to any Africa. I had still not figured out how not to go, but once he was out of the way I would do so. Instead, I told him, 'Be careful that you don't return looking like a cannibal yourself, for when the volcano erupts again you will become as black as cinder and your hair will melt to the roots.'

'Jealous, jealous!' he grinned. 'My dear sister, when I return I will have so much money that I could probably buy the whole country. If you are nice to me I may perhaps send you some American bleaching cream so the cannibals won't mistake you for one of them,' and he left with the last word. I stayed in the car with uncle Buddhi and his chee. Only one visitor was permitted into the airport lounge with each embarking passenger. My mother was that visitor.

Between the first news of Africa and their departure, Mrs. Perera's sewing machine did not cease to spin. My brother Rasitha got bush shirts in all sizes until the age of five. My father got safari suits and bush shirts in all shades of khaki, beige and brown. Ammi went to the video parlour and rented all the videos with jungle films and copied the style of clothes in Hollywood. I got a chance to see Born Free, Hatari, the Nun's Story and many classics during a matter of weeks. When my mother's wardrobe was completed it was difficult to say if she looked like Audrey Hepburn as a nun in the Congo or Elsa the lioness, in the bush.

They went. They tried to take me, but I refused. Normally my refusal does not mean much, but I convinced them I was too good to be taken out of school and too bad to be innovative in a new country. I was one of those absolutely mediocre mediocrities. A genetic calamity when compared to the talented TM Mozart.

Prior to their departure, Dagma called. She had started urinating. She did not know why, but gallons and gallons were escaping her bladder. She could not come to say goodbye. Nenda hurriedly told Ammi to lie to Dagma about the date of departure for Dagma was nothing but a living misfortune. If one saw her face before leaving for a new venture, one was sure that one would be struck by bad luck. 'That uncle Cecil,' she said, 'had nothing wrong with his heart, now he has something wrong with his heart.' Perhaps she was right. Since their return from that rocket hospital in India my granduncle Cecil, though his heart was twenty years younger, looked about forty years older. He had never spoken much in his life, he had Dagma for that, but now, he did not speak at all. Even when he said good morning, he would gasp like the fish we took out of water before beginning the dissections for zoology in school.

They left. Tears poured down all the faces. Nenda, Magi, Dasa, the boarders, my grandmother, Mrs. Adonis, Mrs. Perera the seamstress, Roswitha, Sharona's mother. They all stood and cried. It became like the flood that Viharamahedevi with her alabaster beauty was sacrificed in order to stem. Only Thathi and uncle Buddhi remained calm. They packed uncle Buddhi's car with the luggage and said they should leave unless they wanted to miss the flight. My brother Rasitha went from arm to arm. The tragedy was not Africa, the tragedy was not that my parents were leaving and the tragedy was not that some of us were remaining. The tragedy was that this sweet little baby could no longer be cuddled and pampered by all these women who were beyond child bearing age. Except me, but I was another story.

I held back my tears like Atlas holding the world. I didn't want my mother to reconsider taking me with them because I appeared to be sad. Africa had no cricket. I had to seek my bowler in this country, not Africa. They got into the car. There was no room for me, even though I could have got a visitor's pass since three people were departing. But my mother's Hollywood clothes occupied too many suitcases and uncle Buddhi's vehicle was a car, not a bus.

As they kissed me farewell, Thathi said, 'Study well. Whatever you have in life people can steal from you, but not your education.' Then Ammi hugged and kissed me. 'Don't waste time with Sharona. Study every day. When you finish your A' levels we will send for you to attend an African university.'

'Yes, Ammi,' I said, wiping my face. I still did not like being kissed.

I decided not to do my A' levels or else fail it for the rest of my life. I took my brother Rasitha into my arms. I wondered when I would see him again, or if I ever would? He barely spoke, but he grinned at me and plucked a handful of hair from my head and went with my parents and his, to Africa. I stayed behind. TM Mozart was at the foot of Mount St. Helen in America.

Our life together was over.

11

On the night before the holiest day in the month of July, on a lonely stretch of road close to Jaffna, thirteen soldiers of the Sri Lankan army were ambushed and killed by the Tamil Tigers.

They died like dogs. Mutilated and decimated. All thirteen were between the ages of eighteen and twenty two. All Sinhalese.

Twelve self-loading rifles, a repeater shot-gun, twelve grenades, seven bayonets, seventeen magazines and two hundred and ninety rounds of ammunition did the job.

The twelve self-loading rifles, the repeater shot-gun, twelve grenades, seven bayonets, seventeen magazines and two hundred and ninety rounds of ammunition had been the property of the Sri Lankan army.

The Tigers borrowed it. For the light of Eelam, the Tamil speaking homeland in the North and East of Sri Lanka.

What the Liberation Tigers of Tamil Eelam borrowed, they did not return. What they killed, they did not replace. Their cause was worthy, the world had to understand it.

Their demarcations and demands were unclear. The Sinhala politician spoke no Tamil. The Sinhala Buddhist monk who preached non-detachment and longed for the Buddha's second footprint upon Adam's peak spoke no Tamil. But the noise for Eelam was heard. The bomb, the bullet, the massacre, the sorrow.

The explosion that had mutilated the bodies of the thirteen Sinhalese army officers between the ages of eighteen and twenty two, traveling in Jeeps on this lonely road in Tinnavelli on the night before the Esala (July) full moon poya day, the night before the celebration of the Tamil Vel festival in honour of Lord Kataragama, and the night of the Sabbath was detonated by an electronic device that had once been part of the inventory list of the Sri Lankan Cement Corporation. When the thirteen Sinhalese soldiers lost their lives on that lonely night before the full moon, the Sri Lankan government realized that the detonator had been stolen. They struck it off their inventory list.

It was war. Thathi called from a telephone in Africa. His short wave radio had broadcast the massacre on BBC. 'How is everything?'

he bellowed through the telephone. I held the receiver six inches away from my ear and shouted back. 'Here of course, everything is okay. They did not even show it on television.'

'BBC said that the soldiers were killed because they had raped Jaffna Tamil girls.' Nenda heard Thathi through the receiver I was holding six inches away from my ear and grabbed it from my hand.

'LIES, LIES, ALL LIES,' she shouted. 'Don't believe a word of what BBC says, those Tamils are all over the world and are giving us Sinhalese a bad name. Those BBC people are foolish and they believe everything those Tamils tell them. Those innocent young Sinhala soldiers were killed because the army captured one of the Tiger leaders. It was REVENGE. NOT RAPE!' I didn't know where Nenda got her information, I knew nothing of either revenge or rape.

She returned the telephone to me. 'Chooti, how is school?' Thathi asked.

'Okay.'

'Are you studying?'

'Yes.' It was Poya, but I had no problem lying to my father. If the BBC could lie on a Poya day, so could I.

'If you have time between school and classes, learn Tamil. Since I am here I have had a lot of time to think. I realized the mistakes we as a nation have made. I regret that I never learned Tamil. We were foolish. We learned the language of our coloniser but not of our neighbours and friends. That was a mistake. You are still young, you can still learn.'

'Alright Thathi,' I echoed like a hollow tree trunk. I was sick of studying. I was sick of school. I had no bowler. There was not even a batsman. I had my own problems, I didn't have time to learn Tamil. Fashionable people studied French, not Tamil. I was stuck on a zoology table with a dead cockroach pinned on wax which I had to dissect and dismember. My friends studied culture. I studied dead animals. Harini studied French. Sohani studied Greek and Roman civilization. Deepa studied English literature. Marshmallow studied German. And I, I was mutilating cockroaches. After the cockroach I had to begin with frogs. I wondered where it would all end. Karma had really brought my life to a dead end. 'So Chooti, I will stop now. Read the newspaper everyday, study well and don't forget the Tamil classes. Remember, everything you have in life one can rob from you, but not your education.'

I wondered whether it was the lack of education that made the Tamil Tiger rob the detonator from the cement cooperation, or whether the cement corporation kept detonators due to a lack of education. 'Your education will enlighten you and put you on the path to happiness. Life is nothing but a quest for happiness. And happiness is nothing but a fleeting moment.' My father was still on a soliloquy.

Was the struggle for Tamil Eelam happiness? Or, the extermination of thirteen soldiers between eighteen and twenty two a fleeting moment of happiness? I felt no happiness when I killed the wretched cockroach for dissection. Just disgust. I hated cockroaches, but I could not kill them, not for wisdom, and certainly not for anatomy. My father was still speaking. 'I remember when I was a child, your grandmother keeping me on her lap and telling me stories - that was happiness.'

Even though I rejoiced at their departure, I must admit I missed them. My brother Rasitha, Ammi, Thathi and even TM Mozart. I missed my grandfather, whom I thought of as a Buddhist cacophony on the armchair. I still missed Podian the driver. Life was no longer the same in this rambling house down Cemetery road. There was no more happiness. 'Okay Chooti, I will stop now, this call is getting very expensive. If someone comes to Colombo from here, I will send a short wave radio so you can listen to BBC. I did not ask my father why I had to listen to their lies! I said alright and the line went dead.

The mutilated bodies of the thirteen soldiers had to be put into plastic bags for burial. Extremities switched and shredded. They had been thirteen poor boys from poor parents, from villages. They had joined the Sri Lankan army as a source of income. Not patriotism. They were the pawns in the game of chess between the Tamil Tigers and JR.

An eye for an eye, a tooth for a tooth...

After the great wave had come and separated Lanka from India, the Dravidians from South India had crossed the few miles of water, seen the copper sands and the copper waters in the river that ran through Tinnavelli and called it Thambapani (copper sands), and Tamra Varuna (copper water). They had settled down on that copper coloured earth. In peace. To prosper. The copper had now changed hue. The copper sands splattered with red and the crystal clear water that had taken the colour of the copper sands, now took the colour of blood. Red.

The Sinhala mob wanted revenge. Revenge for the killing of thirteen nameless soldiers who died on that night before the full moon on a quiet stretch of road, close to Jaffna.

The army became a single rabid dog. They got into their vehicles and went on a random spree of shooting. Thirty-nine Tamil speaking civilians in the north died in retaliation for the death of thirteen Sinhala soldiers. Those who died were neither terrorists nor soldiers. The Sinhala mobs arrived in the North, took an example from the patriotic soldiers and continued looting where the shooting had stopped and the soldiers had been ordered back to their barracks. There was no compassion.

A hush entered the country. The Sinhala pride rose like the ferocious lion on the flag carrying its golden sword. The Buddha's footprint and the Buddha's decaying tooth were forgotten. I wondered if the Buddha had given the lion the sword during a secret visit which had not been chronicled by his adherents.

Nenda and Magi united in the moment of crisis and spent day and night in front of the Television. Nenda wore white, so did Magi. They were in mourning. The television set telecasted archaic soap operas from America which had been shown when JR first introduced television to our country. In between the soap operas some of JR's ministers showed their faces and spoke of universities and higher education. The massacre remained in the North.

It was called censorship.

The gate bell rang early in the morning. No one answered it, we were all sleeping.

It rang again. I put the pillow over my head and continued to sleep. Be it devil or angel at the gate, I would open it only when sleep took her leave.

The bell ringer kept his finger on the bell and did not release it. Sleep took her leave before the morning sun had begun to shine. Nenda wobbled to the window and shouted through it, '*Kawudha? Me udé paandara yakku gas nagina welaawata minissu aheranne?*' (Who is this, trying to wake up people at a time when devils are climbing trees?) Magi and I followed. We stood close behind Nenda at the window. I had my pen knife in my hand, Magi a rolling pin and Achi, the broom. '*Enappa Nanda Haamu… Me mama. Mama.*' (Enappa Madam Nanda, this is me. Me). A little light flickered in the labyrinth of my mind. It was barely visible. 'We don't know anyone called mama (me), tell us the name.'

'Ennappa, Nanda Haamu, it is what a pleasure to be hearing your voice, even if I am on the other side of the gate and not seeing yours beautiful face.' The voice outside the gate was male. And it was Tamil. 'Who is this 'I' outside the gate? That is what I asked,' Nenda repeated. 'Nanda Haamu, you have forgotten me no! Ennappa, I am very sad. How can you forget me? Podian.'

'PODIAN?' Four voices of disbelief echoed the name we had not dared to mention over the last few years. 'Podian, Kandapola uncle's driver, Podian?' Nenda needed evidence. 'Ennappa Nanda Haamu, what other Podian you knowing?' the voice laughed over the gate. 'How do I know it is you? As if I can remember your voice!' Nenda was dying to open the gate, but we were now learning to be wary of the Tamil man. It had never been like this, but, since the rise of the Liberation Tigers of Tamil Eelam, the fungus of suspicion and mistrust had entered and destroyed the barrier of language that had never been united, but tolerated.

Although Podian was not a Jaffna Tamil, the killers of the thirteen Sinhala soldiers were. In this moment of ferocious patriotism and forgotten compassion, a Tamil man was a Tamil man. Their common language brought them together and the difference of their origin was not important to us, the Sinhalese. Blinded by zealous politicians and monks impregnating simple minds with the fear of being pushed into the sea when the Tamils created their country called Eelam, we had now begun to be wary of those who had escorted us through our long history as a nation. 'Ennappa Nanda haamu, you wanting to remember my voice, so I will sing the song Mister Tissa always play on gramaphone record when he dance with madame, practicing steps from dance class he and Mister Buddhi visit with the Madams.' And so he began. '*Bom bom bom bom, Bombay merrai hai, bom bom bom bom, Bombay merrai hai, ladies are nice, they're so full of spice, come bom bom bom bom bom Bombay merrai hai!*'

Nenda lost her wobble and sprinted to the gate to open it. There stood a man I had never seen before. The Podian I remembered did not look like this. This Podian was small, black, ugly, toothless, yellow eyed and trousered. Our Podian had not been so ugly and had never worn trousers, only a sarong.

But, it was him. He first went up to my grandmother and fell down at her feet and worshipped her. 'Madam Haamu Beet, Madam Hamu Beet…,' he cried kissing her feet. He could speak no more. Nor could we. Then he got up and kissed Nenda's feet. 'Nanda Haamu. Nanda Haamu, you are still looking so beautiful like the day I saw you last.' Nenda smiled in ecstasy. Then Magi. 'Ennappa Magi akka,' he said clutching her feet, 'Look at me Magi akka, I am like skeleton. No food in this world taste better than the food you had fed to Podian every time I have come to this house. Every day I have been thinking 'Podian, you have to make money only to see Cemetery Road family and eat Magi Akka's food. So I am now here.' He got up from Magi's feet and came towards me. 'Enappa this is small baby no?' he said holding my hand. I was no longer a small baby, I was taller than him. 'Ennappa baby, you must not be remembering me. I carried you when you were baby and everyday when I was here I drive you to your school in the Flower Road. But it is long time gone. I am sure you not remembering me now baby.' I smiled at him, 'Of course I remember you,' I said. I could never forget Podian. He was a part of my life. We all walked into the house for breakfast. Happy.

JR was worried. He didn't know how to hold the funeral for the thirteen dead soldiers who were from thirteen different villages in the country. It was not possible to have thirteen different state funerals at the same time. JR contemplated having the funeral in Jafffna since the thirteen soldiers died in an ambush in Tinnavelli, close to Jaffna. But the police did not like the army having the funeral in Jaffna. 'They died like dogs, you can't bury them like dogs,' was the argument against Jaffna. So they decided to have the bodies flown to Colombo and have one mass funeral in the cemetery on Cemetery Road where I lived. JR and his affiliates knew that the Sinhala anger was like a magma chamber about to erupt. They also knew that flying thirteen bodies in plastic bags was the final push this chamber needed to explode. But, against all wisdom, they decided to fly in the thirteen plastic bags of mutilated bodies. The Sinhalese were like the yellow lion represented on the national flag. Standing on three legs, the fourth carrying the sword. No animal could stand on three legs and not stumble. Either it stood on four legs, or it stood on two. But three? JR, his ministers, his affiliates, his cronies, gave the power to the three legged lion. Wisdom was nowhere to be seen.

It was not the first of the month. But Magi began to make kiribath to celebrate Podian's return. 'You are a dirty fellow,' said Nenda teasingly. 'You went without saying a word. I don't know why we even let you step into this house again!'

'Ennappa Nanda Hamu, you knowing? I am a foolish man no? Not clever and educated like you and big Hamu.'

'Why did you go?'

'Enappa, how not to go? When government say come, must go. I went.'

'But you should have said you refuse to go.'

'How can poor foolish man like I, say no to government? They come, put us in lorries and then into the sea and we go.'

'But you should have come and told Mister Tissa, he knows a lot of people in the government I am sure you could have stayed.'

'What to do Nanda hamu? I am knowing only now, what I should be knowing then. Now, too late. What has happened has happened. So I tell myself, one day enappa I return. And I stay. If government try to send me back, I stay and shout till they kill me. If they not kill me I will hide in big house in Cemetery Road and no one will find me.'

'You don't have to hide. You were born in this country no?'

'Ennappa, Nanda Hamu, when all politicians having wisdom like you no war in the world no. Only peace.'

'How was it in India?' Achi asked.

'Ennappa big hamu! Yindia? All over the place people, people, people! And vary dirty! Here is paradise. Not like Yindia.'

'So what did you do there, did you work as a driver?'

'Ennappa no. There when working as driver, having to go to kovil every day and donate gold jewelry to Gods to protect life. Not one God, to all the Gods. There protecting life on roads too difficult for one God. And me, poor man, where I having gold to donate to gods to save life? So I not drive. People driving like mad mans on roads. Everywhere cars, everywhere Bajaj, everywhere loud buses, bicycles, dogs and cows.'

'Cows also?' Magi had returned to the conversation between making tea and milk rice.

'Ennappa! You have to see that Magi akka. Cow sitting all over the road and waiting. Holy animal no, so have to sit and wait. Can't push holy animal around no. But kill holy animal in accident! Ennappa I don't want to think what is happening. I think having to go to jail or paying money for foolish animal sitting on road and doing nothing.'

'So what did you do if you didn't drive cars?'

'I work in shop.'

'What shop?'

'Condiment shop. I carry flour sack, rice sack, saffron powder, cardamom, from delivery lorry to shop. Hard work, but good boss. He tell me Podian, you do everything in this shop, be honest and you can sleep between the gunny bags and I will not be charging you money.'

'You slept all these years between gunny bags?'

'Sometimes between gunny bags, sometimes on top gunny bags. Not so bad Nanda Haamu. That way I not having to pay money to landlady to live in room and I am being able to save all money I make to get into plane and come back to my country.'

'And you never married? If you married you would have got a good dowry and could have slept in a nice bed no? Without sleeping on gunny bags.'

'Apo Nanda Hamu, dowry or no dowry, me not marrying. Marrying woman getting lorry full of children and me having more problem coming back to my country.'

We laughed heartily.

'So one day I am counting money and thinking, enough! So I go to tailor and tell him, make me cheap trouser only to wear one time in life for I am going in plane back to my country. Tailor asking me why one time? I say, 'when I am gone to my country I am not coming back and when I am not coming back in plane I am not needing trouser. In my country I can wear sarong and be happy.'

'Apo Podian, don't throw the trouser away, you look smart in it,' said Achi smiling.

'Trouser not comfortable big Madame, I am meaning to ask you if you can lend to me old sarong from Tissa sir so I can wear in house?' Nenda brought Podian a sarong. It was my father's newest sarong.

'Enappa Nanda Haamu, this is good sarong no?'

'It does not matter, by the time Mister Tissa and family return to this country this sarong will be old, so at least you can wear it without it just aging in the almairah.'

'Thank you Nanda Haamu, you are being very generous to me. And I am coming back to country without bringing you any present. I am meaning to buy some gold bangle for you and Magi akka, but when I have enough money for plane I say, 'Podian now is good time to go.' But when I get job here again driving car I buy gold bangle for you, Magi akka and this small baby, from big Madame's Mister Niser in Pettah Bullion Exchange. He is surely giving me good discount price.'

We all laughed. It was good to have him back.

Magi announced that the milk rice was ready. Podian went into the kitchen escorted by Nenda and Magi. While he ate they related the stories of the last few years. Of my grandfather's death and of my brother Rasitha's birth. Of my parent's crossing water and of my brother TM Mozart going to a university at the foot of the volcano. They told him of Kandapola siya's new driver who was an absolute imbecile. But I don't know if they said anything about the situation in the country which was beginning to explode like a volcano. I think they forgot. They were happy to have the Tamil man back in their lives.

13

Sharona and I decided to go to the funeral. We knew that neither of us would get permission to go, so we checked the obituaries in the 'Daily News' during the last week and saw that most Budddhist funerals where flowers were specially not requested were at four in the afternoon. The Buddhists liked to give flowers to the Lord Buddha; therefore, most good Buddhists didn't want flowers at their funerals. It was a typical Buddhist sacrifice, like being vegetarian.

Sometime between three and four in the afternoon, Sharona told her mother she was coming to my house to do a school project about ancient Egypt. Around the same time I told Nenda that I was going to Sharona's house to do a project on ancient Egypt. If my mother had been here we would not have got away with this lie, for neither Sharona nor I had anything to do with ancient Egypt in school. But my mother was not there. Where Nenda was concerned, the dissection of cockroaches and frogs was not very different to the mummified pharos in the pyramids of Egypt. I took a plastic bag and put a white skirt, a white blouse and a folding umbrella into it. Then I held a Life magazine belonging to my grandfather with a picture of Tutankhamen, showed the magazine to Nenda and left the house. Sharona did the same. We scaled the wall to Mrs. Adonis's garden, hid the plastic bags and the Life magazine in the deceased Cleopatra's kennel, put on the white clothes over our shorts and t-shirts, opened the parasol, concealed our heads so that Roswitha would not notice that we were on the road, and joined the crowd on Cemetery Road walking towards the cemetery.

The cemetery road was full of people. All in white, walking in the same direction with colourful lion flags neatly folded in their pockets. They were all Sinhala. Sharona and I were Sinhala too, but we had not brought the lion flag.

After we passed Roswitha's line of vision, we folded the umbrella and took up the spirit of the people who were walking beside us. They were not sad people, they were angry people. Amongst these angry people were Buddhist priests who were angrier than the lay people. Ecstatic with attachment, not a molecule of detachment was visible. As Sharona and I walked towards the funeral on this poya day, we realised that the Buddha's compassion had died. We did not know if it had died with the thirteen soldiers who were killed in the ambush, or if it had died before. But, the fact was that it was dead. Dead like the soldiers in plastic bags awaiting burial. There was no more hope for unity.

The leader of the Liberation Tigers of Tamil Eelam was not much different from the leader of the red fungus who had killed and killed and finally said, '*I am not a murderer, I am a Bolshevik.*' I don't know what the liberation leader would say the day he is captured. I probably wouldn't understand, since he would undoubtedly speak in Tamil and I had still not found the time to study the language. But, I could not believe that those jewelled and multi-coloured Gods belonging to the Hindus tolerated murder. Lord Shiva had assumed the form of the Natarajah (lord of the dance) and kept his standing foot on the dwarf of ignorance not letting him rise. Lord Kataragama, the God common to both Hindu's and Buddhists is not only the god of war, he is also the god of wisdom. Podian the Tamil driver had sacrificed a goat so I, the Sinhala child could live. But now it was over. The mistakes made by men and women without wisdom leading this country in their megalomania and their obsession for power had brought us to an abyss. There was no point in asking who was to blame. The weed of anger had sprouted from the drops of blood upon the soil. Perhaps they were all to blame. One to a lesser degree, another to a greater degree. Racial unity was a fragment of the past. A shadow, a memory, a photograph.

We still spoke separate languages. No one had succeeded in making us speak one language, or even learn the other. Even though they had all realised it was vital to our existence as a multicultural, multi-ethnic, multi-religious island beyond the tip of India. Nationality, chauvinism, patriotism had defeated compassion. Attachment had defeated peace. Racial hegemony conquered human life. Buddhist hegemony conquered human life. Perhaps Natarajah had ceased to dance and let the dwarf of ignorance free.

And no one knew.

14

When Sharona and I reached the funeral premises, pushing through the mass of people who were also pushing, no plastic bags and no coffins were to be seen. Even if they had been there, we probably would have not seen them for it was worse than Dudley's funeral; there were more people here than I imagined lived in our small country. Everywhere I looked there was someone I knew. Most of those someones were people working in the shops down Cemetery Road or people who sold flowers at the temple on Cemetery Road. Even the man who used to look after the slippers at the temple on poya days was there. I wondered if they had all been friends of the soldiers who had died in Tinnavelli?

The slipper protector saw me and pushed his way up to me. I tried to escape him, but it was too late. 'Hello baby,' he said, 'did your grandmother allow you to come here today?'

'Yes.' I lied.

'That was not very wise of her, they are expecting trouble.'

'How do you know?' He smiled as if he knew a lot, but said nothing. 'I think you and this other baby should hurry up and go home before trouble starts.'

'Why should there be trouble?' I asked naïvely, 'This is a funeral no?'

'When those buggers kill our boys you think we will be still? No! Baby, go home now.' I said alright and moved away to another place where we thought we would see better. I wonder how the rubber slipper protector at the temple got his information. He was only a rubber slipper protector at the Cemetery Road temple, how would he have information about what was happening in the country? I paid no heed to what he had said and tried to push my way forward holding Sharona's hand.

'Aney I don't know,' said Sharona who was getting tired of being squashed between stinking armpits. 'I don't know if it was a good idea to come here today. See, one hour has gone and still no funeral.'

'We are here and we are staying,' I told her vehemently. I wanted to see what was happening. 'For you it is easy, your grandmother is old, she won't notice that you aren't at home, but my mother is young and will realise that I'm not at your place after she finishes reading 'Polyanna'.' Sharona's mother loved to read.

'Your mother won't realize anything. Today they are showing a two hour special of 'Dynasty' on the television and your mother will not budge.' Normally we had only twenty minutes of 'Dynasty' without advertisements, but today, there was to be two hours of 'Dynasty' without ads. I too had been tempted to remain and watch 'Dynasty', but my patriotic curiosity got the better of me.

I was glad we had come early. The crowd gathered behind us by the thousands. Most people working in Sinhala shops around Cemetery Road and its surroundings were at the cemetery. I wondered if they all had observed poya and closed the shops, for there was no Sunday that they usually did not work. 'Sharona, see that man over there, he is the one who makes *Gothamba roti* near the rail tracks.'

'I know,' she replied. 'Strangely enough, there are no Tamil people at the funeral no? Not a single person from the sari shops down the road.'

'Sharona use your brains,' I scolded her, 'You think Tamil people would dare to be seen here?'

'Why not? The Tamil people selling saris down our road did not kill the soldiers.' I didn't respond. Her observation may have been naïve, but it was true. The Tamil Tigers who killed the thirteen Sinhala soldiers were not the Tamil people selling saris down our road. But, would our passionate descendants of Vijaya the bandit prince and Sinhabahu the slayer of his father understand this difference? If I had been born Tamil and had been the daughter of a sari seller, I certainly would not have dared to come to this funeral even if I had wanted to. That would not have been detachment, it would have been suicide. On the other hand, were we not the compassionate result of the three visits of the Buddha, the footprint and his tooth relic?

More people were filing in and Sharona and I were being squashed forward and sideward. Through rare gaps we occasionally managed to glimpse the huddled white clad bodies of strangers, mourning and wailing. I presumed they were relatives of the thirteen village boys who had died. Suddenly the woman standing next to Sharona fainted and fell at her feet. Sharona pushed me to the side in fright. We left the woman and proceeded to push ourselves forward. It was hot, sunny and sweaty. The lamentations from the front reduced, I presumed the mourners were fainting one after the other.

Another hour passed, no corpses arrived. The lamentations were giving way to anger. Anger had always been there, but now it was increasing. The *Kadala* (gram) seller from the temple pushed past me and started shouting, 'Give our bodies back to us, give our bodies back to us.' Like a chorus of a Greek tragedy the others followed. The kadala seller pushed past us again, he smelt of liquor. When he sold kadala on poya days in front of the temple, he did not smell of liquor, he smelt of Lifebuoy soap. The slipper protector saw me again. 'Baby, I am very angry that you are still here, didn't I tell you to go?'

'I have been trying,' I lied. 'But I can't get through the people standing at the back.' The flower protector took over my protection. '*Oong...* everybody, move, move to the side. This baby is going home now.' The people moved a bit to the side. Sharona and I escaped to another place where there was no slipper protector. He too had the same smell that the kadala seller had. Alcohol.

Suddenly I saw the main priest of the Cemetery Road temple addressing the mourners and the government. There was no one from the government there, but he was addressing them by proxy. The more he gesticulated and poured words, the more agitated the mourners became. The soldiers who were supposed to protect the crowd from madness became wax dolls. Still no corpses arrived. Not yet. And no funeral took place. The afternoon was giving birth to a beautiful sunset, unusual for a month during the monsoons. Suddenly the mourners dashed forward and Sharona and I got caught in the movement of the mob. She started crying 'I want to go home.' I realized it had been extremely stupid for us to come here. It was time for us to leave. But I didn't know how to get out. The mob was moving forward and I could not move back. We were pushed, squashed, pressed and moulded into the crowd.

Now people were shouting, screaming, gesticulating and pushing. Anger had overcome the crowd. There was no sorrow to be seen. People were throwing stones at the soldiers and police officers standing paralyzed. Unable to move, unable to control the crowds, unable to bring reason. They had seen the writhing head of the angry Medusa and turned to stone. I held onto my head and hoped that Sharona held

onto hers. I hoped we wouldn't get stoned. I didn't know how to explain
a hole in the head to my grandmother who thought I was doing a project
on ancient Egypt. I tried to move against the crowd and leave the
cemetery. We pushed, trod on and stuck our elbows into the people
who blocked us. There was no mercy. Claustrophobia was just beginning
to overcome me when I turned blind. A scalding, burning, tearing,
carving blindness entered my eyes. I couldn't see anymore.

I was blind.

15

In the holy city of Benares in northern India, the Buddha held his first discourse on Esala full moon poya day. It was the discourse that set in motion the wheel of his doctrine. The doctrine of avoiding the extremes of self-indulgence and self-mortification. 'Self-indulgence is low, coarse, vulgar, ignoble and unprofitable,' he had told his first five disciples, 'self-indulgence retards one's spiritual progress and self-mortification retards one's intellect.'

Perhaps the Buddha should not have spoken of self, he should have spoken of the other self. Today would be the perfect moment for him to detach himself from Nirvana and remind these worshippers of his decaying tooth and single giant footprint of what he had once said, *'When a man sees a dead body on the charred ground, he thinks of his own body. He says to himself, truly my body is of the same nature as that body on the charred ground. It has not got past the condition of becoming that body.'* But the Buddha did not come down from Nirvana, instead someone let loose to the demons from hell.

Amongst these demons, saffron robed Buddhist monks mingled - with canisters of kerosene oil and set fire to all the sari shops, Indian sweet-meat shops and even Muslim jewelry shops. The odd Tamil speaker who tried to escape the fire was caught by the mob and burned alive. In that ravaging madness which had blackened the glow of the Esala full moon, there was no reason, rationality or compassion. The Tamil, Muslim and even odd Christian became the victim of indulgence, immolation and mortification. The Sinhala Buddhist patriotic spirit was high, soaring above the flames, into space. *'Only through a fearless comprehension of mortality will the mediator arrive at a clear view of reality.'* But, the Sinhala mob had no fear, no comprehension, and they couldn't give a damn about mortality. The Buddha was happily tucked away in Nirvana and there was no law to protect minorities in a city that spoke a different language to the masses. The police turned a blind eye. The Army took a holiday. The navy waited for Ravana to strike the ocean. JR and his ministers opened a bottle of champagne.

I don't know how Sharona and I made our way home before absolute insanity spread over the cemetery walls and entered the city of the living. Either it was the rubber slipper protector from the temple or the kadala seller smelling like alcohol who came to our rescue. Perhaps it was someone else. I don't know, neither did Sharona. Our eyes were a burning wound that teared and blocked our sight. Providing we still had sight. We stumbled down Cemetery Road without our slippers, our clothes disarrayed. The umbrellas were lost in the crowd. Fortunately it was night and Roswitha was night blind.

Neither Sharona nor I went home. We were scared to go home. Sharona was afraid of her father's wrath and I was afraid of being deported to Africa. Without speaking a word to each other we opened Mrs. Adonis's gate and went into her garden. She was sitting on the verandah looking at the flower pot. 'I think I know what you two have been up to,' she said without smiling. We were crying. 'This is perhaps the only time that crying will help you two after doing things you are not supposed to do,' she said. Tears were the natural antidote to the tear gas in our eyes. 'But come,' and she took us to her bathroom and washed out our eyes. Our sight started returning. She then inspected our eyes and said, 'You two look like you are having an acute case of conjunctivitis, you can't go home yet. I will call your parents and say that you are both at my place having dinner and that you will return shortly before bedtime.'

'Thank you, but first say that you were helping us in the project about ancient Egypt,' I told her. 'Egypt? Whoever studies Egypt at your age?' The smile returned to our faces. Mrs. Adonis picked up the telephone and lied. 'Thou shall not lie,' was a fundamental Buddhist precept. But what difference did the lie make? Outside Mrs. Adonis's walls, everything the Buddha had said was a blazing lie. Buddhism had become a gangrene.

She fed us, lent us her slippers and took our white mourner's clothes to wash. We sat with her in shorts and T-shirts and thanked the planets that Mrs. Adonis was not a Tamil. If so, she would be dead. 'I presume you two have some explaining to do?' she said. Sharona and I looked at each other and remained silent. 'What came into your heads to go to the cemetery on a day like this?' We remained silent. 'I would like you to think and give me an explanation.'

'We went to the funeral.' We answered dutifully.

'Who's funeral?'

'The funeral of the thirteen soldiers of course,' Sharona replied.

'Did you know them?'

'No.'

'Did you know what they looked like?'

'No.'

'Did you know any relatives of the soldiers?'

'No.'

'Then why did you go?'

'I don't know,' Sharona and I said.

'See children, this is what I'm saying. It's a tragedy that thirteen soldiers were killed. But, it is the tragedy of their families and loved ones. Neither you two nor any of the other thousands at the cemetery, who did not know these soldiers personally, experienced a real tragedy. You were there because of sensation. You wanted to be where the action is. Curiosity overcame rationality. You robbed even the loved ones of these soldiers the chance of having a proper burial ceremony for their sons, brothers, friends, whatever. Look at the result.' We looked. 'Look at the flames riding the sky. We now have not just thirteen dead soldiers, we have thousands of dead civilians. Is that what you both wanted?'

'No.'

'You, in this country, have the heritage of one of the greatest men that ever lived. Prince Siddhartha, known as the Buddha. He preached compassion and rationality commanded by reason. He preached that life was subject to sorrow, do you understand this?' Sharona and I were experts on Buddhism we knew what Mrs. Adonis was preaching.

'We know,' Sharona replied. 'Life brings disease, old age and death; that is sorrow.'

'Right,' Mrs. Adonis replied, 'This sorrow is caused by ignorance which creates attachment. Do you understand that?'

'Yes,' Sharona replied again. 'That is, when you own something and you lose it you are sad, so it is better not to be attached to something you own, then you are not sad when you lose it.' Mrs. Adonis smiled and began to speak again.

'This sorrow can be eliminated by the elimination of desire. The 'middle path' is the way to eliminate desire. Do you both know the middle path?'

'Yes,' we replied together and elaborated: 'Right understanding, right thought, right speech, right action, right livelihood, right effort, right mindfulness, right concentration.'

'Good,' said Mrs. Adonis, you two are excellent Buddhists.' and she smiled. 'Now tell me was it the middle path you observed today?'

'No,' we replied immediately. It was becoming clear to us that our text book Buddhist brilliance was not the real thing.

'And burning and destroying the livelihood of the Tamils because thirteen soldiers were ambushed and killed in the North, is that right action?'

'No,' we replied together. It was more than right action gone wrong. All eight precepts of the middle way were no longer right. Buddha's Buddhism had gone fundamentally wrong. We pondered in silence. The minutes dragged by.

Endlessly.

Kerosene became a murder weapon. When the flames died, the looting began. No one stopped the mobs. Not the Buddhist priests, not the dharmishta president. 'It isn't going to get better,' said Mrs. Adonis pessimistically.

'You are right,' said Sharona, even though she knew less than me about the happenings in our country. 'I must say Manuka, you are lucky that your big brother is gone and your little brother is too small to enter the army. By the time uncle Tissa and them return with Rasitha, all this will be over. Fortunately my brother has one leg shorter than the other so they will never take him into the army.'

'Sharona,' said Mrs. Adonis thoughtfully. 'I may not live for very long and I'm extremely happy about it, but mark my words child, this is not the end. This is only the beginning.' We looked at her in disbelief. We hoped she was wrong.

'All this is because of the language problem,' I quipped, trying to intelligently cover my misdeeds of before, 'If they had introduced English when the British left we would not have this problem.' I was young, gullible. I repeated what I heard and reduced the problem of our ethnic disunity to the question of language.

'It is easy to put all the blame on language, but it is wrong to put the blame only on language. Do you know children, that when the British left, after one hundred and fifty years of colonisation, only six percent of the population spoke English?' Sharona and I nodded our heads in disbelief. We had been taught to believe we lived in the most literate country in south-east Asia. Mrs. Adonis read our thoughts. 'Don't go by statistics. Speak to the people. Writing one's name in English is not literacy. It is only literacy to those who make the statistics. The government.'

'If language is not the problem, what is?' asked Sharona. I realised that she had seen too much that day. She was after all a few years younger than I was and could not digest as much. She was determined to leave Mrs. Adonis's house enlightened. Mrs. Adonis thought a bit, then she walked into her living room and brought out a piece of paper.

I will read to you what the great Mahatma Gandhi once said at the Indian parliament, '*No cabinet, worthy of representing a large mass of mankind can afford to take any step merely because it is likely to win the hasty applause of an unthinking public. In the midst of insanity, should not our best representatives retain their sanity and bravely prevent the wrecking of the ship of state under their care?*' She re-read it, and emphasised the words worthy, hasty, unthinking, insanity and care.

We were in the third day of murder, rioting, looting and arson. But JR, the dharmishta president had not showed his face on television. From the dharmishta Buddhists there was no sympathy. Nor was there empathy. There was simply apathy. 'I saw this once, before the two of you were born. During SWRD's time.' Mrs. Adonis broke into our thoughts. 'My husband knew SWRD. I told my husband, speak to the prime minister, tell him it is time for emergency. My husband refused. I went to the prime minister without telling my husband where I was going. The prime minister heard my tale. He gave me a cup of tea and a banana, smiled and said, 'Mrs. Adonis, it is an exaggeration to call the situation an emergency,' and he sent me home.' She pondered a bit longer, 'On my way home I saw my Tamil seamstress burned alive. She asked me to help her. I could not, I turned away and left. A few meters further, her Muslim brother in law was hacked to bits with a mamoty. I was glad that he had not seen me.' She thought a bit more. Sharona and I were silent. 'Those days we said that it was the 'Sinhala only' call that had agitated the masses. We blamed SWRD. But now, SWRD is dead but the mobs are still alive. Wisdom has been forsaken for power.' She read Mahatma Gandhi's speech again. She now emphasised the full sentence, '*win the hasty applause of an UNTHINKING PUBLIC.*'

'Baby, baby…' Podian had been sent in search of me. He opened the gate and entered. 'There, your Nenda is scolding you. She is saying she not knowing what Egypt you are doing, but she knowing, when you leave house you not return even when the devils is climbing trees at midnight.' Three days later Nenda still thought I was occupied with Egypt. Time had obviously stood still. For all.

'She is such a nuisance,' I told Mrs. Adonis, 'Since Ammi and Thathi are away, she thinks she is the boss.'

'She not nuisance, she good, wise woman,' Podian defended her. He widened his sarong and squatted on the ground close to Mrs. Adonis's feet.

'Podian, why did you return?' she asked.

'I come back because this my home, no?' he replied chewing beetle.

'You see the problems outside?'

'Ennappa Adonis Hamu, that is problem with Tamil man from Jaffna, I'm poor Tamil man from plantation, I have no problem.'

'Podian, don't take it too lightly.'

'I am not taking nothing too lightly. In Yindia it is worse. All the time Hindu killing Muslim and Muslim killing Hindu. Ennappa, It is worse there because many more peoples living. So, few less by religious fighting not making difference.' He laughed. 'So I tell myself, Podian, one thing only you have to do in life is, save money working hard and return to my country to family in Cemetery Road. Bad time I know now with problem, but sometimes countries have bad times and sometimes good times. It is like having monsoon and having drought. It is like Lord Kataragama being same god for war and wisdom. It is here now, but it will go soon and then no one not knowing it has ever happened.'

'Podian I wish I had your optimism,' said Mrs. Adonis sighing. 'Now go, take these children to their homes, they have had a long day.'

But Podian was in a chatty mood. 'Adonis Hamu, I was telling Magi akka and Nanda Hamu: before going on repatriation, I wanting only two things to see before I die. Not a lot for man to ask no? Only two things. It is the wonderful Taj Mahal standing like white skin Kandyan Hamine and the most holy river Ganges in Varanasi. I am telling Podian, you, when you are in good health you can bathe in Ganges, otherwise you only look at Ganges.'

'Why only in good health? All the Indians go there to bathe in bad health and hope to get good health after bathing no?'

'Enappa Adonis Hamu, that is maybe good for Yindian, but not for Ceylonese man like me. Mali Hamu telling me one day, only getting cholera when in the Ganges, so I am very scared. So I think to myself, Podian for you, looking only is enough.'

'So when you were in India, did you see what you wanted to see?'

'Ennappa Adonis hamu, how to? All nice things in Yindia only in the north no? Bandaranayake Madam sending me with repatriation to south.'

'So what is the problem, you could have gone to the north no?'

'Ennappa no! When I am in Yindia I am only thinking of coming back to Siri Lanka. I am no longer thinking of Taj Mahal or the Ganges. I only think Podian, save all the money you make working to take plane to come to Siri Lanka. One day, when all these new problems with Jaffna Tamil is over, I am going with Nanda Hamu and Magi akka to Kataragama Devala to thank Lord Kataragama for sending me back to my country. Lord Kataragama can give the message to Lord Vishnu from whose feets the Ganges is flowing, that I have been in Yindia but not having money to see the holy river.'

Nenda shouted out of the window 'Ko, where is that man? Has he got planted like the Mara tree and cannot remove the roots?' Podian laughed. 'Apo... that Nanda Hamu is worse than the fire outside, come babies, must hurry up and go before Hamu getting too angry. I am always telling Nanda Hamu, 'Hamu, not Mara tree, Bo tree. Bo tree only, tree of Buddha's enlightenment, not Mara tree.' But Nanda Hamu very stubborn... she saying, when you getting planted and not moving in life, it is the *Maraya*, like the Mara tree, not the Bo tree which is Buddhist tree. Buddhist tree not getting planted. It is tree of detachment.' Podian laughed. 'Then I am telling Nanda Hamu... I am foolish man, I am not understanding your Buddhism. How can tree be tree when tree not attached to ground?' Then Nanda Hamu telling me, 'Podian, you foolish man not to understand simple things.' She telling, it is all changing when I am dead. Then I will re-be born clever and understanding more. I am then telling Nanda Hamu, 'I am only hoping

I am re-born near your house.' Then she telling me, 'Podian no hope of that. I am praying to enter Nirvana in this life so that I will not have to suffer rebirth again.'

Nenda shouted again. Podian laughed. 'I am making her shout and getting angry so she not go to Nirvana. They say angry people not taken to Nirvana only people not having anger.'

We laughed on that Esasla poya day while the city of Colombo was ablaze. We laughed with the Tamil man. We laughed with him, not at him.

Nenda shouted again and we got up. 'Mrs. Adonis, thank you. You won't tell?' We had been asking this question every day.

'It is all right girls. My lips are sealed. Don't forget Mahatma Gandhi's speech. You two are the future. Do it right. Don't make the mistakes of the past.'

If neither Sinhala, nor Tamil nor English could save our people from insanity, we may have to learn Esperanto. Perhaps an artificial edifice of words could save us where everything else seemed to have failed. When murderers climbed Adam's peak where butterflies flew to die, perhaps it was better to die ourselves than live this lie.

Sharona and I left Mrs. Adonis's veranda with Podian behind us. He did not stop chattering, 'Babies, this is good country. You know the story of Sura and Asura?' No we didn't. 'Sura are gods and Asura are demon protectors of forest.' I asked if they were like Ravana. 'Yes,' he replied, 'All same family but different time.' He continued, 'You know Asura king Padmasura, strong king captured all the Sura gods and kept them in his forest Lanka. The Suras very sad and went to Brahma the creator and asked him to help to free gods. Brahma only creator, he can't solve problem. So he said, 'I can't, not my job, you go to Lord Vishnu.' So Sura gods went to Lord Vishnu, protector of the worlds and asked favour. But Lord Vishnu scratched his head and said, 'Sorry. I am only protector of worlds, I can't help. You go to Lord Shiva.' So Sura gods went to Lord Shiva. Lord Shiva destroyer of world, very powerful god. If anyone could help it was Lord Shiva. But Lord Shiva had other plans. He is deep in meditation so he cannot be bothered killing Asura king. So he say, 'It is beneath my dignity to fight Asura king, I will send my son Kartikeya to kill him.' and Lord Shiva continued to meditate. *Oooom*. Now babies Sharona and our baby, Lord Kartikeya is son of Lord Shiva and Shiva wife is Parvati. When Kartikeya baby, Shiva wife Parvati give her son Kartikeya a Vel. Lord Shiva knowing Kartikeya can kill any Asura with his Vel. So Lord Shiva sending his son to Lanka to kill Asura king. Lord Kartikeya coming to Lanka and killing Asura king in one blow with his Vel. But Asura king not wanting to die and pleading Kartikeya for mercy. So, Kartikeya say, 'Alright, I make you into peacock.' So Asura king becoming peacock and Kartikeya stay in Lanka falling in love with village native girl Valli. They call their village Kartikeyagama (village of kartikeya). But now they are not calling it Kartikeyagama any more, they call it… guess what?'

I had no idea. Nor did Sharona. 'Ennappa, what you babies learning in your schools no? You not even knowing where Buddhism people and Hindu people are meeting to be holy. Kartikeyagama is today known as Kataragama.' He laughed gently at our ignorance. 'So, when I not seeing Ganges river starting at Lord Vishnu's feet and flowing through the Lord Shiva city of Varanasi, I am going to Kataragama and maybe seeing Lord Shiva son and telling him thank you my lord for sending me back to my country.'

'Podian I hear your voice in the darkness. Will you hurry up and come into the house without lying to the children,' Nenda hissed through the window. Sharona and I parted. Podian hummed Bombay merai hai, while I walked next to him in eloquent silence. Lord Shiva's son had married the native princess and built the temple where the Hindus and Buddhists, Sinhalese and Tamils come to pray. We pray. After praying, we kill each other.

The paradox of my country.

16

Sometime during the flames we ran out of bread.

The flames subsided. We had been eating rice every day. I was sick of rice. I wanted bread. 'There is no bread,' said Magi. 'Then I can't eat,' I fussed. I had nothing else to do, so I fussed. It wasn't a question of bread or rice. I was bored. The earth had stopped rotating and along with its rotations it had stopped all telephone connections. We could make no calls and we received no calls. I had run out of readable Barbara Cartlands and Mills & Boons. The television set re-repeated repeat telecasts, all of which I had seen. Sharona had become a bore and I had nothing more to do. I wanted bread. Not rice.

'I will go to the Kadé and buy loaf of bread,' said Podian.

'You are not going anywhere,' said Nenda, aware of the danger outside.

'Ennappa, why not? What can happen to me?'

'Don't bother to find out,' scolded Nenda, 'You are staying.'

'Ay, ay sir,' said Podian, 'you are like army captitain no, Hamu.'

'I am worse,' said Nenda. I had to eat rice, or starve. I starved. There was still no bowler in my life, perhaps the loss of a few pounds would help me find a new bowler when the earth resumed its rotation again. I put on an Englebert cassette and stared at the Ceylon tile roof.

Magi barged into my room. 'Podian is not there. Have you seen Podian?'

'No,' I said and continued to stare at the tiles.

Then Nenda barged into my room. 'Have you seen Podian?'

'I said no once, and I'm saying it again. NO.' And I continued to stare at the roof.

'Get out of that bed and call the neighbours and ask if they have seen Podian. Something has happened, I know something has happened. Podian would not disappear like that.' A strange hollow sensation entered my body. I knew it was not repatriation this time. I went to Mrs. Adonis. She always sat on the verandah; she knew who walked this lane at all hours of the day and night. 'Mrs. Adonis have you seen Podian?' I asked. 'Yes,' she replied, 'He stopped here and asked me if I needed something from the boutique. He said he was going to buy you some bread.'

'Did you ask him to bring you something?'

'No. I told him that I have everything I needed and that he should not be walking in the streets at times like this.' The first teardrop was forming in my eyes.

'He said not to worry he will return before anyone notices he is missing.' The teardrop rolled down my cheek.

'Has he not returned yet?'

No. He hadn't returned.

17

He did not return.

Magi did not cook.

No one wanted to eat. Neither rice nor bread.

Podian did not come. Nenda and I walked to the boutiques down the road and searched for Podian. No one knew him. Not any more. Uncle Buddhi came. Achi and I drove in uncle Buddhi's car looking for Podian in all the boutiques that were beyond walking distance. There was no trace of him.

The flames had died. The smoke had cleared. Charred skeletons remained. The sari shop where Ammi had bought the sari I wore for uncle Buddhi's eldest son's wedding was razed to its foundations. No saris left. Only the gray remains of fire. The shop where Ammi bought Nenda's sari for uncle Buddhi's eldest son's wedding was in worse condition. It did not even have a foundation. The Muslim jeweler who spoke Tamil had his jewelry shop, but the gold had been removed in the course of the four day Buddhist revival. The Bombay sweet-mart where I always drank a Faluda on the way back from school was still emanating smoke. 'Baby, BABY,' someone shouted from across the street. The rubber slipper protector of the cemetery road temple had built himself a pavement shop on the foundation of a Sari shop. It was free. 'Baby, baby, come here with your grandmother. See I have some nice silk Kanjipuram saris straight from India. I will sell you one for a special price.' I ignored him. The Kanjipuram sari he tried to sell me looked strangely familiar and much like the sari I had wanted to buy for uncle Buddhi's eldest son's wedding. 'Come baby, come,' he shouted. I pushed my grandmother into uncle Buddhi's car and we drove to another boutique in another area to search for Podian.

We did not find him. Nor did he come. Uncle Hubert was sent for. He came. He was given a photograph of Podian and me. Podian next to the Hillman and me on top of the Hillman. He was asked to locate Podian. Achi pleaded with him and said, 'Hubert, don't step into this house until you have found Podian.' Uncle Hubert left with the photograph promising to find Podian.

I don't know what uncle Hubert did with the photograph, but before long we received a telephone call through the recently repaired telephone lines saying that someone who was living in 186 Cemetery Road needed to be identified at the police station at the junction of Cemetery Road and the Parliament road. We didn't wait for uncle Buddhi to drive us, we walked. Achi held onto my dead grandfather's walking stick and I held onto her hand. She supported me and I supported her. Neither of us needed another's support, but on this special journey we didn't have the strength to walk alone.

The policeman took our identity card numbers. He wrote them down in a large book, taking all the time in the world to do so. Then he looked at the clock patiently ticking on the wall and stated that his duty had ended and we must await his colleague to proceed with the task we had come for. 'But we only want to…' Achi began. The policeman's stomach rumbled like that of Ravana's brother Kumbhakarana who slept six months without food. He left.

We held onto our identity cards and awaited his replacement. The replacement recognized us. He was the rubber slipper protector's younger brother, and had been an assistant slipper protector before becoming a policeman. We told him we had come to identify a missing person.

'Person?' he asked, we have no persons, we have three bodies that need to be identified. 'Bodies?' Achi asked, 'dead bodies?' 'Yes,' he said, 'bodies.' I don't know what Achi and I said, or did. 'Aney I don't know Madam,' he continued, 'when I came to the police station this morning there were three bodies that had been thrown over the wall into our premises. We don't know who they are because they were not carrying identification cards. And because they are dead they can't even talk and tell us who they are.' He laughed. I saw Achi's dark face turn white and her hair became the colour of snow before my eyes. She held onto my hand and said to me, 'I don't know if I'm strong enough to take this.' This time I knew she meant it.

'Achi you wait here. I will go.' I knew I was not strong enough either. But someone had to see if our Podian was one of the policeman's bodies. The policeman ordered a cup of tea for Achi and took me inside. He told me it was incredible how much I had grown in the last few years. I could not say how he had grown because I had never looked at the face of the temple rubber slipper protector's brother on poya days when I visited the temple.

Three bodies lay on the ground. In a pile, a heap, a dump of disrespect. The policeman tried to kick them apart. But the dead were stronger than the living, they refused to move. Then the second police officer offered to help him. But first he had to wash his lunch packet rice off his right hand. One of the bodies was wearing the same sarong my father had never worn, which Podian had received after returning from repatriation. But it was not an unusual sarong. Red and yellow tie and die. I was sure that half the population in this country owned such a sarong. I suppressed my fears.

The first body wasn't wearing my father's sarong. Podian didn't own a blue and black striped sarong. The second body was in trousers, now torn. Podian had only one green pair of trousers. These trousers were black. I turned to return to my grandmother. Podian was not here. The sarong which covered the third body was a sarong that could belong to the entire population. Red and yellow had been the two auspicious colours for the last new-year season. But the policeman called me back. 'Ho, ho, ho he shouted after me, this one you have to look at as well.' I wished my father had never owned such a sarong.

The face that stared at me with its dead vacant eyes and body covered with bruises and cigarette burns, was that of the little black man who returned to us after repatriation. He looked different. I suppose that was the difference death made. He stared at me. Lifeless, rigid, empty, different. The stiffness of death had eliminated his vibrancy. Lacking vibrancy, it was not Podian, it was another. I hated that wretched man for returning after repatriation. I wished he had remained in India for us to scold him for leaving without telling. Why had he come? The Police officer had been observing my face. '*Meya naeda* (this is him, isn't it)?' he asked, kicking his stomach. I did not want Podian to be kicked by that Police officer, or anyone for that matter. Not even in death. I nodded my head. I think it was an affirmation. Yes, that third dead body which revealed its dead face to me was Podian. His dead right hand still clutching half the loaf of bread he had bought for me. The other half was missing.

I left the space at the back of the police station and returned to my grandmother. 'Achi if dead can talk those dead bodies will be talking Tamil,' I said. 'Podian?' she asked quietly. I nodded in affirmation. 'His heart has failed and he has died a natural death,' said the police officer who had followed me. He then went to wash his hands. Achi aged further before my eyes.

The policeman washed his hands and returned to us. 'This baby seems to have lost her speech today,' he said laughingly. 'We will send for the body,' said my grandmother, 'that man has been one of our employees for the last twenty years. We will perform the last rites.' 'You will perform last rites for a Tamil man?' he asked. Neither my grandmother nor I replied. If dead bodies did not speak how did he know that it spoke Tamil?

I held on to Achi's hand while she held on to her stick and we left the police station. We now needed the third leg for support. The police officer stood up and asked us to visit again when we had time and whenever we needed anything. As he stood up, his shirt collar opened and I saw the pendant of Lord Kataragama hanging from the chain around his neck. Lord Kataragama had hung from Podian's neck as well. I couldn't remember if Lord Kataragama was still around Podian's dead neck. I tried to leave Achi's hand to look at Podian again. But she held me firmly and didn't let me go. I think she recognized the pendant herself.

She also recognized the twenty two carat gold chain that carried the pendant. That was the gold chain aunty Lydia had given Podian before leaving for the commonwealth. This gold chain now hung from the police officer's neck.

My grandmother recognized it, I did not.

18

When the dog died, I cried. When the cat died, I cried. When the rabbits died, when the squirrel died, when my grandfather died, I cried. When Podian died, I couldn't stop crying. I had betrayed him. I was the Sinhalese, he was the Tamil.

I belonged to the masses, but I could not protect this little man from my own lot. The police officer said that he had died a natural death, but the holes on his body resembled the cigarette burns in my party dress. They had the same diameter, the same radius. The difference being that my dress was replaceable and meant nothing to anyone except me, while Podian was the personification of life that meant a lot to everyone who lived down Cemetery Road.

I saw my existence through the hole in my dress, but I could not see through Podian's holes. I could only look into them. I saw pain, suffering and betrayal. The victim of Sinhala Buddhist passion that had over-ridden the boundaries of moderation, detachment and compassion. If this was supposed to be the new version of Buddhism that had evolved after the death of thirteen Sinhala soldiers, I did not want to be a part of it. Podian's burns, bruises and death, reflected our national spirit.

When my grandmother and I walked out of the police station that day, all the police officers were sitting on the verandah drinking tea and smoking cigarettes and protecting the Sinhala nation for the Sinhalese. All their cigarettes were the same size as Podian's burns.

Achi didn't utter a word while we walked back home. She only became very old. She had me help her to the armchair in the television room where my grandfather died and said, 'I never thought that our people could ever sink so low.' The rest of the household and Mrs. Adonis gathered around her in silence in that small television room. 'Put on the TV my child,' she told me, 'Perhaps the president has the sense of humanity to condemn this action.' My grandmother spoke for all the Sinhala Buddhists, and she wanted re-assurance from her president that we, as a nation, had not sunk to the level of a hyena. My grandmother was older than I was, she had more to lose. I at least could live to see better times. I still had hope.

The rioting, killing and looting continued for four days, but JR hadn't the time or inclination to address the nation, or enact emergency. On the fourth day he showed his face. Not a furrow more and not a furrow less. He said that he understood the frenzy of the Sinhala mobs. His absence of four days was not apathy. It was not sympathy either, it was empathy, towards the mobs. I switched off the Television set. I understood Sinhala politics.

The normally garrulous people living in our house were silenced. We stared at the empty television screen. It was too painful to look at my grandmother. 'The Lord Buddha has not come here three times,' she said. 'That is a lie. He has not come here at all.'

'Now leave me on this armchair where my husband died and let me die. There is no more reason to live.' We still hung around. But Achi chased us away. 'Go,' she said, 'do what you have to do, I have done what I had to do.' And she closed her eyes. I went to my father's study and blindly picked a book to read. I returned with this book to my grandmother and watched her breathe. I started reading somewhere in middle.

Once upon a time there was a king. One night, three clever thieves broke into the king's palace and stole many goods. But the king's guards caught them and brought them before the king.

'Did you, or did you not commit this robbery?' the king asked.

'We did, your majesty,' replied the robbers.

'Are you guilty or not guilty?' asked the king.

'Not guilty,' replied the robbers.

'How can that be?' asked the king.

'It was easy to break into your palace your majesty, because the mason who built your walls did a poor job. The mortar was extremely loose. Therefore your majesty we are not guilty, the mason is guilty.'

'Call the mason,' ordered the king. The mason arrived. Fearful.

'Are you guilty or not guilty of putting the mortar very loosely when you were building my palace?' asked the king. 'Not guilty your highness,' answered the mason.

'How is that?' asked the king.

'The labourer I appointed to mix the lime has done a bad job. Therefore I am not guilty, the labourer is guilty.'

'Summon the labourer,' commanded the king. The labourer was brought before the king. 'Are you guilty or not guilty of improperly mixing the mortar when the mason was building my palace?' asked the king.

'Not guilty,' replied the labourer.

'How is that?' asked the king.

'When I was mixing the lime a beautiful girl passed by and my mind got distracted. The girl is guilty your majesty, not I.'

'Summon the girl,' said the king. The girl was brought before the king.

'Guilty or not guilty of distracting the labourer?' asked the king.

'Not guilty,' said the girl. 'If the goldsmith had given me my jewelry on the day he promised, I would not have gone by the day the labourer was mixing the lime. So the goldsmith is guilty.' said the girl.

'Call the goldsmith,' ordered the king. The goldsmith was brought.

'If the goldsmith is guilty of not giving the jewelry to the girl the day he was supposed to, take him and keep him against a large rock and let my festival tusker elephant gore him to death.' Seeing the executioner, the goldsmith began to weep.

'Why do you weep?' asked the king. 'I weep because two such magnificent tusks as your majesty's festival elephant has, will break when they bore through my emaciated body and strike the hard rock I am tied to.' said the goldsmith.

'What is the alternative?' asked the king.

'I saw the pot-bellied prosperous Thambi aiya on the street. If it was Thambi aiya that festival elephant would gore, then his beautiful tusks will not strike the rock behind him and will not get broken.' The king summoned Thambi aiya and had him gored through his round middle by the festival tusker.

My grandmother was still breathing.

In the story, it was the Muslim, now it was our Podian; when there were no more Podians the Muslim's turn would come again, or the Burgher, or the Malay. Someone was always there to blame. As long as there was someone else to blame, we need not blame ourselves.

My grandmother did not die. She had one more thing left to do. She had to take care of Podian's funeral arrangements.

Uncle Buddhi came. Achi and he traveled to many temples before they found a Buddhist priest who was willing to give the Tamil man his last rites as a Buddhist. They found one. Detached. Closer to Nirvana than to life. Far more evolved than any of those monks who preached Buddhism on JR's television screens during prime-time television. He told uncle Buddhi, 'I am proud that there are people like you and this Hamu still living in this country.'

We had him embalmed. He lay in a coffin in our living room. Head, west. He looked smart in the green suit he had worn to get onto the plane in order to return to us after repatriation. Now he wore this suit for the second and last time. Uncle Buddhi, Dagma, Kusita, uncle Hubert, Mrs. Adonis, Roswitha, Sharona and the rest of us followed the funeral procession down Cemetery Road, to the cemetery.

Podian had no other family. We were his family. His home was our home.

Our country, his.

19

Achi didn't die. She went to Pettah with Mrs. Adonis and bought two urns. Both for Podian. Then they cashed in their pensions and bought two air tickets; for her and Mrs. Adonis, to Benares. They bought one piece of hand luggage for both of them and secured one urn between two voile saris. The other urn was kept under lock and key in Achi's almairah.

Nenda and Magi got into a panic when they realized that Achi and Mrs. Adonis were going to Benares with Podian's ashes. They called uncle Buddhi. Uncle Buddhi called Thathi and consulted him on the course of action. The two ladies were not to be deterred. Thathi thought and he thought. While he was thinking, uncle Buddhi who was paying for the telephone call to Africa, offered to go with the two old ladies to Benares and row the boat down the Ganges in order for Achi and Mrs. Adonis to empty Podian's ash. That way, they would return without drowning. Neither Achi nor Mrs. Adonis could row or swim. Uncle Buddhi was good at both.

Podian had always wanted to see the Ganges. Ganges, the great and mighty river that began at the feet of Lord Vishnu, the almighty protector who sat on Mount Meru. The Ganges meandered through the city of Benares until it reached the Gulf of Bengal. Lord Vishnu, the god of samsara, incarnation and reincarnation, death and rebirth carried the same wheel of power which was marked on the soles of the Buddha's feet. It was this same Lord Vishnu who incarnated himself as Rama and came to Lanka to kill the mighty Ravana. Podian did not give a damn about Rama or Ravana. In fact, he said, 'Enappa baby, I think those days before Lord Rama coming to Lanka better days for this country. Those days we in this country having precious stones and big palaces built with gold. Now only having Buddha's tooth.'

Achi and Mrs. Adonis saw it as their duty to show Podian the Ganges. They both liked duties. Hence, on that first Saturday after the monsoons, they embarked on the aeroplane with uncle Buddhi following them with the hand luggage of ash. Uncle Buddhi's eldest son, who now had a wife and a car, drove us to the airport. He could not be bothered buying a ticket and entering, therefore, he drove around the car park while I bought a ticket and watched the three of them go, with Podian in their hand luggage.

In Benares, uncle Budddi hired a boat with a boatman and they all made their way early one morning and emptied the urn full of Podian's ash in a spot where the rising sun cast a golden image and the water had no ripple. Lord Vishnu now had the duty of protecting our Podian and bringing him back to us through Samsara. Death and re-birth.

Achi and Mrs. Adonis wanted to return immediately with the empty urn. Uncle Buddhi tried to show them Benares. 'Aunty, you have come here for the first time, to this great city of Shiva, I will show you both some beautiful Shiva temples and the famous gardens where the Lord Buddha held his first discourse on Esala Poya day.'

'Buddhi,' Achi is supposed to have said, 'I am sick of the Buddha and I am sick of Shiva. I want only to go home.' Mrs. Adonis had seconded her. 'Buddhi, let that Shiva dance as his Natarajah. The world thinks he has his foot on the dwarf of ignorance. But that is a lie like everything else. The dwarf of ignorance is free.'

'Aunty, Mrs. Adonis, if there is nothing you believe in, why did you waste money coming to India with Podian's ash? You could have strewn it somewhere in Sri Lanka.'

'Buddhi, we didn't do it for us. We did it for him.' Mrs. Adonis agreed. 'And we didn't do it for any Vishnu sitting on a mountain above a stream, we did it because that poor foolish man Podian wanted to see the Ganges once before he died.'

Uncle Buddhi told them 'Okay, I came with you to do something which you thought was necessary, which I think was unnecessary. Now you come with me and do something that you may think is unnecessary, but I think is necessary.' Achi and Mrs. Adonis opened their ears. They loved necessity.

Uncle Buddhi continued, 'Aunties, everything has failed. Politics has failed, religion has failed, medicine has failed, science has failed, humans have failed. But, there is one thing above all that, which has not failed.' Achi and Mrs. Adonis were all ears. 'Music.'

And so they roamed the city of Benares and helped my uncle Buddhi buy the best Sitar in the whole of India. Where everything else had failed, music remained. *Om.*

***

In the meantime, Nenda, Magi and I took an express private bus to Kataragama with Podian's second urn. We disembarked at the banks of the Manik Ganga and walked towards the river with the urn. I tucked up my skirt and carried the urn. Nenda and Magi raised and tucked up their saris. We walked together into the crystal clear waters on whose banks Kartikeya, the son of Lord Shiva had married his native princess and built their shrine of worship. Kataragama. We walked until the water began wetting our clothes and then we stopped. The river had become too deep. In this deepest spot, I opened the gold coloured urn and emptied Podian's remaining ash into the water. He swirled, and then he twirled. He was ready for his passage.

We watched him leave us. Specks of darkness upon the clear waters of the Manik Ganga. I looked at Nenda and Magi. Their own Manik Ganga of tears was carving a valley down their cheeks. I could not cry anymore. There were no more tears.

We climbed out of the river. Nenda and Magi untucked their saris and went into the Kataragama temple. I did not. I had nothing to pray for.

Buddhists in their white clothes and Hindus in their multi-coloured saris were going into the temple to worship Lord Kataragama. The sweet smell of incense and sweet-meats offered to the gods circulated in the air and entered my nostrils. It made me nauseous. What is the point of worshipping a dead deity while the living were massacred before one's eyes?

I remember Podian's dead face on the hard floor of the police station, under the framed picture of the Buddha hanging on the wall. Twisted and contorted in pain. What was this religion that was supposed to take us to Nirvana? I stared into the spot where Podian's ash had been emptied. I watched the cascading swirls of water make their downward journey to the ocean. I wondered why my family emptied Podian's ash into the water when they wanted him to return through Samsara, back to us. Wouldn't it have been better to bury the ash in the garden under the Karapincha tree?

Everything I had been brought up to believe was nothing but a load of bull. But, perhaps in the midst of all this bullshit there was a small grain of truth. Perhaps one day I would begin to search for the truth again. For the moment, I was spiritually dead.

Like a *Mandala* made of butter, I waited in the blazing sun for Nenda and Magi to arrive. The sacrificial goat bleated in panic as the holy resonance 'Om' activated the living.

Epilogue

The road
to Nowhere

I went out into the world. I saw what I was meant to see. What I did not see, I watched on television and what I did not see on television, I saw at the travel agent's where colour posters and travel catalogues filled the shelves. I traveled.

The world was full of countries. The countries were all different. Some had palaces, others had hovels. Some had cherry blossoms, others, cactuses. Some had deserts, others had mountains. Some had lions in the wilderness, others had lions in zoos. No one was interested in my lion. Everyone spoke, no one listened.

One person spoke to me. He told me the meaning of Manuka. He was a biologist, examining curative plants before extinction. I was one of them. Not curative, but bordering extinction. I was old and Latinized. Discovered even before Captain Cook landed in New Zealand in 1769. Latin: Leptospermum Scoparium, indigenous to New Zealand. Also Latin: Melaleuca alternifolia, indigenous to Australia. I think my father had traveled a long way with his pocket-sized note book. I was too old to consider it a solace that I was not a direct descendant of the aborigine, but a direct descendent of a bush. The tea tree.

An extremely resilient evergreen, varied in growth and height, of pleasant smell but bitter taste, between five centimeters and fifteen meters in height, brewed and drunk by the Maoris before Captain Cook anchored in seventeen hundred and sixty nine. Suitable as atmospheric cleanser, disinfectant, honey, oil, cosmetic etcetera. Especially recommended for those suffering from allergies.

The pre-extinction botanist sneezed every morning and every night. I refused to become his antiseptic. I told him to get lost. He went his way, I went mine.

By the time I returned to my island, I had seen what karma had in store for me. What I had not seen, I was not meant to see. It did not belong to the syllabus of my Karma. My karma was my own. It was non-social, non socialist and non-conformist.

Besides memories, I had a suitcase full of dresses. They were party dresses with cigarette burns. One dress had a burn bigger than the others. It had been my favorite dress. Black, short, sexy. Karma had given me a varied syllabus. I got my own set of holes to see the world beyond the Indian Ocean.

I was unsure whether to be thankful or angry towards that rubber slipper protector who had betrayed me, and perhaps caused karma to change its syllabus. I hoped he was dead. After he berated my grandmother for permitting a young girl such as myself to be a part of the chaotic rumpus at the cemetery, the day the thirteen bodies of the soldiers were to be flown down from Tinnavelli, Achi refused to take the responsibility for my protection. I had to go.

I carried with me the little hole which karma had given me and boarded a rickety aircraft, more like a flying sarcophagus than a mighty monster that conquered the skies. I thought death would come. But it did not.

In Lanka, the war which began with the death of thirteen soldiers in Tinnavelli, raged on for years. In the South, the poor village woman's sons joined the Sri Lankan army. It was army or unemployment. In the North, the poor Tamil woman's sons were conscripted to the LTTE. Nobody asked them whether they believed in the cause. They had to join the 'Boys'.

In the South, the leaders got rich, they got fat and their children went abroad to study political science in order to return as presidents, ministers or business men. Those politicians' sons who lacked brains to study, resorted to thuggery. But no one joined the army.

I circulated, mingled, intermingled, learned, un-learned and waited for karma to complete its syllabus. The day she completed it, I was permitted to return. Alone.

Everyone had died. Achi had died. Roswitha had died. Sharona's grandmother was dead and a generation of young men had died. Only Mrs. Adonis was alive; feeble, but alive. I opened her gate and joined her on the verandah. She was still staring at the flower pots her dachshund Cleopatra had raised her short legs to piss upon. 'She was the best dog I ever had. You don't get dogs like that any more.' I couldn't remember much of Cleopatra. She had been run over by a steamroller shortly after JR started building his road to the right up to the new parliament.
'How are your children Mrs. Adonis?' I asked her.
'How can they be? They are getting older, richer and greedier. One tells me to sell this house, the other tells me to extend it, the third tells me to

move into their house, the fourth tells me to rent the rooms to strangers, the fifth tells me to build an upstairs. Fortunately the sixth and the seventh are still abroad.'

I didn't know what to say. I had neither house, nor children.

***

JR ruled for twelve years. He did everything possible to the constitution and to the entire concept of government in order to stay in power forever. But, after twelve years the planets refused to cooperate and he had to go. His minister of the orange bridges acceded to his post. In the final battle between the planets and man, the planets were stronger. They had their own karmic logic. They now chose to support another.

JR's destiny was the destiny of all men and women. Ravana had a time to go. Sinhabahu had a time to go. So did Kuveni, the Portuguese and the Dutch; the English colonizers, Dudley and Mrs. Bandaranayake all had a time to go. Nothing more, nothing less. 'Man' was a victim of time.

JR was followed by Premadasa who was followed by Mrs. Bandaranayake's daughter. Another gender, another party, another road. Not left. Not right. Not center, nor diagonal. I don't know where we went. We went here, there, everywhere and finally nowhere. The road to nowhere.

***

As I sat in the fading light on Mrs. Adonis' verandah, my little brother Rasitha opened the gate and came and sat on my lap. 'Akki, there, Nenda wants you to come for dinner.' I looked at my brother's thin, cheerful face, awkward gait, coarse, curly hair. The Capricorn. Yes, there was a future. Here. I would teach my brother compassion, not patriotism. 'Malli, do you know the story of the Ravanaya?'
'Of course I know. That is the story of Rama and Sita.'
'Silly boy, I said the Ravayana, not the Ramayana! This is a story that begins before Rama, the story of an ascetic; a magnificent, compassionate, dharma abiding king of Lanka.'

We held hands. I was glad that he had been born. The night owl began its song before the monsoon arrived with the storm and I began my story...

> His name Ravana,
> a Raja of renown
> Noble and compassionate,
> of splendid Lanka town
> Protector of his people,
> Upholder of his word
> The terror of his foes
> And Dharma's faithful Lord
> Commanded by his mother
> Faithful Ravana went
> Along with his brothers
> To achieve the state of saint
> Shiva, whom he impressed
> Granted Ravana boons
> Longevity,
> And a long victorious sword.
> Again commanded by mother
> The noble Yaksha dame
> He again embraced austerity
> And plucked away nine heads
> Brahma witnessed this act
> And feared the tenth last head
> Came to ascetic Ravana
> And returned him his heads.
> He further offered boons
> Of indestructablility
> And more power than men.
> He knew this king of Lanka
> This son of Yaksha Raksha tribe
> Knew the art of war and peace
> And acted,
> With wisdom as his bride.

He married the pious Manodhari
A buxom lass from Land
She bore his favourite son
Indrajit,
The faithful fervent lad.
Brahma returned to Amravati
And glanced at his product
What he saw with his eyes
Was similar to a god's own land.
Lanka. Jeweled, splendid, ripe.
Scintillating for Aryan,
To strike…
T'was Ravana's creation.
His.
Ravana,
The Raja of renown
His charm, his goodness, his wisdom
Is he here? Is he here? Is he here?

Acknowledgements

I wish to thank:

My father, for the tireless effort of answering all my questions with unfamiliar tempo and for his philosophy that nourished us.

My mother for tirelessly believing in us, even through moments of disbelief and for constantly pushing us further. If not for her, we would have stopped a long time ago.

Nenda, for gifting me her interpretation of the world that made my existence more mysterious and exciting.

My brothers for their diversity, eccentricity, geniality and inspirational existence.

My husband, for tolerating my eccentricity.

My babies, for giving me the space to dream and to write. Their births made it possible.

Canice and the rest at Rumors for lending me their ears.

My friends Conall, Paula, Indu, Michael, Princo, Dolly, Vitta and Seneka for the moments of laughter and realization.

Kollu for a comfortable bar stool.

Fawzie and Willie for the comfortable cement floor and the Baila.

Kosala, who always believed in me.

Perry, who related tales from the Classics.

Laura who revealed the mysteries of language: the sorcery and power.

Herr Zollitsch for the techniques of language that made me finally understand what I spoke.

Dr. Balakrishnan who nourished the soul with poetry, mathematics and food.

My publishers, who kept asking me the hated question, 'How long more?' If not for them I would be writing for the rest of my life.

Sundi, who was the planetary catalyst that connected me with the above.

And to all those friends and family I did not mention by name, but who escorted this process. Thank you.

Glossary

Achi: Maternal grandmother

Aiya: Elder brother

Akka/Akki: Elder sister

Amma/Ammi: Mother

Asura: Anti-God

Atha: Grandfather

Bodhi Puja: Veneration to Bo tree

Brahma: Hindu god of creation

Devas: Gods

Dharma: Doctrine/Buddhist teaching.

Duwa: Daughter

Ganga: River

Goday: Not-fashionable

Hamu: Mistress

Jataka tales: Tales of the Buddha's many lives

Kadala: Gram

Kadé: Roadside shop

Kanya: Zodiac sign, Virgo

Kakki: Shit

Kaliamma: Hindu goddess of death

Kiribath: Milk rice

Kiriamma: Paternal Grandmother

Kovil: Hindu temple

Lagna: Zodiac sign

Mahamaya Devi: Mother of Lord Buddha

Mahappa: Uncle

Malli: Younger brother

Mallung: Asian green salad

Mantra: Chant

Meena: Pisces

Nenda: Aunt

Nirvana: Realm of non-existence, extinction

Pali: Daughter language of Sanskrit. Language of Buddhist texts

Pattini: Hindu Goddess
Pol: Coconut
Pottu: Spot on forehead
Poya: Full moon
Putha: Son
Rajah: King
Samsara: Cycle of death and re-birth
Sarong: Cloth tied on waist, male atttire
Sinha: Lion
Siya: Grandfather
Sura: Gods
Thali: Thick gold chain. Tamil attire
Thambi Aiya: Muslim elder brother
Thatha/Thathi: Father
Varanasi: City of Benares in India.
Veddha: Lankan Aborigine.
Vel: Lance
Vishnu: Lord and protector.